Tornado Weather

Tornado Weather

Deborah E. Kennedy

FLATIRON
BOOKS
NEW YORK

TORNADO WEATHER. Copyright © 2017 by Deborah E. Kennedy. All rights reserved. Printed in the United States of America. For information, address Flatiron Books, 175 Fifth Avenue, New York, N.Y. 10010.

www.flatironbooks.com

The Library of Congress Cataloging-in-Publication Data is available upon request.

ISBN 978-1-250-07957-2 (hardcover)
ISBN 978-1-250-15492-7 (international, sold outside the U.S., subject to rights availability)
ISBN 978-1-250-07958-9 (ebook)

Our books may be purchased in bulk for promotional, educational, or business use. Please contact your local bookseller or the Macmillan Corporate and Premium Sales Department at 1-800-221-7945, extension 5442, or by email at MacmillanSpecialMarkets@ macmillan.com.

First Edition: July 2017

10 9 8 7 6 5 4 3 2 1

To Joyce and David Kennedy

One dog yelping at nothing will set
ten thousand straining at their collars.

—JAPANESE PROVERB

But fish do not build cathedrals.

—JACQUES COUSTEAU

Tornado Weather

Where They Killed
All the Indians

(May)

Fikus pulled up to the corner of Hate Henry Road and Rocky Way and flipped on the ambers. The crossing bar swung out and nearly hit a feral dog scooting its way through gravel to the other side. Damned cur, he thought. Damned nuisance. Better not bite her.

"Daisy! You ready back there?"

He found her in the rearview, giving him a thumbs-up. My God she was cute. So cute it hurt Fikus's gut a little to look at her. Those dimples. Those crooked front teeth.

"Prepare for flight!" he said, and grabbed the remote that worked the wheelchair lift.

In the Bottoms, the cottonwood seeds were flying, pushed by a hard wind from the east. Dry snow. Christmas in May. It wouldn't be dry for long. There were thunderheads gathering into knobby purple towers over the county dump. Lightning flickered between the clouds like children's flashlight beams. Secret signals, Fikus thought. The day had turned eerie. Tornado watch. Strange green sky. Lilacs, gust-bent and fragrant, growing over the old Udall place's garage, focused on him with the strange concentration of a periscope. When Fikus was a kid, Willa Udall slaughtered pigs there and made homemade sausage in her bathtub. Now the house was haunted, or so some said, with the ghosts of the pigs and the poor deceased Udalls. Hard to tell them apart, said the believers. The people and the pigs. The Udalls always did have squat noses.

Fikus hopped out of the bus and watched as Daisy rode the platform down to the street. The white swirled around him. A cottonwood seed landed on his tongue and he stuck it out at her. Then he swallowed the thing and patted his stomach. "Mmm-mmm good."

"Ewwww," Daisy said, scrunching up her nose. "You're gonna grow a tree inside you."

"Mayhaps a whole forest. And then I'll spit it out, oh, I don't know, just here—" He poked her tummy. Something hard hung there. Metallic, felt like. Bejeweled. He spied a chain around her neck. She cupped the necklace or whatever it was and laughed. He tickled her chin and she laughed again. See? She wasn't scared of him. He was forbidden from touching the children but did it anyway because it was an idiotic rule and he wasn't hurting anyone. Leave that to the priests and the perverts, he thought. "And then you'll have a woods for your belly button. What about that?"

"No thank you."

"You know your neighborhood used to be all trees? That was the Bottoms, back in the day. Prettiest, wildest place in all of Colliersville, Indiana. Trees and Indians. Indians and trees. As far as the eye could see. Now look at it. Three streets toppling into the river. Sad."

"Indians?" Daisy asked.

The wind whipped up more cottonwood seeds, drove candy wrappers down the street. The little dog sat down under an oak ten feet away. He licked a sore spot on his leg, then raised his nose in the air and howled.

"Native Americans," he hollered at Daisy, who had clapped her hands over her ears. "Feathers, not dots."

The dog stopped howling and lay down in a pile of white fluff.

"What happened?" Daisy asked.

"To the trees or the Indians?" Fikus said, although it amounted to the same thing.

"The Indians," she said.

"Oh, well . . ."

"Tell me. Please."

Fikus took a deep breath. It wasn't a pretty story and the bus was idling. But he couldn't tell her no. That face. That voice. He should have had a child when there was still a chance.

"So, this young chief," he started, "braids down to his ankles, decides to steal this Englishman's daughter, right? There was a fort on the river, you know, where that barge sank a few summers back."

"Fikus!" It was Tiara, Fikus's eleven-year-old neighbor. She was halfway out the bus window, a scowl on her sharp face. "What's taking so bleeping long? I'm worried about Murphy."

"Who's Murphy?" Fikus asked. Had a kid from someone else's route snuck on the bus when he wasn't watching? It wouldn't surprise him. His bus was a madhouse.

"The fish I won today in the spelling bee duh," Tiara said. "I want to get him home and in the tank before he dies. Or before we all die in a goddamned tornado."

"Gimme a minute, Tiara."

"Fine," she said. She showed him her skinny right wrist clad in an oversize plastic watch. "One minute. I'm counting."

"Fine," Fikus said back.

"So . . ." Daisy prompted.

"So," Fikus said. "Where was I?"

"There was an Englishman's daughter and a fork."

"A fort. Doesn't matter. Anyway, the Englishman goes crazy. Just insane, thinking his beautiful daughter's going to be deflowered by this savage longhair, and he gathers up a militia. The Englishman and his cohorts are kind of a ragtag bunch. They've got arrows, some rusty muskets, and only one cannon, but they're determined. They think God's on their side, so they hump it over to the Indian camp and they let loose. They go crazy. They turn those teepees to tatters, into toilet paper. They burn. They rape. They pillage. They hang men, women, and children from the nearest tree. They take moccasins and put them on their own smelly feet. It's a slaughter, and when it's all over, they chuck the bodies into the Ranasack." He took a deep breath. "The end."

Daisy wasn't looking at him. She seemed to be thinking. Rain began to fall in big, cold drops and her wheelchair got a sheen to it. "What's 'deflowered' mean?"

"Oh, well," Fikus said, "it's just a saying."

"But what does it mean?"

"Forget it. My point is, the Bottoms is where they killed all the Indians. The ground's soaked with their blood. Anything you grow here, grass, rhododendrons, dandelions, cucumbers, is seething with sin."

Fikus was trying very hard to be a more spiritual person. He'd been raised a Lutheran, but his mother and father's starched faith and the stiff services they took him to as a child did nothing to expand his world or his understanding of it. Now, in late middle age, he hoped to discover new sides to the story, to find out that everything—from human action to the prevailing wind currents to the soil and the life that sprang from it—was connected. Maybe even in a cosmic way. There were books on Buddhism, Sufism, the New Age movement, and Hinduism waiting for him back home. Not that he'd been able to get very far in them yet. His nightly routine usually left only enough time for a quick dinner, followed by whiskey, a few episodes of *Star Trek: The Next Generation,* and bed, which wasn't really bed, since he slept in his recliner, but he hoped to do better. He had goals.

"Are daisies seething with sin?" Daisy asked.

"Oh, I don't know about that." Fikus had gone too far. He was always going too far.

"But my home's haunted." Daisy's eyes were fixed on his face now. "That's what you meant."

"This land is full of ghosts, just full of them."

"Where you live, did they kill the Indians there, too?"

Fikus considered the question. Maple Leaf Mobile Home Park was up the hill and around the corner from the Bottoms. It was not, as far as he knew, the scene of an Indian slaughter, but it might as well be. The misery that went on there. It warranted its own monument. "We killed the Indians everywhere, sweetie. Especially in Indiana. Ironic, isn't it?"

"Maybe that's why I see ghosts," Daisy said. "I saw my mom

out on our dock just a couple weeks ago. My daddy said it was the fog but I know it was her."

"How?" Fikus asked.

"She had her curlers in."

Fikus started to give Daisy a push toward home but didn't get very far before a man everyone called Basketball Juan ran up to meet them, tossing Daisy the bright orange ball he carried wherever he went. Daisy caught it like a pro and tossed it back, a perfect chest pass. Juan said something to Daisy in Spanish and then the two high-fived.

Juan had a scar that ran from one ear to the other and a way of smiling at you like you weren't really there, eyes wide and expressionless, mouth usually full of bright pink gum. Fikus didn't trust him. He didn't trust that dog—hovering like a bad smell—or the day, either. And then there was the fact that Hector, Daisy's father, was nowhere to be seen. Hector made a point of meeting the bus and escorting her home nearly every day. A teacher at the high school, Hector typically snuck away during his planning period, and, Fikus presumed, having settled Daisy comfortably in her room with a book or a doll or a TV show, headed back to school to teach the final class of the day. Locking the deadbolt behind him, most likely, the Bottoms being the Bottoms. On the rare days when Hector didn't show, Daisy was met by her babysitter, Marissa, a pretty junior who had the same free period as Hector. "This is my 'Make a Difference Hour,'" she sometimes announced to Fikus, shaking her dark ponytail proudly. "Honors students are encouraged to leave campus, to go out into the community and serve. Sometimes, if I'm lucky, I get to take little girls home and make brownies." Daisy would look up at the older girl in mute adoration and, for some reason, that look hurt Fikus's gut, too.

"Were you supposed to maybe get a ride to the high school?" Fikus asked Daisy. "Hang out with the cafeteria ladies like you sometimes do?"

That was another arrangement of Hector's. When he had to stay late to grade or conference with a displeased parent, Hector would ask Daisy's teacher to drive her to the high school, where, according to Daisy anyway, she became Shellie Pogue and the other cafeteria ladies' favorite helper. Fikus had been informed of all this at his annual August training session. He was given two bulging red folders, one labeled "Daisy Gonzalez" and another "Alex Nelson," so he would know how to handle any issues that might arise from Daisy and Alex's "situations." That was how his boss at the bus garage had put it. *Situations*. The folders were at home as far as Fikus knew, probably languishing under the newest Thích Nhất Hạnh he had yet to even think about reading.

Fikus leaned in toward Daisy, cupped his mouth, and lowered his voice. "Does your dad know you're hanging out with that guy?"

She smiled and nodded. "Juan's my friend. He's teaching me how to play basketball."

"Oh. Basketball."

Someone inside the bus started screaming. This time it wasn't Tiara, and that meant it was most likely Asperger's Alex. The screaming grew louder, more insistent. It was definitely Alex. "I've crapped my pants, bus driver!" he shouted. "Crapped my pants! Crapped my pants! Crapped my pants!"

Alex had to say things four times and he wanted you to do it, too. If you didn't, he would start honking like the geese that lived on the man-made lake behind his house in Wyndham-on-the-River and he wouldn't stop until you said you were sorry, sorry, sorry, sorry.

"I hear you, Alex!" Fikus said. "I hear you, I hear you, I hear you!" He looked at Daisy, at her corduroyed legs and Velcroed shoes and small brown arms downy with dark hair. Then he glanced at Juan, who was smiling vacantly while he dribbled.

Fikus had certain rules he was supposed to follow as a bus driver in good standing with Colliersville Community Schools. Number one, don't touch the children. Whatever. Number two, do not come to work intoxicated. Hungover didn't count, right? Right. Number three, never let a child go home in the company of someone who wasn't her parent or guardian. He thought about telling Juan to go away, to play with someone his own age for a change, but Tiara appeared again, waving one hand in front of her nose and thrusting the other one out over the street. In that hand she had a plastic bag half-full of water. An orange fish the size of a sugar cookie fluttered at the bottom.

"Fikus!" Tiara said. "Seriously. It's been a minute. Plus, it smells like shit on this bus and I think it's killing Murphy."

"Just one more second." Fikus turned, expecting to see Daisy still sitting there, but Juan was already wheeling her away down Hate Henry Road, the mangy dog following right behind, nosing at the dirt and weaving from pothole to pothole.

A day late and a dollar short, that's how Fikus's own mother often described him. He was always late and told kids violent stories they couldn't possibly process. Plus, he was balls at discipline and, as far as he could tell, a bad Buddhist/spiritual person. He sucked at being present and mindful and couldn't for the life of him meditate. Fikus sighed heavily and pulled himself back onto the bus. Tiara was in his seat.

"Move," he said. "Go back and sit next to Sammy."

"Can't. Sammy's got Alex's poop in her hair. She played in it."

It turned out Sammy hadn't played in it. Alex had wiped it on her, trying to clean off his hand. But Tiara was right about one thing. The whole bus smelled like shit.

"I am a mess, bus driver!" Alex said. "I am a mess I am a mess I am a mess!"

"I know, Alex!" Fikus said. "I know I know I know. Let's get you home home home home."

Tiara found a spot far away from Sammy and Alex. Fikus put the bus in gear and drove up the hill, watching in his mirror Daisy disappear down the street. As he pulled out of the Bottoms, there was a flash of lightning and a spooky, charged delay. Then thunder so loud it rattled the bus windows. The girl, the man, and the cur were cut off from his vision by a sideways sheet of rain mixed with a wave of tumbling white seeds. The seeds seemed to silence things as they fell. To bring a hush. Like snow. Like Tiara telling everyone to shut the fuck up, they were making Murphy nervous.

Alex pulled his backpack down over his head and his books and pens and papers fell in a heap on the floor.

"I am too good for this world," Tiara said. "I am before my time."

Fikus turned the wipers on high and dabbed at his forehead with a handkerchief. The cottonwood seeds stuck to the glass in white splotches. Those seeds. This storm. He remembered his horoscope from that morning's paper. It had dealt in some way with weather. Hadn't it? Said something about an ill wind blowing no good.

Spilled Milk

(A month earlier)

Colliersville's one full-time police officer texts me at four A.M.:
The milk spills today.

It's my alarm clock, that text. And my one-way ticket out.

The buzz of it wakes Maria. "Who the fuck?"

The room is cool and dark and smells like aerosol because Maria does her hair in the corner and the spray's stuck to the walls and the floor. We sleep on a futon mattress under the window. The window frame is a mess of peeling pink paint that, when I worry it with my fingers, gets stuck under my nails and reminds me that if I were a real man I'd have scraped and sanded and stained that shit long ago. Or at least insisted our douche of a boss/landlord do something about it.

My phone vibrates again, knocking itself against a water glass.

"Seriously," Maria says.

An amber line of light from a buzzing pole outside slices her in half. She's naked and the light looks like a belt. It reminds me where to put my hand. Down the block a dog is barking. In the apartment below us a teakettle shrieks. So does someone on TV, yakking about skin lightener. The mind-blowing results. I had thought when I moved here that I'd at least be able to hear the river but everything else is too loud and it's too quiet. Unlike my phone, which buzzes a third time.

I cup the screen and squint. What's his name? Randy? Richie? Who cares. He thinks he's Dick Tracy. *Did you get that last text?* Whatever his name, he's clearly the anxious type.

"Who is it?" Maria asks again, sitting up. Her breasts sway. Shatter me. Propped up against the wall with that same line of light across her thighs she looks like someone I should paint. It's her hair. Blue black and thick. When she braids it, it's a rope to throw to a drowning man. Then there's her waist, rounded but with ribs showing. Also her arms folded over her chest and the way her lips purse at the edges because she's annoyed and wants to say something she shouldn't. If I could paint I would give her her same eyes but take the sadness out, the waiting-for-everyone-to-screw-her-over out. But I can't paint. All I can do is write. It's a very sad story.

"My mom," I say.

"Yeah right."

I lean over and kiss her where her neck is sticky and whisper a song she likes about hips not lying.

"How about you be a hip then," she says. "Stop lying."

"I'm not lying."

She shrugs. "Sure."

"Time to make the doughnuts."

"We got toast."

"Yum."

"And eggs."

"Good enough."

The kitchen light casts a green net and cockroaches run for cover. Maria wears a T-shirt and nothing else while she fries the eggs. She hums and dances in her bare feet, and her heels on the brick-red linoleum floor are dirty. Water could run under her arches.

"She's a lady," I sing, grabbing her by the waist and spinning her. "And the lady is mine."

There are no cabinets in this kitchen, only a series of shelves made from two-by-fours and concrete blocks. Also a few plastic chests of drawers flanking the refrigerator, which never stops whining. Maria pushes me away and gets on tiptoe, pulls the salt and pepper down from the shelf next to the stove. When she cooks she likes to tell me stories about how, before she met me, she was wild, a partier, if not the Colliersville "it" girl, at least its "id" girl. Stripped at Miss Kitty's. Ran with white boys. Drank everything in sight. Snorted it, too. I've calmed her, apparently, helped her grow up. Everyone says so. She's worried she'll go back to her old ways if I leave her and, like every asshole before me, I promise never to leave her.

She puts ketchup on my eggs and slides the plate toward me across the card table. The plate sticks on a crusty puddle of old jam, and before I can do anything, before I can say, "I'll get that," Maria is back with a wet rag, wiping the spot clean. The eggs are runny. Jealousy eggs.

My phone buzzes again. I've got it in my pocket now but the vibration makes a fart sound against the metal chair and Maria looks up from her food to stare at me, toast triangle dangling from her fingers.

"Who the hell is texting you a million times before the sun comes up?"

"I told you. It's my mom."

"Your mother certainly has a lot to say this morning."

"She can be that way. Verbose."

"Actually I wouldn't know, would I? Seeing as how you haven't introduced us."

For five months now Maria and I have been a team, the dairy's most dynamic duo, and for two of those, lovers, but she doesn't know who I really am and soon I'll be dead to her and everyone else and I'll go back to my life in New York and write the exposé I was hired to. Before I know it, this entire time will come back to me only in dreams and an ache behind my eyes. Also faces. Maria. Small forehead, wide mouth caked in hot-pink lipstick, deep dimple in the chin. Basketball Juan and his shaving scar. Mrs. Gutierrez and her thick eyebrows, tiny nostrils, and teeth like cards falling. Nina Morales, who everyone says is a witch but only because she's a lesbian and has a wart on her nose. The cows, too, those eyes. I think the cows are wise. I think they've forgotten everything we've ever known and I'll say so in my article, but the editor will strike that entire section. *Come on,* she'll say. *You're better than that.*

I took the job at Yoder Dairy for the article, for my career, and for justice, but in just a few weeks it became all about Maria and this one-bedroom apartment next to the stairs. I'd had my eye on her for a while but who didn't? Maria, who's been in the States since she was eight and can speak better English than anyone, Maria and her black lace bras and animal-print pants and *TVyNovelas* magazines. Maria and her soft body and kind heart and hard mind. There isn't much that gets by Maria. Except for me, of course. Not much she doesn't see coming.

Except today.

"Who is it, Ramon? I mean really." Maria's big eyes narrow. A loose hair hangs from the arm of her T-shirt. One end's in her eggs. "Tell me the truth."

I don't answer her. If I'm quiet, if I pretend to be affronted, she'll give up and be sweet. If I say something, things will get ugly. Thrown dishes and screaming and threats. I eat fast and stare at the food. By the time the toast's gone she's hugging me and apologizing for being so cray-cray.

"It's my fucking period. I'm sorry, baby. Tell your mama I said hi, okay? Tell her her son's the handsomest man this side of forever."

"She's sick," I say. What's one more lie? "In the hospital. I'll have to call her later."

"Poor thing. You should call her now."

"No time."

Which is true. Maria glances at the cat clock over the stove and dribbles coffee on her shirt. "Oh shit." We race each other to the bedroom and dress, grabbing clothes from the floor and laundry baskets and bags—you can indeed live without furniture, without HBO and artisan cheese and good coffee and air-conditioning—and we're out on the street with the others before I can think of what sickness my perfectly healthy mother might be suffering from.

Mrs. Gutierrez is at the front of the line as usual. She tells us good morning, clutching her fat purse closer to her side. There are Nutter Butter cookies and homemade tamales in there. Also romance novels. She reads to me and Maria at lunchtime. Maria likes the cowboy ones best because the men wear chaps and the women aren't white for once.

"Good morning, Mrs. Gutierrez," we say.

"Good morning you two," she says. "Another day in paradise."

All of us live in the Ranasack Apartments because Helman Yoder, our boss at the dairy, owns the building and rent is peanuts. Of course, we don't get paid anything either, so you do the math. Our Bottoms neighbors don't like us much. There's a whack-job militia man down the street who thinks it's good fun to use printouts of Mexican faces for target practice and a few others who tend to spit when we walk by. The river floods at the first sign of rain, and no one ever comes to clean it up. No one comes to clean anything up. The streetlights are always broken and the yards are littered with pop cans and diapers and driftwood. Apparently Señor Yoder doesn't believe in home repair. Windows leak and pipes leak and walls leak. We borrow five-gallon buckets like cups of sugar. When the river rises, the air smells like garbage and death.

Colliersville, Indiana, voted Most Livable City in America three times running.

When the bus pulls up, Mrs. Gutierrez waves us in front of her. She wants to sit with Mr. Aguilar and who can blame her? He always knows the weather report. Plus he's a gossip and good-looking and a recent widower. I watch them flirt for a minute. It's my last chance.

There's a whirring sound and the heavy creak of metal on metal. Instead of opening the door, Fikus Ward, the bus driver, must have activated the wheelchair lift. We watch the platform settle on the ground, empty except for a single white shoestring, and then rise again. Someone at the back of the line claps and the door finally opens.

"C'mon, baby," Maria says. She takes my hand and pulls me forward, tenderly. Remembering Mama, I guess.

Even though there's nothing around our necks, we march single file because that's what we did at first and habits don't break. Plus, it makes getting on the bus easier and faster. No squeezing, no jostling, no fights. Fikus is eating an Egg McMuffin and flipping through AM radio stations. He drives the bus badly—all hit curbs and crossed centerlines and jerky pedal work—and Ulises has tried a hundred times to take the wheel but Fikus won't budge, just grunts and says, "Mine mine mine mine," off-gassing Old Crow all over the place.

He looks like rain has been falling on him for a hundred years. Except when Maria gets on.

"Good morning, Señor Ward," she says to him, painting her accent on thick.

"Morning, darlin'." Then he eyes her all the way down the aisle.

The only reason I don't punch Fikus in his frog face is I'm pretty sure he doesn't know any better. It's like Ulises says. *Boy ain't right.* And, unlike Señor Helman (or Señor Hell-man, as we call him from the privacy of our rooms), he has a heart in the right place, even if it pumps dumb.

The bus used to belong to the Baptist church. Maria and I sit in the same spot every day, in front of Ulises and right under a picture of Jesus blessing the little children. The children have pink, fat cheeks and sparkling eyes. Jesus stretches from one window top to another. He's like Greenland on a globe. All out of proportion. There are Bible verses spiraling out from his enormous head:

"Many waters cannot quench love"; "Jesus wept"; "Before I formed you in the womb I knew you."

Maria's had two abortions. She says never again. She says, "With you, baby, everything's different."

There are twenty-nine of us total, most in our thirties, but there is a small pack of teens that sticks together and dreams of better jobs in bigger cities, and a few oldies but goodies who boss them around. When we take our seats, we're as quiet as the birds. Not until Fikus drops us off at the barn do we say much of anything and even then we conserve our words, use only what is absolutely necessary to get the job done, because talking takes energy and it's going to be a long day. It's always a long day. Twelve hours typically. One time last month, when there was an accident with Big Bessie and her calf and all the milking machines malfunctioned at once, twelve hours turned to thirteen, then fourteen, and three women fainted dead away on the dairy floor, pale and panting and cold to the touch. Señor Helman had us carry them inside his house and stretch them out on the pretty area rug in the living room because the nearest hospital, he said, was too far away. His wife put wet cloths on the women's heads and gave us glasses of lemonade and talked too loudly about tough economic times and stubborn cows and the heat. "Haha! But I bet you're used to that." Then she shrugged and haha-ed again and mumbled, "Poor souls," because she thought she was safe and none of us could comprehend a single word she said.

Everyone thinks we don't speak the language and we like it that way. That's how we hear things we shouldn't, things about no-good sons and out-of-wedlock, pregnant nieces and wives with alcohol and Percocet problems. Birdy Yoder or, as Maria puts it, Mrs. Yoder If You're Nasty, falls into the latter category, a straight-up opioid and bourbon addict who started using when Helman decided to fire his nice white staff and hire us, Team Brown. Ulises was party to that particular information, overheard a whispered kitchen sink fight during which Helman refused to refill his wife's prescription and she hissed that he cared more about "his Mexicans" than his own family. When Birdy saw Ulises standing there in the doorway she did what any good white wife would do— frowned and froze. But Ulises immediately assumed a sort of Speedy Gonzales demeanor, stammering and twirling his mustache, and I bet Birdy thought, Phew. I bet she was thinking, Thank God they're illiterate *and* dumb. Otherwise . . .

Birdy being indiscreet is also how we found out about Wally, his love for dresses and lacy thongs and pink hair ribbons, and his "perverse thinking he was born this way, oh my God Helman can you imagine? We were there in the delivery room, both of us fully conscious. He came out of me an intact boy, there is no doubt in my mind. Why is our son doing this to us?" That was me in the doorway that time. I was there to tell Helman about a heifer gone dry and, because they both expected me to, I launched into breathless, broken Spanish, making all kinds of mistakes, slaughtering the subjunctive, and Helman said, "I can't understand you. Speak English," so I did, haltingly, like an Indian in a John Wayne movie. Palm raised, fingers straight as arrows. *How.*

In reality there are only a few of us who speak only Spanish. Jesus H. for one. Also Julio R. and Carlos S. and Elena V. and Elena's four daughters, who all have painful acne, long legs, and perfect asses. Then there's me, the one they call Ramon but whose name is really Gordy, who writes the Queen's English and plans to blow the doors off this entire stinking operation in, oh, six hours or so.

Poor Mrs. Yoder, I think. Poor soul.

We smell the dairy before we see it. At five A.M. even odors seem loud, and once the scent of manure leaks in through the bus windows we huddle closer together and hope, perversely perhaps, for a crash, a fire, mad cow—anything that will take us back to our beds, even if we don't have beds, just hot, musty cushions and the bodies of others.

"I'm hungry," Maria whispers.

"Ask Mrs. G for a Nutter Butter."

"Uh-uh, no more of those. I'm watching my figure."

"I'll watch it for you. So will Fikus."

She smacks me on the arm, then looks down at her nails. They're a mess of chipped glitter polish and jagged edges. Her hands are smooth on top, callused on bottom. They feel so nice that way, rubbing my back at night to get rid of the day knots. I pull her wrist up to my lips and kiss her veins.

"If you leave me for your text girl, I'll kill myself." She takes her wrist back and draws a nail across the underside. "Just like that."

"You would never," I say.

"What do I have to live for, huh?" Maria gives me a crooked smile. "This job? Fuck this fucking job."

Like me, Maria is a "milker/general laborer/herdsman." That's what it says on our checks, anyway. "Sexist much?" she says, come payday. We're all milkers/general laborers/herdpeople, except for Mr. Aguilar, who's a "herd manager," and a lot of the youngest workers who feed the beasts and sneak out as much as they can to smoke. No smoking for me and Maria. When the first milking's over, she and Basketball Juan and I lead the cows out of the parlor and into the pasture to make sure they all get enough to eat before the next round. Then we inspect every single fucking teat for cuts and sores and signs of irritation, sometimes by squinting, other times with touch. The teats feel like deflated whoopee cushions.

We all love the cows. Love them as much as we hate them. On weekends, we eat pig. Pork rinds, bacon, chorizo. To celebrate our fourteen-hour paycheck I brought home steaks and Maria said, "Take them back. My God, I can't eat Bessie."

"I should go back to stripping," Maria says now. "Anything is better than this."

Behind us, Ulises amens. "Jesus Christ I hate this place." Then he crosses himself. "Please forgive me, Lord. I am a sinner. I know not what I say."

At the entrance to the dairy are life-size metal cows that in the morning dark look almost like the real thing. There are three of them and we've named them after the members of the Yoder family—the big boss man, Helman; his wife, Birdy; and their wannabe trans son, Wally. Cow Helman has long horns and a raised tail. Cow Birdy is fat and docile looking. There are silver flecks on her rump where the paint's worn off. Cow Wally is small. His head is on the ground like he's getting ready to charge. A few of the guys put a dress on Cow Wally a couple months back. A dress and a bright pink wig. Everyone thought it was pretty funny, everyone but Maria, who, the first chance she got, ripped the dress and the wig off Cow Wally and burned both in a barrel behind the apartments. Then she gave the presumed guilty parties— Ulises and Julio R.—a talking-to, called them bullies and bastards and worse. She made me swear I had nothing to do with it—I

didn't—and promise that if the like ever happened again I would
kick the ass of whoever was responsible for such a cowardly and
dickless prank. "As if the poor kid doesn't have it hard enough,"
Maria likes to say. "The kid is fucked." She's right. So I leave Cow
Wally alone. I leave Human Wally alone, too, but I'm not above
taking a pee break on Cow Birdy's back right hoof when no one's
looking.

"Morning, Wally," Maria says to the statue version. "Let's make
it a good day."

The gravel drive up to the barn is pitted and Fikus hits every
hole. The manure smell grows overwhelming. I reach out and
palm the cool bus window and my phone buzzes one more time.

"Your poor mother," Maria says, angling away from me. "I'll
have to send her a get-well card."

The text reads, *Bringing reinforcements. B ready.*

My editor and I made an agreement with the authorities. I
would go undercover, wear a wire, get the scoop, and gather evidence, foolproof, bulletproof, do what the cops had been unable
to do themselves, and in return they would offer every worker am-
nesty, even Basketball Juan, who's slow and might be a danger to
himself. American citizenship.

"No ICE," I'd told the cop. Randy. That's it. Randy.

"Cool," he'd said.

What did he mean by reinforcements? And even if everyone
gets to stay, they'll be jobless and it will be all my fault. Where
will they work then? How will they live? They won't go back
home. I know that much. They'll stay and rot next to the Ranasack like the washed-up carcasses of fish, of frogs, of puppies that
have lost their way.

And they'll hate me for a while. They'll sit in the plastic chairs where I used to sit, drink the same swill beer I used to drink with them, and say, *Ramon. Fucking Ramon. Did you know his name was really Gordy? What kind of name is that?* They'll keep it down in front of Maria but still they'll curse me, toss out the T-shirt I left behind. Rip up my picture. They'll forget me like they've forgotten what it was like to live near the ocean where they grew up. They'll say, *The ocean? What was that? We'll never see* that *again.*

I will. I'll see it. I'll take the award money—my piece will impress the hell out of people who read such things—and buy a ticket to Cancún. That's the big difference between me and Basketball Juan, between me and Maria and Ulises and Mrs. G. A plane ticket. A credit card. The option. I'll hate Cancún, all bikinis and beer bongs. I'll pick it as penance. I'll drink the water.

But for now, I'm one of them. For now, I'm we and they're me and there's the bus ride coming to an end and Maria's head on my shoulder.

"Ramon," she whispers to me as we pull up in front of the barn where the lights blink on, an almost hello. "I think we should end this. You know, see other people."

I jerk to attention, alarmed, then Maria kisses my jaw and laughs. Her teeth are smeared with lipstick but she's still the most beautiful woman I have ever seen.

"Just kidding." She kisses me again, on the lips this time. Lingering. "April Fool's." Her fingernails trickle down my face and she shakes her head like, Don't cry, baby. Don't cry.

Collarsville

(May)

Daddy and Uncle Scottie are in a militia, which they say is a lot like high school only in the militia no one tells them what to do because they're the bosses and they can chew gum and eat whenever they want. Also they shoot things. Paper targets mostly, but once in a while birds or squirrels or trees. And they do this agility-training stuff on an obstacle course Uncle Scottie built in our backyard out of old burn barrels and fence posts and sometimes they pretend it's end-times and the government's right there in their faces demanding that Daddy and Uncle Scottie and the other guys—there's maybe ten in toto; it's a pretty exclusive group—surrender their firearms and then it is so on. That's when they start shooting up the ground, the barrels, anything that's around. They shoot up the sky if they feel like it, and even though it's May it feels like the Fourth of July and I'm like, This doesn't resemble school in any way. This is anti-school.

It's not like my dad thinks. I don't skip. Much. My grades are going to shit on account of Mr. Gonzalez, who is my math teacher and history teacher and walking, talking torment. He hates me. Seriously. He effing hates me and there's really nothing I can do about it because as far as I can tell I never did anything to bring on the hating in the first place. The fact that he teaches two of my classes is bad enough, but Benny said he heard that Mr. Gonzalez was telling my other teachers that I was a loser from way back, like a born loser, and so now they're following right in Mr. Gonzalez's tiny footsteps, giving me grief if I'm a second late and grading my papers and tests extra hard.

At least I'm doing halfway decent in art class, which is good because I'm pretty sure that's what I want to do with my life. Be an artist. Starve. What the fuck? Art's my only A, but even Mr. Sawyer told me I need to be careful not to lose my line. Mr. Sawyer thinks art is all about having a line in your head and following it, putting it on the page in a way only you can, and he's worried I might have stopped seeing my line. You're talented, he says, but talent's not everything.

It's because my last name's Seaver. That's according to Benny and Benny should know because his sister's married to my third cousin and my cousin gets pulled over for a DUI every two weeks while Benny's sister can drink like a fish and hit a few mailboxes and go home completely unmolested.

Benny likes the word *molested,* not because he's a cho-mo or anything, but because he says it makes him sound learned. Benny's like that, smart and sophisticated, and he promised me five months ago when we were drunk and smoking out at Spencerville Fun Spot that once he got his license and his dad's cast-off Camry he'd drive us as far away from Colliersville as he could. "Into the ocean if that's what it takes," he said, and even though we were hammered and Benny was feeling a little high on account of I'd just blown him and let him cum in my mouth, I'm going to hold him to that promise because it's really all I've got.

Well, besides Daddy and Uncle Scottie and my bunny, Chiggers, who, according to Uncle Scottie, isn't really long for this world because of how fat he is and old, too. I guess in a way I have Benny, but he's a boy and beautiful and his skin is slick like a seal's and sometimes when we're together it feels like he could just slide right out of my grasp into the ocean. Not that we're close to the ocean here in Colliersville, Indiana, or Collarsville as I like to call it, landlocked as we are and choking on dust, but Benny doesn't belong here and I know I have to do extra-special stuff to keep his interest, hence the blow jobs and the swallowing, but soon that won't be enough. I have to be smart and get good grades like that Italian slut Marissa Marino, who moved here in December with her hair and her skin and her I'm-going-to-be-valedictorian-as-well-as-head-cheerleader-you-just-watch-me glow (and believe me, Benny does watch her), and that's why one Sunday while Daddy and Uncle Scottie are in the living room, cleaning their guns and cuing up *Road House* for the hundred-billionth time, I decide to shed a little light on the "why Renee can't seem to pass history" dilemma.

"Daddy," I say, handing him and Uncle Scottie beers from the cooler Dad keeps next to his recliner, "I got a little bit of a problem with a teacher at school."

"Oh really?" Daddy takes a long swig of beer and runs one of my old T-shirts through a puddle of gun oil. "What's the trouble?"

Daddy's distracted, but still, I can tell my timing's impeccable. Apparently Mr. Yoder—who owned, or used to own anyway, a big-ass dairy out on Route 20 where Colliersville meets Spencerville through a tangled chicken-wire fence—came to the militia meeting tonight because the police raided his business a few weeks ago and he's out for revenge or something. I guess Mr. Yoder showed up dressed in Revolutionary War garb, white wig and everything, and kept saying, "Give me liberty or give me death," and it's weird, but bad news just charges Daddy and Uncle Scottie up, especially when it comes with a new member. Blessing upon blessing, Mr. Yoder's not only a crossbow enthusiast, but also a mover and shaker in the Colliersville Chamber of Commerce. So, there's sort of a spark in the air tonight you can almost smell, a "we finally know people who know people" excitement coming off Daddy and Uncle Scottie in waves, stronger even than their usual Old Spice/Axe body spray combo I'm so used to.

"This Helman Yoder development is gonna take us to the next level," Uncle Scottie says.

Dad agrees. "No doubt about it. Helman will see to it that we step up our game."

I don't know Mr. Yoder from a wheel of cheese, but his son, Wally, is in my class and we used to be sort of friends way back when in fourth or fifth grade, but he thinks he's a chick now or something—wears skirts and tights to school and uses the girls' restroom even. I heard he works at the Hair Barn, giving mani-pedis and eyebrow waxes to old ladies. Wild. He doesn't say much when I run into him in the bathroom, preening in front of the mirror and slathering on the same shade of lipstick as Marissa the Italian Slut, just averts his eyes and plays with his hair. But that's fine with me. Now that Wally's a girl, it's like we have nothing to talk about.

"Daddy," I say again. "I need your help."

Daddy looks up from his rifle, a shiny blue-gray, walnut-butted Winchester he likes to call Cher in honor of that singer from the seventies who used to be beautiful but is suffering from melty face like the rest of them. "Spill it, sugar," he says. "Tell me all about the asshole."

Uncle Scottie laughs and shakes his head. That's his response to a lot of what Daddy does and says and even though they're not really brothers and he's not technically my uncle, just an old friend of the family, they get along like they're related, doing pretty much anything for the other and having the occasional fistfight to clear the air.

I take a seat in Daddy's recliner and pop it up so I'm relaxed and dig in. "It's this Mexican guy, Mr. Gonzalez—"

"Spic teacher?" Daddy says.

"Well, yeah," I say. "Mr. Gonzalez hates me, Daddy, he really does, and you think I'm skipping, but what's really going on is he's flunking me on purpose and telling all my other teachers that I suck or something."

"What right does he have . . ." Daddy says, going red about the temples. "What right . . ."

It's feeling too easy, but I go with it. "I know, Daddy. That's what I thought. What right?"

Gonzo's as legal as they come—born in Chicago, according to Benny, and a Bottoms dweller like us—but there's lots of illegals living right next door now, thanks to Mr. Yoder, who brought them here to milk his cows. Well, not *technically* next door, but down the street in the Ranasack Apartments, which, like the rest of the Bottoms, used to be nice. Daddy says he can remember a time when people took some pride in their places, mowed their lawns, planted flowers by their front stoops, kept their boat docks waterproofed and up straight. It's as if everything's sort of gone downhill. Literally. The three shoulderless streets and two gravel alleys tip toward the Ranasack like cigarette ash left too long, and Daddy blames the illegals for the difference. Whenever we run into a group of them, playing basketball in the apartment parking lot or hanging out around Tony's Pizza or the bank or the PO, he makes sure to get between me and the men especially, who, Daddy says, have one thing on their mind, that being the rape of young, helpless white girls like myself. Benny thinks it's all bullshit, says my daddy and his precious militia make the KKK look like a bridge club, but I'm not sure. Daddy says there's a right way and a wrong way to do things.

The wrong way is my dick of a cousin Josh's approach. A few nights ago I caught him writing, "Spics go home!" on someone's truck with a Sharpie. He was drunk off his ass and in the company of his stripper bit on the side. She was plowed, too, and wrapped up tight like a Christmas present in a bright blue Band-Aid dress. She kept stumbling on her six-inch heels and telling me I was pretty for a Seaver. "That's because all the Seavers you know are men," I said, and pushed Josh toward home. "Go back to your girlfriend."

"Excuse me?" said the drunk girl.

"Your *real* girlfriend," I said.

Josh wants in Daddy's militia so bad everyone can taste it, but Daddy and Uncle Scottie won't budge. They have their standards, regardless of what Benny might say about it.

"Your teacher says you suck?" Uncle Scottie asks, eyeing me suspiciously from under the brim of his hat.

I just ignore him and forge on. "I study, Daddy, I really do. And I work hard. You've seen me. I get home and go right to my room and do my homework until it's all finished, but Mr. Gonzalez is poisoning that place for me. Just poisoning it."

I have this way of dealing with Daddy. Some, and by some I mean Uncle Scottie, would say that I'm spoiled, that Daddy's wrapped around my pinky finger, but it's a lot more complicated than that and no one, not even Uncle Scottie, not even Benny when he's quiet and listening and so beautiful and empathetic I want to eat his face, can really understand what Daddy and I have. It's just us. It's been just us for three years now since my mom up and left with that horrid Irish guy who came through town selling fake limbs, only the problem was the fake limbs were even a little fake. They didn't work, didn't stay on, didn't move right—ask poor Carl Nickels, who's in the militia but mostly moves targets around since he lost his leg below the knee to sugar diabetes. Carl was the first guy in town to buy one of the blarney dickwad's fake legs and was so jazzed thinking he'd finally be able to drive again that he strapped it on and took off full tilt, only to have the thing come unhinged at 60 mph and his El Camino split in two by a telephone pole. By the time people realized it was all a scam, though, my brilliant mother was elbows deep in love with the dude and skipped town with him and his truck full of plastic arms waving good-bye.

I have one of the arms. It got left behind by accident, flew out of the truck bed and landed, fingers up, in our lilac bush. It's sitting on my bookshelf in a vase. I painted a tattoo on it, a whole sleeve of tangled things—roses, words ("Mother," "Benny"), bullets, bunnies. It's a souvenir. I have a dress of hers, too, an ugly one with the armpit ripped out, and a seashell earring box with four pop-beads inside.

I can tell by the diamond commercials on TV that Mother's Day's approaching. None of us gives a shit. None of us has any mothers. Dad's died of a heart attack before I was born and

Scottie's drank herself blue and right into the ground a few years ago. Mother's Day, shmother's day.

Anyway, Daddy and I bonded after Mom left, got really tight because we had to. Watched a lot of movies, mostly Disney princess crap because that's what I was into then, fell asleep on the floor together sometimes, ate popcorn and Little Debbies and Corn Nuts just to survive. Things were tough for a while, things were downright scary because Daddy lost his job and then almost lost his mind, but now here we both are, on the other side of all that, stronger, better and better for it, and Daddy's got a j-o-b he kinda loves at the junkyard off Route 20. It's a pretty easy gig. He feeds the dogs, watches a little TV, packs a little heat. I take Benny there a lot, that is when we're not hanging out at the Fun Spot, which is a badass location because it's like history just froze everything in place, and trees grow up right through the rides and wooden clown faces rot in the rain. Benny's into that sort of thing, old stuff with long stories. That's why he likes the junkyard, which he says is like a cemetery for cars. When we go there we get lost in the jungle of truck cabs and tires, throw flowers. It's spooky and wonderful at night, strange shadows and varmints scurrying in the high grass and wheel wells.

"Mr. Gonzalez, you say?" Daddy holds Cher up to the light and tilts her back to really let her shine.

I nod, doing my best to sound choked up. "I just don't know what I'm going to do."

"Maybe you should go in, have a meeting with him, Hank," Uncle Scottie says. His gun's clean and packed away. I can tell by how fast he's finished and the fact that he's sitting on the edge of his chair that he's itching to get home to his pretty girlfriend—Patty?

Penny? It doesn't matter, won't last more than a few weekends. He'll take her out to Sharkey's, turn her around the dance floor a few times, and she'll get drunk and accuse him of looking up some other broad's skirt. Before you know it, Uncle Scottie'll be alone again and begging to sleep on our couch out of sheer loneliness, moaning about crazy women, can't live with 'em, can't kill 'em. *Except you could,* Daddy'll say, like he always does. *If you had the balls.* We're very big on balls around here.

"Think that'll help, honeypie?" Daddy asks me now. He lays Cher lovingly in her case and snaps it shut. "Giving Mr. Poncho Gonzalez a good talking-to?"

"Not sure he's the type that'll listen to reason, Daddy."

Uncle Scottie whistles and shakes his head.

Meanwhile, on the TV, Patrick Swayze's telling a whole bar full of mulleted, wannabe bouncers, "I want you to be nice, until it's time to not be nice."

"Well, all righty then," Daddy says, drinking his beer down. His gaunt, handsome face narrows to a point.

Chiggers bangs against his cage in the kitchen and I text Benny right then: *Gonzo's reign of terror ends now.*

Colliersville High School is the kind of building you look at and just know there's lead paint in there somewhere. It's ancient, so old my dad went there, and sticking out between the windows are these hideous yellow panels, for decoration, I guess, but I can't help thinking that they look like dead teeth in a rotting face. Inside it's almost worse. The first thing that hits you is the smell: old sweet potatoes, body odor, and hunger. People think that hunger doesn't have a smell but they're wrong. Half the hunger's the real and sad kind—Colliersville's got its share of poor kids— and that smells like shit breath and sugar, but the other half is pure desperation to get the hell out of Dodge. That's the kind of stink I have and mostly I don't mind it. I'll wash it off someday, soon maybe, when Benny takes me to the ocean.

Next up on your tour of Collarsville High, after the wall of smell, is the big, bright hallway where the rumbly-stomached, genuinely poor kids stand so they can make fun of your outfit. Not that I blame them. They have to have something, so what they have is judgment. I'm a Seaver and I used to be a poor kid, kind of still am if you compare me to Marissa the Italian Slut and her Wyndham-on-the-River friends, but Collarsville is weird that way. I'm cute, or at least I was in elementary school, and ever since I punched Lauren Tewksbury in the throat for calling my mom a hussy, I've had a reputation for being mean, so the poor kids leave me alone. After all, I was one of them back when Daddy lost his job and we had to shop at the Apple Mart, the little grocery store tacked on to the foodbank to make the impoverished feel like they have agency. Those are words Mr. Gonzalez loves to say. "Impoverished." "Agency." "Marginalized." Ba-lo-ney, if you ask me, which of course he never does.

Me and the other Apple Mart kids—Uncle Scottie's real niece Balinda with the big swimmer shoulders and George, Carl Nickels's two-legged son, most of the McElroys, and this Taiwanese kid whose name no one can pronounce but you know not to mess with on account of his killer eyes and weird upper-lip tic—we're the ones who remember what this town was like when it was all woods and farmland. Back then places like Wyndham-on-the-River were just stink bogs filled with birds, and we all bonded in the foodbank aisles over the generic cereals and wilted produce and our unspoken knowledge that the only thing standing between us and outright homelessness was our parents' spotty ability to get up and go to work in the morning. It brings you together, that knowledge. It's an invisible thread yanked tight and double knotted.

Benny wouldn't know anything about it. His family has money. They own a couple gas stations in town and one down in Fort Wayne, not to mention a huge Wyndham-on-the-River McMansion with an in-ground pool out back and a genuine fountain out front. When he meets me in what he calls the Gauntlet Hall the morning after my talk with Daddy and Uncle Scottie, he's wearing a pressed wine-red shirt and expertly faded jeans. His hair, dark like chocolate and shiny as the barrel of Daddy's gun, is elegantly mussed. It's going in so many directions I get a little lost staring up into it, but that's usually how I feel whenever I'm around Benny, like I'm on a hilltop somewhere spinning in circles like that girl who played the nun in the spring musical last year—"the hills are alive, with the sound of mucus"—and then someone says, "Now walk a straight line." Yeah right.

"Morning, pork chop," Benny says. He throws an arm over my shoulder and guides me through the smell and scoffs and flying spitballs to his locker, which is decorated on the inside with poetry torn from magazines and posters of Barack Obama and the women of the Supreme Court. Benny's a bit of a leftist, which makes him a weird match for me, I know, but I guess it's true what Uncle Scottie says after every one of his breakups: Opposites attract.

Benny grabs his trig book. "I hate this town so much I want to shoot myself in the face."

I glance over his shoulder down the row of lockers to Wally Yoder, who is awkwardly adjusting his bra. What does he have in there? Socks? Kleenex? Regardless, the result is lumpy and the left side is visibly bigger than the right. For a second, I can't help feeling sorry. Benny and a lot of the other boys aren't always so nice to him. Machismo crap. Then there's the scandal surrounding his dad's dairy and the whole transitioning into womanhood thing. I want to help him but not enough.

"Sweet cheeks," Benny says. "I have a proposal for you."

Here it comes. The invitation I've been waiting for. Everyone's been talking cummerbunds and tulle and blowouts for weeks. Also dinner reservations in Fort Wayne and limos and disc jockeys versus live bands—the pros, the cons. To hokey or to pokey. It's lame, it's ridiculous, it's girly, pretty in all sorts of pink kind of bullshit, but I can't help it. I want to go to prom with Benny, or, at the very least, I want him to want to go with me. I try to look up at him but can't. A hole is growing in the toe of my right shoe. Under my left is a blue band camp flyer.

"Let's do something exciting today," Benny says. "Go wild. Get in trouble."

The disappointment makes my back sweaty. Also my nose itch. I don't say anything for a moment.

"C'mon, kid." He punches me in the arm.

"You mean like skip and go to the Fun Spot?"

"Nah. I mean like rob a bank. Steal a plane. Blow up a building."

"Kidnap a brat and hold him for ransom?"

"Now you're onto something."

"Whatever," I say. "You're all talk. Remember what happened when I sliced into that fetal pig in bio? You practically fainted."

"That was different," Benny says. "That was a smell thing. I'm talking about indulging in real criminal behavior here. Something for the papers. Something for the interwebs. Let's put Colliersville on the map."

I can never tell if Benny is serious. His dark eyes say he is, but his perfect mouth is grinning at me. Those lips. Those white teeth. I want to make out with him until we're both stunned and out of breath, until we forget where we live and who we are.

"We could break into my dad's junkyard," I say, because where we go doesn't matter—Fun Spot or junkyard, clowns or cars or clown cars, as long as Benny's there and I can touch him and feel for a moment no one's on his mind but me.

Benny snorts. "We did that last week."

His eyes drift over my shoulder. Wally's gone now, probably to the girls' room to touch up his mascara, and Marissa the Italian Slut is in Benny's sights. The dead giveaway's the sticky pink blush spreading up his neck and the way he keeps sniffing like his allergies are back. No one but Marissa makes him lose his cool like that. Certainly not me.

I lean up against the wall so Benny can, if he so desires, get a good view of my boobs. I'm proud to say that, if they aren't my best feature, they're at least a close second to my legs. No Kleenex necessary, in other words. My body's my biggest asset, ask anyone, even Uncle Scottie, who's gotten drunk at our house a few times and slurred something about my filling out real nice. What's not so great is my face—Stridex doesn't come with a money-back guarantee—and my feet (flat and too long) and my hair: limp, lifeless, the kind of blondish brown that can't make up its mind. My eyes are okay, I guess. Blue. Nothing like Benny's deep, dark magnets or Marissa the Italian Slut's light brown M&M's eyes that make all the boys melt in her hand. The warning bell rings. We have five minutes to get to class or else. Benny's still staring Slut-ward.

"Count me out, Benny," I say. "I've got all the excitement I can handle with Gonzo."

He finally looks at me. "Fine, fine, rain on my parade. You mi-litia girls are all the same. All bluster and no bullets. So what's your dad going to do to poor Mr. Gonzalez anyway? Blindfold him? Take him out behind your house and use him as a human target?"

"Daddy's just going to talk to him. You know. Scare him a little."

Benny whistles, a perfect imitation of Uncle Scottie. Then he shuts his locker and drapes his arm around me again. "This can-not end well," he says.

"*Au contraire, mon frère.*" I grab some of my worthless hair and chew on it. French is one of Benny's turn-ons, so I'm applying my-self like hell in that class, but I can tell it's not working today. I smile up at him and grab the sides of his face, kiss him hard and quick, because what choice does a girl have? He's bored with me. "This will end exactly the way I want it to."

God must have an extra-special hate just for me, because first period is geometry with Mr. Gonzalez and guess what? Last period is history with Mr. Gonzalez. So, I start and end my day in exactly the same way—staring at Mr. Gonzalez's pockmarked mug and wishing I were anywhere but where I am, I were any-one but me.

"Renee Seaver," he says when there are exactly two minutes

left in history class and the whole, miserable day, "come here, please."

Which of course means I'm in trouble. Everyone who's had him knows that Mr. Gonzalez calls you by your first and last name when you've done something wrong. The first-name treatment's reserved, as far as I can tell anyway, for students of color and kids like Marissa (olive skinned, but I don't think that counts) who always have the right answer when he calls on them about the top five causes of the Great Depression or the first seven digits of pi. Then there are the last-name kids, "Sloan," "Daugherty," "Nelson." Those are the jocks with at least a fifty-fifty chance of getting athletic scholarships to a state school.

Most teachers have their desks at the front of the room, but Mr. Gonzalez sits in the back behind a mountain of paper and books and confiscated cell phones. I guess it's his first line of defense in case someone like the Taiwanese kid goes all postal, but what it really does is just reinforce how short he is. A Mexican Napoleon avenging himself on anyone lucky enough to be blessed with height. Room 323 is Mr. Gonzalez's own island of Elba, although it's more like us kids are the ones in exile. Take that, Gonzo. Someone knows her history.

"Ms. Seaver." He rubs his forehead. "I got a call from your uncle today during my planning period."

Ah. Uncle Scottie. Or Daddy masquerading as Uncle Scottie. I manage to look confused. "Really?"

Mr. Gonzalez shuffles some papers and almost knocks over his Starbucks thermos. Standing above him like this, I can see his bald spot. It's slightly wet with sweat. Up close he smells like creamed corn.

"It seems I've been invited over for dinner tonight," he says.

The room has that end-of-the-day roar, and I lean in. There's no way I heard him right.

"Sorry?"

"I guess that means you'll be cooking."

I don't know what I expected, Daddy making a quick but memorable visit to the principal's office maybe, or him and Uncle Scottie meeting Gonzo at his sad-man Honda in the teachers' parking lot and giving him the what-for. Either way, I was hoping they'd leave me out of it.

The bell rings and the roar rises and gets sharp with the squeak of chairs pushed back and knocked over. Next to Mr. Gonzalez's leaning tower of cell phones is a pink plastic-framed picture of his daughter. I've seen her around the Bottoms some, playing basketball with a retarded illegal who lives in the Ranasack Apartments. The picture's a good one. She has dime-sized dimples, a coffee-colored face, and a mermaid necklace hanging around her neck.

"You can bring Daisy to dinner if you want," I say.

"Thank you, but I've arranged a sitter for her." Mr. Gonzalez riffles through a stack of papers. "Let's just hope you're better at the culinary arts than you are at the Cultural Revolution." He hands me my last test.

A D+. Bright red like communism, bright red like the period stain I found in the girls' toilet at lunch. The plus sign mocks me as I shuffle out the door, where Benny's waiting, his eyes plastered to his iPhone. We walk together not talking, not touching, to the diesel-soaked outdoors, me getting on bus number 1989, the one Marissa and her crowd call the ghetto bus, and Marissa and Benny boarding number 2010, the very year of our Lord we're living through right now. The rich bus. The bus that's twenty years

ahead of me, Balinda, Wally, and Twitchy Taiwanese Kid there in
the back. Maybe it's just me but I swear the windows in 2010 are
cleaner than the rest. How else would I be able to see Benny slide
in next to Marissa, take a lock of her hair, and twist it tenderly
around his finger?

Uncle Scottie's depression-gray Ford Bronco's in the drive
when I get home, and the front windows are wide open, despite
the fact that a rainstorm is gearing up in the west and a black cloud
full of eyes, a puffy Mount Rushmore, looms over the roof, staring me down.

From the front walk I can hear Daddy shouting, "The new
powder, numb-nuts. Use the *new* powder."

Cake or bomb, I wonder, and take my time going in.

It's not something I think about often, but when I imagine
Benny paying a visit to my house—he never has, just as I've never
been to his place—I see everything through his eyes and wish
Daddy and Uncle Scottie spent less time on the militia and more
on home repair. The used-to-be-peach siding's green with mold
and the canvas lawn chairs on the front stoop are full of holes
and rusting up their sides. The window screens are the worst,
ripped as they are and ready for the mosquitoes to push themselves through at night. When Mom was still here the house was
lots nicer—flowers out front, not just weeds, everything with
that woman's-touch shine to it. We even had a pretty sign under
the porch light that said WELCOME TO THE SEAVERS, but that sign
was one of the first things Daddy used for target practice when the
militia got going two years ago.

I can't help wondering what Gonzo will think, especially now that the militia's all but taken over the side yard with a new set of targets plastered with President Obama's face tricked out to look like the Joker from *Batman*. Nailed to the trees are a bunch of cheap straw sombreros Carl Nickels brought home from his job at the card and party outlet. The guys had a field day with those, drawing thick black mustaches on the brims to sort of symbolize illegal immigrants. Then they made some margs and shot the hats up while Uncle Scottie played a song about El Paso on his guitar. If Marissa the Italian Slut ever left her gated community and drove past my house she'd probably confuse it with the junkyard where my dad works.

Turns out it's neither cake nor bomb.

"We're making cornbread," Daddy says to me from the kitchen, "and I've been schooling Scottie here on the importance of fresh baking powder. Fresh powder, my dear, is paramount."

Scottie rolls his eyes. He's wearing my mom's old flowery apron. I can see them both through a hole Daddy made in the living room wall right after he lost his job, back during the scary times. The hole started out as a mistake, a fist through the drywall Daddy didn't feel like puttying, and then one day he took a sledgehammer to it, singing the praises of the open floor plan. It's almost finished now, but a few loose wires can really fuck you up. Get your arm too close to the edge and you'll come away with black fingers and a peeing-yourself sort of shock.

"Fresh powder," I echo. I drop my backpack near the front door. "It makes the bread rise better."

They're drunk, or at least three-quarters of the way there. They've stacked their Milwaukee's Best beer cans in a pyramid on the coffee table.

"Right you are, pumpkin," Daddy says. He sidles over and gives me a wet kiss on the cheek. When he's like this I actually miss my mom.

I glance around the living room, taking in what for Daddy and Scottie has clearly been a very good day. In addition to the beer-can pyramid, the coffee table's sporting a few girlie and *Field & Stream* magazines and a mostly eaten bowl of microwave popcorn. Scottie's gun and Cher are both out, resting barrels up against one arm of the couch, and there are a couple of Netflix envelopes on the floor. Chiggers is in his cage against the sliding glass door, gnawing on a few wood chips and gazing out at the agility course.

"So what's the plan, you guys?" I ask, letting Daddy lead me into the kitchen.

"Dinner with Chi Chi Rodríguez, of course," Daddy says. He motions to the counter. An Apple Mart taco kit, half-open, and an onion share some space with a bottle of Pepe Lopez tequila and a mountain of dirty dishes. "Tex-Mex followed by a short introduction to basic firearm safety. That is . . ." He glances at Scottie. "If there's time."

"If there's time?" I ask.

Scottie shrugs and stirs the batter. "Could get a few extra visitors."

"Just some militia business, sweetie," Daddy says. "We may or may not have pissed off a few guys from the Spencerville chapter."

"Turns out they wanted Helman Yoder." Scottie greases a cake pan with a fingerful of lard. "We stole their only arrow guy."

"You're kidding."

"Don't you worry your pretty little head about it." Daddy chucks his empty into a box by the fridge. It bounces off the others and lands near Scottie's bare feet. "Everything'll go smooth as cream."

The last time Daddy told me not to worry my pretty little head, a bunch of neo-Nazis from Michigan and their waxy-eared kids landed in our front yard for a weekend's worth of assault rifle training. It was like something you'd see in an al Qaeda recruitment video, all ratty tents and AK-47s. One of the fascists' little girls got shot, a calf graze and not much blood, but still. I held her while her dad wrapped the wound. She was chilly and soft, like the other side of the pillow.

"So when's Mr. Gonzalez coming?"

Uncle Scottie shoves the cornbread in the oven and sets the timer on the microwave for ten minutes. "Could be anytime, right, Hank? I think he said he'd come straight from school, but I can't quite remember."

Daddy's doing his best to chop the onion. "Can't seem to summon that-there memory myself, Scottie my boy. I guess it's like warfare, this whole entertaining-at-home business. You got to be ready for any and all eventualities. Uninvited guests. Collapsed soufflés. Tornado watches."

"There's a tornado watch?" I ask.

"Yeah," Scottie says, "but I can tell this one'll just blow over. The clouds aren't the right color green."

I flip open my phone and study the screen for a second. It's an ancient Nokia piece of junk, not nearly as cool as Benny's iPhone loaded up with apps, and I'm limited to 160 letters per message or Daddy gets a bill that makes him scream and threaten to go old-school on my ass and make me pick out my own switch. I want to tell Benny that I'm scared and that it's a new feeling and it hurts. I want to beg him to come over now and rescue me, but

he'd probably say, "From what?" and I wouldn't know how to answer. How can I explain Helman Yoder and the rest of it to a kid
who hates his parents for not getting him a new flat-screen for
his bedroom? I settle for *I'm screwed. Gonzo disaster. Help.* I know
it'll probably be hours before he responds. That's usually how it
works and even then, after I've wasted most of my night envision-
ing him rolling around naked on a puffy rug in Marissa the Italian
Slut's perfect pink bedroom, he sends me something disappoint-
ing, something fucking inadequate, and I begin to doubt his
sincerity in promising to drive me away into the sunset. I begin
to think he might not love me after all, at least not the way I love
him, and that thought makes it hard to breathe.

"Renee, sweetie," Uncle Scottie says. "Do us a big favor and set
up the card table in that little nooky area there. And your pop and
I need another round of beers. Cold ones are in the cooler behind
the couch."

Just then the doorbell rings.

I run to the door to make sure it's Gonzo and not one of the
Spencerville hicks pointing an Uzi through the peephole. "It's
him," I say.

"*Entrez-vous, amigo,*" Daddy shouts.

And it all goes downhill from there.

"**My daughter was born smart**," Daddy says halfway through
the meal, which, because he forgot to brown the meat and Uncle
Scottie used the old powder, consists of broken taco shells, some
sliced onions, and a handful of lettuce. "She came out of her
mama's magic baby door talking in complete sentences and the
like. And she's one hell of an artist. Did you know that?"

Mr. Gonzalez hasn't looked at me once since we sat down at the card table and started passing around the taco shells. In fact, his eyes have barely strayed from his plate, a situation that gives me a clear view of his bald spot. I think of Daisy and glance at his left hand. There's a wedding band on his ring finger, bumping up against a hairy knuckle.

"'Course," Daddy continues, "all of those complete sentences were in English because that's the language we speak here in the ole U.S. of A. Do you speak English, Mr. Hernandez?"

"Gonzalez," he says to his plate.

"What's that?" Daddy says. "My hearing ain't what it used to be since I got a gun. Repeated blasts near the ear canal, etcetera."

"His name's Mr. Gonzalez, Daddy," I say, looking over at Uncle Scottie for some help, but he's concentrating on trying to fill a split shell with lettuce.

"It just keeps breaking more." Scottie stares at the sad remains of the shell. "Every time it breaks just a little more. Like a heart. Like my heart. Did I tell you, Hank, that Paige dumped me because I said that lady on that show where people see dead people was pretty?"

Daddy nods quickly. "You mentioned it once or twice today, Scottie, and sad as you are, I have to ask you not to stray from the main topic at hand, which is Renee, her God-given intelligence, and the shitty grades this guy keeps giving her because, well, hell if I know. My daughter seems to think it's on account of her last name, a little something she just so happens to share with me. I think it's time you started talking, sir. Did some explaining of yourself."

A long moment of silence follows, broken only by the sound of Chiggers kicking wood chips over a new poop. Then Uncle

Scottie starts to cry noisily, the tears leaving wet tracks on his face, and outside there's a deafening boom that rattles the walls, followed by what sounds like shotgun spray against the house.

Mr. Gonzalez jumps in his chair and his hands tremble over what must be the crappiest dinner he's ever not eaten.

"Daddy." The bangs outside get louder, closer. "Do you think . . . ?"

Daddy puts both hands on the table like he's about to do a push-up. His veins are blue puffy paint. "Could be, sugar bear. Could be."

Scottie wipes his eyes and gets up, grabbing his gun on his way to the door. Daddy follows him, yanks Cher up to his shoulder, and weaves a little. A few bullets hit the front screen door, at least it seems that way to me, what with the pinging sound of metal against metal. Me and Gonzo, we duck. We throw ourselves under the table like it will do any good and then, as Daddy and Uncle Scottie plunge out the door, it occurs to me that Benny might have made up that whole thing about Gonzo trashing me to the other teachers, that maybe most of what Benny's told me since we became friends, well, started taking each other's clothes off when he moved here after my mom left, is a lie. Like, "Renee Seaver, you're special." That one. And, "Renee Seaver, you're the coolest girl in Collarsville," and, of course, big, huge, fat duh, "I'll take you away from here, Renee Seaver."

Because it's not Benny crouching next to me on the peeling linoleum with the bunny hair and dead ladybugs. It's Gonzo, who, if he weren't here tonight trying not to get killed, would probably be home with his crippled daughter doing something inspiring, like teaching her to kick a soccer ball with her wheelchair feet. So I do something crazy. I mean I do something totally

schizo. I put my right hand over Gonzo's to stop it from shaking.
It's a furry paw and damp like the rest of him and all of sudden I
remember the night my mom left with the Irish guy and how I
spent most of it with my fingers wrapped as far as they would go
around that fake hand that fell out of the truck. It was hard and
felt like my mother's when I was little and she would grab hold of
me to keep me from wandering into traffic. Like she cared. Like
anyone ever really cares about anyone else.

And then I can't help it, I'm thinking of Benny and our first
time, and how the whole thing, the kisses, that feeling of his weight
on me, just busted me wide open on a cool spring night like this
one, the sound of spring peepers somewhere in the corner of the
junkyard drowning out Benny's sighs coming soft and fast in the
back of a rusty red Buick with torn upholstery and a chopped-off
top. Moon directly above us. Daddy back in the office nodding
over a plastic 7UP bottle half-full of vodka. Emptiness like an entire sky spilling out of me when it was all over and Benny turning away to look across the hoods of all those dead cars. I'm that
empty tonight, all alone with my bad grades and bad skin and bad
love. And I'll never get out of here, except in a body bag.

"Oh no, Chiggers!" I say, and peek out from under the table to
make sure he's okay and not some bloody mess of fur and guts.
But Chiggers is fine. Chiggers is bored. Behind him, the world has
gone black and white. All we're dealing with here is a hailstorm.

I tug Gonzo out from under the table and we go to the sliding
glass door and gawk. The spooky stuff falls from the sky and
bounces off the ground like a plague of Ping-Pong balls while
Daddy and Uncle Scottie run in circles, trying to save their targets, guns still clutched tight. It's a lost cause. Most everything out
there, including the sombreros, is shredded to soggy confetti.

"See, Mr. Gonzalez? It's okay," I say. "It's just a storm."

Gonzo doesn't react at first. He mumbles something under his breath—a prayer, probably—and watches as tree branches whip like cheerleader hair around the house.

The wind's dying down but the damage's been done. The neighbor's shed roof sits suspended in our elm tree like a lost kite. Uncle Scottie's Bronco is pitted with dents. Scottie leans his cheek against the driver's-side door and cries some more.

Me, I don't let go of Gonzo's hand. For a while it sends tremors up my arm, but, finally, when the hail slows and there's a bright wave already melting against the door, I feel it relax and go still in mine.

Blood Curse

(May)

Josh didn't understand why she didn't just cut it already.

"It's down to your knees," he told her, pushing a handful of marijuana seeds and buds around on the kitchen counter. "It's not even pretty anymore."

Shannon tried to shrug off his casual criticism—Sticks and stones, she told herself—but it hurt more than she wanted to admit. She'd always assumed he loved her long hair. In bed in the early morning when he was sweetest he liked to grab a handful of it and say he felt like he was living with a princess in a fairytale.

"Rapunzel," he'd whisper. "Let down your golden hair."

Her hair wasn't golden, it was dark brown, and she'd considered dyeing it, got so far as to call her best friend, Rhae Anne, at the Hair Barn to make an appointment, but Rhae Anne said hell no, she wasn't going within a foot of that.

"It'd take me eight hours," she said. "And why would you want to be blond like everyone else?"

It was a question Shannon couldn't answer. She'd spent a year of her life second-guessing almost everything she did, from how she brushed her teeth ("Too loud," Josh said) to the way she walked ("Like a lesbian") and the way she laughed when Josh's brother was around ("Like you want to fuck him"). Self-doubt had become a habit with her, a reflex. She'd always been shy, but now it was as if there were a spotlight on her, its brightness always picking up a flaw she had no power to change.

She opened the door and stood for a moment, watching Josh and feeling the cool morning air on her cheeks. It was foggy now but it would be sunny later, warm, maybe even hot. From where she stood Shannon could just make out Hector Gonzalez's back deck and busted-up gas grill. Squirrels in the trees dropped nuts down and scattered a spiderweb. That poor man. He'd banged on her door the night before, frantic, wondering if she'd seen his daughter—"Anywhere anywhere," he kept repeating, eyes wild—but Shannon could only shake her head. She'd just gotten home from work herself and hadn't seen Daisy in a couple weeks. Even then, it was a fleeting glimpse—Daisy being wheeled home by Hector or a high school girl, Daisy tossing a basketball in the Ranasack Apartments parking lot. At the time, Shannon thought, I should volunteer to watch her once in a while. But she hadn't.

"Can you believe it about Daisy?" She fiddled with her braid, letting it drop against her side when Josh looked up. "I wish there was something we could do."

Josh went to the closet, probably, Shannon thought, for rolling papers, which he kept in a large wire basket behind the sugar. "I'm sure she'll pop up soon," he said. "They always do."

"They do?" Shannon was pretty sure that wasn't true, that

missing girls hardly ever "popped up" after they'd disappeared. Or little boys for that matter.

"Christ, who cares?" Josh's back was still to her. While he hunted, a few cereal boxes hit the ground, followed by an open bag of flour. White powder made a cloud at his feet. "They're Catholics, right? They breed like rabbits. One disappears, another's born the next minute. Problem solved."

Shannon's hand went to her heart. "She's an only child."

"Whatever," Josh said. "I'm guessing she wasn't kidnapped at all. She probably just ran away to give her dad a scare. Kids these days, dying for attention. Bet she's hiding out in the apartments as we speak." He turned, stepping in the flour, and held something out to Shannon, a tidy gray box tied with pink ribbon. "Can we stop talking about her?"

Shannon nodded and took the box.

"Open it." He glanced at her from behind two long locks of hair, and for one brief moment, he was the Josh Seaver she fell in love with—handsome, vulnerable, possibly running a fever.

She palmed his forehead. "Are you okay?"

"I'm fine," he said, ducking away. "Open the box already."

She thought of how it all began, their odd and quick courtship. It would have been a good story to tell their children, but there were no kids to tell it to and probably never would be now. Josh, who'd been living in Maple Leaf Mobile Home Park with a few buddies, had, on a beautiful April day, come into the Laundromat where Shannon worked, obviously sick. He'd shoved a load in one of the washers and slumped down in a chair by the front windows, shivering under a stained *Duck Dynasty* blanket and cursing the perfect weather. Shannon ignored him just as she ignored all Seavers, but halfway through the spin cycle, Josh fell off his chair to the floor and didn't get up. He just lay there, blinking up at the ceiling and sweating. Shannon ran over to him, worried about a seizure or an overdose or worse. "Are you okay?" she'd said then, just as she'd said today. But instead of shrugging her off, Josh reached up and touched her hair. He seemed to marvel at it.

Under normal circumstances, she hated it when strangers took such liberties—her hair was like a pregnant woman's belly, inviting an intrusive touch, just asking to be manhandled—but these weren't normal circumstances and Josh wasn't really a stranger. She'd known him all her life. They'd grown up together in the Bottoms, playing cops and robbers and cowboys and Indians and staging epic, all-day snowball battles in and around the old Udall place. But she'd never known him to be gentle. "Sweet Shannon," he'd said to her that day, his fingers still holding her hair. "Sweet Shannon Washburn."

Her heart was touched, and when her shift ended and his load was dry, she took him back to her house, settled him on her couch with a better blanket and the remote, and told him to rest. He followed her orders, sleeping for twelve hours straight. Like a baby, she thought. She fed him chicken soup and Gatorade and tea and toast. One night, when she leaned over to put the thermometer under his tongue, he gave her hair a quick tug and kissed her. "Shannon Nightingale," he whispered, his breath sugary from the Gatorade. "Mother Shannon Teresa." Stay, she thought. Ditch that disgusting bachelor double-wide and move in with me and stay for as long as we both shall live. Or as long as we can stand it. He did. It was the one time Shannon could remember a wish of hers coming true.

The present was a silver bracelet. Three charms—a tiny heart, a rose, and a shiny, red-bowed box with her birthday carved on both sides—dangled from the links. Shannon smiled but the smile felt strange on her face. Josh wasn't a gift giver. He hadn't given her anything for Valentine's Day or their anniversary. Touched as she was by this unexpected display of thoughtfulness, she couldn't help wondering where the money had come from. At the same time, she didn't dare ask. To bring up anything having to do with their finances was to step on a landmine. Suddenly this man whom she liked to think of as a gentle giant would explode with rage and threaten to join Hank Seaver's militia. "But why?" she often asked. "To teach *them* a lesson," he'd say.

Josh had been out of work for a month, ever since he'd lost his school janitor job to one of the Mexican immigrants living down the street in the Ranasack Apartments. Josh claimed his boss let him go because the man (who, according to Josh, "was borderline retarded and carried a basketball around everywhere because he thought he was Michael Jordan or some such shit") agreed to work for practically nothing, but Shannon had heard from Rhae Anne that Josh actually got canned for failing his second of three drug tests.

"Do you like it?" he asked now.

"It's beautiful. Thank you. But what's the occasion?"

"Do I need an occasion to get my woman something nice?" Josh pulled the bracelet from the box and fastened it around her wrist. "That should take your mind off of missing Mexican girls."

Shannon bit her lip. She felt a sudden need to cry. Not here, she told herself. And not now. "I might stop at Granny's for a while after work. Is that all right? If I leave you on your own for dinner?"

"Sure." Josh was back to searching through the closet. A line of white footprints trailed him. "I'll have leftovers or something."

"Okay. Well."

Shannon looked down at the bracelet, gave it a shake, and listened to the charms tinkle. The links caught in her arm hair and she gasped. Josh didn't hear her. He'd pulled his favorite papers from the basket and was busy rolling a clumsy joint. She stood for a moment longer in the kitchen, but there was nothing more to say, and she was going to be late for work if she didn't hurry. The flour. She sighed. She'd clean it up later.

It had rained the previous night and the river was high. Hate Henry Road was a swamp and halfway out of the Bottoms she got stuck in the very same spot she had a foggy night a few weeks ago when Rhae Anne called her for a ride home from the Hair Barn. "Larry's gone and picked up another shift," Rhae Anne said, and Shannon told her she'd be right over, not letting on that she and pretty much everyone in town knew Larry wasn't working overtime at all but was instead spending most evenings with a Mexican beauty, who, after Helman Yoder's dairy farm got shut down, had turned to stripping and was now, rumor had it, doing her best to get knocked up with an anchor baby.

On that night, Shannon was sure she would just sink like a stone and never be heard from again—she imagined the headline in the *Colliersville Record*: QUICKSAND CLAIMS ONE OF OUR OWN— but then she closed her eyes, concentrated, pressed the gas, and somehow she was inching her way up the road, checking her rearview for a sign. She liked to think it was her mother who freed her. Maybe that was Rita's ghost, right there, rustling the ditch grass, a breath of her. Memories of elegant feet making dents in the dirt.

This morning there were no ghosts, no Ritas, and, no matter how many times Shannon hit the gas, no going anywhere. The streets of the Bottoms were deserted. To her left Shannon saw a makeshift "Come home soon, Daisy" shrine that had quickly taken shape on Hector Gonzalez's lawn. It spilled over Hector's driveway like a small but bulging baseball diamond in a motley pile of offerings, much of it—namely the posters and paper lanterns and stuffed animals clutching tiny felt bouquets—soggy and drooping. There were toy-sized plastic wheelchairs topped with random objects: skateboards and peacock feathers and baby bottles. Also, strangely, a tattooed fake arm propped up next to some wax fruit, a clutch of dog whistles, and a few Disney DVDs. Boxes of chocolate still in their cellophane wrapping leaned on large baskets of flowers, and a stack of Bibles towered over a garden gnome out of whose mouth came a dialogue balloon reading, "We love you, Daisy!" Candles of all shapes and sizes, most nearly melted, others with wicks totally intact, formed the shrine's sloppy spine. Someone had tied a wooden cutout of Jesus to Hector's dying ash tree and taped Jesus's hand to a laminated picture of Daisy. Her smile tilted up at him.

"I hate you, Hate Henry Road!" Shannon shouted out her window. Her voice echoed back, mocked her.

Hate Henry Road had gotten its name from some long-dead, tarred-and-feathered white politician, who, according to local lore, dared to marry an ex-slave. Shannon pitied the man, pitied his wife even more, but still, the name was perfect. She'd gotten stuck in the snow and mud so often that her boss at the Laundromat, Mr. Breeder, joked that he should invest in a tow truck just so he could bail out "my little damsel in distress" and get her to work where she belonged. Of course, Chuck Breeder would never think of driving the five miles from his new house in Wyndham-on-the-River to pick up any Bottoms damsel.

"He might get his wingtips wet," she mumbled to herself.

She glanced down at her cell phone. She could call Josh, but there was a good chance his Jeep wouldn't start, it'd been so long since he'd driven it, and anyway she hated his method of freeing her, which basically consisted of pulling his Jeep right up on her bumper and hitting the gas. It worked more often than not, but it'd made her beaten-up Accord look even more destined for the junkyard than it had before.

Shannon's mother would have cried if she could see the state of the car's rear end, scratched as a skating pond and pulling away from the rest of the body like rock from an old hill. She'd loved that car, loved it enough to name it Miss Scarlett because of the paint job, which over the years had faded to an uneven and watery tomato red, and when Shannon thought of her mother, which was at least every day since she'd died of what Shannon's granny called "the galloping girly part cancer," she often thought of her behind the wheel of Miss Scarlett, mannish sunglasses over her brown eyes, a travel coffee mug from the Flying J Truck Stop in her hand. Rita Washburn had worked at the Flying J for twenty-five years and even into her fifties was the most popular waitress there, pocketing the best tips on account of her sweet voice and pretty legs. That's how she was able to pay cash for Miss Scarlett and finally burn the mortgage on the Bottoms house Shannon had grown up in, the house that was now Shannon's, although she couldn't bring herself to change anything her mother had done to the place, even the pink, iridescent rose wallpaper in the guest bathroom that Josh said made him want to puke or go gay.

Rita had been that kind of woman, persuasive. She was beautiful and smart and sometimes mean and Shannon never questioned her judgment about anything, even when she was sixteen and punk was in and Rita made her promise she wouldn't get "one of those stupid dyke haircuts" like the rest of the girls at school. Shannon could still see her mother at the breakfast table, Flying J nametag already affixed, saying, "Tell me you'll never cut your hair," and for a while Shannon was just careful to make sure Rhae Anne, who went straight to beauty school after graduation, never cut it above her shoulders. When Rita died, though, Shannon just started skipping haircut after haircut. She'd made a promise and she wasn't about to break it, even though it got her more attention than she wanted.

Shannon put the car in gear and revved the engine once more, thinking as she always did that maybe this time would be different, that there'd be a sufficient shift in the car's position, in the road's surface chemistry, to send her on her way. She leaned forward and held her breath. "Mom," Shannon whispered. "You there?"

"Shannon?"

It wasn't Rita. It was Irv Peoples, her neighbor from two doors down. Shannon had probably talked to him only about five times in her life, despite the fact that they'd known each other since Shannon was a little girl. Irv had a beer gut and a small head and a way of not looking at you when he talked. Rhae Anne once told Shannon that Irv had killed a man over a fish, but Shannon didn't buy it. With his sloping shoulders and slack middle, he reminded her of a broken horse. Lately he'd been out a lot, clearing trails in the woods between the Bottoms and town, a red-handled ax in his hand and a miner's hat on his head.

He'd pulled up alongside her in his truck and leaned out, long fingers toying with the door handle. Hummed something. "Crazy" maybe? He had on a work shirt and a baseball cap, the bill of which was pulled down low over his large-pored face.

"Hey, Irv."

"Need some help?"

"I seem to have gone and got myself stuck."

"Lucky for you I'm an expert at such things."

Shannon tried to smile but it was like the smile she'd attempted for Josh. Unsuccessful. She was thinking of Daisy Gonzalez, of Hector, of what he would do if Daisy never "popped up." She was also thinking of herself, which was inexcusable given the private hell Hector must be going through. Still, self-pity would always win the day, especially when the source was love or something like it. She glanced down at the bracelet. It was pretty, sweet even, but it didn't fix things. Josh had grown tired of her before she'd had a chance to grow tired of him. She was certain of this, gifts or no gifts, and loving him felt like trying to rebuild the same wave-ravaged sand castle over and over and over. A lost cause. A losing battle. And one that made her feel increasingly desperate and powerless.

Shannon imagined a second, follow-up headline in the *Record*, her obit basically: DEAD WOMAN, ON THE CUSP OF A CHILDLESS MIDDLE AGE, MISSED BY FEW. The tears that started back at the house threatened again, but Irv was out of his truck and approaching her open window, so she choked them back.

"You okay?" he asked.

"Me? I'm fine."

"How about I give you a push?"

"If you think it'll work."

He shrugged. "Got any better ideas?"

"Fresh out."

"Well, there you go then." He gave Miss Scarlett a playful punch. "This car used to belong to your mother, I believe."

"Yes," she said.

They were quiet for a moment. Shannon got a whiff of lilac. Also of Irv. Wood chips and beer and animal. Definitely animal. Odd. Maybe he didn't shower often. Or was the bachelor equivalent of a cat lady—was there such a thing? Did men collect pets, too, to remind themselves that just because they were alone, they weren't dead yet? A part of her wanted his little log cabin to be full of kittens or snakes or, better yet, domesticated rodents. Ferrets, perhaps. Guinea pigs.

"Have you heard about Hector's daughter, Daisy?" Shannon asked. "She's missing."

Irv nodded. His shadowy face grew more so, and he crossed his arms over his chest. The biceps were strong and freckled. "I'll station myself at your bumper and when I say so, give it the gas, okay? I mean, all you've got."

"Thank you," Shannon said. She felt chastised, a little girl who'd spoken out of turn.

"Don't thank me yet."

Irv disappeared around the back of the car and an oriole shot past Shannon's window like a neon-orange baseball. It dipped back, landed in a roadside sycamore tree, and trilled a few warning notes. Then a shrill and joyful song seemed to float upward on an invisible current of air. Hey, Mom, Shannon thought. Is that you? Rita had always wanted to fly. Not in the corny way that everyone wants—to be given wings and bird bones and, somehow, the permission. No. What Rita had wanted was to get on a plane and go somewhere because she never had. Disney World, maybe. Paris. Timbuk-fucking-tu. Shannon wanted that, too, but they'd never gone anywhere. Shipshewana didn't count. Neither did Spencerville Fun Spot, especially since when Shannon was a girl she and Rita could get in there for free anytime they pleased. Her grandpa had owned the place.

"Mama," Shannon whispered. The oriole shook its tail and cocked its head, hopping to a higher branch just out of sight.

"Go!" Irv yelled from behind her. "Bring it!"

Shannon pushed the pedal. Irv groaned. She could see in her rearview mirror his thin cheeks straining, brown eyes going buggy. There was another groan, this one from the car, and she was moving. She was up and out.

Behind her, Irv gagged, heaved. He slumped against the sycamore that had the oriole in it. Shannon hoped he was okay but didn't dare stop.

"Thanks!" she yelled back at him.

"My pleasure," Irv said. Then he straightened up and walked slowly back to his truck, sadness on him like a second shirt. Shannon decided that she was probably wrong about the pets. Irv didn't collect animals. He was a loner. A lone wolf. So, what did he do all day? What was Irv's life like? Did he have a family? A woman to see to his needs? Shannon had no idea. She'd never thought to ask him about himself and he never volunteered anything. Irv Peoples. International Man of Mystery.

Breeder's Laundromat was on Beacon Street, sandwiched between a pet store and an accountant's office. There were faded suds painted on the front windows and posters advertising specials on detergent. Over the door was a large banner declaring WE SUP-PORT OUR TROOPS. Mr. Breeder had it hung there when local boy Kenny Garrety signed up and shipped off to Iraq a few years before. Mr. Breeder often said if he could do it all over again he would enlist in the army the minute he turned eighteen, just as Kenny Garrety had. Unfortunately, Mr. Breeder's father needed him to step in and take control of the family business. "Otherwise," Mr. Breeder said with a sigh, sometimes staring wistfully at the banner, "I would have spent my life engaged in hand-to-hand combat with the enemy and I would not have ceased until the enemy was begging for mercy. That or six feet under." He was very patriotic.

Shannon had worked at the Laundromat since high school and did her job well. She knew what to expect of Mr. Breeder, who called her "darlin'" and came in every Monday to check on her and every Friday to do the accounts. She was friends with most of the customers, who had their routines, too, regular as a drying cycle. There was Josh's aunt Pam Seaver, who always brought in two loads of whites in a white basket and one of colors in a blue basket; and Jack McElroy, who washed his sheets four times a week and his underwear once; and Zane Bigsby, who liked to take every washer in the place because, as he said the first day he came in with a girl under each tattooed arm, "I got needs, motherfuckers." Also the Tucker boys, whose clothes were always heavy and often deafening—metal in the pockets, Shannon supposed—and little Tiara Peacock with her dirty mouth and quick eyes.

Shannon didn't necessarily love them all—Zane's girls often laughed at her and played with her hair like she was a doll made for their own amusement, and the Tuckers scared her some with their barely concealed carries and growly voices—but in a way they were like her own relatives, familiar, maddening, easy to take for granted. When a customer died, like Mr. Blister had the summer before of skin cancer ("Now that is just wrong," Rhae Anne said when she read the obit in the *Colliersville Record*), Shannon always went to the funeral, and it was guaranteed that she'd see a few other Breeder's regulars there, shy around the family, a bit on the periphery, but still committed to getting through the ceremony because that's what good people did. Mr. Breeder liked to say the Laundromat was its own little community, "a miniature Colliersville, Indiana, if you will," which, if you asked Rhae Anne or Larry or Josh, was pretty microscopic already. Shannon didn't mind the smallness or the sameness. It made her feel safe.

Not that Breeder's was immune to change. It took on a slightly different character when Helman Yoder began employing the immigrants at his dairy the year before. The workers all moved into the Ranasack Apartments, which Helman bought so, in his words, "his employees could have safe and family-friendly housing." Family-friendly Shannon's right ankle. The place was cockroach infested, full of mold, and a known firetrap. None of the apartments had washer or dryer hookups, so when the dairy was going full steam, Shannon could count on at least three Ranasack families a day lugging heavy bags of mud-crusted work shirts and jeans and socks through the doors. Post-shutdown, she still saw at least five groups a week, most of them hauled into town in a gray minivan with Michigan plates. Too many people, not enough seatbelts.

There was something about the children in particular that hit Shannon in a physical place, started aches she couldn't explain. They reminded her of the wonderful summer her mother invited a Puerto Rican waitress named Camila to live with them because her mail-order husband, according to Rita, "beat the snot out of her." At twelve, Shannon didn't understand how a beautiful girl could be got through the mail like a prize off a cereal box and she told Rita so. Rita said wait, "It'll all be clear someday," and it was, all except the weekend she spent helping Camila cover their front lawn in white crosses made of plastic forks. That she'd never figured out.

Mr. Breeder did not share her fascination with his new clientele. Like Josh, he swore the whole lot of them symbolized a death knell to freedom and the American way, so when the families jammed the machines with Mexican coins, which had happened four times in the last five days, Shannon was careful not to tell Mr. Breeder about it. She fixed the machines herself if she could with an ice pick and a few well-placed kicks to the side. When the jam was too bad she called Rhae Anne's cousin Scottie, who had his own hired handyman business and seemed to Shannon a sweet guy, even though he had the tendency to grumble that the Mexicans were taking jobs away from bona fide documented Americans. Shannon just flirted with him, paid him from her own salary, and hoped the little doe-eyed kids always turning up at her elbow didn't understand English yet.

Sometimes when the Mexican families took over the Laundromat Shannon closed her eyes and pretended she was back with Camila, the two of them painting their toenails while Camila told stories about her childhood in a village so small everyone had to share a car with four different-sized tires and one working window.

"The Caribbean," Camila said just before she went back to her husband and disappeared forever, "is magic."

Shannon knew, of course, that Puerto Rico and Mexico, or, as Mr. Breeder called it, "Meheeco," weren't the same place, but still the Mexican customers made Shannon wonder where Camila was now, if her husband was cruel or kind, if she still kept forks near her bed.

A small family of death knells was waiting for her when Shannon pulled up to the curb that morning. There were four of them, a tiny girl and boy sitting at the feet of a toothless grand-mother and next to her a pretty young woman staring blankly across the street. They were huddled together on the stoop in front of the Laundromat, their bony shoulders holding up Good-will T-shirts.

"Good morning!" Shannon called to them. "Sorry I'm late."

Technically she wasn't late. She still had five minutes before Mr. Breeder would be there at seven, but they looked as if they'd been there for hours. They said nothing, just shrugged and parted like a broken chain to let her pass.

When Shannon turned her key in the lock, the sound was scratchy and hollow, and a few ancient mosquito carcasses hov-ered near the front door handle, trapped between panes of glass. She flipped on the lights, and the street outside went dark against the fluorescent glare. Inside, the Laundromat smelled of baby powder and overheated electrical coils. Always. A bulb over the north row of washers blinked and hissed—she'd call Scottie about that later—and the cement-block room was cool.

Shannon strode to the cramped space in the back to get her cash drawer from the safe. When she returned, the girl was whis-pering to the boy and they laughed behind their hands, maybe at her, but Shannon didn't care. She smiled at them, and while the boy just looked down at the worn-out Velcro straps on his shoes, the girl returned the smile, her lips parting over two large front teeth jagged at their edge. The girl was cute, even pretty, if you didn't count her teeth, and maybe she'd grow into them. Children did sometimes.

She reminded Shannon of Daisy Gonzalez and not just because

both girls had unfortunate teeth and black hair and brown skin. It was the strange mixture of vulnerability and fun in the face, of fragility and goofiness, that suggested a sort of sisterhood.

"Shouldn't you be in school?" Shannon asked.

At first the girl giggled and shrugged at her. Then the toothy smile disappeared behind a set of chapped lips, and her large eyes widened in distress at something she seemed to see over Shannon's shoulder. Shannon glanced behind her, but the room was empty except for the women dropping clothing into three superload washers.

"What's wrong?"

The girl started to say something but was interrupted by the clank of the metal bells against the doorjamb and Mr. Breeder walking in, carrying his satchel of bills and accounts. He was just in time to see a yellow liquid puddle around the little girl's feet and trickle down a crack in the floor toward a row of chairs pushed up against the wall. The girl's brother inched away from her, but his shoe soles were already covered in urine, and he left wet spots as he went. Sticky by the sound of them.

Later, Shannon would tell people that the whole incident might have blown over if the girl had cried and run to the bathroom in shame or if the grandmother, busy with a box of All Stainlifter, had scolded her and even smacked her wet behind.

But the girl didn't cry. She laughed.

Mr. Breeder dropped his briefcase and clenched his jaw. His face, which was naturally red on account of high cholesterol and rosacea, turned almost purple. "Get out!" he screamed at the girl, and in case she didn't understand, he grabbed her by the shoulders and half carried her toward the door. "Get out, get out, get out!" he yelled at the old woman and her daughter and the little boy. He yanked up the lids of the washers and tossed the wet clothes at their heads. "Don't make me tell you again."

Shannon had never seen him act like this and even though she wanted to run after the girl and clean her up and tell her everything was going to be fine, accidents happened all the time, she just stood there like she was one of the pinball machines in the corner, nailed down and out of order, her heart pounding hard inside of her and her skin going prickly like it did when Josh got on his kick about how, at thirty-six, she was drying up like a granny apple and how she'd probably never be anyone's mother at this point, thank Christ for small miracles.

"Get out," Mr. Breeder said once more even though the whole family, having grabbed their wet clothes in their arms, was already gone.

Mr. Breeder insisted on making the sign himself, which was why the "an" sound in "Mexican" was spelled with an "en" and not an "an." Then he hung the placard—fashioned out of the side of an empty Tide container—in the center of the front window and asked Shannon if she thought the message sufficiently clear.

"I want it so even a monkey can understand it," Mr. Breeder said.

" 'No Mexicens,' " Shannon read back to him, having joined him outside. "Not much room for interpretation there."

Mr. Breeder smiled for the first time all morning. "Good."

"But don't you think, Mr. Breeder—"

"Chuck," he said.

He was always trying to get her to call him by his first name and she did when explicitly ordered to, but she never thought of him as anything but Mr. Breeder. How strange, she thought, that someone with such a surname didn't have children. "Don't you think, Chuck, that this sign is going to seem insensitive?"

"Insensitive?"

"Well, I mean since the little girl in my neighborhood, you know, Daisy Gonzalez, has been reported missing. And she's. Well. She's Mexican."

Mr. Breeder sighed. "Shannon, Shannon, Shannon. You know the Ranasack people are killing me. You of all people should know. They're cleaning me out. They come here and stay for hours and use all the toilet paper in the restroom and steal my magazines and make a mess and a racket. If something doesn't change I'll be forced to go out of business. And you'll be out of a job. Think about that. Besides, this sign is clearly not about Daisy. I was watching the news last night—I saw the reports. Her dad works at the high school. He went through the proper channels."

"The proper channels?"

"He was born here, so Daisy's American. More or less."

Shannon remembered Josh's words from earlier that morning, the thing he said about one Mexican being as good as the next. Bunnies. Girls as rabbits. *Problem solved.* "I'm just worried a sign like that at a time like this could strike the wrong note. Send the wrong message."

"Trust me. This is exactly the message I want to send."

While Mr. Breeder secured the sign with duct tape, the pretty woman Larry was seeing on the side walked in, her curvy body stuffed into a tube top, hoodie, and animal-print jeans. Shannon recognized her right away. She'd seen her riding with Larry in his truck around town, cruising all the streets except the one in front of the Hair Barn. The woman had high-heeled patent-leather peekaboo shoes on her feet, a pink phone up to her ear, and a shimmery bag slung over one shoulder. Her hair was long too, not as long as Shannon's, but wavy and black and thick.

"No," Mr. Breeder said, following her in and wrinkling his nose. His voice was quiet and his words came out in a slow sputter. "No. No more of you."

She ignored him and threw her bag down on one of the washers the old woman and her daughter had already loaded with quarters. When she saw that the washer was primed for her, she smiled into her phone and opened the lid.

Mr. Breeder, meanwhile, hovered over her, his breath short. "Can't you read?" He pointed to the sign, which was facing the street and hanging at a slightly drunken angle.

The woman turned around and seemed to see Mr. Breeder for the first time. She took him in from the top of his bald head to his tasseled shoes, leaning back so she could get a better view of her attacker. Her graceful neck turned cobra, coiling and then swaying back and forth. She snapped her phone shut. "Yes, I can read," she said.

"I said no more of your kind here," Mr. Breeder shouted. "Read the sign."

Never once taking her eyes off Mr. Breeder, the woman unzipped her bag, turned it upside down, and let a shower of frilly things—bras, panties, negligees—tumble into the open washer. The final insult was the way she emptied her Woolite bottle, slowly and with relish, the way you would drizzle syrup on a sundae.

"That all your own hair?" she asked, turning to Shannon and leaning down to grab her braid between her fingers and her thumb.

Shannon nodded.

"You get tired sometimes?" Her voice was low. There was hot-pink lipstick on her perfect teeth. "I get tired sometimes."

"Well, it's a little much in the summer—" Shannon started, but Mr. Breeder had had enough. He held up his hand to silence them and looked at Shannon, his cheeks shaking with fury.

"Darlin'," he said to her. "Call the police."

Shannon didn't move. She was riveted by the girl's stare and the grip of her broken nails on her hair.

"Fine," Mr. Breeder said. "I'll do it myself."

The cops did indeed come. Well, *the* cop, Randy Richardville, lights flashing. And his two deputies, Jack and Zane. Right behind them was the press.

By the time Shannon got to her grandmother's the story was all over town, at least that's what Granny told her and Granny tended to be in the know, thanks to her weekly visits to the Hair Barn for a shampoo and set. Also, Granny never turned off her TV, and local news, along with junk food and a never-ending game of solitaire, seemed her main source of consolation for a life lived alone.

"Breeder's flipped his lid for good," Granny said, hobbling down a dark hallway into the kitchen, where Shannon stood with an angel food cake in her hand. Granny's rubber-tipped cane made sucking sounds against the hardwood. "What the hell was he thinking?"

Shannon put the cake down on the counter and grabbed a knife from a beer mug next to the toaster. Her grandmother's house used to smell like Pine-Sol, but that was years ago when Granny was still spry. Ever since Rita died, Shannon cleaned the house when she could, and it'd been too long between visits. There was an odor of spoiled milk about the place and of microwave dinners and unwashed sheets.

When Shannon was a girl, she used to love to visit her grandmother's stately home on Peach Street, to get lost in the upstairs bedrooms while Granny made a pie or ironed Grandpa's shirts. Granny always left her alone to wander the house, to go from room to room, picking up knickknacks and making up stories. Back then she didn't like to share Granny or her house with anyone if she could help it, not even Rhae Anne. The only time she remembered playing with another person at Granny's was the summer Camila lived with them and her memory of those days was sketchy. Mostly she recalled walking with the beautiful girl through the back hall where the linoleum—yellow roses on a silver background—echoed their steps back at them. And their breathy version of "Follow the Yellow Brick Road." Together they traced the chains of flowers from doorway to doorway, their feet kicking up dust motes that spun in the half-light of the hall like disturbed spirits. At one point, Camila had whispered, "I want to stay here forever."

"Forever," Shannon whispered back.

But the passing years had been cruel rather than kind. Grandpa Washburn died broke. Spencerville Fun Spot, the amusement park he'd built with his brothers, was shut down by the state in the eighties after one too many accidents involving drunk employees and the Tilt-a-Whirl. That private catastrophe was followed by a string of bad investments and old-people scams. Then Granny got sick. Rita, too. Time turned the floor flowers gray, and the house, once so beautiful, seemed to be falling apart around Granny without her really noticing. Or caring. She lived in squalor with only her television and a fake bird for company. The bird, which Granny had named Johnny Carson, was a battery-powered parrot that cocked its head and chirped incessantly. It was a present from Rita and for that reason, Granny refused to get rid of it or power it down.

"Polly want a cracker," the bird squawked from its perch near the refrigerator. "Land ho!"

"How are you, Granny?" Shannon asked.

"Don't change the subject, missy. Tell me all about the showdown on Beacon Street. Inquiring minds want to know." Granny maneuvered herself up to the table and looked up expectantly at Shannon, who put a slice of cake in front of her.

Shannon was early. She usually got to Granny's around dinnertime, but there was no point in her staying at work. She'd spent most of the morning trying to help customers get through a tangle of TV reporters, who, with their cameras and microphones and antennaed white vans with their own pictures on the side, reminded her of a swarm of gnats. No one could do any laundry if they couldn't get in the door, and Mr. Breeder, eager to talk to anyone holding a microphone, forgot Shannon was there at all. At one point she heard Larry's mistress, restrained by a puffing Randy Richardville, tell Mr. Breeder that she planned to sue him for everything he had. "You'll be speaking to my lawyer," she said, and Mr. Breeder, calmer now that he had reinforcements, replied, "Just make sure he talks American."

Shannon didn't want to think about any of it. "You obviously saw the news," she said. "Why don't you tell me?"

"Well," Granny said, drawing the word out and putting her fork down with a flourish, "Breeder's saying that all the Mexicans do is crap on his floor and break his machines, and that foreign hotsy-totsy is calling him every name in the book. But I don't know. She didn't look like the kind to drop trou in the middle of a Laundromat to me."

"It was a little girl. She peed her pants and there was some on the floor. Mr. Breeder saw it and went nuts."

"And who cleaned it up?" Granny asked.

Shannon didn't respond.

"I thought so. You gotta quit that job, girl. I've told you and told you. You're too good for that place, just like your mother was too good for Driving K's."

"Flying J's," Shannon said automatically.

"You know what I mean." Granny ate her cake quickly. She usually had two pieces to Shannon's one, said angel food cake was mostly air anyway, and Shannon supposed she was right. "All this on top of that Daisy what's her name going missing. I don't recognize this town anymore."

"Daisy Gonzalez," Shannon said. "She lived next door to me. I mean she *lives* next door to me. She and her dad. I don't know them well, though. They sort of keep to themselves."

"That's modern times for you," Granny said. "Not knowing your neighbors. When I was your age we practically lived in our neighbors' houses. Children running back and forth, shared dinners, sleepovers. You'd forget whose kid was whose. We'd do anything for each other. And now what? We sit tight in sealed rooms? We have decks instead of porches. We Tex-Mex instead of talking."

"Text," Shannon said.

"Yo ho ho and a bottle of rum!" Johnny shrieked.

"Anyway, the way things change, you start to long for death,"

Granny said. "I guess that's how it's supposed to work. When I go I won't miss this place, I'll tell you that much."

"Argh, matey!" said Johnny. "Prepare to walk the plank!"

Shannon leaned against the counter, tired and fighting off a headache. "Hey, Granny, do you know Irv Peoples?"

Granny glanced up from her cake. There were crumbs at the sides of her mouth. "That shut-in roadkill collector?"

"Is that what he does? He collects roadkill?" So she was wrong about the kittens and/or rodents. Live ones, anyway.

"I believe so. Don't make that face. It's not his hobby or anything. It's his job. At least that's what your mother told me. They were friends of a sort. Didn't he use to shovel your walk in the winter? And clean your gutters?"

Shannon nodded, remembering Rita at Christmas, baking thank-you cookies for Irv and a few other men around town who came by the house to help with odd jobs. Shannon couldn't recall ever having to shovel snow or rake a single leaf, and she certainly didn't have Josh to thank for that.

"I bet he still does," Shannon said, "but he's always so quiet and secretive about it I never have a chance to thank him."

"He's a nice enough guy, sure," Granny said, "but why Rita saw fit to buy property in such a cursed place as the Bottoms was, is, and forever will be beyond me. Not that she ever listened to her parents. So stubborn."

Shannon reached back and grabbed the end of her braid. Then she snapped a few split ends off and threw it back over her shoulder. "Do you think I should cut my hair?"

"Why?"

"Josh just kind of said something about it. That maybe it wasn't pretty anymore."

"Josh is a dead end."

"Don't start."

"Don't you 'Don't start' me. I promised your mother on her deathbed that I'd keep an eye on you and it would be breaking my promise to turn a deaf ear and a blind eye on your relationship with that boy. He's a Seaver and Seavers are Seavers no matter what. They don't change. They are born trash and they stay that way, world without end, amen. You know, I wouldn't be a bit surprised if a Seaver's behind that girl's disappearance. Hank, maybe. Him and his gun club buddies. The whole thing stinks of Seaver."

Shannon sighed. She didn't believe any of the Seavers had it in them to hurt an innocent young girl. They were all bark, no bite, especially Josh, who rarely did anything now beyond roll joints and blow pot smoke at the fish tank in an effort to intoxicate their neon tetras. Sometimes he filmed the results—fish rotating slowly at the bottom of the aquarium like tiny, bright hotdogs—and posted them to Facebook, tagging his cousins and half cousins and cousins twice removed. *LOL,* they'd comment. *ROTFLMAO. Haha looks familiar!*

Granny was still talking. "You need to find yourself a decent earner," she said. "That's what I had in your grandpa. He didn't set the world on fire but he worked and he worked hard and he made me comfortable most of the days of my life. But that Josh. I hear he lost his job to a Mexican. Apparently *he,* meaning the Mexican, is actually willing to do a decent day's work, unlike Josh, who—"

"How did you hear that? About Juan taking Josh's place?"

Granny winked. "I have my ways."

"Ah. Rhae Anne."

"Maybe. But it doesn't matter who I heard it from. It matters that it's true. Josh Seaver simply cannot, or will not, keep a job, and in my humble opinion that's no man at all."

Shannon knew what was coming next. Once Granny got going on Josh's essential worthlessness as a man, a much longer and tiring monologue was sure to follow, so Shannon left her cake untouched and grabbed a mop and five-gallon bucket from the utility closet. While Granny treated her to an exhaustive list of Josh's faults—bad temper, lack of ambition, too many tattoos—Shannon dumped a capful of bleach into the bottom of a bucket for the second time that day, cut it with water from the tub, and let it sit for a moment while she stripped Granny's bed, throwing all the linens in a garbage bag for later. Mr. Breeder let her use the washers and dryers for free after hours. Access to the equipment, along with catastrophic health coverage and all the bleach she could ever want, was what Mr. Breeder liked to call "the perks of the job."

"And don't even get me started on that boy's dope habit," Granny shouted from the kitchen while Shannon pulled a set of striped sheets tight over the mattress and shook a light blanket out on top. "Your cousin Paulie tells me he sees Josh over at that what's his name's house almost every week buying dope by the suitcase and him as unemployed as a doornail so I guess you're paying for that and my God, honey, is there anything you don't do?"

By the time Shannon left her grandmother's house it was dark and a full moon was hanging low over Tony's Pizza, closed by the look of it. She passed the Hair Barn, bright and still bustling, and made a right on Beacon, heading for Breeder's. She could go home, but Josh would probably be there and she could catch his hopelessness quick as a cold. Chances were good that if she went home right then, she'd walk in on him not-so-surreptitiously surfing porn. It had happened before, several times now, and if she complained, he called her crazy, a jealous bitch, asked her if she was on the rag. But was it crazy jealousy to wish your boyfriend didn't spend much of his free time ogling other women? Especially when those women had bodies that looked as if they'd been polished and painted, and overlarge lips and eyes and breasts like a Barbie doll's or a Disney princess? Rhae Anne told Shannon not to take Josh's porn habit personally. "All men look at it," she said. "Larry does. Josh does. They all do. It's no big deal." But Shannon did take it personally and didn't know how not to because Josh, who once declared he'd never need porn again as long as he had Shannon to satisfy his every need, could hardly be bothered to glance at her now. Shannon felt that without any real notice or time to change the trajectory of things, she'd been replaced by a bevy of Asian beauties and blond MILFs and barely legal teen queens whose dial was always set to sexy, who had no other job but to be sexy, all day long, all night even. Such beauties weren't burdened with body odor or dead mothers or ailing grandmothers or insurance payments. At least for the ten minutes it took for men like Josh to get off on them. They had no desires of their own beyond being fucked by the man on-screen, longer faster harder, and being looked at, loved for their poreless skin. So easily placated, those women. So ready-made for pleasure.

But when the cameras stopped rolling, Shannon supposed porn stars were just like her. They took off their fake eyelashes and cake makeup and went home to apartments with leaky faucets and countertops strewn with unpaid bills and men with porn habits who would call them crazy menstruating bitches out of self-defense. Shannon shook the bracelet and read her birthday on the gift charm. Off by a day. Nice, Josh. Very nice.

The bracelet, she realized, parking in the same spot she had that morning, was a bribe and nothing more, an inelegant move in the unhappy chess game that had become their relationship. It was like the time Josh made her a home-cooked meal to keep her from asking about his job search. There was a catch. There was always a catch. Literally. The bracelet had yanked out most of the wrist hairs on her right arm. But what was he trying to make up for this time? What had he done or failed to do and when would she find out?

She did not want to think about any of it, so she stepped out of the car, a slow burn spreading up her back, and almost ran into the old woman from before, the grandmother type Mr. Breeder had chased out the front door. The woman was standing on the Laundromat steps, a plastic pitcher in her hand. A dark liquid splashed out onto the sidewalk, coating the concrete in something viscous and iron smelling.

Shannon stood transfixed, watching the woman shake the last drops of liquid onto Mr. Breeder's cardboard sign, now letters-down in a puddle. Her cell phone buzzed in her pocket.

"Rhae Anne."

"Oh my God, Shannon. What the hell?"

"What the hell what?"

"The Mr. Breeder thing, duh. And that Mexican woman who's going to sue him. It's all anyone's talking about."

"Oh."

"Well, that," Rhae Anne said, "and Daisy Gonzalez gone missing. It's like we're living in the Bermuda Triangle all a sudden."

A hair dryer whirred on Rhae Anne's end and Bob Seger sang about Hollywood nights, high rolling hills.

"And listen to this. Larry told me that the Ranasack Apartments people, you know, Helman Yoder's illegals, are putting some sort of voodoo on Breeder's in revenge for that sign he put up in his window. Larry said they drew a bunch of blood, the whole kit and kaboodle, even the kids, donated it I guess in some back alley behind Tony's—*that* must have been sterile— and they're going to throw it on Breeder's steps or something. Can you believe it? And there's talk it's all related, that the voodoo people might have taken Daisy and that they're going to demand ransom from rich whites—Mayor Rodgers, maybe, or that carpetbagger Mike Marino—to get her back. Bermuda. Effing. Triangle."

"Wild," Shannon said.

The old woman turned and stared at Shannon. She put her finger to her lips. In the moonlight, she looked like something out of a fairytale, all except the Reeboks on her feet and her Daytona Beach trucker hat. Shannon watched as the woman took off down a narrow alley, pitcher flopping against her hip.

Rhae Anne drew a long breath. "I said to Larry I said, 'We really should call Randy Richardville,' but he was like, 'What's he gonna do?' And Breeder is kind of an ass. Are you listening to me? Larry said that it's supposed to bring about nine hundred years bad luck, that blood, so you'd better call in sick tomorrow. Get that stuff on you and poof, you're gone. And you know what I think? I think the whole town's in for it."

Shannon looked down at her feet. The blood had leaked down the sidewalk onto her sandals. In the amber glow from the streetlight it looked like tar or quicksand.

"Listen to me, Shannon," Rhae Anne said. "I don't know how Larry knows all this. Guess he got it from the Internet or something, but anyway it's serious. I love you, girl. I'd kill you if something happened to you."

Shannon knew she was supposed to laugh. Rhae Anne did it for her. "You okay, sweetie?"

Now, Shannon told herself. I should tell her. About Larry and that beautiful woman with the pink phone and stockpile of sexy lingerie. That the woman threatening to sue Chuck Breeder was the same woman keeping Larry out nights. I should tell her. Right now. "Hey, Rhae Anne. There's something—"

"Oh shit, honey. Gotta go," Rhae Anne said. "Mrs. Hochstetler and her monthly mom perm. Talk soon, okay?"

"Okay."

Shannon put her phone back in her pocket. She looked around her, up the street. Down. Only storefront windows stared back, dark beneath metal awnings and broken neon signs. She was alone with the sky and the moon. She looked down at her bracelet, recalled the sight of Josh's unwashed, bent head as he secured the silver clasp. The charms shook there at the end of her arm, hung out over the pool of blood where reflections of white clouds were scudding, small ships on their way home. Wait, Shannon thought. Wait for me.

Hate Henry Road was dry now. As Shannon slowed down to steer Miss Scarlett around a series of potholes, she saw Irv Peoples out of the corner of her eye. He was walking through the patch of woods that mercifully divided the Bottoms from the concrete plant. He had on his miner's hat and the bulb was shining shakily through the trees as he walked, ax in his fist making a scraping sound against the earth.

"Irv!" She pulled the emergency brake and jumped out to meet him where the oaks stopped and the pines started. He blinded her for a moment with the beam of his headlamp. Then he took the hat off and rested it in the crook of his arm.

"Can you do something for me?" She blushed. "Again?"

"You got blood on your shoes."

Shannon crouched in the grass. There was a tree stump at her left shoulder. She slid up next to it and glanced at Irv, felt the weight of the whole day pulling her down. Bermuda. Effing. Triangle. She could just make out his dark eyes and thin-lipped mouth. "There's a curse on Breeder's Laundromat," she said. "Could be Colliersville, too. The entire town."

Irv nodded, adjusting the ax against his leg. "Sounds about what we deserve."

Shannon threw her braid over the stump. "Cut it."

She knew she was acting like a crazy person, but what did it matter? She was as good as dead anyway. Not that she believed any of what Rhae Anne said about the blood curse, the voodoo. It wasn't an ugly thing, it was a beautiful thing and they'd done it, hadn't they? Shown the world. Shown Colliersville, anyway, that they wouldn't be ignored. Blood like a river in the center of town to rival the Ranasack. Blood like a heart beating. The stain would be there for years. Mr. Breeder'd have to get all new concrete or move out. Wondrous. Shannon wanted to be wondrous.

"Cut it all off," she said. "Please." But not for Josh. Not for him. For her.

"You sure?"

"Yes."

Irv didn't say anything more. He'd never talked much. It was, as Rita had said, just his way. He sighed and put his hat back on. Then he hoisted the ax over his right shoulder. When he was done with her hair, she'd ask him to chop up the bracelet, too. To splinter it, turn it to shavings. Or maybe she'd wrap it around the tattooed plastic arm now languishing in Hector's driveway, the oddest offering in the "Come Home, Daisy" shrine. Either way, Shannon would be rid of it. Good riddance, bad rubbish. Irv's blade flashed in the moonlight and Shannon knew everything was about to change. She closed her eyes and waited for the cut.

Natural Disasters

(May)

"It's not the way I thought it would be," said the young woman behind the blue curtain.

Birdy nodded. "I know."

"Life, am I right?" the woman said. "Fucking life."

"Yes, of course. Life."

For once, Birdy was in complete agreement with the young woman and would not have minded the chance to expound on the subject of life as an exercise in disappointment, but the issue was, her feet were on fire. They were itching and burning and the skin felt stretched impossibly tight. She raised her covers and looked down, half expecting to see a five-alarm blaze and maybe a few hunky firemen doing their best, but her feet were just her feet—slightly swollen and in dire need of a pedicure—and they were all alone at the bottom of the bed. Nothing there for company save a pair of discarded hospital-issue socks with tread on the top and sole and no heel to speak of.

"When do the good times start?" the young woman asked. "Huh? Do you know what I mean?"

"I do."

The young woman was Birdy's roommate. From the shadow she cast on the curtain, she seemed to be pulling her hair into a ponytail. Good, Birdy thought. Straighten yourself up a bit. Birdy was often ashamed of the girl, whose slovenliness and stubborn vulgarity of speech struck Birdy as deliberate attempts to appear as common as possible. Birdy had been trying to transfer rooms since the day Helman committed her, but so far such efforts had gone nowhere and so she was forced to hear all about the young woman's "difficult as fuck relationship" with her "sort of boyfriend," who, when it came to choosing between Birdy's roommate and his "lame long-term sig-oh," was having a hard time knowing when to "shit" or "get off the pot." Birdy couldn't remember the woman's name and she'd never even asked Birdy for hers, so the woman talked to Birdy like someone she'd known all her life, no preface, no preamble, no pleasantries, which made sense really, because there was nothing pleasant about the psych ward of a large county hospital.

"No one ever promised me a goddamned rose garden, but still," the woman said.

"Still," Birdy whispered. Her feet had stopped itching, but now the fire had somehow jumped her body and was burning near her hairline. Her follicles were tree trunks and her skin the wildfire raging out of control. Birdy could almost hear the roar of the wind and the flames. She reached her hand up, touched her head. Nothing there either. All systems normal, except for the sweat dripping down the side of her face. Birdy supposed it was withdrawal—the doctors and nurses warned her it might be like this—but the knowledge didn't comfort her much. She wanted desperately for all of this to end, to go home where she could pretend young women like her roommate didn't exist outside of reality television shows and *Judge Judy*. But she knew she was stuck where she was for another forty-eight hours at least, and in the meantime, she'd settle for the day nurse, who often called her "Betty," coming in with a cool cloth, a sharp word, and a tranquilizer. She pressed the red call button beside her bed.

"She's not going to like that," the young woman said.

"Like what?" Birdy asked.

"The nurse was just in here. Don't you remember? Like ten minutes ago. She said if you pressed that call button again in the next hour, she was going to eat you for breakfast. Also lunch. Maybe dinner, if there was anything left."

"Oh, well." The flames, the smoke, the burn. Birdy gritted her teeth. Who did this trashy woman think she was? "This is an emergency."

"That's what you said before."

Birdy was in for alcohol abuse and prescription painkiller addiction. Helman told the admitting nurse—a man with a full sleeve of tattoos and dime-sized holes in his ears—he was worried that if she didn't get help soon, his wife might end up hurting herself. Birdy tried to tell the nurse that she didn't know how she could possibly hurt herself when she couldn't feel a thing, not her bad back thank God, not her legs or arms or hands, not even her own nose, but there was such a faulty connection between her brain and her mouth that she had no choice but to sign whatever paper was put in front of her.

The woman behind the blue curtain was in for exhaustion.

"I'm so tired," the woman said now. Her hair in a neat ponytail, she seemed to have moved on to her makeup. Birdy watched her apply what appeared to be mascara. Also eyeliner. So the boyfriend would be here soon. That was the only time the woman took any real care with her appearance.

"I thought I was tired before, but I didn't really know tired until now. I want to sleep and sleep and sleep and never wake up."

"But if you did, that boyfriend of yours would be sad."

"Yeah, right. He doesn't give a shit about me. All he cares about is his own skin."

Birdy supposed that was true. She thought the same might be said of Helman. Just look at what he'd done to their family. Ruined them. He could blame the overzealous cops and the overreaching government all he liked, but neither the cops nor the government forced him to transform their respectable and reputable family business into something illegal and shameful. Did Randy Richardville insist that Helman go into deep debt purchasing more cows than their more than competent staff could possibly milk in a day? No. Did President Obama put a gun to Helman's head and tell him he had to partner with that shady handlebar-mustached broker from Texas who, the night Helman invited him to their home for dinner, spilled two—not one, *two*—glasses of red wine on Birdy's best Oriental rug and, insult to injury, used the prettiest part as an ashtray? Most certainly not.

Couldn't Helman and Mr. Mustache have done all their dirty work on the phone? Over the Internet? Perish the thought. Helman had this weird obsession with looking men in the eye. And shaking their hand. Mr. Mustache must have been very steady and firm, because, the dinner done and Birdy's rug a clear goner, Helman declared that they'd be firing all their nice, English-speaking employees and swapping them for Mr. Mustache's human cargo, scheduled to arrive in a week. Then Helman went and bought the crumbling Ranasack Apartments, putting poor Wally, who was not what you'd call handy, to work painting and sanding and scrubbing. Window dressing. That's all that was. Birdy wouldn't put a cow she liked to bed in that place, but Helman insisted on housing all their new workers there. He did all of this without consulting her, without asking her opinion on a single thing, and soon the dairy was buzzing all day and night with Spanish and the kind of behind-the-hand, sideways-glance laughter Birdy was sure was aimed at her. Even that laughter sounded like a foreign language. Exposing herself to the workers' contempt even for a few minutes was painful. It stung like a sunburn.

The most time she'd ever spent around any of her husband's employees was a few hours one awful and unseasonably hot day in mid-March when everything went wrong—a bunch of sick cows, malfunctions in the milking machines, no vets or repairmen around for miles, and Helman stubbornly refusing to let the workers go home at the normal time. He hoped, it seemed, that they would be able to bring about some miraculous cure for both the cows and the machines. What happened instead was several women passed out from exhaustion. Birdy wanted to call an ambulance, but Helman vetoed that, opting to have a handful of men carry the sick women into the house, where Birdy did what she could, putting cold cloths on their heads and speaking soothingly. She imagined herself a Melanie Wilkes–type figure, weaving her graceful way through rows and rows of ailing soldiers, but then one of the workers, a butch sort of person in a Daytona Beach trucker hat, shattered Birdy's fantasy, shooing her out of her own living room and wielding the cool cloths like whips. *"¡Vayase!"* the woman said, her voice full of contempt. Then, "Useless. You're useless."

So Birdy hid. She divided her days between long, drawn-out shopping trips to Fort Wayne and marathon viewings of *Gone with the Wind, The King and I,* and *Lawrence of Arabia* in her locked upstairs bedroom.

Helman had started sleeping downstairs in the guestroom when the illegals arrived in town anyway, swore it had to do with safety, with "protecting what was his," and to that end he kept a shotgun under the bed and a crossbow in the closet. After dinner, he disappeared, checking on the apartments, he said, but Birdy wondered what else he was up to. It was as if she didn't exist to him anymore. When she threw out her back doing toe touches to an old Richard Simmons video, her only comfort was a slim hope Helman might notice her, pay her some mind. But Helman had no time for her. It was Wally who took her to the doctor and got her first prescription filled. And it was Wally who fluffed her pillows and brought her trays of food, morning, noon, and night. Helman could hardly be troubled to ask her how she was feeling. He was too busy, Birdy supposed. Too preoccupied with "bringing the dairy into the twenty-first century" to acknowledge his wife of twenty-two years. His concern, his love for her, seemed to have evaporated, turned to thin air. So Birdy turned to thin air as well. She took her pain meds as ordered and drifted. Eventually, she didn't bother to drive to Fort Wayne. She didn't watch what Helman so dismissively called "her shows." She lay on her numb back and dreamed about being a young girl, going to sleep in her big white four-poster bed, surrounded on all sides by stuffed animals her father had won for her at the Spencerville Fun Spot.

It wasn't as though Helman never visited. He did. Twice. But he didn't stay long. He sat in the plastic chair by her bed and played with his hat. That or he took his glasses off and cleaned them on his shirt repeatedly. The only things he seemed to have to say to her were about the looming court case with the county and what measures they'd have to take if he got jail time, but it was all a bit beyond Birdy at the moment and she stopped listening once he uttered the words *plea bargain*.

She'd tried unsuccessfully to get him to talk to her about their son, about Wally and how he'd changed—the dresses that had begun appearing in his closet, the tights and bras and high-heeled shoes—but Wally's troubling transformation seemed the last thing Helman wanted to address. He kept changing the subject to something he referred to as "constitutional justice" and the help he hoped to get from Hank Seaver and his Bottoms ilk.

"Hey, babe."

Birdy looked up. It was her roommate's boyfriend. He'd paused at the edge of the blue curtain, not even bothering to greet Birdy or give her a smile. What a winner, she thought. Standing there, shaggy, unkempt, stinking of marijuana. At least he usually brought flowers. Cheap, wilted grocery store daisies and sunflowers with slimy stems, but it was more than Helman had done for her.

"Got you something," the boyfriend said, thrusting the bouquet away from his body like it was a baby with a leaky diaper.

"I see that," said the woman.

"Aren't you gonna water them?"

"Water them yourself."

"Wow. The gratitude. It's blowing me away."

"You want gratitude? Spring for roses next time."

"I thought you liked carnations."

"You don't know me at all."

The couple's interactions oscillated between cold indifference and hot, weepy desperation. The visits often ended with an argument about when they were finally going to get the hell out of Colliersville.

"We've got to cut bait," the boyfriend said now, and Birdy watched his shadow drop the flowers on the windowsill. "Why are we still here, for fuck's sake?"

"Can I heal first?" the woman asked. "Huh? Would that be okay with you?"

"Sure."

"Thank you very much."

"So healing. How long does that take? Roughly?"

The woman did not answer.

"The longer we stay, the worse off we'll be," the boyfriend said. "The worse everything will be."

"So you've finally dumped what's her ass?"

"I thought we agreed not to talk about her."

"I never agreed to that. You agreed to that. You agreed with yourself about that particular situation."

The pretty day nurse came in then, dragging a computer and a cart of Dixie Cups filled with pills. Birdy sat up straighter and patted her hair. The nurse looked annoyed and slightly harassed, but not as if she wanted to eat Birdy for breakfast.

"What is it, Betty?" the nurse asked.

"It's Birdy."

"That's why you called me in here? To tell me there's birds outside y'all's window? Most people would be happy about that, but, as you're so fond of reminding us, you're not most people, are you, Mrs. Yoder?"

Birdy sat up even straighter and raised her voice so the nurse could hear her over the young woman and her boyfriend arguing about how he probably bought his live-in "for reals roses like every single goddamn day." "My name isn't Betty. It's Birdy."

"And you white people say our names are weird." The nurse crossed her arms over her chest. "What is it you need, *Birdy?*"

"Is one of those cups for me?"

"Afraid not. These are for the second floor."

The young woman behind the curtain had told Birdy stories about the "poor fucks" on the second floor. Lots of lost causes up there, apparently. Schizos, the woman said. Catatonics. Seriously clinical cases roaming the halls with towels draped over their heads and drool running down their chests. A barren sadscape.

"I feel like my skin is burning," Birdy told the nurse. "Like it's on fire. Can I have something for the pain?"

"I gave you something for the pain"—the nurse paused and glanced at the computer screen—"thirteen minutes ago."

The fire was in Birdy's belly button now. It radiated out from her inny in waves of heat and agony. Birdy glanced down at her hospital gown. No scorch marks. No plumes of smoke. She folded her hands over the blaze. "Whatever you gave me isn't working. Maybe the dose wasn't strong enough."

The nurse sighed and craned her neck. She was clearly more interested in the fight behind the curtain than in Birdy's dosage. The young woman and her boyfriend had moved on from his "pussified" inability to break it off with "that bitch" to his unlicensed gun collection and lack of gainful employment. Birdy thought she heard something about a roadkill dog and lost or squandered milk money but couldn't be sure. None of it made much sense.

"While you're here," Birdy said to the nurse in a tone she hoped was reminiscent of the one her own mother used when demanding what was her due, "I would like again to request a room transfer. The constant arguing and cursing I've been subjected to since I came here is a detriment to my health. I'll never get better with all this negativity swirling around."

"You're in the psych ward, Mrs. Yoder."

"Your point being?"

"There's not much but negativity swirling around."

"I'm accustomed to a more civilized environment."

"That's not what I heard."

"Excuse me?"

"Doesn't your husband run a dairy?"

"Well, yes. He used to."

"Lots of mud involved? Cow shit, too?"

"Yes, but . . ." Birdy could feel the tears welling up. "I was born to better."

She touched her naked throat and thought longingly of her mother's strand of Akoya pearls, which, unless one of Helman's new workers had stolen them or Wally borrowed them for a day at the Hair Barn, would be resting in a tortoiseshell jewelry box on her dresser next to her bottle of Chanel No. 5 and her silver-plated hairbrush and hand mirror. Yes, Birdy Yoder, née Rodgers, had married a dairy farmer—for love and when he was still the handsomest man in town—and yes, there was bound to be mud on her kitchen floor as she spoke and burned, but that did not mean she'd forgotten where she came from. She had grown up in a beautiful brick home on Peach Street complete with a walled garden and a solarium. Her father, Colliersville's most beloved family physician, had made a name for himself and his hometown by pioneering a procedure that eased the pain of IUD insertion, which had proved controversial but not terribly so; and her mother, Eileen, was the daughter of Colliersville's most long-standing mayor. Now Birdy's brother, Rupert, seemed poised to break his grandfather's record. Birdy had even gone to finishing school in Massachusetts, where she learned art appreciation and how to enter and exit political discussions, not to mention crowded rooms, with grace and poise. She spoke French and was an accomplished dressage equestrian. The Rodgerses were good stock, the right sort of people. None of that was canceled out by a little back pain or problem with the pills. Or manure, for that matter.

"Born to better, huh?" the nurse said. "Weren't we all."

Birdy was going to reply *I think not,* but just as she opened her mouth to speak, the grocery store carnations hit the blue curtain that divided Birdy from chaos, from trash and the people who talked it, and the flowers that didn't stick to the canvas fell to the floor with a damp thump.

"I can't do this anymore!" shouted the young woman's boyfriend. "You're impossible to please. Plus"—he stopped dramatically at the edge of the curtain—"you're a cunt." Then he stormed out, clipping the day nurse in the shoulder as he walked by.

"Hey!" the nurse said. "Watch yourself."

While the nurse's back was turned, Birdy grabbed two Dixie Cups of orange capsules from the cart and, without thinking, without caring, swallowed the lot in two big gulps. The thin plastic coating dissolved against the roof of her mouth, releasing a cascade of tiny, sweet-tasting beads that chased one another down Birdy's throat like bubbles. Scrubbing bubbles, she thought. Ahhh, the relief. Where's the fire? What fire? She saw steam rise from somewhere, heard the hiss of flames being doused. She crumpled the cups and held them. Maybe they would melt, turn to wax figures, birds in her palm. Maybe they wouldn't.

"Told you," said the young woman behind the curtain, throwing herself against her pillows in a pout. "Only cares about his own skin."

Birdy was ten years old again and at the Spencerville Fun Spot with her father. Her mother and brother had stayed home. Her brother was sick with something. Rupert was always sick with something back then. The air smelled like fried dough and body odor. Gasoline, too, from the demolition derby that had taken place a few hours before in the muddy arena next to the mini–golf course. It was late and Birdy was getting sleepy. She and her father had ridden all the rides and all that was left was for him to win her an animal to hug on the way home. Almost all the games involved guns of some kind, but there was one, tucked between the Sitting Duck booth and the Deer in Headlights stand, that didn't. It was called the Frog Prince. Birdy's father paid fifty cents for the chance to flip rubber frogs at rubber lily pads. The goal was to get the frogs, wet and slippery and many of them missing hands and feet, to hit a pad and stay. A pretty young woman in a tight waitress's uniform kept the men in frogs. The players were all men. Birdy wondered why. Couldn't a girl flip a frog just as well as a boy? The pretty woman's nametag read "Rita." She was probably in high school or just out of it. When she leaned over, Birdy could see all the way to her bra, which was black and lacy. Birdy wondered if she'd ever look like that, have breasts, own a bra that pretty. Her father's frogs landed. Every single time. The pretty girl told Birdy's father he could pick out whatever prize he wanted from the assortment of stuffed animals, black-light posters, and plastic assault rifles hanging above their heads. Birdy's father said, "It's up to the boss here," and Birdy picked out a huge purple dog almost as tall as she was.

"The boss?" the pretty woman said. "Nah, she's a princess. Beautiful enough to be anyway."

Birdy blushed with pleasure. No one had ever complimented her looks. Not her mother or her father and certainly not her brother, who liked to make fun of her poochy girl belly and pigeon toes.

"I thought you were the princess," her father said to the woman. "A princess waiting for her prince among all these frogs."

"Maybe I am," the woman said. "Waiting, I mean."

Birdy's father laughed, showing all his teeth, even the silver-capped ones in the back. Birdy was ready to go now. She put her hand in her father's and squeezed.

"I think the princess is tired," he said.

"Of course," the woman said. She leaned forward again and patted Birdy on the head. "Sleep tight, Snow White. Don't let the bedbugs bite." She winked at Birdy's father, who bowed gallantly.

Birdy's father carried both her and the dog all the way to the car. Then he buckled them both into the backseat, kissing Birdy on the forehead and scratching the dog below his chin. When they set off into the night, everything grew dark and soft. It was as if the velvet sky had swallowed the moon. "I love, I love, I love my calendar girl," her dad crooned from the front seat. "Yeah, sweet calendar girl . . ."

Birdy felt safe, there in the dark next to the dog. It had been a perfect day and a perfect night. She couldn't remember ever being this happy, this content and at peace with the world. Her dad steered the car over a wooden bridge and the thwack of the tires over the planks told Birdy they'd be home soon. Ranasack, Ranasack, Ranasack, she sang to herself. All the way back, all the way back, all the way back. Then something went wrong. The car seemed to swerve. Birdy jerked in her seat, heart pounding. A wave of water had washed up over the car and was pouring through the windows. Her father was gone, pulled from the car by the current, and Birdy was all alone with the stuffed dog, left to drown. With her head just above water, she screamed until her lungs ached.

"Wake up," the woman next to her was saying through the curtain. Her voice was bored but kind. "You're okay. You're having a nightmare."

Birdy woke to the blue walls of her hospital room and the beeping of monitors down the hall.

"Thank you," she said to the woman.

"Don't thank me. You were screaming bloody murder. I only said something so the rest of us could hear ourselves think."

Wally showed up at Birdy's door sometime later, bringing with him a stack of old magazines from the Hair Barn and some dry chocolates. He did a kind of sashay into the room in black capris, a camo crop top, and combat boots. He'd painted his lips a throbbing-heart color. He was full of news. There was a curse on Breeder's

Laundromat, he said, and Basketball Juan Cardoza had been questioned about Daisy Gonzalez's disappearance. Juan would probably be let go soon, though, and as far as Wally knew, there were no solid leads in the case.

"We're all sort of waiting with bated breath for someone to find her but really these things never end well, do they? Personally I think Benny Bradenton's to blame but who asks me anything? No one. Anyway, how are you?"

Birdy found it difficult to follow Wally's rapid-fire dialogue even when she was her best self and she was not her best self at the moment. She'd started shaking when she woke from her nightmare and it only got worse as time went on. Tremors took over her hands. It was hard to hold the chocolate still enough to bite.

"I'm fine," she said. Then, haltingly, because her tongue had grown thick inside her mouth, she asked him how he and Helman were getting on without her.

"Don't worry about me, Mom," Wally said. "I'm fine, too. Actually, I'm thinking of suing dear old dad for emancipation, and then you'll both be rid of me and won't that be a burden lifted? But if I do, it's not about you, okay? Remember that. This is a daddy issue only, a 'need to be free to be me' kind of thing."

Birdy wanted desperately to persuade him against such drastic measures, but her mind was as fuzzy as the cotton that used to swaddle her precious pink pills. The wildfire from earlier had been replaced by an earthquake and a fog, the quake pretty serious on the Richter scale, the fog heavy and low hanging. She managed to say something to Wally about how much she loved him and how he should make sure to eat well-balanced meals, especially at breakfast time, but then she gave up, her teeth chattering and her head swathed in clouds.

"I know, I know," Wally said. "Breakfast. The most important meal of the day."

Birdy nodded and her son and the room around him seemed to jump and vibrate like a plucked string.

"I had Jell-O pudding for breakfast!" the young woman behind the curtain volunteered. "Breakfast of champions."

"That's nice," Wally said. He shot Birdy a look like, Why is this woman talking to us?

Birdy smiled at him, or she thought she did. It was hard to know exactly what her face was doing, but she was grateful her son seemed to recognize immediately, without her having to tell him, her roommate's inherent lack of quality.

"So you said the police have someone behind bars?" the young woman asked eagerly. "For kidnapping that Mexican girl?"

"For now," Wally said, "but last I heard they're going to release him. No real proof he had anything to do with it. Personally I think they're picking on him because he's an easy target. Poor Basketball Juan."

Birdy's roommate scoffed. "I'd save my pity for someone who actually deserves it. Poor Juan? Poor Juan my white twat."

Wally ignored her and focused on Birdy. It seemed that in addition to gossip, he had a request. "Mom," he said, "I'd like you to call me Willa from now on."

Birdy dropped a chocolate in her lap. She tried to pick it up but failed, smearing a streak of brown across the front of her robe. Wally leaned in, grabbed the truffle, and held it up to her lips.

"Willa," he said. "Willa as in Cather. You know, the writer. As in *O Pioneers!*? Or *My Ántonia*? Or how about *A Lost Lady*? Actually, that one really fits. I feel like a lost lady most of the time."

So did Birdy. She was a lady. She was lost. And she'd read

My Ántonia in high school. But what did a story about bohemian immigrants and Nebraska have to do with her child? Her feet joined her hands in the shaking. The bed began to bounce.

Wally rested his hands on Birdy's ankles. "Steady there, girl," he said. "You had to know this was coming."

Maybe, but she'd hoped it wouldn't. She thrust her hands under her hips and clenched her jaw. She tried to tell Wally that she was worried about him, that life was hard enough without courting trouble, but it all came out in a jumble of words. Muddy waters. Wally looked pained, fiddling with his shoelace.

"You're the one who's always told me to just be myself and that people would love me for who I was," he said. "If they didn't it was their problem. Remember?"

Yes, she remembered. She remembered everything about Wally with a clarity that surprised her because in many other areas, her memory fell short. He was born in this very hospital on an unseasonably warm day in February. There were complications—a twisted umbilical cord, a feet-first positioning—and he came out C-section. Hardly breathing. Nearly purple. Birdy's miracle baby. It had taken her four years to get pregnant and he almost died in the delivery room. When the nurse cleaned him off it was clear he was beautiful, one of the prettiest babies born that year, that same nurse swore. It was his big brown eyes, which he'd inherited from Birdy's mother, his thick black hair (courtesy of Helman), and his puckered pink mouth. So kissable. And he stayed beautiful all the way through childhood and into adolescence. It was only recently that he'd grown gawky, awkward, pimply. Birdy preferred to think of Wally at eight, milking one of the cows in a bright green field, a swirl of honeybees behind. She had a photograph of that very moment on her nightstand at home, and the charm of it wasn't just in the fact that Wally was young and sweet. She'd taken that picture when she too could pass for young, when she and Helman were happy, or at least Birdy was, and before she realized it wouldn't always be that way.

"So?" Wally said. "Will you do it? Call me Willa, I mean. Not Al. Or George. Or Ishmael. Willa. Will-a. Will you?"

Birdy's limbs would not stop trembling. There were fissures opening up in her skin, leaving in their wake a path of destruction, potholes and water main breaks, collapsed bridges and broken promises.

"Mom? Are you there?"

How to answer him. How to answer *her*. Wally. Willa. Was he her son anymore? Or was he her daughter? Was she still Birdy Rodgers now Yoder or had ten days in the hospital turned her into Betty the dirty dairy farmer's wife with nothing to show for herself but small-town scandal and a sexually confused child? Did any of it matter anyway?

"You're impossible, Mom," Wally said. "What am I going to do with you?"

Another unanswerable question.

"You need to stop this," Wally said. "The drinking. The pills. Or you're going to die and leave me all alone with Dad. Please don't do that. Can you hear me?"

She heard him and tried to nod, but the world was tipping and she had to grip the sides of her bed to keep from falling off the edge. She thought she saw out of the corner of her eye the woman from the horrible dairy day shuffling by. There was the trucker hat, the beaky nose, the narrow, disapproving eyes. The woman did a double take, stopped in the doorway, hovered. Why was she here?

To point out to Birdy just how useless she was? Birdy closed her eyes, put her fingers in her ears. See no evil. Hear no—

"Okay, well," Wally said. "I'm out then."

No, Birdy thought. No. Stay. Please stay. But she couldn't form the words. There was a tsunami between her and her brain, her brain and her mouth. And her son was on some other shore, out of reach.

"Willa!" she cried, but when she opened her eyes, he was gone, the magazines and chocolates and a lingering scent of nail polish remover the only signs he'd ever been there in the first place.

Birdy started to weep into her shaking hands. What kind of mother was she? What kind of woman?

"I wouldn't worry about your boy," Birdy's roommate chirped. "Everybody loves the gays now. I mean, look at that Ellen person. People fucking love her."

They pumped her stomach. That was pleasant. Pumped it empty and then hooked her up to an IV and gave her a chalky substance to soothe the pain in her throat. They told her to rest and she did, but not for long because Helman was sitting in the plastic chair again, staring at his hat. His fingernails were dirty and he hadn't bothered to shave. He had, however, put on his best pair of work pants and a clean white shirt, and his hair was freshly washed.

Birdy's throat was sore from the tube they'd shoved down during the pumping, but still, she had things to say. Now that Helman was actually here, she didn't want to waste her chance.

"It's about time you came to visit." Her voice came out as a raspy whisper.

"I know."

"Wally's been here quite a bit." Not true, but Birdy didn't care.

"Has he?"

"He told me he would like me to call him Willa from now on."

"Willa." Helman glanced at the roommate's half of the room. It was empty. The young woman had gone to the cafeteria for lunch, offering to bring Birdy back a sandwich or Jell-O pudding cup, but Birdy declined. She would eat later. "Like the tree?"

"No," Birdy said. "Like the writer. He also told me he plans to sue you for emancipation."

"Really?"

Birdy wondered if he'd even talked to their son once since she'd been in the hospital. Helman always was a terrible communicator. He didn't call to tell her he'd be coming, so, of course, he came at the worst time.

"You should not have brought me here," she said. She took a drink of chalky stuff and swallowed hard, chasing it with water. "Do you realize I've been sharing my room with a stripper? That there is nothing between me and filth but a flimsy canvas curtain?"

"I'm sorry, Birdy," Helman said. "I really am."

Birdy did not trust Helman's demeanor. It was not like him to be contrite. Maybe it was seeing her in such a state. She decided to pile it on. "You should be sorry. Do you realize what you've done? You've put me in jail. A glorified jail with nurses instead of wardens but it amounts to the same thing. And I've been told I can't get myself out for another two days."

"I know. They told me that, too."

"Why?" she asked. "Why did you do this to me?"

Helman stood up and walked to the window, peered out, seemed to study the scene, which Birdy knew from doing the same consisted of a circular drive, a water feature on the fritz, and a cheerless parking lot that stretched to the horizon.

"Aren't you going to say something?" Birdy asked.

Helman did not turn to look at her. He stared straight ahead, hands folded over his belly, so tight and flat in youth but now spilling over a garish bronco belt buckle. He'd left his hat behind on the chair, its bill dented in the center and stained with sweat.

"I'm leaving you, Birdy," he said.

"Excuse me?"

"I've come to ask for a divorce."

Birdy cleared her throat. She blinked away the pain. "You can't be serious."

"I am. Serious, I mean. Don't make this more difficult than it is."

"Don't make this more difficult? Me?" Birdy's whispers were growing shrill. Mrs. Damish, her favorite teacher at finishing school, had taught her to keep her emotions in check. No matter how ugly or upsetting the situation, ladies were always in control of themselves. They preserved their pride, their dignity, their self-respect, by never allowing others to get the upper hand.

"On what grounds?" Birdy asked finally.

"Grounds?"

"What are your grounds for divorce? I've been a good wife to you, faithful, caring. I gave you a son. You're the one who ruined everything. What possible reason could you have for leaving me?"

Helman faced her then. With his piercing blue eyes and infectious smile, he'd once borne a passing resemblance to *Butch Cassidy and the Sundance Kid*–era Paul Newman, but his skin had grown pouchy and loose and the lines around his mouth made him look perpetually dissatisfied. "I don't love you anymore," he said.

Birdy smoothed her covers. "Oh. I see."

"And I'm pretty sure you don't love me either. Otherwise, none of this would have happened."

So that's what he thought. That's how he accounted for her retreat from the world. She had no idea his understanding of her, of marriage, of humanity, was so limited, so misguided. Cows. He understood cows. And pasteurization. He'd taught himself to say "hello" and "good-bye" and "you're fired" in Spanish. Otherwise he was entirely clueless.

"I think," Helman said, "with all that's going on, you know, with the dairy and the case and whatnot, that this is really the best thing. For both of us."

So there was another woman. That's what that "best thing for both of us" statement meant. Wasn't that exactly what Birdy's father told Birdy's mother—"Going our separate ways is really the best thing, for both of us"—when the truth was he'd fallen in hopeless love with the black bra'ed moonlighting waitress with her frogs and lily pads and talk of princes and princesses? Together, the bra and frogs and lily pads, not to mention Birdy's father's hopeless romanticism, conspired to lay waste to Birdy's happy family, all of it coming to an ugly climax the day Birdy's mother threw her father out of the house. Literally. She tossed everything that belonged to him out the window—shirts, pants, watches, ties, every volume of *Decline and Fall of the Roman Empire,* his collection of stethoscopes and antique medical implements, his razors and bottles of aftershave, the heavy blue-plated radio he kept in his study as company on late nights. A few ties and shirts didn't make it to the lawn. They stuck to the window casing like white flags, distress signals. The rest lay on the grass in a heap, the radio on and tuned to a baseball game going into extra innings. Boys from the neighborhood kept walking by to check the score.

"Does she work at the fair?" Birdy asked Helman.

"What? What are you talking about?"

"Never mind."

The day nurse came in to take Birdy's vitals. Helman watched for a moment while the nurse strapped the blood pressure sleeve around Birdy's upper arm and pressed a stethoscope to her chest. Then he put on his hat and stood, a sure sign he was ready to leave. Birdy knew all his signs. She supposed she would have to unlearn them.

"Good news," the nurse told him, pulling the stethoscope from her ears. "Your wife is going to live."

Birdy had her tornado dream again. This one was familiar. She'd had it a million times before. She was in a house that wasn't exactly her house. It was her childhood home mixed with her farmhouse mixed with an apartment she'd seen on TV years ago—plush curtains framing windows that let in darkness and wind and rain, wall-to-wall cream carpets, potted tropical plants scattered here and there among a wealth of elegant, Regency-era furniture. Birdy looked down. She was in a gauzy, flowing night-gown, aquamarine as usual. She ran her hands over the fabric. So soft, so fragile, like something Bette Davis would have worn and not the most convenient attire for surviving a storm, but when the firemen came later to check on her at least she could say she was fit to be seen. On her feet were two impossibly tiny, high-heeled silk slippers with feathery pom-poms over the toes. She did a quick two-step and took herself to the window. That

was how she moved in this particular dream—like she was a pos-
session, a polished settee to be moved around the room until she
found exactly the right place for herself. She watched the black
clouds whirl and mass themselves into a funnel shape. She wasn't
afraid. More fascinated. How insignificant I am, she thought. How
replaceable. Still, she had no desire to die. The minute the train
sound rent the air and the tornado—solid now and big shouldered—
puts its toe down in the north field, she would get to lower ground.
Then she would be safe.

She took herself to her basement door, but the door and the
wall around it weren't doing so well. They looked more like snow-
melt than the solid wood and plaster she was used to. The stairs
leading to safety weren't there either. There was just this wavy
mess. The mess was getting on her shoes. This was new. This was
a strange development. Should she run through it like one would
a waterfall? Should she take herself through to the other side? But
what was on the other side? The nice firemen with their dimpled
chins and kind, capable arms? Or something sinister? The woman
in the hat shooing her. Useless. Useless. Birdy did not know what
to do with herself. She stood there and waited as the howling at
her back grew louder and louder. There were splinters in her hair.
Glass in her arms, carpet in her mouth. I am becoming something
else, she thought. I am becoming my house which is not my house.
Well, look at that.

Birdy woke on her own. It was early morning. Sunlight was just start-
ing to stream in through the window and a band of it traversed
Birdy's chenille spread in a wide, dusty stripe. The blue curtain
had been pulled back and Birdy's young roommate was gone. In

her place was the fierce day nurse, stripping the bed and mumbling to herself about "white woman mess" and "white woman stink."

"Where is she?" Birdy asked, feeling a moment's elation at having the room to herself.

"Gone home, presumably," the nurse said. "No insurance, couldn't afford to stay. You know what she says to me? She says, 'Thanks, Obama.'" The nurse blew air out the side of her pretty mouth. "Because it's *his* fault her workplace is a pole."

The roommate's boyfriend bouquet lay in a heap on the floor and the soft whiff of rotting petals imbued the room with something bride-like. At least that was Birdy's opinion. The nurse was merely annoyed. She swept a litter of brown-tipped petals into a wastebasket and murmured, "Sweets for the sour." A whole carnation, stemless and shriveled, skidded along the tile, coming to rest against Birdy's ankle.

"Hey, Mrs. Yoder," the nurse said from across the room, "you're finally getting what you want."

Birdy thought of Helman and his sweaty, dented hat. "I can't imagine what you mean."

"You're getting a new roommate. It's like transferring rooms, only better. And since you were born to better, you should be happy to hear the woman is minor Midwestern royalty. Heir to a casket company fortune. Or something like that."

Birdy shuddered. How morbid. And tacky. Coffins indeed. When Birdy got out of this horrible place, one of the first things she would do was put on her mother's strand of pearls. Then she would wear them every day for the rest of her life. I'll never take them off, she thought. Not to sleep. Not even to shower. Then the world would know what kind of woman she was and, when she saw herself passing a mirror, she would know, too.

The nurse picked up something shiny off the ground and dropped it in her scrubs pocket, mumbling, "Mine now." She started to leave but ducked her head back in the room and gave Birdy an almost smile. "I'll be right back with your eight A.M. dose."

"That won't be necessary," Birdy said.

"What's that?"

"I don't need my eight A.M. dose, thank you very much."

"Really?"

Birdy took some lotion from her bedside table and massaged it into her skin. Her hands were the wrinkled and much-veined hands of a woman in late middle age, the fingernails losing luster, the knuckles somewhat swollen. Arthritis would hit soon, Birdy supposed. First the knotting, then the pain. Her mother's hands were gnarled and clawlike at the end. Birdy's would probably look like that, too, in ten, maybe fifteen years' time. But for now they were steady and mostly straight and Birdy wondered what sort of work they might do.

"Really," she said.

The nurse shrugged. "Suit yourself."

Birdy supposed there was nothing else to do but suit herself now. She would check herself out of this hospital, tomorrow or the day after that, and then there would be decisions to make, decisions about Wally, where they would live, what their lives would look like without Helman. For a moment it was as if she were standing on the edge of a sheer cliff, everything falling away from her, the scornful woman in the trucker hat, Ms. You're Useless herself, at the bottom, daring Birdy to be something other than a rich white woman with cool rags for once. Birdy touched her naked throat. She could feel the pearls there, taking shape. One by one.

Red Herring

(May)

The bloodstain reminded Randy of a Darwin fish. It had the same curved but smooth top like the flight of a line drive, and the matching convex bottom intersected it, fanned out into a tail. Also two feet seemed to jut out from the underbelly. Commas. Sharp turns. The blot, big enough to warrant two traffic cones with police tape wrapped around, looked like it could up and walk away if it wanted to. Instead it stayed put, and Randy couldn't really believe he was here again, in front of Breeder's Laundromat, staring at dried blood on the sidewalk.

"Randy."

"Yeah, Jack."

"Are you thinking what I'm thinking?"

"Doubt it."

"That this is Daisy Gonzalez's blood."

"Then definitely no. Didn't you read the paper? This blood is from the Ranasack Apartments people. It's some sort of statement."

"But Chief."

"Yeah, Zane."

"This is the same spot, isn't it?"

"The very same."

Three years before, Tina Gonzalez had died on this sidewalk. Still unsolved, the accident was one of the saddest Randy had ever witnessed. Someone had hopped a curb, hit Tina and her little girl (*Daisy, Daisy, where are you?* The thought an ulcer in his gut, burning), and kept driving. It happened on a day like this one, blue sky, white puffy cartoon clouds. The only so-called clues found at the scene were two fake legs lying near Tina's body like those of a spooning lover. Strange and spooky enough, they were clean of fingerprints and struck Randy more as red herrings than anything else.

"I see Saturn," Zane Bigsby said, pointing at the blood. "Rings and all."

"I see Uranus," Jack McElroy joked.

What Randy would never forget from that day, besides Daisy giving the ravaged Hector a wan smile from the back of the ambulance, was Tina's handprint in blood, fingers seeming to stretch toward Daisy's impossibly tiny left shoe, left behind.

Randy rubbed his face. His stubble felt like sand. "Tell Em I'm going to be in the Bottoms if she needs to get ahold of me."

Jack and Zane shot each other a look.

"What?" Randy asked.

"Well, it's just—" Jack started.

"No offense meant, Chief, but we think you're barking up the wrong tree there."

"Yeah," Jack agreed. "It's like it's not even a tree. It's a bush. Or maybe some kind of houseplant."

Randy sighed. "What are you talking about?"

"You're going to question Basketball Juan again, right?"

"I don't know, Jack. Maybe. Why?"

Zane shrugged and picked his ear. "It wasn't him."

Randy agreed but didn't want to say so. "What makes you so sure?"

"A hunch," Jack said. "A gut feeling."

"And besides," Zane said. "He's too nice."

"And he kind of loves her."

It was true. During interrogation Juan Cardoza had broken down in sobs, making the kind of sad, donkey-like sounds men do when they can't control themselves and don't care who's listening.

Maria Pinto, Juan's beautiful interpreter and the same woman who shouted down Chuck Breeder a few days before in front of the Laundromat, basically called Randy, his deputies, and their suspicions absolute bullshit. "Seriously?" she said. "This is the guy you think took Daisy? Look at him. He's a mess."

Juan had a disfigured face and a lazy eye that watered even when he wasn't crying. On top of that, he seemed unable to sit still for long periods of time. Like a child, he kept reaching for things that weren't his and whining. And then there was the basketball situation. Em had tried to confiscate it when Juan came in the station—"The weirdest things make the best weapons," she said— but the man refused to hand it over. He clung to it like it was a life vest and the ship was going down.

"No no no no no," Juan kept saying, shaking his shaved head and backing away from Em into a corner between the water cooler and the file cabinet. "No. No. No. No."

Maria stepped in, whispering something in Juan's right ear. Whatever she said calmed him, and he was able to answer Randy's first set of questions without much difficulty. "How do you know Daisy Gonzalez?" "She's my friend." "Where did you last see her?" "Basketball court." "When?" "After school." "What were you and Daisy doing the day she disappeared?" "Playing." "Playing what?" "Basketball." "But then you stopped playing, right?" "It started to rain. I went inside." "Where did Daisy go?" "Home." "Did you go with her?" "No, I went inside." Randy showed Juan the picture of him and Daisy that had been anonymously sent to the station the night the girl went missing. Juan started to cry. He held his basketball in front of his face and wept.

Maria, stunning and furious, stood and stuck a pointy finger-nail in Randy's chest. "You know what I think?" She was so close he could smell her—hairspray and vanilla. "I think you have no idea what's happened to Daisy and that scares you to death. You know that if you don't solve this case you'll lose your job and so you need a scapegoat, an easy target, and who's better than Juan, a weirdo Mexican who can't speak English and thinks a basket-ball's his baby? Pathetic. That's what you are. A fat fish in a small pond. A big-mouthed bass swimming around all self-important like you know something when what you're really doing is shitting in the water."

Randy supposed he should have reprimanded her, and Zane and Jack were prepared to haul her into a holding cell for assaulting a police officer, but Randy let her rant because she was right. He was a big fish and Colliersville was the tiniest pond imaginable. He was also pathetic, a force of one, three if you counted Jack and Zane, but who counted them? They only worked part-time, pre-ferring to moonlight for the fire department because that job came with a cot and regular meals and instant female regard.

People gave Randy grief all the time, said he was small potatoes,

Barney Fife blah blah blah, and to a certain extent, it was true. Still, just because Colliersville was a quiet town with a relatively low crime rate, that didn't mean it had all been bike derbies and lollipops. Randy had met quite a few lowlifes in his day and no mistake. Fellows missing their conscience, guys who'd just as soon stick their mother's head in a juicer as wipe their own behinds. A few women, too, blowsy broads whose idea of fun was to leave their kids tied by the ankle to the bathroom radiator for the night while they went out to Sharkey's for four blenders' worth of margs. The majority of the criminals he'd had the misfortune to meet since he'd taken over for his father eight years before had been a pack of unfortunates. Fatties, a lot of them, and dirt-poor and dragged through the ditch and gutter and muck by their thumbs. Faces like worm-eaten wood. Teeth even worse. Hair just barely hanging on.

Randy realized, looking into Maria's bright eyes, that he'd never seen Niagara Falls. He had also never seen the Statue of Liberty, the Grand Canyon, or the redwoods. That was police work for you. Long hours. All ugliness, no beauty. A life half-lived.

"Juan's a red herring, like the legs," he said to himself. And the stain. He'd forgotten for a moment where he was. He'd forgotten Zane and Jack were even there.

"A herring, Chief?" Zane said. "What do fish have to do with it?"

Randy sighed. "I'm talking about the logical fallacy red herring. Not the fish."

"What do dicks have to do with it?" Jack asked.

Everyone in town had a theory about what might have happened to Daisy Gonzalez, and Randy was, of course, party to them all. He kept a careful record of every lead and accusation in a notebook he carried in his back pocket. Most of the ideas were far-fetched, ridiculous even, and clearly voiced to settle scores. Shellie Pogue came to the station to cast suspicion on her former best friend and current nemesis, Helen Garrety—"She hasn't been right since her grandson went to war," Shellie said, "and really, what is she doing out there all alone on that farm of hers with those 'organic' herbs?"—and Helman Yoder, himself in hot water and awaiting trial, told Randy he thought that Gordy/Ramon person, who acted as Randy's informant in the dairy shutdown, might have skipped town with the girl as "insult to injury." Fingers had been pointed not only at Juan Cardoza but at Hank Seaver, Fikus Ward, and a handful of other unsavory elements living in Maple Leaf Mobile Home Park, including the Tucker boys, Jack's uncle Lloyd, and Irv Peoples, the hermit roadkill collector whom Randy heard had a stash of axes in his garage and loved the sight of spilled blood.

Randy was ashamed to admit, even to himself, that he had no idea who had taken Daisy or what they might have done with her/were doing to her at that very moment. Which meant that Maria was right about that, too. He was a failure at his job and it was just a matter of time before someone with enough power to do so stripped him of his badge and sent him home to his wife, who, Randy supposed, would greet the news the way she greeted everything these days: with a shrug and a "That sucks, sweetie," just before turning back to her computer to play *Candy Crush* or *Words with Friends*.

"Personally," Jack said, "I think some out-of-town pedophile's to blame. You know, some twisted fuck with kiddie porn all over his computer."

"Could be," Zane said. "Or maybe it's a desperate woman who

couldn't be a mom on her own so she had to steal someone else's kid to fulfill that particular dream."

"Dude," Jack said. "You might be on to something."

"I'm always on to something," Zane said.

Randy couldn't listen anymore. He got in his squad car and headed down Main Street toward the Bottoms, Jack and Zane be damned, going first to the old Udall place because it was sunny and the bugs weren't too bad. The house, at the corner of Hate Henry Road and Rocky Way, was a squatter's spooky paradise and Randy made an effort to walk through or at least drive by every few days to satisfy himself that someone hadn't turned it into a makeshift meth cookery or, worse yet, an underage brothel. It was one of the banes of Randy's existence, just as it had been for his father. Twenty years ago, a rotating set of Seavers and Tuckers, on the run from their daddy's whip and ma's open hand, slept curled up together on the kitchen floor, usually two or three at a time, one blanket and one pillow between them. They had animals for company, mostly rats. And river fish for food. And a space heater shaped like Yoda. They filled the house with farts and bad singing. Also beer cans. They painted one bathroom a hideous bloodred and hung a picture of José Canseco in the hall. After the Seavers and Tuckers came the oversexed and hopped-up teenagers. They turned the house and its immediate environs into one long rave. House music. Ecstasy. Plastic water bottles. Tie-dyed everything.

Then silence. Ten years of it. During which time there was a five-hundred-year flood and a few fish swam through, died in the corners and in the one pink toilet. Carpenter ants took over the attic. An ash tree fell on the front porch and the garage caught fire. Spontaneous combustion. The fire would have burned down the whole Bottoms if Hank Seaver hadn't run over there with his garden hose, screaming at the top of his lungs at the neighborhood to help him for "Christ's sake get up get up get up the Redcoats are coming! The Redcoats are coming!" After they put the fire out, everyone roasted hot dogs and marshmallows over the ashes and Hank, armed with a fifth of Jim Beam, led the company in a toast to the Bottoms, Colliersville, and America. Also to the Colts and the Pacers and God, Jesus, and big-breasted women. Amen.

Eventually the city council voted to have the old Udall place torn down, but the demolition bids came in high and everyone just forgot about it the same way they forgot about Nan Udall, who'd had a heart attack while in her closet looking for a camisole and was pulled out the front door one beautiful morning in 1979, feet first, nothing but bones.

The house, which had fallen into disrepair after Nan's death, seemed to lean ever so slightly to the west. Everything—windows, doorjambs, roof peaks—was just askew enough to make you dizzy if you looked long enough. Peels of pea-green paint lay on the grass like feathers. What wood there still was was rotting, turning to honeycomb. Wasps buzzed greedily through the warped windows. Fun-house mirrors. Randy went inside but was stopped short by a fallen beam. That was new. As were a few signs of recent habitation—a musty blanket, an ashtray full of roach clips and lipstick-stained cigarette butts, a balled-up pair of women's panties shedding glitter.

"I like what you've done with the place," he said to the empty rooms. The only answer was the José Canseco picture crashing to the hallway floor. Randy ducked under the beam and was hoping to investigate further when his phone rang. It was Cat.

"Hi, hon," he said. "What's up?"

"Can you pick up some dish soap on your way home tonight?"

"Sure."

"And also some TP? The situation's growing dire."

"Of course."

"Good day, sweetie?"

"Just fine," he said. "Can't complain."

He could complain, but what would be the point? Especially of complaining to his wife, who loved him in her way but had long ago stopped listening anytime he talked about work. As far as Randy could tell, Cat was the only inhabitant of Colliersville who couldn't care less about the disappearance of Daisy Gonzalez. She was much more intrigued by the kidnappings and killings she read about on the Internet than the crimes that scarred her own hometown. When Randy asked her why this was, she acted like the answer was an obvious one. "It's only interesting if it happens to other people," she said.

Which might explain why she'd stopped sleeping with him several years before. Randy gazed sadly down at the discarded panties, felt a faint memory of desire stir within him, but he'd buried his sex drive so deep under layers of loyalty and long-term commitment that it wasn't difficult to dismiss the feeling as a fleeting animal urge that had nothing to do with real life and everything to do with the sort of erotic fantasy Cat found so repugnantly male. All those lingerie fetishes, that fixation on breasts and asses and the lace that held them in place. Sex was, by nature, sexist, she often said, born of men's compulsion to a) dominate women and b) transform them into glorified vessels for their seed. Cat had gone to college, Randy, too. That's where they met. But Cat stuck it out for all four years, graduating with a degree in liberal studies, whereas Randy left after two to join his father on the police force. He wondered if this was why he and Cat couldn't talk to each other—a basic education mismatch. And because they didn't talk, they didn't touch, either.

Before he'd completely given up, Randy used to argue with her. *Can't sex be fun, too?* he'd say. And then there was the whole intimacy thing. *Doesn't sex bring people closer together?*

No, she said. *I don't think so.*

Once, over too many beers at Sharkey's, Randy had made the fatal mistake of confiding in Jack and Zane that he and Cat had stopped making love. "Like stopped?" Jack asked, confused. "You mean you bang like once a week? Or once a month? You don't mean stopped as in stopped for real."

"You do do it on y'all's anniversary, right?" Zane said. "Everyone gets laid on their anniversary."

Randy shook his head. "Never," he said. "She said it hurts and she's just not into it and if I love her I'll understand and respect her wishes."

"She said that?" Zane asked. "Respect her wishes?"

"Yeah," Randy said.

"Sounds like feminazi bullshit to me," Zane said.

Jack agreed, sucking suds off his mustache. "Two words," he said. "Lesbian."

Randy was convinced Cat's sex strike had more to do with her cousin Frannie than feminism. Frannie had given birth to a son, Kenny, now serving a tour of duty in Iraq, when she was only fifteen. Cat swore Kenny was a child of rape, that Frannie's pregnancy was the result of a sexual assault by a much older man—a man Cat absolutely refused to name because naming him would acknowledge he was human and he was much more on the level of pond scum—and that that was why Frannie didn't stick around to raise her own son. "Just couldn't face Kenny's face," Cat said. Cat seemed pathologically afraid of motherhood, and so Randy suggested, as gently as he could manage, that she get on the pill. But Cat refused to ride that particular physical and emotional rollercoaster. *The hormones,* she said. *Killers. Why don't you try pumping your body full of them and see how you like it.*

Cat made an impatient noise that sounded like static in Randy's ear. "You there?"

"Yeah, sorry, hon," Randy said. "But I gotta go. Another call coming in."

"Okay," she said. "See you tonight."

"See you tonight."

The other call was Em, his receptionist, phoning from the station.

"Randy," Em said. "We've got a situation."

Randy massaged his forehead. "This about Daisy?"

"Afraid not, but on the plus side, this one's got 'fun' written all over it."

"Fun? Yeah, right."

"I mean it. Dispute at Miss Kitty's. Catfight."

Cat hated the word *catfight.* With a passion and not just because of her name. She said it deprived women of their personhood. Personhood? What was that exactly? Then Randy made a mental note—*toilet paper, dish soap.*

"You're joking," he said to Em.

"I'm not," Em said. "And word is, it's getting serious. Someone could lose an eyelash."

"Be there as soon as I can." He was about to hang up.

"Oh, hey, one more thing," Em said. "Yuhl Butz came by earlier."

"He did, did he?" Yuhl was one of the many men in town determined to find Daisy before Randy did. Perhaps that was unfair. All the search teams had the same stated goal—to find Daisy alive and well and reunite her with her father—but Randy couldn't help seeing them as walking, walkie-talkie-ing reminders of his own incompetence.

"He found a girl's hair tie on the side of Route 20," Em said. "Actually, I think it was a bloodhound that sniffed it out. Could be absolutely nothing, but—"

"Could be something," Randy said.

"Should I send it to the lab?"

Em loved sending things to the lab. It made her feel like she was on *CSI*. Or *Bones*. She was crazy about police procedurals, the bloodier the better, and, inspired by an episode of *Major Crimes*, she'd even drawn up what she called a Daisy Gonzalez "suspect map," which she'd constructed in the break room with butcher paper, thumbtacks, and red yarn. Hanging between the window and the refrigerator, it linked the pictures of possible perps to their motives and their relationship to Daisy. Randy was often in awe of Em, and not a little bit frightened of her. She should have been the cop, he thought. Not me. She'd be a lot happier out in the field, investigating kidnappings and breaking up stripper fights, than she was in the office, where she divided her time between answering the phones, filing, and watering the plants she insisted they keep around because they gave the mostly spartan station a "homey feel." If they switched roles, Randy could be the receptionist, flirting with Lance the lab tech and making sure the African violet got enough sun and the spider plant not too much. Of course, Lance wasn't really his type. . . .

"Randy? Did I lose you?"

"Nah, I'm here," he said. "Sure, send it off. Can't hurt."

"That's what I thought. Can't hurt."

Randy hung up then. He would have to scout out the Udall place later. On the front porch he found a few rolling papers and what looked to be a bra strap. Should he have Em send them to the lab? Across the street, Juan Cardoza was shooting baskets. He stood at free-throw distance, his aim perfect. Nothing but net every time. An older woman in a trucker hat sat on a nearby picnic table, watching and working her way through a box of chocolate doughnuts. When Juan saw Randy he grabbed his basketball and ran inside. The woman stayed where she was, chewing slowly. Her weary stare told Randy she knew his type and wasn't impressed. You're not fooling anyone, that stare said. You might have a shiny gun and a shiny badge and a shiny black-and-white car with flashing lights and a dash cam, but you don't scare me. You don't scare me at all.

Randy didn't have the heart to face a bunch of combative strippers just then, so instead of driving straight to Miss Kitty's, he took a detour at the Spencerville Fun Spot and parked next to the defunct ticket booth, watching butterflies flit in and out of the rusty window bars. He put his head back and let himself dream about his high school girlfriend, Kimberly, who had long ago moved to California and was rumored to be dating a filthy-rich restaurateur famous for transforming Midwestern staples like tuna-fish casserole and ambrosia salad into haute cuisine. Randy knew that Kimberly was as old as he was, forty-five if she was a day, but when he thought of her—and lately he could lose whole hours thinking of her—he imagined her as she was when he met her, young, gap-toothed pretty, and tanned. Small breasts and long legs. Dark brown hair that caught the sun better than any blonde. Two perfect ass cheeks (male repugnant fixation). A way of saying his name that made him feel like royalty. Not as conventionally pretty as her older cousin Rita, maybe, but smart and sexy and with that deep, raspy voice that went right to your spine.

More and more, Randy caught himself zoning out on the job. He liked to park his car in some remote location where he was confident he wouldn't be seen or harassed and then relive the one perfect day more than twenty years ago when he and Kimberly ditched school to come here to the Fun Spot, where they rode the Ferris wheel for hours, making out and laughing at the carny operator, Pa Tucker, a Kentucky transplant with a ruined face and a habit of picking his nose and wiping it on kids as they ran by. They talked about getting married after graduation and maybe having a couple of kids of their own, buying a house in the tree streets. Kimberly, whose parents owned a double-wide in Maple Leaf Mobile Home Park, dreamed of sturdy walls, hardwood floors, a fireplace that, "you know, burns real actual wood. Not one of those electric things." Randy had grown up in one of the better houses in the Bottoms, so he wouldn't mind, he said, "trading up." On that beautiful, flawless day, Kimberly eventually grew tired of the Ferris wheel with its view of cornfields and Pa Tucker's scabby head, so she skipped away from him in search of an elephant ear and a lemon shake-up. As lovely as her retreating figure was, Randy did not enjoy the feeling that came with watching her get farther and farther away. Every once in a while she would turn and laugh and call for him to follow, a string of silver bells tinkling against her ankle, but she was growing smaller, less distinct, with every step, and that bright sound—her laugh and the bells—so pretty at first, morphed into something harsh and jarring.

Randy woke to his phone ringing. Em again.

"Um, are you on your way? To Miss Kitty's? Had another call. Things are getting out of hand."

"Yes, definitely." Randy sat up and rubbed his eyes. He checked himself in the rearview. He'd drooled some on his shirt collar. "Got a little sidetracked is all. You know, police work. Never a dull moment."

"Speak for yourself. I'm bored to tears over here."

"How's lab Lance?"

"Still married."

"Well, you'll have that," Randy said. Married men tended to stay that way. Look at me, he thought. I'm the poster child for inertia. Just as the Fun Spot—not so fun anymore—was the perfect example of entropy. The barnlike structure that once held the Matterhorn was falling in on itself in an almost circular pattern, the boards taking on the form of hourglass sand, and the lemon on the lemon shake-up booth had faded to gray, looking more like the shadow of the Death Star than a piece of fruit. While he scanned the ruined buildings, twisted metal, and collapsed roofs of his childhood, something caught his eye—a shiny object directly under the Ferris wheel, reflecting light in fits and starts. A breeze-buffeted candy wrapper, he supposed. That or a part from the ride, jostled loose by time and weather.

He started the car. "This is me, heading to Miss Kitty's," he told Em.

"Oh good," she said. "While you're there, get a lap dance for me? I hear they're half off on Tuesdays."

Randy had never, in all his years of policing, seen Miss Kitty's in such an uproar. The last time the sleepy strip club seemed to wake up from its stupor was St. Patrick's Day 2007, when the owner and Jack's second cousin, Stan McElroy, splurged and booked that midget porn star who called herself Mabel in Miniature. People came from all over to watch Mabel go through her routine of old-fashioned burlesque followed by naked knife juggling. Even Randy had made it out, using his badge as an excuse. "I'm here to keep the peace," he'd said, but in truth he was simply curious. Mabel did not disappoint. She was beautiful and perfectly proportioned for her height. It was like looking at a Barbie doll on a slightly larger scale. You wanted to pick her up and change her dress, put her in a Jeep with Ken, and roll them into the sunset.

The commotion that greeted him today was of a different variety. Two dancers in G-strings were onstage, locked together like exhausted boxers. Randy recognized Maria Pinto right away. The other dancer was a dirty-blonde, strong in the shoulders. A small crowd of mostly male onlookers had taken sides in the scuffle, sloshing beer on themselves and tossing dollar bills on the stage. The women scratched each other, pulled hair, threw kicks that failed to land. Then they slipped in their six-inch heels, growling and gasping for breath. It was like a naked mud-wrestling match, only instead of grime, the women were covered in sweat and money.

Randy pulled out his shiny badge and announced his presence to the room. The effect was immediate. The blonde, who had Maria in a half nelson, let go. Maria snapped to attention, spotted Randy, made a face like, Not you again. The men went silent, a few of them frozen in the act of tossing cash. Randy took advantage of the break in the action to rush the stage. He grabbed both women by the arm and, trying hard not to look at their breasts (male repugnant fixation), led them to the dressing room behind the DJ booth. At one point, the blonde muttered something about tacos and twats and Maria tried to take a swing at her, but Randy was in the way.

"I will arrest you both," he said. "In a heartbeat."

The dressing room was a mess of G-strings, wigs, Red Bull cans, and stilettos. Scotch tape and glitter littered the floor. A cell phone was going off somewhere, the ringtone a tinny version of "Like a Virgin," and there was a brunette mannequin head staring at Randy from a pile of feather boas.

"We need to stop meeting like this," he said to Maria.

"Tell me about it."

She and the blonde sat down and crossed their arms over their chests like pouty schoolgirls. Randy took his cue from them and put on his best "disappointed principal" face. "What's this all about, ladies?"

The blonde spoke first. "She called me a thief."

Maria rolled her eyes. "You *are* a thief."

"Prove it," the blonde said. She had short legs and a small waist. Pimples peppered her forehead.

"I don't have to," Maria said.

"So . . ." Randy prompted Maria. "She—" He looked at the blonde. "I'm sorry. I don't know your name."

"Brianna," the blonde said. "Brianna Pogue."

"Thank you," he said. "So, Maria, you're accusing Brianna of stealing money from you."

"No," Maria said. "She stole from the high school. From her own mother, even."

"Oh my God." Brianna leaned back and folded her arms behind her head. "You're just making shit up now."

"I don't make shit up," Maria said to Brianna. "I don't tell lies. That's your department."

It was Brianna's turn to roll her eyes. "Jesus titty-fucking Christ."

Randy stared down at the table, at Brianna's wide palms drumming the surface. Someone had carved her initials into the wood. STD. Or maybe it was a joke and the joke was on him.

"I don't understand," Randy said. "Help me out."

"There's nothing to understand," Brianna said. "She's spreading lies about me, probably because she's tired of spreading her *legs* for every Tom, Dick, and Hay-sooce who dares put a dollar up her hooha." She turned to Maria, lit a cigarette, blew the smoke in her face. "Why don't you just go back where you came from?"

Maria was out of her chair before Randy could stop her, pointy finger in Brianna's chest this time. "You are the ugliest person I've ever seen," Maria said, "and I'm not just talking about your greasy mug or your cottage cheese thighs. I'm talking about your soul. Your racist, thieving, disgusting, cottage cheese soul. Who steals from their own mother? Who takes the food right out of our children's mouths like that?"

"You have no idea what you're talking about."

"Yes I do. Daisy told me."

"Daisy?" Randy asked. "What does any of this have to do with Daisy?"

The cell phone rang again. *Touched for the very first time. Like a viriririrgin . . .*

Maria grew icy. She spoke slowly, deliberately, like a witness in a courtroom, coached and calm. "Daisy informed me just a week before she disappeared that Brianna stole a bunch of money from the high school cafeteria till while Shellie wasn't looking. A lot of money."

"Lying whore!" Brianna shouted, arms pinwheeling at Maria's face.

"Thieving slut!" Maria spit.

Randy broke them up. "Hey there." He felt less like a capable principal now and more like a babysitter charged with solving an unsolvable dilemma. He wished he could put both women in time-out. "You two simmer down."

They sat down again and faced the mirror. Maria rubbed coconut oil on her legs and watched herself while she did and Brianna plucked the small space between her eyebrows. Their chests were still heaving.

So Brianna was Shellie Pogue's daughter, Randy thought. Shellie was the head cafeteria lady at the high school, and the last time Randy questioned Hector Gonzalez, Hector had mentioned something about Shellie watching Daisy once in a while when he was particularly busy grading tests and papers and prepping for the next day's class. Shellie would wash dishes in the back or wipe down cafeteria tables and Daisy would "help" her. Probably, Randy supposed, by making a mess. Randy would have to talk to Shellie again, but this time he'd have to distract her from her desire to point the finger at Helen Garrety and ask her what she knew about her daughter's supposed theft.

Stan McElroy peeked in then, a chicken wing in his hand.

Heavy metal poured through the open door. "Maria," he said, "you're going on in two minutes. Pick out your song."

Maria shot Brianna a scathing look. "'Crazy Bitch' seems appropriate."

"Yeah it does," Brianna said.

"I'm truly sorry," Maria said, hand on hip, "that business is so bad you had to resort to stealing. I feel responsible."

"You feel responsible?"

"It's too bad all your old clients prefer me to you, but really who can blame them when you can't be bothered to wash your pussy on a regular basis."

"I'm not going to dignify that with a full response," Brianna said.

Maria laughed. Then she leaned over Brianna, dropping a condescending kiss on the blond girl's forehead. "My God, you're an idiot."

After she left, Brianna wadded up a Kleenex, wiped the kiss off, and threw the tissue across the room.

Randy waited a moment for Brianna to settle down. When she started brushing out her fake eyelashes, he launched what he supposed was a relatively safe line of questioning. "Is it true about the money?" he asked. "If so, I'd suggest you return it."

Brianna put a dab of concealer in the middle of her forehead and spread it around. "Or what? You'll book me? Of course it's not true. Maria hates me is all. Has it in for me. Just ask anyone here."

"Why would she have it in for you?"

"How should I know? Green-eyed monster, probably." Brianna drew a beauty mark next to her thin-lipped mouth. "En. Vy."

"I see," Randy said. "But back to the cafeteria thing . . . I was just wondering . . ."

"Yes?"

"If you'd seen her lately."

"My mom?"

"No. Daisy."

"No."

"No?"

Brianna swiveled around and faced him. Randy couldn't help himself. His eyes drifted to her chest. Her breasts were flat and pancake shaped but they were also young and bare and it had been a very long time since Randy had been in a small room with a naked woman.

"Stare a little longer and I'll charge you," she said.

Randy blushed and coughed into his hand. Then he stood and started to let himself out of the dressing room. He needed a vacation. And a real lead in the Daisy Gonzalez case. And a drink. "Take care of yourself, Miss Pogue."

"Oh I will," she said, turning back to the mirror and teasing her hair into a beehive. "Besides robbery, taking care of myself is what I'm best at."

Back in the main room of Miss Kitty's, Maria was onstage, spraying down a bronze pole with Windex. She rubbed it clean in rhythm to the first few notes of her song, and the motion was sensual, sexy, but instead of watching her dance, Randy fixed his eyes on a television hanging above the bar. It was tuned to CNN and a breaking news alert about a suicide bombing in Iraq.

A cute bartender who introduced herself as "Cherry Pi, Pi like the mathematical symbol not the dessert" gave him a beer.

"On the house," she said. "You look like you could use it."

He smiled gratefully at her. "That obvious, eh?"

"Eh," she said.

Randy glanced back at the television. He couldn't believe what he heard. The closed-captioning was a second behind the audio feed but there it was. The boy's name in yellow letters superimposed over a shot of desert, wailing women, smoking tanks.

"Holy shit," Randy said.

Cherry paused and set down the glass she was polishing. "What?"

He pointed to the TV. They both stared, openmouthed, at the screen, watched until, inexplicably, the story changed to one about red wine and weight loss.

"It's a small world, isn't it?" Cherry said. Her big blue eyes seemed to glow in the gloom. She poured herself a shot of Apple Pucker and downed it in one gulp. Then she did another. Circling her smooth neck was a tattoo of black, tangled briars. Blood dripped from the branches. "He was my prom date. Senior year. What a sweetheart." She adjusted her leather bustier. Randy watched as the pink moles at the tops of her breasts rearranged themselves into a straight line. Orion's belt, he thought. Or maybe his knife. "Well," she corrected herself, "he was."

Honor

(May)

We turned the Humvee into an ice-cream truck for the afternoon. It was Winter's idea.

"Hearts and minds, people," he said. "Hearts and minds."

We knew he wanted to do it to impress that Shiite girl whose brother was dying of some horrible cancer, but no one teased him. We just followed orders.

"Chocolate?"

"Check."

"Vanilla?"

"Check."

"Cookies and cream?"

"Check."

"Pistachio?"

"Who the fuck eats pistachio?"

"My old man, that's who, so suck my dick and put it on the truck."

It was sweet, the whole operation and Winter's puppy love for that girl with her beautiful copper eyes and the way she had of shuffling every day in her bright pink shoes between her house and the hospital in town armed with comic books and a basket of burned bread. That was Winter for you, falling in love with someone he'd probably talked to only once and had never really seen because she wore what looked like a heavy black sofa cover everywhere she went.

"How we going to hand this out?" Junior asked. "There aren't any spoons."

Petes shook his head. "People've got tongues, haven't they?" Petes was so big he never went by just plain Pete. His sheer girth warranted the *s*. "Use your imagination, Junior."

The ice cream came from some rich guy in Austin, Texas, who wrote a letter to all of us explaining that he'd been transformed by September 11. "Irrevocably," he said. He also apparently had more money and patriotism than sense. The ice cream was vacuum-packed in dry ice and when Winter opened one of the fifty boxes, plastered all over with American flag stickers, the freezing steam turned his pale face almost blue.

"My what?" Junior asked.

"Forget it," Petes said.

Henzlick was the only one of us who seemed annoyed by Operation Get Rid of It Before It Melts. "So the girl's brother likes Superman and carbs," he mumbled as we stacked the individually wrapped cups in sweating towers on the Humvee's floor. We called the truck Hoosier in honor of my home state. "How do we know he likes ice cream?"

"What kid doesn't like ice cream?" said Petes. "That's un-American."

"Then just because I'm lactose intolerant I'm un-American?" Junior said.

I shoved him, and he shoved me back. I took the CD Winter tossed my way.

"Scott Joplin?" I said. "Who's he?"

"Just load it."

We were supposed to be on the hunt for these three guys who, according to the major, were deputies of deputies of Abu Bakr al Baghdadi. Really, truly, horrible, evil men, the major said. Insane. They'd kill you for refusing to diaper your goats. Winter got the orders to scour the streets in Sadr City, go house by house. We'd been assigned such searches before. They gave Junior the shakes and usually ended with us in a tiny room, shining our flashlights in the faces of people so terrified they peed themselves and then had to usher us out across floors wet with their own urine. Before our last raid, we'd been given family pictures of five men wanted for the bombing of a Sunni farmer's market. The pictures were bright, beautiful. They were taken at a wedding. This time we just had a few rough sketches of the men to go by, pen-and-ink drawings that could have been anybody. Winter took the drawings and taped them up next to one of Hoosier's windows.

"We'll get to those later," Winter said. "Move on out, boys."

Hoosier was cool inside and smelled like sugar.

"We're going to be in a world of shit," Henzlick said.

Henzlick didn't usually question Winter. Like everyone else, he seemed to think that Winter was pretty much as good a soldier as you'd see anywhere—knew enough Arabic to get us through some hairy checkpoints, handsome but not pretty, smart but not superior, and brave without being reckless like the last lieutenant we'd had—Uhrick, that crazy German from Pennsylvania who almost got himself killed running into a burning building after some kid's pet bird. Uhrick was dead now. Helicopter crash. I thought about him sometimes, but mostly his face was just a flash that would come to me at unexpected moments, a charred circle framed with parrot feathers. Lots of people were dead now.

"What's your problem, Henzlick?" Petes threw an ice-cream cup at Henzlick's head.

"Yeah, Henzlick," Junior said. "What's your supreme unction?"

"The raid, asshole," Henzlick said to Petes, dodging the ice cream. He ignored Junior, which is pretty much standard operating procedure around here. "You think they're not going to notice that we're screwing around instead of doing our job?"

The ice cream hit the sketch of a bearded man who was supposed to be the ringleader. In the drawing, the man had big alien eyes and a slit for a mouth.

Petes wiped at the line of ice cream streaked across the man's face like a milk mustache and licked his finger. "Hmm. Tastes like chicken," he said.

Winter didn't seem to hear any of this. He was too pumped up. We'd stopped on the girl's street, a run-down Shiite block where almost every building was riddled with bullets. "Petes, put Hoosier in park. Let's do this."

Of course there was a crowd of kids. When we first got to Iraq we used to joke that the kids must have had metal in their arms the way they flocked to Humvees like shavings to magnets. But those kinds of jokes didn't fly anymore. We'd been in the country two years now. The war was almost three times that old and nobody back home even remembered what we were doing here.

Winter motioned to Junior to open Hoosier's back door, a spot everyone called the panty hatch because Petes had spray-painted it to look like the seat of a woman's polka-dot underwear. "Garrety," he said to me, "cue the music."

The first few notes of "The Entertainer" hit the hot air. Winter and Petes started tossing cups of melting ice cream at a hundred outstretched brown hands. I took a few vanillas and handed them to a young girl whose fluttering fingers made me think of butterfly wings. I felt indestructible. I threw the cups far and wide. Petes went into the stretch, pretended to pick off a runner at first. We were doing a good thing, a right thing. The music encircled us like a benevolent force field. Bombs could not hit us here. The children must have felt the same way because they skipped and shouted, dancing along the roadside where less than a week ago IEDs had burst from below piles of trash.

"C'mon, Henzlick," I said, pushing a tower of chocolate his way.

Henzlick kicked the ice cream back at me. "Nope. No dishonorable discharge for me, thanks."

The plan was to hand out the ice cream, and then, if we didn't see the girl, move to another block and hand out some more, but Hoosier was surrounded. The kids just kept coming back. They filled their ragged T-shirts with cups, shouting, "My sister! My sister!"

"How do they know English?" Petes asked.

"All the schools we're building," I said. Then we laughed because we had to. The only thing we'd built in the last six months was a boxing ring where Junior was forever challenging Petes to rematches that all ended the same way—with Junior's face on the mat and Petes picking him up gently the way you would a sleeping kid, saying, "Nigger, I told you. Give it up."

Junior said he'd get the trots just holding the ice cream, so instead of joining me and Petes and Winter he climbed down into the crowd and tried to teach a pack of street kids a new game. Bloody strips of old bandages flapped at their skinny ankles. Flies buzzed face wounds. "Repeat after me," Junior said. "I scream. You scream. We all scream for ice cream."

"You are seriously fucked up," Petes said.

A boy, probably about four years old, tugged on my sleeve. "For Mama," he said. His voice was smoky.

I handed him two cookies and cream. "This is the best," I said.

The boy smiled. I didn't know if he understood me. It didn't matter. Winter was a genius. These kids needed this. We needed this. This is what it's all about, I thought. This is why we're here. Dessert in the desert. We're winning this war.

But then the boy was gone and I realized that there were too many people. Their shiny black heads made me dizzy. We'd never have enough ice cream for all of them. We'd never have enough. Handfuls of gravel hit my helmet and chest.

"Gotta cut and run," Petes said, looking at Hoosier's empty floors. "We're pretty much out anyway."

Winter stood for a moment longer, scanning the crowd. He reminded me of an explorer, the kind you see all the time in children's history books, striking a strong pose on a mountain crag, pondering the country's destiny. The hot sun turned the sharp planes of his face into something heroic and beautiful and I thought of the talk the two of us had a few nights before when everyone else was watching a movie in the chow hall, a piece-of-shit action flick with Ben Affleck as the star. Winter and I both agreed Ben Affleck was a douche, or at least played a good one on TV, so we were sitting on our bunks, Winter with a book, me in front of a blank laptop screen. I wanted to write an e-mail to my grandma back home in Indiana, but every line was a false start. *Dear Grandma, I found the arm of a girl in the street today. Grandma, there are no trees here. Grandma, I feel like I might die soon.*

The last message I got from her was full of bad news—deer in her garden, Mom on the run again, a girl named for a flower gone missing and feared dead because, as Grandma put it, that was the way of the world.

Colliersville isn't the same since you left. Nothing's the same anymore. Amen, Grandma. Amen.

While I tried to think of something to write to Grandma to make her feel better, Winter laughed and threw his shoe at me. "Garrety," he said. "Earth to Garrety."

"Dude." I threw the shoe back. "I'm writing to my fucking grandma."

"Well, stop writing to your fucking grandma and listen to me."

"What? What is it? I'm listening, okay? You've got every ounce of my fucking attention."

Winter was looking in my direction but it was as if he could see through me and the thin white walls of the tent to the city beyond. His face was filled with light. "We're here for the right reasons. Years from now, history will show we were the real heroes. Don't ask me how I know. I just know it." And I believed him. I wondered if he would be president someday.

Today with the ice cream and the swelling crowd, he was just as sure. "Cut the music, Garrety," he said. Then he got on Hoosier's loudspeaker system and launched into Arabic. All I caught was, "Sorry. No more."

More gravel hit the truck. Junior climbed back in. "That gift horse/mouth thing," he said. "Whatever the fuck. That's what they're doing."

"Be happy they're not shooting." Petes started laying on Hoosier's horn, trying to clear a path to drive through. The kids dispersed slowly, heading back to the homes we'd be searching later for guns and clues.

"Now that that's over," Henzlick said, "can we start looking for the Three Stooges?"

The air inside Hoosier had gone back to hot and stale. There would be a sandstorm that night.

"We got one more stop," Winter said.

Henzlick leaned his head back and pulled his sunglasses down off his forehead. "Wake me up when it's over."

Petes gave everyone but Junior and Henzlick a cup of chocolate. "We earned this shit," he said. He ate his cup. Then he ate three more.

By the time we pulled Hoosier up to the hospital, there were only five cups of ice cream left, two chocolate, two cookies and cream, and one pistachio. Winter had stashed them away in one of Hoosier's floor compartments.

"Why the fuck you do that?" Petes asked.

"I happen to know she's got family," Winter said, blushing.

"She?"

"Miss Pink Shoes," Junior said, pointing out the window at the girl, just then making her way out the hospital doors.

"Excuse me, guys," Winter said. "Urgent business to attend to." He grabbed a cup of pistachio and hopped out of the truck, brushing dirt off his uniform. He looked like a sixteen-year-old kid about to ask the homecoming queen to the prom.

"He's got it bad," Junior said.

Winter approached the girl and spoke to her for a moment. Watching him work was like watching the salesman of the month.

No one could say no, not even a shy, heartbroken girl. They headed back into the hospital and we lapsed into silence. Typical Baghdad street sounds filled the quiet—chickens squawking, high, keening prayer chants, distant gunfire.

Then Petes said, "I'd give anything to hear the howl of a train at night."

"Cicadas," Junior added.

"Ernie Harwell," I said.

It was a stupid game and we knew it, but we played anyway because it was something we could all understand.

"I'd give anything to eat Cincinnati chili," said Petes.

I licked my lips. "Red velvet cake."

"Henzlick's mom's pussy," Junior said.

I glanced over at Henzlick. He was sitting underneath the picture of the bearded man whose face was still marked with a splatter of chocolate ice cream. There were drops in Henzlick's curly hair like pearls. He didn't seem to notice. His gaze was fixed on the hospital's exit where Winter was now gingerly leading the girl through a group of women carrying children and baskets of purple and blue cloth.

"Anyone know her name?" Petes asked.

Henzlick mumbled something but no one paid much attention.

"My money's on Bathsheba," Junior said, wiping sweat from his forehead. "Hot biblical shit."

A few more minutes clicked by. I closed my eyes. If I concentrated hard enough I could leave the guys behind, get back to a summer afternoon in Colliersville where it would be warm and quiet, except for the whir of hummingbirds at their feeders. I could lie under the sycamore in my grandmother's backyard, hang out in my old tree house until I got bored, then ride my bike into town, drink a Coke outside Tony's Pizza, hover near the high school for a glance of the girls' track team all stretched out on the sidewalk, after which I could hunt down Brianna Pogue, because no one's as fun as Brianna Pogue, even though she's as old as my mom, and we could re-create the send-off she'd given me at Miss Kitty's the night before I flew here—pizza and, of course, strippers and Brianna offering this piece of arm-around-the-shoulder-beer-breath advice: "Kenny Garrety, don't ever fall in love. And don't die over there."

I promised not to do either because that's what you do at parties like that. Talk. Bluster. Brag. I'm pretty sure she knew I was already a little in love with her anyway, and not just because she was kind enough to rob me of my virginity when I was a freshman and covered in zits, but because she was sexy in the way snakes and thunderstorms are. No choice but to surrender. I thought of her body spread out below me, her eyes vacant and dreamy, her mouth in a hot scowl, and even with all the guys around, I got hard for a minute.

Petes said daydreaming was how fuckers got killed. The trick, he said, was to remember at all times where you were, to stay focused, to not let yourself, for even a split second, be too happy, but we all did it, even Petes, who liked to talk about a girl from home named Wanda who gave the kind of blow job that would make you believe in God if you didn't already. "I mean like a nice God," Petes said. "Not the Old Testament asshole or anything. A kinder, gentler God who lets you into heaven no matter what."

"Gentlemen." Winter was standing outside the panty hatch, his hand hovering just above the girl's shoulder. "I've invited this lovely young lady to ride back with us. Save her the long walk home."

I looked at Henzlick to see if he would protest this final breach of military command. He was staring at his boots. Plain black.

"This way her ice cream won't melt," Petes said.

Winter and Junior helped the girl into Hoosier. Henzlick offered her his seat but she bowed and sank down next to me on the floor, watching Junior as he secured the panty hatch. Only her eyes and pink shoes peeked out of that awful black sheet. When Junior gave the panty hatch an affectionate slap, her eyes got wide. Then she clapped her hands to her mouth. It was too late. A giggle escaped and the sound was like something taking flight.

There was a bombing.

That's what we told the major the next day when the inquiries began. *There was a bombing on the north side of the city and we got stuck. The road was blocked for hours. Otherwise we would have been there. There's no doubt in our minds, sir, yes, sir. We would have prevailed.*

It was Winter's idea that we all say the same thing. *Synchronize our stories, if you will.* He made the suggestion before we'd heard that the three men we were ordered to apprehend were spotted blowing through a checkpoint at dawn. We figured that realistically, only part of our story was a lie.

"The carnage at the bomb site, sir. Well, you can't imagine."

"Pardon me, Private Garrety?"

"I'm sorry, sir. Of course you can imagine. Of course you've seen . . . I just meant. It was horrible to behold, sir."

The major's office was the only room in the barracks not covered with a thin layer of grit. It smelled like the major, who smelled like Head and Shoulders.

"I know of no such bombing," the major said, crossing his hands behind his head, "but I have been told that several men in this company were seen yesterday in Sadr City tossing what looked to be cups of ice cream into a crowd."

"Sir?"

"And that these same young men were thought to have brought a woman on board their Humvee at sixteen hundred hours for purposes unknown."

The major liked inspirational posters. The one behind his head said, "Success comes in cans. Failure comes in can'ts."

"Private Garrety?"

"Yes, sir."

"Would you care to respond to these reports?"

"Well—"

"At best we are talking about insubordination, which will bring with it a dishonorable discharge. At worst, treason. And we haven't even gotten into what's going to happen to the girl."

"The girl, sir?"

The major sighed. "Are you really so naïve that you don't know about the Shiite tradition of honor killings?"

"Killings?" I said. That was part of the approach Winter suggested we take. *If you feel cornered,* he said, *ask a question. If you feel worse, ask another.* "How is that honorable, sir?"

"Young woman is discovered to have been in the company of strange men for hours," the major continued. "Anything could have happened, including rape. In accordance with fundamentalist beliefs, the girl has to be killed. The family's honor must be preserved."

"Rape, sir? Are you serious?"

The major stood up and walked in front of his desk. He leaned back on his palms and looked at the ceiling, which was starting to droop in one corner from a leaking toilet on the second floor. "Tell me what happened and don't give me any crap about a bombing. As your shitty luck would have it, yesterday was the only day in the last month that there wasn't a bombing on the north side of the city."

The treason thing and the talk of so-called honor killings—that was all bullshit. I knew enough to know the major was just bluffing, casting everything in a bleaker light so I'd be tempted to confess.

"Whose big idea was it, Garrety? This ridiculous stunt?"

I looked at my hands. They were the hands of another man, bony and brown. I shook my head.

The major leaned toward me. I could see sleep caked in his eyes, a piece of egg wedged in his front teeth from breakfast. "Would it change your mind if I told you there's a promotion in this for someone, maybe even a holiday in Kuwait? I've heard tell the women there are sweet and sticky where it counts."

Dear Grandma, It's beautiful here in Kuwait. Different from Colliersville. No tiger lilies or thistles, but pretty still. Palm trees everywhere. And the women are sweet and sticky where it counts.

I stood up. "I'm sorry, sir. I got nothing."

The major let out a low growl. The wrinkles on his red forehead deepened. "Get me Winter," he said. "Now."

Winter was sitting against the wall, his elbows on his splayed knees, face in hands. When he saw me he tried to smile, but the effect was frightening, like the smile a skull can't help but make because all the skin's been removed.

I made a swinging motion with my arms and laughed a lame laugh. "Batter up."

For a moment, Winter didn't move. "She might die."

"Who?"

"Don't do the question bullshit with me. Save that for the major."

"The girl."

"Sihaam."

"That's crazy—"

"I didn't know. It was supposed to be fun. It wasn't supposed to get her killed. What the fuck kind of hellhole are we in? Where they chop off a woman's head for eating ice cream? What is this place? Did you know it's Mass Graves Day today? That's their idea of a holiday. Mass Graves Day. Let's celebrate finding a bunch of bones in a huge hole. Fuck. This ain't Kansas, I'll tell you that. This ain't Georgia or Iowa or Indiana for that matter—" Winter's low voice cracked. He was standing now, swaying in front of me, a skinny, terrified punching bag.

I tried to pat his back, but the gesture was awkward, wasted. My hand felt like a flipper. "The major's just making shit up now, Winter. No big deal. We'll probably just get a reprimand, you know. Lose a week's salary. Get some dick duty for the next month. Don't worry about the girl."

"Sihaam, goddammit. That's her name. Have the respect to call her by it."

"Sure. Okay. Sihaam."

Winter walked to the major's door. His hands were shoved deep in his pockets. "It means arrows."

"Really? Arrows."

"Things that are straight. Beautiful."

"Also lethal."

"Shut the fuck up, Garrety."

"Okay."

"I thought you of all people understood."

"Sorry."

I walked back to my tent and there was Junior, on his bunk, cutting his toenails. His feet were like everything about him—pale, long, and slightly sour smelling. "He's gonna cave," he said, "and then guess what, Garrety? We're all fucked. Fucked hard, like Henzlick's mom at a cowboy bar."

I was annoyed and nauseated after my meeting with the major and seeing Winter so shaken. Junior's calluses did little to help the situation. "At the cowboy bar? What does that even mean?"

Junior took his toenail clippings and dropped them into a sock he called Suzie. He kept it tied to the leg of his bunk. The sock was the source of endless speculation. Why did he keep stuff in there? Why was it pink? Who was Suzie? Junior stubbornly refused to answer any questions. He guarded the thing with his life.

"All I'm saying is it's rodeo time." Junior waved the sock around his head like a lasso. I tried not to gag. "Giddyup."

The tent was empty except for me and Junior. Petes and Henzlick were somewhere else. They'd already seen the major. Junior, too. He was the first one called.

"I mean, I pleaded ignorance," Junior said, stretching out and letting out a long sigh. "And the bonus there is people believe that of me. But Winter. Not Winter. He's a smart dude. The major will grill him and grill him. We are talking mutiny on the barbie."

"That's one of the stupidest things I've ever heard you say and that's saying something." I could feel heat rising into my face. "And he's not going to cave. He's not."

Junior turned over in his bunk and faced the wall. It was late afternoon. Someone outside the tent was bouncing a tennis ball in the dirt. The sound was like a fist hitting dough.

"Whatever, man," he said. "He's just a fucking guy."

If it were my story to tell, which it isn't, I'd start with the picture the girl made sitting on Hoosier's dirty floor like some sort of flower, black petaled, folded in for nightfall. Then I would talk about how we all comported ourselves like officers and gentlemen the whole time. There was no crotch grabbing, no spitting, no farting, at least out loud. I would mention that Junior didn't say "fuck" or talk about how he wanted to take Henzlick's mom from behind. Not once. I would add that Petes drove slow and steady, careful to avoid every pothole even if it meant waiting five minutes for a man to pull a line of mangy donkeys across the street. Then I would pause for a moment and say, "It began to get dark," because it did and because it takes time for darkness to come over the desert. It's like a cloud or a hand brushing the light out slowly. I'd spice up the story with some local color, saying that we drove by a bombed-out mosque overrun by feral dogs and a morgue doing good business. *Mass Graves Day.* "Taking the scenic route," Winter had called it. "Stalling," Henzlick had mumbled, but we ignored him. I might even touch on the music, say that as we neared the girl's home, Hoosier's walls echoed with "A Breeze from Alabama" and that Winter tried his best to get the girl to dance. But even he couldn't persuade her to go that far. I'd end with how I wish it had ended. We knew Winter, our hero, was going to tell us that we could skip the raid, and there was a feeling of lightness that spread through the truck. This was a reprieve. This was mercy. The girl kept laughing.

A week later, we went on a raid to the same block we were supposed to search before—before Henzlick was made section leader, before Winter turned out to be just a guy after all. We were looking for a man and a woman, brother and sister, who supposedly had a weapons stash that would make Charlton Heston piss his pants. It was the kind of assignment that sent Petes to his Bible and Junior to the toilet.

"This shit is so wack. It's wack, man." Junior was twitching, trying to double knot his boots.

Petes swatted him on the back of the head. "Don't try to talk ghetto, Junior. It doesn't become you."

"What does become him?" I asked.

"Feather boas, I'm guessing," Petes said. "Rhinestones."

Junior pulled his shoestrings tight with his teeth. "Fuck you and the whore you rode in on."

We were sitting in Hoosier, waiting for Henzlick to give us the go-ahead. It was dusk. Winter wasn't with us and so, even though there was a familiar stink about us—one part Junior's feet, one part Petes's breath, one part Henzlick's hair gel, and one part my sweat, which for some reason gave off the faint odor of urine—nothing was the same. Winter would probably be moved to another squadron. Someone heard from the major that there was talk of sending him home. He'd sort of gone Section 8, though no one called it that anymore. Post-traumatic stress disorder. That was its new name. PTSD. Junior was always saying he was going to fake him some PTSD and get his ass back to the States. "I'm gonna wig out!" he yelled. "Attempt suicide! Get me a nice nurse for a wife."

We had a new guy, Jhon, a pretty actor from California who signed up for the guard after September 11, never thinking he'd actually end up fighting a war. We called him "Jahon" because of how he spelled his name and teased him about being a drama queen, though he never really said much.

"Why do we always get the shit jobs?" Junior said.

No one answered him. The curfew was just taking effect, so the streets were deserted and silent. We could smell cooking coming from the houses. It was easy to forget that people actually lived in such shacks, made of mud and aluminum scraps as they were, patched up between bombings. I thought of my grandmother's house, its solid wooden walls, the bleeding-heart bushes out front, and something in me started to ache.

"It's too bad about that girl." Petes rubbed at his bloodshot eyes.

"Shut up, Petes," Henzlick said.

"Well, it is," Petes said.

"We don't really know anything," I said. "The major was probably lying about that honor killing stuff."

"Winter said the major got a call while he was in there, confirming it. Throat cut. Her cousin did it." Junior made a slicing motion across his neck.

"Junior, shut the fuck up." Henzlick squinted out into the street. He looked like that shortsighted brainy kid you loved to torture in elementary school. We all hated Henzlick. We couldn't help it.

"Holy shit." Petes jumped up and stared out Hoosier's front windows. "Fuck me running it's her."

"Who?" Jhon said.

We were up and beside Petes in a second, following his gaze to a woman being escorted across the road by two severe-looking men, a basket swinging from her hand. She had the same shuffling walk as Sihaam, the same tilt to her head. I looked at her feet for a splash of pink but they were hidden. Maybe it was one of her sisters. There was no way to tell with that black garment covering everything.

"She shouldn't be out," Henzlick said. Then he scrambled out of the truck and hustled over to the woman. She shrank away from him, ducking behind the younger of the two men like a girl playing hide-and-seek.

"She's scared, poor thing," Petes said.

"With Henzlick coming at her like that, can you blame her?" Junior said.

Henzlick motioned to the men that they needed to take the woman home. Over and over he pointed toward the row of houses, his long arms making exaggerated arcs in the twilight. The men just stared blankly at Henzlick, who looked like someone doing a hopeless dance without a partner.

"Maybe we should help him," Jhon said.

Petes shot Jhon a look. Junior gave him the wanking motion. Jhon shrugged. "Fine."

The woman reached into her burka, the fabric spreading like a crow's wing over her hand, and as she did so, her companions slowly started backing away from her.

"Where the fuck are they going?" Petes asked.

"Do you guys think it's really her?" I thought about what was under that cloth, her arms, probably beautiful, her heart, things so unique they couldn't possibly belong to another woman, secreted away like treasures. The air around her seemed to glow as the sunlight hit the sand and Hoosier's hood, reflecting back amber like her eyes. Something was about to happen. Winter. Winter would know.

Wallflower

(June)

Rhae Anne liked Wally Yoder well enough. He was personable and clean and smart. Good company. He was also a talented manicurist, a natural with the orange stick and nail buffer. Better even than Tina Gonzalez, and Tina Gonzalez had been very good. He could cut hair, too. And style it. Rhae Anne was jealous of how he handled the round brush and watched him sometimes out of the corner of her eye in an attempt to uncover his secret. Incompetence wasn't the problem. The problem was the middle-aged lady clients. They didn't like change, and Wally, who painted his nails and once in a while tried to get away with wearing a wig to work, was too much change all at once.

They didn't even know what to call him. His workstation plaque said "Willa" but he'd been born Wally and they were used to referring to someone by the name stamped on their birth certificate. They quite simply did not know what to do with him, so what women like Viv Hochstetler and Shellie Pogue and Una Prokus and Velda McElroy did, for the most part, was avoid him.

That meant more work for Rhae Anne and with prom season upon them—kill her now—she had more work than she could handle.

"Wal—I mean Willa, could you get that?"

The phone was ringing off the hook with calls from mothers who, convinced they'd be able to do their daughter's hair for their special night, were in full-on procrastination panic mode, realizing too late that prom was far more high stakes than it had been when they were teenagers. Whereas the mothers had thought an elegant French twist or natural down-do would suffice, their millennial offspring demanded Los Angeles–style blowouts and ropy curls and intricate braids and glitter and flowers and birds shoved in, everything piled high and sprayed for dear life. Heaven forbid an errant strand fall while the girls grinded on their horny dates to gangster rap. Perish the thought that any part of them—hair, face, breast line—resemble their fine-enough, everyday selves. They wanted to be Cinderella for the night. Kim Kardashian. Or the slut who read the news on Channel 12.

Wally understood. Or so he said. "We're basically told from the moment we're born we should be pretty pretty princesses and prom's like the first opportunity to really be one I mean outside of Halloween of course or a coming-out party but who has a coming-out party in Colliersville not me I'll tell you that for sure!" He laughed at his own joke and answered the phone. "I'm sorry we're booked you realize prom is tonight right?"

"Willa?" Rhae Anne said.

He raised an eyebrow and hung up. "Yes?"

"Can you be nicer to the disappointed customers?"

"Oh, sorry," Wally said. "Sure thing, boss."

Wally said the Hair Barn—a small, freestanding shop painted to look like an outbuilding but really more the size of an unhappy teenage girl's bedroom—was his only safe space in town, the only place he could be himself, so Rhae Anne was lenient, letting him get away with more than she should. School was a nightmare, he said. He didn't talk to anyone unless forced to and lived in daily fear for his life. He was sure one of these days a jock or that dick Benny Bradenton was going to take him out behind the woodshed—well, technically field house—and beat him until he saw not only stars but whole constellations, solar systems, "multiverses." Home, Wally said, was worse.

"You know Helman."

Rhae Anne did. She hadn't hired Wally because she felt sorry for him. Not exactly. She'd hired him for his persistence—he'd spent much of the winter haunting the Hair Barn, résumé and nail kit in hand, begging for a chance to show her what he could do—and his skill. But in the back of her mind was a nagging concern for the kid, a sneaking suspicion that to be born the son of Helman Yoder, trans or not, was a rough portion. A bad hand. So pity was part of it.

"Hello Hair Barn otherwise known as Prom Day Head-Quarters. Get it? *Head*-quarters? Anyway, what can I do you for?"

"Willa!" Rhae Anne said. "Tone it down, okay?"

Wally blushed. "Okay, okay. It's just the excitement's contagious, you know?"

Rhae Anne certainly did not know. She was finding it hard to breathe. Prom season always affected her this way. So much hairspray, so much pressure, so many moms, too many memories. She thought, against her will, of her own prom, of Larry leaving her alone on the dance floor to go get drunk behind the school with a bunch of football players and their dates. Rhae Anne would never forget how it felt to stand under a disco ball in a butt-bowed gown,

"We've Got Tonite" blaring from the speakers some audiovisual nerds had dragged in for the occasion, all the pretty girls around her drooping like lilies and forced to submit to being cherished, to being held tight against polyester coats, all whispered to and wanted. Rhae Anne's feeling at that moment was not one of smallness or insignificance. Instead, it was as if she were a giantess towering over the dance floor, her bloated figure (her period would come that night) conspicuous and sympathy inducing. All she could think at that moment was, I deserve this. I must deserve this or it wouldn't be happening.

Marissa Marino was in Rhae Anne's chair. Her mother had thought ahead and scheduled an appointment for a blowout and style back in March. "She doesn't even have a date yet," Tessa Marino explained, trying to sound embarrassed, "but I figure, better to be safe than sorry." Everyone knew that Marissa would get a date for the prom, just as everyone knew now that she hadn't been to school for an entire week.

"Because trauma because shame," Wally had whispered behind his hand as Marissa walked into the Barn, head down, a thinner, self-conscious shadow of her mother. "And her all Miss Perfect Attendance. Not anymore."

The day of Daisy's disappearance, Marissa was supposed to pick the little girl up at the bus stop and babysit her until Hector got home. She told Randy Richardville and the slew of reporters who'd interviewed her—before her mother and father got a lawyer who put a stop to any and all such impolite questioning—that she simply forgot. It had been an odd day she said, her class schedule turned on its head by a spur-of-the-moment pep rally. And then there was the stress of SAT prep and college applications. A small but vocal pocket of the Colliersville population blamed

Marissa for Daisy going missing. "Colleges don't want to hear from you until, like fall," Wally often pointed out. "Even if you're Marissa 'My Teeth Light Up from the Inside' Marino. So that college SAT crap is just that. Crap. And the pep rally? What. Ever."

Shame and trauma and a disappeared Daisy Gonzalez weren't stopping Marissa from going to a high school dance, and she was wearing exactly what she should to her pre-prom hair appointment—a button-up shirt that wouldn't ruin her do later when it came time to don the dress. Also skinny jeans and Ugg boots. She looked beautiful but pale. Her mother did all the talking.

"So what we were thinking is a milkmaid sweep kind of French braid that goes from here"—Tessa drew a manicured finger from Marissa's right temple to her left—"to here. And then soft curls down her back. Also, a gardenia just resting, you know, *resting,* in the braid, but not really *in* the braid. More *on* it. Like it just drifted down from a tree and stayed."

Wally sniggered from across the shop. Marissa blushed but remained silent.

"Where's the gardenia?" Rhae Anne asked.

"In a cooler in my car. Gardenias must be kept at a certain temperature. They'll wilt otherwise." Tessa was a beauty in her own right—tall but not very, curvy but only in the right places, a Sophia Loren sort of face. All of it, from what Rhae Anne could discern, natural, but aided, of course, by money. Tessa was aging in the way women did when they had easy access to fresh fruit, expensive moisturizers, and personal trainers. She'd probably never cleaned a bathroom in her life. Look at those hands.

Rhae Anne glanced in her workstation mirror, wiped away a white fleck of something, and stared for a brief moment at her face, unfortunately freckled, slightly scarred. An ugly beautician. How ironic.

"I have lemon juice in my purse," Tessa said, hovering. "For the gardenia. You'll want to rub some on your fingertips to keep the petals from browning."

"Mom," Marissa said.

"What?"

"We're good," Rhae Anne said to Tessa. "We can take it from here."

Tessa squeezed Marissa's shoulder and found a seat in the waiting area under a strand of star-shaped hanging lights. Rhae Anne watched Tessa cross her legs, study her perfectly shaved calves. What was it like, to look at yourself and like what you saw? To revel in what mirrors gave back to you? It was something Rhae Anne and her best friend, Shannon Washburn, often talked about—what beauty meant in this world and the lack of it, too. Shannon, born to arguably the most beautiful woman in town, was always cursing her own unremarkable looks. "This is why we fuck beneath us," Shannon said just a few weeks ago on a visit to Rhae Anne's. Shannon was drunk and bemoaning her latest knock-down-drag-out with Josh Seaver, which, as far as Rhae Anne could piece together between Shannon's sobbing bouts, had started over the fact that Josh lost his job and then moved on to Shannon's aversion to fellatio and Josh's habit of leaving joints burning in the bathroom. Practically inconsolable, Shannon kept pulling at her crazy-long hair and saying, "We think because we're ugly we deserve the worst of the worst."

Rhae Anne didn't really like the sound of that. Larry was not at all on the same asshole level as Josh, who, Rhae Anne knew for a fact, was cheating on Shannon with high-school-bully/prom-queen-turned-sad-stripper Brianna Pogue. Sure, Larry wasn't perfect—he'd gotten her a set of miniflashlights for Valentine's Day and a Crock-Pot for Christmas and hadn't kissed her in weeks—but he was good-looking and hardworking and also the only man who'd ever paid her any attention. After sixteen years, their love was comfortable, as broken-in and welcoming as the couch at the end of the day. "Fucking beneath us?" Rhae Anne said to Shannon. "Nah, I prefer to be on top." Shannon laughed a little at that. It was the same service Rhae Anne provided her clients. The moment they finished their particular sob story, she swooped in with a silly joke or anecdote, careful to make herself the butt of it all. It was necessary, part of the job. It was also exhausting.

The phone rang again.

"Yellow, Hair Barn," Wally said. "How can I help ya help ya help ya?"

While Wally informed yet another prom mom that she was out of luck, Una Prokus walked in. Without an appointment as usual, Rhae Anne thought, and wearing saddle shoes like a ten-year-old. At least Una never sprang for anything beyond a bang trim and maybe, just maybe, she would trust Wally to do it.

Wally told Una he'd be with her in a minute. "Meantime cool your jets," he said. "Jets or Sharks take your pick."

Una sat down next to Tessa, grabbing a *Highlights* from the magazine rack and crossing her thick ankles. Tessa shot her a smooth smile, but Una didn't return it. Instead, she raised the magazine so that it was level with her bangs. The cover showed a little girl hosing down a golden retriever in a driveway. Blue water everywhere.

"When you're a Jet you're a Jet all the way from your first cigarette to your last dying—"

"Willa!"

"Yeah, boss."

"Can I have a word?"

Wally nodded. They met behind a curtain in the back of the
shop where the two of them sometimes had tea or coffee or snuck
sandwiches between clients. Rhae Anne sat at the yellow Formica
table and folded her hands in front of her.

"You need to be less rude to the customers," Rhae Anne said.
"I mean, I'm glad you feel able to be yourself here, but—"

"It's just how do these women think we can squeeze their
daughters in for a Farrah and a half-foil tonight of all nights?" Wally
again launched into song and his voice was clear and high. "Tonight, tonight, the world is wild and bright, going mad, shooting
stars into space!"

"See?" Rhae Anne said. "That's what I'm talking about. I just
need you to take it down a notch."

Wally bit his lip and looked at his shoes. Chuck Taylors. Red,
with sparkly toes. Rhae Anne hoped he wouldn't cry.

"I know you're going through a tough time," she said. "Still . . ."

It wasn't just the transitioning thing, which, as far as Rhae
Anne could tell, was pretty surface level so far—he'd plucked his
eyebrows into thin boomerang shapes, stuffed his bra, tried to
move around the world more like a woman—but there was also
the dairy shutdown to consider, and his mother's struggle with
pills, which had landed her in the psych ward for a week and a
half. Rhae Anne heard from Velda McElroy who heard it from
Olive May Redburn that Helman and Birdy were talking divorce

and that would mean even more upheaval and probably a move. It was a lot for a teen boy working on being a teen girl to handle and Rhae Anne understood that. She didn't want to have to fire him.

"All I'm saying is when you answer the phone, sound sympathetic, okay? And when you're helping out our more aged clients, just keep in mind that they're a little behind the times."

"In other words," Wally said, tugging at his shirt, "hide my light under a bushel basket?"

"I'm afraid so. Speaking of our aged clients, can you take Una? I'm going to be tied up with Marissa for a while."

"If you think she'll let me."

"Be as 'normal' as you can." Rhae Anne used air quotes for "normal" and rolled her eyes so Wally would know she was on his side. "I have faith in you."

Wally smiled at her and wiped the lipstick from his mouth. It left a purple smudge on his hand and upper lip, where it matched the burgeoning mustache he'd forgotten to shave. "Better?"

"Better." Rhae Anne gave him a shove. From behind the curtain, she watched him approach Una, who dropped her magazine and started to shake her head. Undeterred, Wally took her hand and led her to the station next to Rhae Anne's, saying as he did so just how much he liked her shoes.

"And pardon my bursting out randomly into song, Ms. Prokus." Wally shook out a black cape and wrapped it around Una's shoulders. Una didn't answer, just looked at her lap. "Colliersville High's doing *West Side Story* for the spring musical and I've got 'I Feel Pretty' on the brain."

Rhae Anne went back to her chair. "Let me guess," she said to Marissa. "You're Maria."

"I can't sing," she said.

"Neither could Natalie Wood, but that didn't stop her." Rhae Anne brushed out Marissa's long hair. It was straight and shiny, not a split end in sight. "You have beautiful hair."

"Thank you."

"So, who's the lucky guy?"

"My date? His name's Benny."

Wally was spraying Una's bangs with a water bottle. He stopped. "Benny Bradenton?"

"Yes," Marissa said.

"Benny 'My Dad Owns Three Gas Stations So I've Never Had to Pump My Own' Bradenton? That one?"

"I guess."

"Interesting." Wally narrowed his eyes. "Int-errrr-esting."

"Ignore him," Rhae Anne said. Then she gave Wally a look. *Pol-ite,* she mouthed.

"What's interesting?" Marissa asked.

Wally mouthed back, *Don't worry, boss.* "Well," Wally said aloud, "on the very day that little Daisy Gonzalez went missing I just sort of overheard Benny talking to Renee Seaver—" Wally handed Una a mirror so she could see the back of her head. "I think we should take a few inches off, get rid of the unhealthy stuff, don't you agree?"

"Sure." Una was still looking at her lap.

"Anywho," Wally continued, "I overheard Benny talking to Renee Seaver—Marissa, you know Renee."

Rhae Anne sectioned Marissa's hair for the braid. "Willa, what's all this about?"

"As I was saying, on the very day little Daisy Gonzalez went missing I happened to hear Benny telling Renee that they should do something exciting, put Colliersville on the map so to speak, and Renee was like 'Break into my dad's place of work?' and Benny was like 'No something much more devious not to mention illegal' and Renee was like 'Kidnap a kid and hold her for ransom?' and Benny was like 'Eff yeah,' so I don't know call me crazy but I kind of started wondering if, well . . .'"

Marissa stared straight ahead. Her left eye twitched slightly. "You started wondering what exactly?"

"If Benny Your Boy Toy might have bitten off more than he could chew. Gotten in over his head. Hitched his wagon to a fallen star." He turned back to Una. "So, would you like face-frame bangs or something more jaunty?"

Rhae Anne twisted Marissa's back hair into a clip and started braiding. "Wally, I mean Willa. You can't just go around accusing people like that."

Tessa had left her chair and was hovering again, a mama bird ready to dive-bomb. "I'd appreciate it if you'd leave my daughter alone. She's been through enough already."

"Excuse me, ma'am," Wally said, clearly doing his best to look remorseful. "I'm afraid I like gossip a little too much. One of the hazards of the job."

"That may be," Tessa said, "but that doesn't give you the right to pick on my daughter. Or her date. Or to make that poor little Mexican girl the target of your maliciousness."

Talk of Daisy depressed Rhae Anne beyond measure. It reminded her of Tina Gonzalez, which reminded her very simply of man's inhumanity to man. She and Tina had never been friends—Tina kept to herself, focusing on work and family—but still, Rhae Anne had liked her, respected her. She couldn't believe what was happening to poor Hector now and couldn't stand to have Daisy be the subject of a bitch fight. So, since the one thing she'd learned in nearly two decades of hairstyling was that all it took to make one piece of gossip go away was to offer up another, she said the first thing that came to mind.

"Josh Seaver's cheating on Shannon Washburn with Brianna Pogue."

Una stared at Rhae Anne through parted hair and Tessa folded her arms over her chest, disapproving, as if to say, Two wrongs don't make a right. Or maybe she objected to the subject matter. Cheating=sex and sex=dirty and her daughter had been through enough already. Wally's face lit up as he sifted through a cabinet drawer for a pair of sharper shears.

"Seriously?" he said. "How do you know?"

Now that it was out, Rhae Anne wished she could take it back. She lowered her voice. "I've seen them together a few times is all."

"And they haunt the Udall place!" Una offered. Then she tried to hide behind her bangs again. "I mean, so they say."

"The old Udall place?" Wally asked. "Where that weirdo family used to make sausage in the bathtub?"

"I haven't told Shannon," Rhae Anne said. "I should have said something weeks ago."

Wally let out a long sigh. Then he hacked an inch and a half off Una's bangs, straight across. Face frame it was. "Well well well. Guess you and Shannon need to have some girl talk ASAP."

Una glanced shyly at her own reflection and at Wally. She seemed pleased in spite of herself. Tessa was still at Rhae Anne's elbow, intently watching the milkmaid braid's progress. Rhae Anne's fingers felt suddenly clumsy and numb.

"More customers, boss," Wally said.

He nodded toward Lauren Tewksbury and her mother, who

brought with them the smell of the warm June day—mowed grass, peonies, French fries. They plopped down next to each other in seats by the window and pulled from identical quilted bags two iPhones, also matching. The strand of lights above them flickered like stars and went out.

Marissa sought Rhae Anne's eyes in the mirror's reflection. "Do you need to do Lauren now?"

"Don't worry about them, sweetie," Tessa said. "They can wait their turn."

Rhae Anne wondered if Tessa had said the same thing to Marissa when Daisy went missing. *Don't worry about her, sweetie. Focus on your studies. Everything will be fine and even if it's not fine, it's not your fault. That poor little Mexican girl can wait her turn.*

She shoved her other hand at Tessa, palm up. "I'll take that gardenia now."

"Hold on." Tessa grabbed her purse. "Let me find that lemon juice."

Rhae Anne gave Marissa a few more curls while Tessa fumbled through her bag.

"It must be in the car," Tessa said.

Rhae Anne watched her walk outside, straight-backed and elegant. Her outfit—silk shirt, pencil skirt, suede ankle boots with wooden soles—probably cost more than Rhae Anne made in a week.

"Do you think you could tease that side a little more?" Marissa asked. "I'd really like to be symmetrical tonight."

"Of course," Rhae Anne said, but she didn't oblige her right away. She gazed out the front window at the sidewalk in front of the shop, where at that moment Chuck Breeder was walking by with his lunch. After him came Pearl Butz pushing a poodle in a stroller and an off-duty Zane Bigsby smoking a cigar. A cheap one, judging by the stale smoke that drifted in through the cracks in the door. Just another sleepy Saturday in beautiful downtown Colliersville. The Tewksburys missed the parade. They seemed to be showing each other funny/cute/cat things on their phones.

It's not enough, Rhae Anne thought, taking it in—Chuck and his lunch, Pearl and her poodle, Zane and his cigar. The Tewksburys and their phones. This town, this shop, the job, shampooing, cutting, styling day after day after . . . Dai-sy. Hair. Nails. Eyebrows. Making ungrateful and often entitled women beautiful or marginally more so. And then home to the couch for frozen pizza wolfed down in front of *Dancing with the Stars* with a man who, when he farted in front of her, laughed and blamed the dog. They didn't have a dog.

It wasn't enough. It would never be enough.

"Shit." Rhae Anne burned her right hand on the curling iron trying to extricate the thing from Marissa's thick mane. She brought her fist up to her mouth and bit down to keep from screaming.

"You okay, boss?" Wally asked.

Gritted teeth. "I'm fine."

What she really wanted to say to him was, *Do more.* Get out and do more while you still can. Sing "Tonight" at the top of your lungs. Be as abnormal as you want to be. Go to prom but only if you want to, and never let someone leave you alone in the middle of the dance floor. Throw the fucking bushel basket out the window and let your light shine because what else is there, really? What else? None of us is getting out of this alive. Look at Tina Gonzalez. Look at my own mother and father. You can't look at them. They're buried under six feet of cold, hard Indiana clay.

Marissa's milkmaid braid was perfect—tight but not too tight—
and the curls cascaded down her back in uniformly beautiful
waves. Tessa had located both the lemon juice and the gardenia.
She'd given them to Rhae Anne and sat down again next to the
Tewksburys, who were waiting their turn. The flower was in Rhae
Anne's right hand, the plastic yellow lemon in her left. She let them
fall to the floor. "Oh no," she said, not bending to pick them up.
"Oh dear."

"You don't want the flower to sit too long down there," Marissa said.

"Let me guess," Wally said. "It'll wilt."

Marissa did not look at him. "They're very fragile, gardenias,"
she said to Rhae Anne. "And don't forget the lemon juice. Mom
really wants you to use the lemon juice."

Mom really wants you to use the lemon juice. The demand echoed
in Rhae Anne's head, a nasal mockery of Marissa's real voice, which
was low-pitched and sweet, despite the words. *I'd really like to be
symmetrical tonight.* When she finally got home, when this endless day finally came to an end, Rhae Anne decided she would skip
Dancing with the Stars with Larry and call Shannon instead. She
would suggest that the two of them get together for a pitcher of
beer at Sharkey's and then, drunk and sentimental, Tom Petty on
the jukebox, Rhae Anne would confess everything, beg Shannon's
forgiveness for not telling her about Josh and Brianna a long time
ago, for being a terrible friend. She would plead. She would cry
and get down on her knees if that's what it took. She would say,
Shannon Washburn, I think you're the love of my life, because it was
true. Nothing had been or would ever be more true.

Rhae Anne stepped on the gardenia, crushed it underneath her
heel. She did the same to the plastic lemon. It made a sad deflating-

balloon sound, a sort of squeaky sigh, and the smell of citrus filled the shop. Marissa gaped at her. So did Una and Tessa and the Tewksburys. Then Rhae Anne put her empty hands on either side of Marissa's pretty skull. She knew just how it all would feel when she shoved her hands in—the braid smooth as corn silk, the curls lightly sprayed and buoyant—and what it would look like when she yanked it apart because she'd done it to her own hair as she ran away from the high school gym, crying and shedding shoes and panty hose and bobby pins.

Wally winked at Rhae Anne and smiled at everyone in the shop, even Marissa, who was too busy staring at the ruined flower to understand what Rhae Anne had in mind

"I feel pretty," Wally said. "Oh so pretty. I feel pretty and witty and gay."

Your Sister's Keeper

You never know about some people.

That was the consensus of the Colliersville Baptist Church Saturday Afternoon Knitting Circle regarding the whole Helen Garrety business. Everybody said it was sad, how poor Helen lost her only grandson to the Iraq war. After all, Helen had raised Kenny from a baby and now the only things she had to live for were her herbs and her nutty daughter, Frannie, who, rumor had it, was swaddled away in some cult in Idaho and couldn't care less about coming home to pay her respects. What kind of mother does such a thing? The Frannie Garrety kind of mother, that's who. The kind who gets pregnant at fifteen and skips town when the kid needs her most.

Then there was a terrible snafu at the casualty notification office and Helen, Kenny's true next of kin, heard about his death on CNN.

"They called Frannie instead, and Frannie, idiot that she is, didn't even think to call Helen," said Shellie Pogue. "Can you imagine?"

The women shook their heads.

"It's almost enough to make one question one's faith," Shellie said.

"Almost," Peggy Norquist said.

Everyone was there except Helen—Ruby Rodgers, the mayor's wife, in her broomstick skirt and peasant blouse; Una Prokus, who was fifty-two but you'd never know it to look at her; Peggy, with her purple needles and granny glasses; and Shellie, who held Kenny's obituary from the *Colliersville Record* crumpled in her hand. She'd cut it out that morning along with coupons for Tide, Kraft Singles, and Moon Pies.

The women shared the church's largest basement room with Alcoholics Anonymous, who met there every Tuesday. The orange carpet smelled of twenty-year-old cigarette smoke, bad coffee, and off-brand men's cologne. One whole wall was given over to an illustrated poster of the Twelve Steps and another to a poem a local member had written about her struggle for sobriety. The poem seemed to be about rainbows, Asian carp, Riesling, and God. Shellie read it to herself sometimes when the conversation lagged, wondering why it didn't rhyme.

At the request of Ruby, they were knitting hats for the Mexican children, who, Ruby said, spent most of their mornings shivering away in that Bottoms apartment complex that flooded every spring and summer and was pretty much wall-to-wall poison mold. Shellie made her hat somewhat grudgingly. What about the poor kids who were born here, tried and true? And what was the suffering of a few illegal kids in the face of Kenny

Garrety's death? Kenny was a real American. Kenny was a friend. Kenny was one of the heroes. Well, had been.

"Helen found out about Kenny while she was drinking her morning coffee," Shellie said. She placed the obituary on the table in front of her and smoothed out its wrinkled corners. "Not so much as an 'Are you sitting down?'"

This war was awful, just awful. It had to be fought to teach the terrorists and Saddam Hussein a lesson, but bloodshed was always regrettable, and Kenny had been such a nice boy, polite, shy, handsome if you ignored his wing-flap-like ears and the acne on his cheeks. He would have been a good husband, an attentive father. Pastor Rush had sermonized, and they all agreed, that Kenny was just the kind of young man they would have liked to lead the youth group even though he hadn't been to church since Helen had gone weird and spiritual on them and told them to shove their knitting needles up their fat asses. They forgave her in their way, because they were good Christians and that's how they'd been raised, to turn the other cheek and be their sister's keeper, but it was difficult, watching one of their own stray so far from the fold.

"I just wish she didn't set so much store by that ginko balboa and meditation stuff," Shellie said, passing the obituary around. "It's like she thinks she's an Indian or something."

"You mean Native American." Ruby pulled her red thread tight and crossed her legs. Her skirt rustled.

"Call them late for dinner for all I care," Shellie said. "I think we all know that Helen's as German-Irish as the rest of us."

Ruby drew in her breath. "There really is something to meditation. Dr. Nelson recommended it for me. It's really calmed me down."

Shellie stifled a groan. All this Middle Eastern nonsense. "Meditation, sure, because we all have time to just sit in a dark room and think all day. I'll leave that to Helen, thank you very much."

Then Peggy said, "I'll leave that to Helen, too, thank you very much," because that's what she did, repeated what the last person said. She'd never really had an original thought in her life, unless you counted those toilet brush cozies she made everyone last Christmas.

Shellie glanced at Una, who was reading the obituary to herself, her thin lips moving with each word. "I hate to sound suspicious," Shellie said, "I truly do, but isn't it a little strange? I mean, here he is, dead a week, and there's no mention of a funeral or even a viewing? I know Helen's gone around the bend a bit, but still. You'd think she'd give us all a chance to mourn."

Needles clinked in the quiet.

"I mean, it's unchristian, isn't it? Not having some sort of ceremony," Shellie said.

Then Una, who had a tendency to mumble, said quietly, "I miss her."

"Speak up, Una," Shellie said. People were forever having to ask Una to speak up. "Who do you miss?"

Una also had trouble making eye contact. When she talked to you she usually talked to your hairline, which made Peggy self-conscious about her widow's peak. Now Una was staring at her half-done angora hat. "Helen," she whispered. "I miss Helen."

That was just like Una, Shellie thought. Sentimental little fool. Wasn't it Una, after all, who insisted they give that cat that used to haunt the church a full funeral when they found it, stiff as a wooden paddle, lying in the Rodgerses' pew? Una needed to learn to let go. Shellie, who'd divorced two husbands and buried one, and who'd dropped her daughter off at the drug treatment center more times than she cared to count, could teach Una something about saying good-bye or, better yet, giving up on people. That's what it took. Losing hope they'd ever change. Brianna was a perfect example. Born an angel—pretty, smart, sweet—and now look at her. Up to no good, Shellie was sure, and wasting away to practically nothing. The last time Shellie saw her, nearly a week ago now, she tried to engage Brianna in the most superficial of conversations—"Sleep okay?" "Seeing anyone special?" "Did you hear about little Daisy Gonzalez?"—but it was a nonstarter, a no-go. Brianna simply grabbed a Pop-Tart from the cabinet, said, "See, Mom? I'm eating, I'm fine," and left, a huge canvas purse over one arm. Anything could be in that bag. A change of clothes, booze, makeup, instruments of torture. Shellie had no idea, and she was equally clueless as to how Brianna passed her days or where she spent her nights. This very morning, when Shellie snuck into Brianna's room and found it empty, again, bed still made, she even considered having Brianna declared a missing person, but who would care? All anyone talked about was Daisy Gonzalez, finding her and bringing her home safe to her heartbroken father. Shellie was fond of the girl, in a way. She'd often watched her after school, when Hector was busy with something he clearly considered more important than cafeteria work. Not the day she'd disappeared, though. Not that one.

Cleaning up after Daisy, under the impression she was "helping," had become part of Shellie's routine. Annoying and futile like everything else she did on a daily basis, but sort of sweet, too. And she felt for Hector, who had done his best to continue teaching in Daisy's absence, but who'd been put on what Shellie's co-leader, Bets, called "administrative leave." "Basically time off with pay," Bets explained. "We could be so lucky." The leave came after Hector treated his sophomore history class to a tirade about Colliersville's supposed racist beginnings. Several students objected to his calling their founding fathers "genocidal maniacs" and told Principal Tewksbury so. Shellie wondered how Hector spent his time now. She'd heard from Bets he was basically out of his mind with guilt and grief.

That was understandable. That was pitiable, but what about Shellie's grief, huh? What about her little lost lamb? Would the newspapers, the TV channels, give one column inch or a single hot minute to Brianna Pogue, thirtysomething junkie/loser who sometimes lived with her mother and other times preferred to stay out all night with God knew who? Not a chance.

A knot formed in Shellie's yarn. "I don't miss her," she said.

"Who?" Ruby asked.

"Helen."

"Oh Shellie, how can you say so?" Ruby's hat was almost done. A red number with a jaunty orange flower on one side, it would look good on someone's eighty-year-old grandmother. "She was your best friend."

"*Was* being the operative word in that statement."

For a while no one said anything. The only noises came from overhead, where Pastor Rush's wife, Delilah, was leading a line-dancing class.

"Maybe," Una ventured, setting down her hat on the table in front of her. "Maybe . . ." she said again, then trailed off, staring out the small, mud-spattered window at the lilac bush all bloomed out and the playground beyond that Ruby insisted be handicap accessible, mostly for little Daisy, who'd gone missing before she even had a chance to use the special swing.

Bleeding hearts, Shellie thought. Just a bunch of bleeding hearts in this knitting circle.

"I think I know where you're going, Una, and frankly I agree," Ruby said. "We should go pay Helen a visit. She's all alone out there, after all. She'd probably like the company. We can try to persuade her to let us do something for her, maybe hold a wake here at the church. It's what Jesus would do."

"It's what Jesus would do," Peggy said.

Shellie stood up and tossed her hat down on her seat. "Don't you remember what Helen said to us? How she treated us? She's made it clear she wants nothing to do with us, and I, for one, want nothing to do with her."

Ruby looked at Shellie in that way of hers. "This is no time for grudges. She lost her grandson."

"Oh I'm perfectly aware of who she lost. Remember, ladies, that I was the one who wanted to support Kenny, but no. Helen Garrety spit in our faces. She spit on our flag."

"She did not spit on our flag," Ruby said.

Shellie grabbed her hat. It was lopsided. She'd dropped four stitches in the last two rows. "I'm being metaphorical."

Two years before, on the anniversary of September 11, everyone was doing something, everyone except Shellie, so she baked a cake. Actually, she baked six cakes. She figured she and her fellow knitters could sponsor a bake sale and use the money they raised to buy the soldiers in Kenny's squad some razors, deodorant, comic books, whatever they wanted, and ship everything over in attractive care packages that would say "Our Thanks to You." Inside there'd be respite from a cruel world. A taste of home, in effect. Love in a box.

Helen heard Shellie out, listened to her whole spiel, and

promptly told her to fuck herself. Shellie was shocked. She thought Helen would love her for it. "But I'm doing this for you."

"For me? No you're not."

"Well, okay. For Kenny then. He's one of the heroes," Shellie said.

"He's no hero of mine," Helen said.

"He's your grandson. He's protecting our freedom."

"I would've shot him in the foot if I thought it would've kept him from going."

"But you support the troops."

"No. I don't support the troops."

"Helen."

"Don't Helen me."

"But that's un-American."

"I don't know what that means."

"You're just confused. I can explain—"

"Explain what?"

"Patriotism."

"Give me a break."

"George W. Bush says—"

"Don't use that person's name with me. Don't ever use that man's name in my presence ever again, do you hear me, Shellie Pogue? Do you fucking hear me?"

Then Helen had the nerve to show up at the bake sale, armed to the teeth with Sharpies, and before anyone could stop her, she was writing in sprawling letters on a big table weighed down with cupcakes, pies, and tarts, "Refined sugar kills! Corn syrup equals suicide! Crisco is the devil!"

The proceeds from the sale barely covered the cost of the cakes and one paltry box filled mostly with packing material, as well as six pens, three pads of paper, and two Speed Sticks. They couldn't afford the overseas postage, so Peggy, who worked in shipping and receiving at JCPenney, just sent the boxes first class to Fort Campbell. Helen never apologized. In fact, she came to the knitting circle immediately following the sale for the sole purpose of handing in her needles. Then she said the thing about their fat asses. Shellie was heartbroken. It was around the time she'd buried Buff McBride, her third and favorite husband, and Helen's defection made her feel like a widow twice over. Thrice, even. Before Helen's meltdown, Shellie'd been the knitting circle's de facto leader, the one to whom everyone deferred. Now, what Ruby said went. It was law. Ruby was the mayor's wife. Ruby had a master's degree. Ruby went to conventions on diversity, technology for baby boomers, and parenting as the new black.

"What's that?" Ruby asked Una, who'd mumbled something into her yarn.

"I want to go." Una was ready to cast off. Her hat was as fuzzy as a kitten. "I want to see Helen."

Peggy seconded it and Ruby smiled her satisfied "It's decided" smile. They looked at Shellie, all except Una, who kept her eyes on a spot of carpet littered with cookie crumbs.

"I heard that when they ship bodies home from Iraq they pack them in dry ice to keep them from melting," Una said.

"Now Una," Ruby said in her most motherly, admonishing tone.

But Una was still talking. "And that it's someone's special job to polish the jacket buttons until you can see your face in them. The pants buttons, too."

Above their heads someone fell mid–line dance. The thud echoed through the church.

"Fine," Shellie said. "I'll go. But don't expect me to talk to her."

Shellie had a six-seater passenger van thanks to Buff, who'd been in insurance and overly practical. "Just in case," he said the day he brought it home from the lot.

"In case what? We have five kids?" Shellie asked, laughing and patting her expired womb. Loving him made her glad to be alive most days, and that meant, of course, that he had to die, slow and in agony, despite all the good drugs the nurses gave him at the end.

The van still smelled like Buff: the peppermint candies he liked to swipe from the Pizza Hut, Aramis aftershave, and a subtle end-note of something Shellie couldn't quite put her finger on. Masculinity, maybe. A mysterious, elusive quality men didn't have anymore.

Way in the back Ruby was whining about her seat belt. She kept shoving the buckle over and over into the square receptacle like sheer repetition would make it stick. "It's broken, Shellie. You really should get this looked at."

Who died and made Ruby Ralph Nader? How had she become Ms. Politically Correct All of a Sudden? Ruby, whose husband's last election had been a squeaker because of his friendship with Helman Yoder, on trial for employing a boatload of illegal immigrants at his dairy farm and paying them nothing but cheese curds.

There was Yoder Dairy now, on their right. What a colossal eyesore. With its flaking blue outbuildings and tacky metal cow statues scattered along the fence line, it was starting to resemble Spencerville Fun Spot. The whole property had quickly deteriorated in the wake of the estate sale, and the cows—the real ones—were scattered to the winds, some slaughtered, many sold to mega-dairies out west.

Someone behind Shellie mooed quietly. Una, of course. Always Una.

Prior to Daisy's disappearance, the Yoder Dairy shutdown had been much talked of. It was considered by many to be a serious scandal, and not because everyone in town didn't know what Helman was doing, but because it was assumed he would get away with it. Helman Yoder had been a man who got away with things. For her part, Shellie was conflicted. She found Helman an enterprising man. Was he to blame if certain segments of the world's population would work for free? And he was attractive, too, in a sun-damaged way. Shellie had had her eye on him for husband number four now that he and Birdy were calling it quits. But there was also the fact that he'd single-handedly changed Colliersville forever. Just a few years ago, as Colliersville High School's head cook and lunch lady, Shellie could count on knowing everyone in town. But now, wherever she went she ran into people speaking Spanish behind her back. At the post office and White Swan Grocery and Sharkey's Bar and Breeder's Laundromat and even at work, where the weirdo Juan Cardoza had replaced Josh Seaver as school janitor or, as Juan's work shirt said, "Custodial Technician." Shellie was confronted with whole families of strangers who clearly didn't belong here. Consider the hats they'd knitted that morning. Anyone born and bred in Colliersville knew when winter was coming and how to prepare for it, but the Ranasack Apartments Mexicans were clueless and helpless and a burden on society. Nasty, too, some of them. Bad elements. Shellie not so secretly suspected that Juan or another one of

Helman's former employees was behind Daisy's disappearance. So what if Juan was roughly twenty times better at the janitorial job than Josh had ever been? A good work ethic was one thing, a clean conscience another. If Juan was guilty of kidnapping and even killing the girl, it wouldn't surprise Shellie. It wouldn't surprise her one bit.

She'd shared her suspicions with Randy Richardville and Em Nelson at the police station, hinting also that Helen Garrety might be up to no good, that at the very least she'd lost some of her sanity when Kenny joined up, but Randy and Em made it clear from the looks they'd exchanged that they thought Shellie was the off-her-rocker one. Fine, Shellie thought. Fine and dandy. She just hoped that if the truth came out and she was vindicated in the process, they didn't come crying to her.

The evening was bright and warm. Shellie watched the houses get farther and farther apart until they gave way to woods altogether. Helen's place was five miles out and once Shellie got past Yoder's she could make it the rest of the way with her eyes closed. Two years weren't enough for her to forget the turn onto Hickory at the old Heck's Honey sign or the jog down Decatur Trail to the cattail pond where she and Helen used to wade every summer. At the pond Shellie took a left onto a pitted gravel drive, and out of a meadow of underbrush rose Helen's big green house, flanked by a red barn and a field of neat herbs just starting to poke through the soil.

"I can't believe we used to meet here," Una said. "Remember that?"

Shellie remembered vividly the early years when the circle met in Helen's kitchen, back when Shellie was still on husband number two and Brianna's only drug was sugar. Brianna and Frannie played Barbies together and made fun of Shellie and Helen behind their backs. Things were better. Life made sense. Over pecan sandies and Constant Comment, Shellie suggested and all the knitters conceded her point that Colliersville might be going straight to hell, but the country was in good hands. Reagan, handsome, pre–head twitch, was just what America needed. Personal responsibility. Trickle-down economics. Grenada. Was there anything the man didn't understand?

Later, when Shellie and Helen's girls had grown up and Kenny came into the picture, things changed, but not too much. The ladies all loved Kenny, treating him like a beloved pet. They patted him on the head and gave him treats and spoke to him in funny voices. But then Kenny grew up, too, and he enlisted because it was what his friends did, and Helen met a woman on the Internet who was camping outside of George W. Bush's ranch, demanding he bring her boy home. Helen got a plane ticket and a new suitcase, spent a few weeks in a tent in Texas, and came back to Colliersville a stranger.

"I always loved this place," Una said, sighing, as Shellie parked the van under Kenny's basketball hoop.

Just being in proximity to Helen and her ideas made Shellie's throat tight, so when Ruby said something about the farm still looking real pretty and Peggy said, "Real pretty," Shellie kept silent. She looked out past the ramshackle house to the fields beyond and a line of quaking aspens that bordered the Wyndham-on-the-River subdivision, only half its houses up and streets probably still wet. Ruby lived there in a cream-colored house with her mayor husband and two kids. Ruby, who'd grown up a farm girl mucking out horse stalls, had a perfect two-story and an in-ground pool and a contract with a chemical lawn service.

It seemed to Shellie that the world she knew, or thought she knew, was shrinking to the size of her palm. Soon there'd be nothing left but her sprawling love line and an age spot the color of dirt.

"How do we do this?" Una asked.

Ruby frowned. "We should have brought something."

"Like what?" Shellie asked. "A bag of granola?"

"I don't know. A loaf of bread. Maybe a hat."

" 'I'm sorry about your dead grandson, Helen,' " Shellie said. " 'Here's a hat'?"

"Never mind," Ruby said. "Let's just knock, okay?"

Shellie shrugged.

They approached the front door cautiously. Ruby did the knocking in a self-important way that seemed to say, Do I have to do everything around here? and Una, who because she was Una couldn't help but crowd a body, was right behind Shellie, breathing her sickeningly sweet cough-medicine breath down her neck. Peggy was glued to the bottom step.

Helen must have seen them arrive. Ruby's hand was still hovering near the door when it swung open. And there she was, their former friend, dressed in a long white robe, sparkly shoes, and a lime-green hat that put all their knitting efforts to shame. Shellie stared straight ahead, past Helen's left shoulder where a grandfather clock in the hall ticked off ten seconds. Una coughed. Peggy coughed. Then Helen invited them in for tea.

But the kitchen table wasn't set for tea. The large maple butcher block that years ago held skein after skein of yarn and plates of muffins and half-consumed cups of Earl Grey, orange pekoe, oolong, was draped with a purple cloth and lined with unlit candles. There was something large under the cloth. Some sort of art project, Shellie presumed, or maybe a new herb, psychedelic or illegal, that had to be grown just so.

You got pot under there? Shellie wanted to ask, but she'd promised herself she wouldn't speak. *Or I know. Jimmy Hoffa.*

Helen grabbed one end of the cloth and rolled it back slowly like you would a sleeping bag or a scroll. It was Una who screamed, but thankfully she did it quietly so it came out more as a sad sigh or a moan. Ruby said, "Oh my," which Peggy repeated, and Shellie just drew in her breath.

"I wanted to do him myself," Helen said. "Funeral homes are such soulless places."

Stretched out on the tabletop, pale, slightly swollen, and mostly naked, was Kenny Garrety. There were herbs scattered across his skin, glass beads on his eyes, and flowers between his toes. A sycamore leaf, big as a child's baseball mitt, cupped his private parts.

Helen crossed her arms over her chest, surveying Kenny like he was a freshly planted patch of earth. "They embalmed him already. I tried to get a special dispensation to stop them, but the army has a procedure for everything. The makeup they put on him. Awful. I just got done washing him before you got here."

"Washing him," Peggy said weakly.

Ruby made a gurgling noise and ran down the hall to the bathroom.

"He looks great," Una said, her eyes on her shoes. "So natural."

Shellie had to go ahead and disagree with Una on that one. Kenny looked anything but natural. He'd been a young man when he left for the war two years before, vibrant and funny and sweet. There was still a layer of baby fat on him then, softening his cheeks and pulling his T-shirts tight. He was always laughing, even when something wasn't funny, like the time he brought Brianna, old

enough to know better, home from a party where she took something that made her want to eat her own hair.

Back then, before the war and a bombing that sent shrapnel
through his skull, Kenny looked natural. Now he looked old and
skinny and waxy as the beans Helen had soaking in her sink.
Something bloomed at his hairline like an inkblot on paper. Shellie
wondered if the back of his head was blown away. It was hard to
tell. Helen had placed a plush pillow at the base of his neck.

Ruby came back into the room, blowing her nose into a handkerchief. "I'm fine," she said. "Must have been something I ate."

Helen blinked slowly at her and placed the purple cloth at the
foot of the table under a box of brushes and wet rags. "I'm going
to bury him tonight."

Shellie laughed. She couldn't help it. Then she looked around
for some confirmation. *This is crazy,* she mouthed to Ruby, but
Ruby just bit her lip. Una and Peggy, huddled together under a
scaffold of hanging sweetgrass and sage, were staring past Shellie
to Kenny's uniform, folded neatly on the countertop, and an
American flag with its stars showing. Then Shellie noticed the
shovel leaning up against the cabinets, and a simple wooden box,
roughly six feet long and two feet wide, stashed in the corner by
the refrigerator.

"You're serious?" Shellie asked.

"I am." Helen grabbed a box of fireplace matches from a shelf
over the sink and started lighting the candles.

"Is that legal?"

Everyone looked at Ruby. Anytime there was a question of
legality they turned to her, assuming she was an authority on
most, if not all, of the city's ordinances, but Ruby threw up her
hands. "Rupert never tells me anything."

Helen cleared her throat. "It's completely legal."

"What about Frannie?" Shellie asked.

"What about her?"

"Aren't you going to wait for her?"

"Wait," Peggy said.

"For what?" Helen snorted. "She's been brainwashed by some NRA Mormon wackos who won't let her travel twenty miles beyond the compound. Wait for Frannie. Sure. I might as well wait for the Rapture."

No one said anything, not even Una, who loved to mumble on about the Rapture, how it would come, who'd be pulled into heaven like lottery balls through a tube and who'd be left behind to drown when Christ turned the whole world to high tide. A candle dripped slowly onto Kenny's right arm.

"Besides," Helen said, "Frannie doesn't care what I do. She said her people—*her* people—believe in water burials. Death as rebirth. She's going to bury Kenny in effigy from Idaho. Some crafty lady out there is making a Kenny doll. There's going to be a ceremony."

"We thought maybe we could have a wake . . ." Ruby had one hand on her throat and the other on her belly, which pillowed out under her elastic waistband. "A memorial of some kind. At the church. We'd love to say good-bye. If you'd let us."

Helen shook her head. "No. There was a thing this morning, some pompous nonsense on the tarmac with a gun salute and reporters. It was gruesome. You can say good-bye now."

"You're sure, Helen?" Shellie asked. Her voice sounded alien to her. "Helen" came out squeaky, the name a rusty hinge.

"About what?"

"Burying him tonight."

Helen nodded.

"You have extra shovels, I think," Shellie said. "In the potting shed?"

They stood slightly stunned under Kenny's old tree house, a mess of two-by-fours that rested above their heads like a broken bird's nest in the branches of a sycamore tree. No one was more stunned than Shellie, who still wasn't sure how she'd gotten them all into this. Helen had stayed behind in the kitchen. There were more preparations to be made and besides, she couldn't leave Kenny, not until it was time, so she told them where to find the shovels and where to dig.

The tree house was, according to Helen, Kenny's "sacred space," so they'd trudged there together, dragging their shovels and doubting they'd get it all done before dark.

Sacred space or not, the gods were not on their side. The earth was hard and the tree sent a tough network of roots through the ground, many as thick as Shellie's upper arm. Getting through the grass was the first struggle. The clods came up in small pieces, dirt and grass mixed with rock and the bones of some small animal.

"Chips," Shellie said when she uncovered a jaw and some teeth. "Kenny's dog."

Then came the roots and the clay. They dug in jerky stops and starts, hunched over like the old ladies they would someday become.

"I'm not sure we should be doing this," Ruby said, resting her shovel against the tree trunk. Her fat cheeks were pink and greasy with sweat.

"It's sacrilegious." Una daintily scraped dirt off her saddle shoe.

"Sacrilegious," Peggy repeated.

A bunch of wusses, Shellie thought. All talk and no action. Typical Marxist claptrap. "Oh come on, you guys. There's nothing in the Bible that says, 'Thou shalt not bury your dead in your own backyard.'"

They were silent for a while, long enough for a truck full of teenagers to honk by and an owl to hoot at them from the woods where the shadow of a waning crescent moon was rising. Shellie supposed they were quite a sight, a bunch of middle-aged women digging a grave on a Saturday night. No one was dressed for the job, especially Una and Ruby, who rarely wore pants. Their veiny calves had constellations of mud on them now. Peggy's nails were broken, every one. Shellie knew she had dirt in her hair. She could feel the grittiness itching at her scalp. She missed Buff. And she missed her daughter. Who her daughter used to be, anyway.

"I haven't seen Brianna in four days," she said. "I'm worried she might be in some sort of trouble."

The owl hooted twice more and the wind picked up, bringing a chill.

"She won't talk to me," Shellie said. "She hardly ever comes home. I don't know what I'm going to do."

Una wiped her face on her skirt and mumbled, "She's sleeping with Josh Seaver."

"Excuse me?"

"And she's stripping at Miss Kitty's."

"How do you know this?"

"Heard it at the Hair Barn."

"Oh," Shellie said, shifting her shovel from one hand to the other. "So it must be true."

"Well," Una said. "Yeah."

Shellie knew she was right. In her heart, in her aching back, she knew.

Up in the air, the tree house creaked, and the moon, shrinking to a sliver, reminded them that Kenny was gone. Gone from them forever.

"Let's keep digging," Ruby said. "None of us is getting any younger."

The hole was almost finished, so they took a break. Una had to pee. Peggy was thirsty. Ruby said her sciatica was acting up. They headed straight for the house, all but Shellie, who took a detour through Helen's flower garden. The peonies were out. Pink, fragrant. Brianna's favorite flower. Or had been. What was Brianna's favorite anything now? Shellie brushed the velvety blossoms, remembered the feel of her daughter's baby skin, the heat of her cheek when in fever. You wouldn't have children, wouldn't even think about it, if you knew how it would all turn out.

She stopped outside the kitchen window, glancing in at Helen, who seemed to be blessing Kenny in some way, wafting a round incense holder over his face and chanting a low song while she circled him.

The kitchen was smoky and growing dark. Helen and Ruby stood near the body, which was so still Shellie had the sensation of moving forward even though her feet were planted on the ground. Una appeared from the hallway, holding a long, thin sewing needle. It glinted in the candlelight and trailed an almost translucent pink thread. Helen stepped back and nodded at Una, who, expertly and with grace, removed the glass beads from Kenny's eyes and stitched his heavy lids shut.

"Would you look at that," Shellie whispered.

Peggy sidled up next to her, shivering as she pulled a sweater over her shoulders. Shellie was sure she'd say, *Would you look at that,* but instead she silently tugged at her ponytail.

When Helen started blowing out the candles one by one, Shellie touched Peggy on the shoulder and the two of them went in. It was time. Shellie knew all about this part, the lowering, the sealing up, the sheer finality of the thing that was like all the air being sucked out of the world.

She headed straight into the kitchen, crouched down next to the coffin in the corner, and motioned for Peggy and Una and Ruby to join her. Together they pulled the pine box out from behind the refrigerator and over to the table. It squawked over the lumpy linoleum, the lid flopping open against its side as they positioned it, sanded to gold and smelling of Christmas, next to Kenny. Helen did not cry. She leaned down over Kenny's face and kissed each cheek. She rubbed his arms and stroked his hands and pushed one stray hair off his forehead.

And because the others got weepy then, because they crumpled like Kleenexes, it was Shellie who moved to the bottom of the table and took Kenny's feet. They were cold and smooth and hairless. She remembered helping him learn to tie his shoes. He was terrible at it. So terrible Helen had to buy him Velcro for years.

Shellie looked at her friend. "Ready?" she said.

A few flowers fell to the floor.

Helen gripped the pillow under Kenny's head and took a deep breath.

"Go."

Elderly Care

(June)

It was time for *Star Trek: The Next Generation* but Tiara said she was sick of that show and why couldn't they watch something normal for a change?

"What's normal?" Fikus asked. "*Hannah Wyoming?*"

"It's *Hannah Montana* and anyway I hate that white trash bitch."

"Hey. Simmer down, and watch your language while you're at it."

Fikus lit a healing spirit candle and watched it sputter. He had a bad feeling. He often had a bad feeling, but he was beginning to wonder if maybe something had gone wrong in the astral plane. A disturbance, maybe, in the desire stuff. That could explain it. A wave of unreckoning in the abode of the dead. Fikus said a small prayer for his father and his mother and for Daisy Gonzalez. He finished with a prayer for himself. He'd lost his dairy bus-driving gig when it was shut down and his school route when Daisy went missing. Money was very short just now. So was the spirit candle. Most of it was just a purple puddle on the plate.

"You got a bigger bowl or something?" Tiara asked.

Fikus would rummage through his cupboards again but he knew it wouldn't do any good. "That's my biggest."

"Maybe if he had more room to breathe."

"He's a fish. He's fine." But Fikus said a fifth prayer, this one for Tiara's fish, Murphy, because he had to admit that the thing—a sort of pale goldfish-like creature with pink eyes and a blue-tipped tail—looked listless. It hung out in the bottom of the orange cereal bowl and didn't flutter his fins much.

"He ain't swimming. That's not a good sign," Tiara said.

"Not all fish swim constantly, you know," Fikus said. He checked the oven to see if he'd put in the tater tots. The oven was full of pans. He pulled them out and set them on top of the stove, knocking a six-pack of Gatorade Frost to the floor. The bottles just missed his big toe. "What do you want with your tots?"

"Hmm?" Tiara was plunking the bowl's side and making fishy faces at the water. Her necklace hit the bowl and made a sound like a bell. "C'mon, Murphy. You can do it. You can live. For me. Swim, goddamn you."

She'd brought the fish over as a present of sorts, something to take Fikus's mind off his guilt over Daisy Gonzalez's disappearance and his subsequent lack of employment. Fikus appreciated the gesture a lot more than he appreciated the fish. The last thing he needed was something to take care of. Just look what happened to Daisy when he should have been taking care of her. And who knew what might happen to Tiara if he didn't put a stop to her almost daily visits.

Like Fikus, Tiara lived in Maple Leaf Mobile Home Park. She and her mother were two trailers up B Street in a white singlewide with blue trim and a faded picket fence out front. Hardly a day went by that Tiara didn't show up at Fikus's door armed with something—a homework assignment she couldn't figure out, a videotape she'd "borrowed" from her mother about an obscure disease, an actual gun. Well, an actual water pistol, but Fikus couldn't tell—they looked so realistic now—and he'd screamed and put his hands in the air. "Pow," Tiara said as she pulled the trigger. Nothing came out.

At first when Tiara started coming by he worried what her mother would think, and so over and over he'd sent her home, telling her to find some friends her own age. "I see you on the bus," he'd said, shutting the door in her angry face. "That's plenty."

For a while she stayed away and Fikus was proud of himself. He'd finally managed to put his foot down. But he was also lonely and had to admit that when he heard her knock again on a gray evening in February he was glad. Sure, he'd have to tell her to go away, but at least someone wanted to see him, even if it was a foul-mouthed little girl. "I'm not a complete and utter pariah," he told himself. "Pariah. Pariah should rhyme with tiara, but it doesn't. Funny world. Funny kid." He thought he might let her in, if only so she could warm her paws over the space heater.

But that day it wasn't Tiara on his front stoop. It was her mother. Fikus had seen her a number of times around the trailer park but they'd never officially been introduced. She had a thin face and purple lips and elegant hands, and sometimes, when Fikus passed her house, he'd crane his neck for a glimpse of her, hoping to catch her outside, talking to a neighbor, gesturing. The way she stirred the air. He thought she could be an orchestra conductor if she wanted to, but Tiara said, "Nuh-uh. You crazy? She's a nurse."

Fikus tried to remember her name. Cheyenne? Charlene? Either one would have suited her well. She had a tough brand of beauty.

"What do you have against my baby?" she'd asked him. She had on a man's winter coat and ski pants and heavy rubber boots. Her hands were shoved into purple mittens.

"Excuse me?"

"I said, what do you have against my baby?"

"Tiara?"

"The one and only."

"I, well, I—"

"I'm sorry, Mr. Ward. Tiara didn't tell me you had a stammer."

"I . . . I don't. I just—"

"Yes?" Mittened hand on hip.

"I don't have anything against her. Why would you say that?"

"She told me that she's been trying since January to get you to let her in—'Mama, he's just a lonely old man with only some candles and crystals for company,' she says—but that every time, every time, you slam the door in her face. I ask you, is that any way to treat a little girl who's just trying to get her elderly care merit badge?"

"Her what?"

Frustrated exhalation. Large brown eyes rolled skyward. "Would you do me the favor of letting Tiara pay a call on you? All she needs to get the badge—she's just one step away from full Buttercup Girl status—is to visit with you and write a report about what you did together. She could make you hot cocoa or something. Organize your pills by color. Watch *Matlock* with you. I really don't care. Just let her in the door, for God's sake."

"I would have. I just . . . I thought you wouldn't like it."

"Because she's a girl and you're a weird loner old man?"

Fikus nodded, blushing. He didn't like hearing himself

described in such a way by such a pretty mouth, but he couldn't argue with the assessment.

"Do you plan on molesting my daughter?"

"What?" Fikus blushed harder. Sweat beaded out on his face and ran down his back, ice cold. "Of course not."

"You're a bus driver for the school, so that means, I hope, that they've done an extensive criminal background check on your ass."

"Yes. I suppose they have."

"Tiara's a smart girl, a tough girl. If you so much as tried anything remotely fishy she would claw your eyes out. I trust her. And she wants that fucking badge, God knows why. I told her, 'Sweetie, the Buttercups are a bunch of boring white girls,' but whatever. What my baby wants and works for, my baby gets. I won't have some bent geezer standing in her way. Do you understand me?"

Fikus didn't know what a Buttercup Girl was. He'd never watched an episode of *Matlock,* and he didn't take any medications, except for the occasional sleeping pill. He was on the side of natural medicine. Spiritual healing. He was also on the side of whiskey, which he probably should hide from this shrewd woman and her even shrewder child. Then again, he wasn't sure either of them would care. They would probably say that was his problem, his funeral, same as it had been for his father. And they'd be right.

"Tell her to come on down tonight if you like," he said.

"Not tonight. She's got a crap-ton of math homework and math is not her best subject. We'll be up until dawn. But tomorrow. Okay?"

"Sure," Fikus said.

"Tomorrow," she said. "And every day for the rest of your life." Then she punctuated that thought with a slap on his shoulder. "Ha! I'm joking. You should see your face."

Only it wasn't a joke. It had been four months since that meeting on the stoop with Cheyenne ("Charlene?" Tiara had scoffed. "Are you kidding me?"), and Tiara was a fully functioning Buttercup Girl, not that she cared to go to the meetings—"All they do is make crafty things with cattails and shit. Boh-ring"—and still she insisted on visiting him. Every day. It might be for the rest of his life, too. Fikus didn't expect to live long.

Tiara called what they did together "vegging." For the most part they watched TV—reruns of *Next Gen* or *Xena: Warrior Princess*—or colored pictures of Hindu gods Fikus found in a bookstore in Fort Wayne. "I'd say we were *meating*, but that'd be dumb because you're a vegetarian!"

She *was* a funny kid. There was no doubt about that. She made him laugh and now that Fikus knew there was no danger of Cheyenne reporting him to the authorities, he allowed himself to enjoy her company, particularly when they conducted their "experiments," which usually involved throwing a bunch of about-to-expire food in the blender and mixing in dish soap or laundry detergent or whiskey—"Mama says this shit's the devil's brew and you don't need it"—and then setting it on fire in the driveway. Fikus liked how no-nonsense the girl was. She seemed to smash the dreamworld he lived in, to put him right down on solid ground.

"You know these gods ain't real, right?" she asked him once, giving Vishnu a purple face. "They're pretty, but they're not real. There is no God. Not really. God's just something people invented because they're scared of dying."

"God is everywhere," Fikus said. "He's in everything."

"You mean he's in your nasty hair? You mean he's in your filthy shoes? Your brown teeth? This funky dishtowel?"

Tiara tried to fix him, to tidy his house, and by inches she succeeded. His living room, which had hitherto been a mess of magazines and newspapers and whiskey bottles and half-completed crystal gardens, was now neat enough that you could see your way to the orange shag carpeting. His tabletops were dusty but there was room for a drink, and the bathroom where he kept his hanging plants was less junglelike. The garter snake who'd taken up residence on the radiator had been banished to the outdoors and the bedroom window let in light, ever since Tiara made him pull down the old newspaper he'd taped to the glass for privacy. He grew to love her, even when she called him "cray-cray nasty man," because he knew she loved him, too.

"Should I feed him some more?" Tiara asked now.

"Murphy? How much have you already given him?"

She shrugged. "A handful?"

"You're kidding, right?"

"Why?"

"Never mind. Don't feed him anymore today. Leave him alone and come and eat your tater tots. There are carrot sticks, too."

Tiara made a face.

"No carrots, no tots."

"Fine."

They ate in the kitchen because Tiara had vetoed *Next Gen* and because they had a good view of Fikus's backyard bird feeders, where right then a blue jay was fighting three robins for access to the black-oil sunflower seeds. The jay was winning.

Tiara watched the scene, not saying anything for several minutes. Finally, mouth half-full of carrots, she turned her sharp eyes on Fikus. "Fikus?"

"Uh-huh."

"Do you wish sometimes you lived someplace else?"

"You mean a different state? Or a different country?"

"Sort of."

"I wouldn't so much mind India," he said. "Wanna see the temples there, to get to the bottom of the big questions. Second choice, Russia. I like the idea of steppes."

"Steps? What's so great about going up stuff?"

"Steppes. With two *p*'s. And an *e*. I think. They're meadows. Only huge."

"Whatever. I was talking about living someplace else in town. Other than Maple Leaf. Like, would our lives be different if we lived in Wyndham-on-the-fucking-River? Or on one of the tree streets. Peach. Elm. Maple. They sound so nice. And we live on goddamned B Street. Who came up with that? Seriously."

"Tiara, you have to stop cussing so much."

"Okay, okay, sorry." She popped a tater tot into her mouth and chewed thoughtfully. "It's just that I feel kind of hog-tied here."

"Hog-tied?"

"Held back. You know. And my house isn't a house. It's on wheels. And my neighbors just throw their trash right out the window."

"Well . . ." The girl was so bright. Most times, he had no idea how to talk to her.

"Daisy and me discussed this very issue on the bus the day she disappeared." Tiara rubbed at her throat. The mermaid dangling there, missing some sparklies over the breasts and on the tip of the tail, looked like she could use a dip in the fishbowl. "I'm scared."

"Me too," Fikus said.

"Do you think they'll find her?"

"I really hope so."

"She knew where I was coming from because she was coming from the Bottoms and, seriously, Maple Leaf and the Bottoms, same-same. Apples and apples. But then you got people like Alex, who if he wouldn't fucking repeat himself—"

"Language . . ."

"Sorry. If he wouldn't repeat things a million effing times would sort of have it made in the shade."

"Because his family has money?"

"Our door fell off yesterday."

"What?"

Tiara stood and walked to Fikus's front door (which was his only door) and swung it open. It did not fall off. Then she shouted, "I hate this place! Hey, Asperger's Alex! Can you hear me from your mansion over there? I hate this place I hate this place I hate this place I hate this fucking place!"

"Close that door, Tiara."

"Why?"

"You're disturbing the peace."

"What peace? Here?"

Fikus looked down at Murphy, still listless at the bottom of the bowl. Also bloated. "You're scaring your fish."

"Okay, I'll shut the door, but first come look at something."

"At what?"

"Just come look."

Fikus relented and, in front of them, on B Street, was a small pack of boys holding two dead kittens and a makeshift noose fashioned from an orange extension cord. One of the boys swung a kitten over his head like a lasso, hooting and smiling up at the sky, eyes wild, teeth gray.

Tiara shook her head. "Maple Leaf, represent." Then she sighed, heavily and long. She was so much like her mother. "Now do you see what I mean?"

The Pretty Faces

(June)

Irv was lucky that morning. The buck didn't have a face. It didn't even have a head, which meant it was probably a ten- or twelve-pointer. Usually it took at least a six to tempt a passerby to chop off the head for a wall trophy, and this one was big, full grown, and regal as the mascot in a bank commercial. The midsection was sliced up pretty good. There were guts on the concrete, watery red like a spilled sno-cone. Alive, the buck must have weighed two hundred pounds, and even headless, it took up most of the westbound lane of Route 20 in front of Maple Leaf Mobile Home Park.

It was early morning and the spitting rain left a shine on the sign at the entrance to the trailer park, one of Colliersville's many eyesores, now shrouded in a forgiving fog. Across the street was the Baptist church where Irv went to AA meetings in the eighties, and stapled to the church's front door was a faded blue flyer offering a reward for information regarding the disappearance of Daisy Gonzalez. Irv couldn't read the flyer from where he stood but he'd seen enough of them around town to know what it said: "MISSING. Five-year-old girl with black hair and eyes, last seen wearing a pink shirt and blue corduroys. Wheelchair-bound. REWARD." The pumpkin-cheeked girl went missing on the way home from school. Her bus driver, Fikus Ward, was one of the last people to see her alive.

Irv hadn't thought of Fikus for years, but he lived just a few hundred feet away in Maple Leaf in a shingled double-wide squeezed in between the park's moldy pool and the power sub-station. Fikus had been Irv's first and only partner for a short time in the early aughts, back when working for the county meant something. Borrowed from salt spreading to help Irv get through the summer, Fikus had melted down one day over a deer, that, like this one, had been decapitated by a trophy hunter. He told Irv that deer were his favorite animal, "my spirit animal, Irv, my heart." Then he basically went nuts, left the job that very afternoon talking to the voices in his head and spent some time in the county hospital.

Irv considered visiting Fikus, seeing if he was okay, but he'd found him annoying eight years ago and chances were he still would. People didn't change. That was one truth. Best to let dead dogs stay dead. That was another.

Irv climbed into his truck and backed it up slowly, sliding two big metal forks under the body of the buck. He flipped a switch under the steering column and the forks raised the deer up and into the bed like it weighed nothing. Like it was made of feathers. With the hoist and a rack of rakes and shovels, it was easy to work alone, and Irv didn't miss Fikus, only felt for him. Death and disaster seemed to cling to certain men like wet leaves to a shoe and there was nothing they could do about it. What did that song say?

Some guys had all the luck. Some guys got all the breaks. And some guys were born to scrape flesh off the pavement.

People always asked Irv about the smell. They were fascinated by the smell of death. "How can you stand it?" they asked him, over and over, in line at the White Swan Grocery Store, at the gas pump, after a football game at the high school. "Does it make you go out of your mind?" they wondered, or did he carry something around with him, like a scented hanky, to mask it?

Mostly Irv just shrugged and kept quiet, but if he'd been drinking he might venture to say, "Yeah, you know. I almost never leave home without my nosegay," but no one seemed to find that funny. No one except Rita, of course.

It made sense that people would think the smell the worst part of the job, especially in summer when the sun-cooked flesh and bloated bodies rotted fast and ugly. It was a terrible bouquet of decomposition, escaping gas, and old blood. Fikus used to throw up a lot, took three showers a night to try to wash off the stench, but Irv told him that there was no escaping it. "Stop that before you rub your skin off," he said, but Fikus didn't, and his skin was always pink and raw.

What he hadn't been able to tell Fikus or anyone really but Rita was that the smell didn't bother him so much. What bugged him, haunted him, were the faces, all the pretty faces with their lights turned out. The faces remained in his memory, multiplied down the years like a line of mirrors. Sometimes when he closed his eyes he was sure he could see them all, from his very first puppy to yesterday's raccoon. The only way he'd survived twenty years of it, of helpless things turned to nothing, to stillness and stink, was to imagine the animals living a new life in a strange land where their faces were whole and beautiful again, where there were no roads or cars or fences, just wide-open fields and dense forests and deer paths.

Irv had to picture Rita there too or he'd never sleep. The minute his mind started to process the fact that she, like the animals, was rotting, it shut down and rebooted itself, and he could again focus on the Rita he wanted to, naked and warm and stunning in that highwayless, carless land, petting dogs as they passed and stroking the pony Irv picked up ten years before, dead of what looked like a crossbow wound and on its side, bleeding its heart out across Spencerville Road.

Lately, he'd started seeing Daisy Gonzalez in that peaceful place too, fixed up with a new set of legs and watched over by Rita and Fikus's magic doe. Irv figured the little girl was as dead as Rita, as dead as the departed Bambi leaking behind him, but the search for her was still in high gear. Every weekend men like Irv's boss, Yuhl Butz, strapped on hip waders and safety orange and scoured woods and soybean fields, parking lots and neighborhoods, for a sign of the girl, but so far all they'd uncovered was a goat skeleton, a rusted-out safe full of fancy shotguns, and a Model T Ford half-buried behind a barn.

Irv supposed he should try to make it out on one of the searches, but something held him back.

"Asshole!"

A girl in a Toyota screeched out of the mobile home park, narrowly missing Irv's trailer hitch with her side mirror and flipping him off as she sped by, face distorted behind a cloud of cigarette smoke.

How did she know?

Irv put the truck in gear and called dispatch on his cell phone. If they told him about other pickups, he'd keep driving, but if the roads were relatively clear he'd drop the buck off at the dump—a glorified two-hundred-foot-diameter hole in the ground brimming with deer and dog and kitten carcasses—and take an early lunch.

"Yeah." It was Greta, the new girl who'd managed in just a few short weeks to break two hearts in leaf removal.

"Irv here. More jobs for me?"

Silence, followed by the sound of her opening a potato-chip bag. "Give me a sec, okay?"

"Sure." Then Irv heard a squeak. At first he thought it was Greta being cute, but he held the phone away from his ear and realized it was coming from a ditch in front of the church. It was soft and plaintive. Irv cut the engine and walked across the road. *Why, according to Ernest Hemingway, did the chicken cross the road?* he once asked Rita. *Why?* she asked. He loved her for not saying, "Who?" *To die,* Irv said. *In the rain.*

Lying near the bottom of the ditch in a pool of water was a little dog, a mix maybe between a Yorkie and a pug, its back leg twisted underneath it and bleeding. His brown eyes blinked up at Irv and at the sky where a hawk was circling. The dog's snout was stubby and crinkled, like a crushed beer can.

"Irv, you there?"

Irv nodded into his phone, reaching a hand out to the dog, daring him to bite. The bony dog licked his fingers instead and Irv thought, No. No way in hell. Don't even think about it.

He should have taken the dog to the pound. That's what he should have done. To the pound or the vet, saying, *It's your lucky day,* as he handed the dog to some pretty girl volunteer, who would coo over the thing's bloody leg and darting tongue. But he didn't.

Instead, Irv took the dog home with him, straight home, and so the buck was still in the back, bleeding out the tailgate, and the roads around Colliersville, Spencerville, Auburn, and Angola went uncleaned for the night. Poor Greta. He'd hung up on her by accident and ignored her repeated attempts to reach him. Irv could see the scene at the public works building now. Yuhl would be having his usual conniption. There would be spilled coffee and an excess of drama and worry, but not enough real concern for anyone to come check on him, and Irv thought with an odd sort of pleasure that he, like Fikus, might be going crazy. Did crazy feel like this? Like freedom? Like not giving two shits?

He left his cell phone on the front seat, wrapped the dog up in the reflective vest Yuhl insisted he wear even at high noon—his "Be Safe Be Seen" gear—and took him right to the tub to clean the wounds on his leg and side. The dog shivered and quaked when the water hit him. Irv could feel the knobby spine through the dog's fur, itself tangled and ratted with burrs. The leg was tender at the hip and bleeding in four jagged lines but not too bad. It was as if the dog had been hit by someone on a bike, or maybe the same douchebag who killed the buck might have decided, as a parting gesture, to beat a stray dog and leave him on the side of the road to drown as the ditch filled with rain.

Nothing surprised Irv anymore. He'd seen a mother raccoon, her belly ripped open, dead but still giving birth; a red-tailed hawk with its beak torn off, flying away into the woods, blood falling from the sky; an enormous dairy cow turning one whole block of Elm Street to a river of milk; and two squalid boys pulling a deer carcass home on a sled so their mom could turn it into venison. Nothing shocked him, nothing, that is, except Rita's leaving him alone.

Irv fished one of her old towels from the back of the bathroom closet and cocooned the dog so he couldn't move. Then he set him on the couch in front of the local news, giving him a bowl of water, which the dog quickly lapped up, and a stew bone from the freezer. The dog gnawed it hungrily, drooling and making funny growling noises as he did. The poor thing seemed on the verge of starving, so even though Irv was tempted to give him a whole T-bone, he held back, knowing that introducing food slowly would have the best results. "Maybe some rice and hamburger in a half hour," he said. "Dished up in small portions." The dog did not look up. Some blood joined the drool on the couch but Irv didn't care. He'd throw a blanket over it. Or a pillow. If he had any left from the Rita days.

He poured himself a bourbon and Coke and nuked a lunch of leftover chili mac. Then he added a handful of limp fries to the plate and tossed a piece of garlic bread on top. It was the kind of meal that would have driven Rita nuts.

Your food's all the same color, she used to say, handing him a bowl of salad or popping a plum into his mouth. *You need to eat the rainbow.*

Men wanted Rita Washburn. They couldn't help it. When Irv fell in love with her for real, she was a middle-aged mother, a member of the PTA, and the prettiest waitress at the Flying J Truck Stop. Pushing fifty, she still put the other waitresses to shame. Wherever she went, people smelled lemon pie and possibility, so who in Colliersville would've believed she'd fall for Irv Peoples and his pin head, bowling-ball gut, and job as the most accomplished roadkill collector for four counties? Nobody.

The town's opinion of Irv was that he was different, which, next to being a fag or Mexican or both, was pretty much as bad as it got. (Exceptions were made for little Mexican girls, missing and presumed dead.) There was even a rumor Irv had strangled a guy at Bass Lake over a bluegill. He had no idea where that came from, although Fikus was known to have told some tall tales while he was in his padded cell, and people in Colliersville believed what they wanted to believe.

Rita was the only one who'd really taken the time to get to know him. If he thought of her too much, if he let himself think about what it was like then, loving her, being with her, and what it was like now, he'd end up drunk by nine P.M., listening to Conway Twitty and crying into the cracks in the floor.

"They don't make them like that anymore," Irv told the dog when he'd finished his food. The dog was shaking under Rita's towel, a tender paw exposed. Irv sat down next to him and covered him back up. "She was a breed apart."

Funny then that Rita's daughter, Shannon, should be so mousy and keep-to-herself. Poor girl, Irv thought, motherless and in love with a Seaver besides. Loving a Seaver was about as bad an idea as loving Irv. Ask anyone in Colliersville and they'd tell you that the whole clan was cursed, although "cursed" implied a lack of culpability. Irv believed the Seavers deserved everything they got, and he even suspected they were behind the bad luck that had broken out at the Ranasack Apartments. First, "Spics go home!" appears on someone's truck and the basketball court where the Mexicans played their three-on-three tournaments. Original, that one. Then two young women report to Randy Richardville that a man in a red ski mask was haunting their rooms at night, whispering threats through the screens. Irv was gut sure that was Shannon's boyfriend, Josh, in the ski mask. And what if Josh somehow had a hand in Daisy's disappearance? What about that?

Irv didn't say anything to anyone about this—sharing wasn't his strong suit—but he had an odd feeling, driving by Shannon's house. He kept his eyes open but his head down.

Shannon lived in Rita's old house just up Hate Henry Road from Irv, and a few weeks back he'd helped free her car (another Rita hand-me-down) from their swamp of a shared road. Later, she'd hollered at him when he was on his evening constitutional, keeping the paths around their houses clear for walking, and begged him to chop off her Rapunzel hair. That hair, which flowed almost to her feet, was the only thing that marked Shannon as the daughter of someone special—Rita often bragged about it, said it took hours to wash and dry—and he wondered why a girl would choose to rid herself of something so beautiful, so distinguishing. He didn't question her. It wasn't his right, but still, his conscience smote him. He and his ax were responsible for that, for stripping the world of one of its few beauties, for hacking off something Rita had cherished.

The dog was looking him intently.

"What? What do you want?"

He scratched at Irv's arm, like, *Go on, tell me more.* Irv shrugged. He supposed secrets were safe with a dog.

"I'll be the first to admit that there have been other women," Irv said. "Last long enough on this planet and you're bound to get some action, but there's been no love. No love before Rita and none after." He cleared his throat and launched into his best Humphrey Bogart impression. "It all started over a Reuben at Flying J's . . ."

Rita was nearing the end of her shift when Irv dropped by the restaurant on his way home from work. The truck stop café smelled like hamburgers and coffee. A handful of patrons took up three booths along the front where the windows, fogged to their edges and pink from the sunset, gave the place the cozy feel of a grandmother's kitchen. It was exactly what Irv needed that day. It'd been a record setter: ten deer and a couple dogs. His back and brain were killing him. He was dazed with death and told Rita he had to quit, he couldn't take it anymore. Rita was dazed, too. Up until then, she had no idea what he did.

"I thought you planted trees or something," she said.

Better yet, she didn't care.

"Can't you smell me?" he asked.

"What? English Leather and desperation?"

Somehow, after three cups of coffee, he'd gotten up the balls to ask her to come home with him. When she said yes he had to catch his breath. They'd been neighbors since the eighties but never talked much. He shoveled her walk and plowed her drive. She baked him cookies at Christmas. He never dreamed she'd look at him as anything but the weird guy who didn't get out much.

But then there she was, an hour later, standing in his kitchen in her uniform and hairnet and light jacket, high heels left at the door so she could rub her sore soles and stretch her toes. She stayed over, giving him and his stupid body until morning to muster a hard-on and then thrilled him by climbing on top, dawn creeping up the backs of her thighs, her long hair in his face forming a cave. Safe. He felt safe and loved and a part of something. Like from then on he'd be on the inside, a member of the club everyone else seemed to belong to without ever having to pay dues.

Which is why it came as such a shock when, over a breakfast of eggs and toast, Rita asked if he wouldn't mind if they kept their affair a secret. He wanted to tell the whole world, but she said no, people were, speaking in large generalities, shit sandwiches who wouldn't rest until everything beautiful and sacred in this world was ruined beyond recognition.

"Let's just keep this between us," she said, kissing him, wafting her irresistible scent his way.

He shrugged and said, "Sure, you're the boss."

And she was, the full five years they had together, all the way up until the day she died in a hospice center in Fort Wayne, bald, angry, and only one hundred pounds. Irv wasn't there, of course, people being shit sandwiches and all. He heard about her death from one of Rita's fellow waitresses, who pulled Irv into an alcove outside the kitchen and handed him a note.

The note read, *I love you, you ugly bastard. Don't forget me.* She didn't sign it, of course. She didn't have to.

"That was it," he told the dog, hurrying to the end, which he didn't like to think about. "She was it for me."

The dog barked and a flower of blood bloomed on the towel near his tail. Irv wrapped him tighter and flipped the channel. The cute blond anchorwoman on Channel 12 was saying there were new developments in the Daisy Gonzalez case. Irv pointed to the little girl's picture on the dusty screen. "Think you could find her?"

The dog whined and licked his nose while the anchorwoman teased the town's housewives. "Tune in to *First at Four* for details," she said.

Irv tossed back the rest of his drink, his eyelids drooping. He cupped the dog's head with his palm and leaned back. To dream of Rita, he thought. To dream.

.   .   .

The next day Yuhl was on him from the moment Irv walked in, following him all the way from the front of the public works building to the break room, tsking after him worse than a wife.

"Where did you go? Greta told me she called you four times and you didn't answer. I'm looking at the Corpse Count Log from yesterday and it's blank. Plus, I know for a fact you took your 'Be Safe Be Seen' vest home with you. I checked this morning and it wasn't in your locker and Irv, you know that's a violation of rules twelve and fifteen. . . ."

When Yuhl joined the department six years before, he insisted Irv keep a "Corpse Count Log," so that at the end of the year Yuhl could justify Irv's salary to The Powers That Be. Before Yuhl, Irv didn't have to keep track, just had to make sure the streets were clean for the next day's traffic. Now he had to chronicle each pickup, writing down a short description of the animal's condition and where he found it. Yuhl said the log was his way of making sure that Colliersville's tax dollars were well spent, but Irv despised the thing. It flew into his dreams, flapping around his head like an enormous bat, forcing him to remember in detail what he'd just as soon forget.

It was like the dump, which Yuhl rechristened the Greater Colliersville Carbon-Based Waste Processing Facility. With his nonsensical micromanaging and delusions of grandeur, Yuhl had managed to take what had been a pretty awful job to begin with and make it completely insufferable.

"I told Greta, I told her there must have been some extenuating circumstances. Irv just isn't the kind of guy to fall asleep at the switch like that, I said. So, Irv, what happened? What was the big deal?"

Irv poured himself a cup of coffee from the break-room carafe. His jacket was wet with rain, and the lima bean–colored floor was already muddy from fifty other booted feet. He nodded at a few mechanics passing around a *Playboy*. They smiled and went back to the centerfold, the grease on their hands leaving little black tracks on the table in the shape of frowns.

There was something about the break room—its brown walls, perhaps, or all the "Be Safe Be Seen" literature on the corkboard over a rack of fake plants—that made Irv feel hopeless.

"I got sick," he said.

"Oh." Yuhl pulled on his mustache. "I wish you could have told us, or told Greta at least. She was worried."

Sure, Irv thought, spying Greta through the glass window between the break room and the call center. She was blowing on her nails and smiling up at the new landscaping hire.

"Sorry, Yuhl."

Yuhl coughed. "That's okay. That's all right. It's just that, with Daisy Gonzalez gone missing and that blood curse in front of Breeder's business, people are starting to get concerned. You know. To think there might be dark forces at work."

To hear him talk, Yuhl was the Daisy Gonzalez search team's most dedicated volunteer. He seemed especially keen to make himself useful during the searches held at night near water and liked to brag in the break room about the gear he'd bought to either a) make himself glow in the dark or b) keep his body spectacularly dry.

"Any big breaks in the Daisy search?" Irv asked. "Heard something on Channel 12 about new developments."

Yuhl lit up. "Well, me and the mayor's son, we saw a wheel-chair near the Detroit train bridge, adult-sized but still. We really thought we were on to something." He sighed. His gut pushed against the black buttons of his shirt. "I tell you, Irv. Another day, another setback."

The search team was all volunteer and when Yuhl described some of the weekend scenes when the group got together, Irv thought the whole thing sounded oddly festive. A potluck dinner. Prayers. Hand-holding sing-alongs. Maybe that's why they hadn't found Daisy yet. They were having too much fun.

"Of course, we prayed it wasn't Daisy, and lo and behold, the Lord has given us the chance to carry on, to search another day."

"Amen." Irv smiled tightly and started shuffling back toward the front of the building, curling his shoulders up against Yuhl's earnestness, which he didn't trust. Yuhl seemed determined to fol-low him, and Irv wondered what he'd say to him if he trailed him all the way to the truck and saw the buck languishing there. *Just found the bugger. Ain't he cute? Don't mind the buck. Ignore the blood. Everything's under control.*

"A miracle's coming our way," Yuhl said, stopping at the front doors. "Maybe tonight. I feel it. The Lord gives, doesn't he? He doesn't just take away."

"True. True." Irv took his hat off, put it back on. "Well, I should really make up for lost time. That log's not going to fill itself, is it?"

Yuhl laughed and slapped Irv on the back, wished him Godspeed. "Love to see you out there some night, Irv. On our search. We're doing the Lord's work, you know. To have you join us. Well. That would just do me no end of good."

.   .   .

The dog hadn't moved except to gnaw his way through a granola bar left on the seat. The buck hadn't moved at all.

Irv had a list of pickups from Greta. One was in the same spot on Route 20 in front of the trailer park where he'd found the buck, only this time the corpse was a coyote. "Again? What an odd coincidence," Irv had said, but Greta just stared at him blankly.

The morning was dark and heavy with rain. Irv pulled out of the public works parking lot onto Main Street, where the traffic lights made Christmas-colored pools on the ground. He passed the elementary school, the courthouse, and White Swan Grocery, envying that sweet, slow kid, Trevor Hochstetler, wrestling with a line of carts outside the doors.

"That's the life," he told the dog. "No fuss. No muss."

The dog, wrapped in another pink towel of Rita's, licked his paw. Irv had considered seeing if Shannon might watch him, but she had her work at the Laundromat and he didn't want to inconvenience her. And since Irv didn't want to leave the dog home alone, his only choice was to bring him on his route and hope no one, including Yuhl's wife, Pearl, who waved at him from the corner of Main and Elm, spotted the thing as it let out the occasional yelp.

Main Street became Route 20 just outside of town, and Irv could feel himself growing tense the closer they got to Maple Leaf. The buck was bad enough, but coyotes sort of got to him. They reminded him of his childhood dog, Pepper, a raggedy shepherd mix with a taste for rats and bus chasing. Pepper got hit by a car on Irv's tenth birthday and it was Irv who found him, sliced in half in front of the Nelsons' mailbox but otherwise fine, like one part of him could have gotten up and walked east into the sunrise and the other into darkness.

As he pulled up on the coyote carcass he could see that it was mostly intact, and not alone. Standing next to it, in a bright yellow rain slicker, was Fikus Ward. It'd been a few years since Irv had last seen him, but when Fikus turned his face to Irv's truck lights there was no mistaking him. Sunken eyes. Straw-colored hair. Lips that chewed themselves. Irv killed the engine and told the dog to sit tight.

"Fikus."

"Irv."

"Long time no see." Irv held his hand out to Fikus for a shake.

"Yes sir."

"What we got here?"

"A not so wily coyote."

"Bad spot for animals just now." Irv thumbed the air over his right shoulder. "Buck I got in the back perished in the same place."

Fikus hung his head, his neck jutting out like a vulture's. "Somethin' ain't right, Irv."

Irv agreed with Fikus, but mostly because he didn't think it was the behavior of a healthy man to be standing out in the wet over a dead coyote if he didn't have to. "So what's going on, Fikus? What brings you out here on this lovely day?"

"Daisy Gonzalez."

"Oh."

"I'm going to find her." Fikus's face froze into an odd mask. "Have to."

"I see."

The dog perked up then, gave Fikus a few suspicious barks, and Fikus did a double take. "Where'd you get that dog?"

"Found him yesterday. In the ditch yonder."

"Mary mother of God."

"What is it, Fikus? Are you okay?"

Fikus approached Irv, got close enough for Irv to smell his breath, which was oddly sweet. Whiskey and bananas. His hand shook as he reached out to grab Irv's shoulder. "Help me."

"Help you? How?"

"You got a car. I don't."

Irv thought of Greta's list of pickups sitting in his cab next to the dog. He really didn't plan on getting them all—there was a Saint Bernard out by the water treatment plant, a wild turkey in front of Angola Trinity Lutheran, a freakishly big possum blocking the egress of the Spencerville Army Surplus store, and a family of rabbits scattered across the highway into Auburn—but hitching his wagon to Fikus's star didn't seem like a good idea.

"It's my fault," Fikus said, his gray eyes wide and rimmed with too much white. "I dropped her off in the company of that Juan character and I left because this other kid had shit his pants and I was in a hurry to get gone. She's missing because of me. Please. I'm going crazy here."

Irv did a thoughtful circuit around his truck, checking on the dog and giving the thing a nod and a knock on the window. The dog nosed Irv's knuckle through the glass and drooled on the door handle. Irv had no desire to spend his day looking for dead things. They'd stay dead, wouldn't they? If anything, they'd be a little more dead tomorrow. His job didn't matter. He didn't, either. Not to anyone anymore.

"Okay," Irv said. "But I only got a few hours."

"Thank you," Fikus said, grabbing Irv's hand again and pumping it. "Thank you thank you thank you."

"Don't mention it," Irv said. "Help me with this thing?"

Fikus took a deep breath. "It'll be like old times."

"Or I could just use the hoist. County sprung for one a while back. Pretty nice. Takes the work out of work."

"Nah, I'll help."

"All righty."

Irv took the head and Fikus the feet and they swung the coyote in next to the buck, puffy now and hard to the touch. Then they stood for a moment staring at the coyote and deer, squeezed together like mismatched puzzle pieces, both the color of tree bark.

Eventually Irv said, "You hungry?"

Fikus shrugged. "I can usually eat."

"Flying J's?"

"Fine with me."

Fikus had struck Irv as oddly normal, emotionally stable even, until he took a seat next to the mutt. He kept glancing down at it, curled up and panting happily next to Irv, like it might explode.

"Fikus, he's a dog, not an IED. What's wrong?"

"Seeing ghosts is all."

Flying J's was loud with retiree chatter and the clink of forks against stoneware. It had gone through a makeover since Rita died, from brown-and-orange plaid to a cheery, almost tropical peach and yellow, but new upholstery wasn't enough to shed the smell of thousands of cigarettes smoked and coffee left to burn away to dust on hot plates around since the seventies.

The first few years after Rita's death Irv avoided Flying J's, preferring to eat his bachelor dinners in the privacy of his own home, but gradually it had again become a part of his morning routine, and being reminded of Rita didn't hurt like it used to. There was even a thick-legged young waitress Irv liked because she never bothered him with too much chitchat, just brought him his standing order—French toast if the morning was cool, two eggs over easy with sliced tomato if it wasn't—and threw him a few sad smiles over his newspaper.

"Mmm, bacon," he said to Fikus, who'd stopped just inside the front doors and had gone from chewing his lips to fluffing his hair. Over and over and over. Like a girl at a photo shoot. "Smells like victory."

"Gone veggie myself," Fikus mumbled. Fluff, fluff, fluff.

"Ah," Irv said. "That's your conscience talking, I suppose. I don't listen to mine. Hey, would you stop messing with your hair? You're making me nervous."

Fikus slammed his arms to his sides. "Sorry. Habit."

"Have you considered therapy?"

"I told you. I'm fine."

"Sure you are."

Irv's favorite waitress was at the hostess stand, scrubbing syrup from a plastic menu. "Sit anywhere," she said.

Which was her way of making a joke. It was morning rush and Irv could spy just two empty chairs in the entire restaurant, both at the lunch counter and separated from each other by a broad-shouldered man staring into the pie case. Hector Gonzalez. He had a bowl of oatmeal in front of him and a spoon raised over the rim. Irv watched him for what seemed like a full minute and the man didn't move. Not once. He hardly even blinked, and the spoon just hung, poised above the bowl like a diver suspended in midair while the pies rotated slowly: pecan, lemon meringue, cherry, sugar cream. Irv had taken Hector some food right after

Daisy went missing but hadn't tried to connect with him since. Irv got the feeling the man wanted to be left alone.

Fikus tugged at Irv's elbow and stage-whispered, "I can't eat here. Not with her dad just sitting there like that."

Irv gritted his teeth. "Fine. Let's go, but I'm still hungry."

"I don't know how you can even think of food at a time like this," Fikus said, stepping on one of Irv's shoelaces as they crossed the parking lot to the truck. "Our world is falling apart."

"They ate while Rome was burning. Well, someone did. Barbecue."

"Maybe you should just take me home."

Irv thought about it. He thought hard and unlocked the truck door for Fikus, pushing the dog to the center. He was prepared to turn around and head right for Maple Leaf, but just then Hector Gonzalez emerged from the restaurant entrance and dropped his wallet on the sidewalk. The sight of that heartbroken man stooping to pick it up and the memory of him and his untouched oatmeal and levitating spoon made Irv think again.

"You can't give up that easily, Fikus," Irv said. "You must have some idea of where you wanted to look. What's first on your list?"

Fikus fluffed his hair and pulled a crumpled sheet of paper from his back pocket. "The elementary school."

"You actually have a list?"

"You just said, 'What's first on your list?'"

"I was speaking figuratively."

"She's a real girl, isn't she? Not a figurative one."

"Never mind. Why would she be at the elementary school? I'm sure Yuhl and his crew checked there already."

The dog nuzzled Fikus's leg and Fikus jumped. Then he opened his window, letting the rain in. "You name it yet?"

"Not yet," Irv said.

"It's going to need shots."

"Probably."

"You should put a leash on him at least."

"He's injured. Leg wound. Don't think he's going anywhere for a while."

"That's what I thought about Daisy," Fikus said.

Before he could reply, Irv's cell phone rang. It was Greta, of course, "worrying about him" again. Irv ignored it and put the truck in gear, passing in front of the restaurant entrance where Hector Gonzalez now stood, wallet in hand, gazing out across the rows of cars as if he'd forgotten where he parked. The man was lost. Completely lost. Irv remembered that feeling. It was what happened when your home wasn't a house but another person and that person was gone. Fikus had the same look about him.

"First stop," Irv said. "The elementary school."

General Henry Colliers Elementary School was an old brick two-story with pillars out front and baseball fields in the back. A few years before, the mayor's wife had spearheaded a campaign to tear the school down and build new, something modern and energy efficient and easy to secure in the event of a mass shooting or terrorist attack, but the push ended in what came to shove and the school stayed. Why fix what isn't broke? And why turn our tax dollars over to the government only to see them wasted? That was the gist of the opposition, led by relative newcomer and successful real estate agent Mike Marino, who, according to rumors, had his eye on the mayor's office. Irv had to agree with the man, much as it pained him to do so, but unlike Marino's, Irv's reasons weren't purely practical or mercenary. He found the building beautiful and some things had to be saved for beauty's sake.

Fikus was clearly on the side of Ruby Rodgers. "Should have leveled this place when they had a chance," he said.

Not much had changed since Irv had gone there forty years ago, and as he walked up on it, the days returned to him in sharp snapshots—the snaggletoothed principal telling him he wouldn't amount to much, a pretty brunette girl who moved away before he even knew her name—and smells: spilled milk left to sour, sawdust poured over vomit, a rich perfume on the brunette girl that Rita sometimes had worn, too, toward the end. Youth-Dew. Irv bought the stuff by the bottle now and put it on his pillows.

"Dumpster's in the back," Fikus said. "Let's go."

Irv could have told Fikus there was no way Daisy would be allowed to decompose in a Dumpster that janitors visited every day, but he kept his thoughts to himself because of Hector and that suspended spoon. Also because Irv had watched a young Fikus, yellow hair standing stiff, shoes losing their soles, get his ass kicked over and over by the big kids right where they were standing and done nothing.

They took the sidewalk around the school, rain from the eaves dripping down their necks, and stationed themselves in front of a hulking metal can wedged between an air conditioner and a row of plastic chairs arranged in size from biggest to smallest, all of them tipping off their legs. A few desks were dumped there, too, and some shelves. End-of-the-year detritus. The smallest chair looked to be just the right size for Daisy Gonzalez, and Irv imagined her there, a latter-day Goldilocks, trying all the chairs out until she came to the one that fit her best. Fikus was staring at the chairs like a man transfixed. He tried to fluff his hair but it was too damp. It fell against his skull like drowned worms.

"Well, here we are," Irv said. "You want to do the honors?"

"Actually, Irv, would you mind? Suddenly feeling woozy."

It was like that stupid summer all over again. Irv had had to do all the hard work, all the heavy lifting, because Fikus was forever feeling woozy or dizzy or "not his best self at the moment."

"No problem," Irv said, raising the Dumpster's heavy black lid and peering in. The can was, as he'd suspected, empty. "Nothing here save a pink eraser and plastic grocery bag tied around a chicken bone."

Fikus sighed with relief. "Thank God." He turned on his heels and headed back toward the truck, stepping quickly through puddle after puddle. "Next up, the bank."

Irv had to hustle to keep up with him. "The bank? Really?"

"There's a method to my madness, Irv."

"If you say so."

So Irv drove Fikus all around town, stopping not only at Colliersville Bank and Trust, but at the American Legion, the recycling center, and the high school. They didn't talk to anyone, just rooted around in trash cans mostly, and Irv wondered if the day would land him in jail. That or find him jobless.

The dog rode along cheerfully. His leg had stopped bleeding and his tail wagged almost constantly. Irv thought he'd name him Pooch. It was simple. Manly. And he'd take him to the vet when this horrible day with Fikus was over, get him a cast, some stitches, and a rabies vaccination. Maybe he'd get him a red collar at the pet store and one of those tags: "Hi. My Name is Pooch. I belong to Irv. If you find me, call this number." *I belong to Irv.*

On their fifth Dumpster of the day, Irv, hands full of soggy receipts, finally asked Fikus, "What are we looking for exactly?"

"Clues," Fikus said.

"What kind of clues?"

"We'll know them when we see them."

"We will?"

"Just keep digging."

And he did. For no reason and with no direction. His phone rang and rang.

Eventually, Irv insisted that they eat. They went to Tony's Pizza because it was open and Flying J's was dead to Fikus. That's how he put it. "That place is dead to me."

"Fine, fine," Irv said. "Whatever you say."

Tony's Pizza wasn't good. It wasn't bad, either. Irv and Fikus split a large cheese and Irv gave the last piece to the mutt, who gobbled it and barked for more. Irv's phone had rung ten times. On the eleventh, he turned it off.

"What are you running from, Irv?" Fikus asked.

"What? No one. Nothing."

"All of us are running from something."

"Not me."

"For instance, I'm running from myself. I'm running from the fire inside."

"Must get tiring."

"It does. It is. You wouldn't believe the things I see. The things I hear. I admit it's often too much for one man."

"Sure."

"You wouldn't understand."

They spent some time sitting in Tony's parking lot, Irv wondering just how long Fikus could keep this up and Fikus staring out the window and fingering his rain slicker, his chewed-up lips a beefy mess. Finally, around four, Irv turned to him and asked, "So what's our final stop?"

"The park behind Miss Kitty's. Off Elm."

"Okay," Irv said.

The whole day was one piece of futile ridiculousness after another, so what was one more? It was stupid, the search, and it was dumb, to hold out hope in this world, but, his belly finally full, Irv did sort of wonder if they could find Daisy, the three of them, and maybe, in spite of their past track record, find her alive. Wouldn't that be something? To deliver the pretty little girl into the arms of her grateful father? To just once have the chance to change the story.

The route to the park took them past the Hair Barn and Breeder's Laundromat. Fikus didn't say anything until the steamed-up windows with their trademark fake suds came into view. The now famous bloodstain billowed out from the stoop to the gutter in the shape of a thought cloud.

"Hey," Fikus said, wagging his finger and looking alive for the first time all day. "Remember Rita? Rita Washburn? Doesn't her daughter work there?"

Irv put on his casual face. "Sure. Shannon. Good kid. And Rita was a good waitress."

Fikus whistled. "Good waitress? Great woman. All woman. Fucked her a few times. Years ago now."

Irv almost blew through a stop sign. "What? You what?"

"Oh you know." Fikus slid his index finger in and out of his fist. "Everybody did. Back then. It was right around when you and me started working together. Rita Washburn. Ass like an onion. Brought tears to my eyes."

Elm Street waved in front of Irv like a hair ribbon caught by the wind. I'll kill him, Irv thought. I have a shovel back there. I've got an ax at the house. I'll kill him and throw him in a hole and no one will know because there isn't a soul in the world who cares about Fikus Ward. Not a soul.

"We're stopping at the dump," Irv said.

"That's not on the list."

Irv reached over the dog and grabbed Fikus's list, crumpling it in his palm. "Enough of that."

"But what about the park? You promised."

"I promised? What are you, Fikus? Six?" Irv made a U-turn and hit the gas.

The Greater Colliersville Carbon-Based Waste Processing Facility was waiting for them behind a rise of earth that many in town swore was an ancient Indian burial mound. Fikus was one of the believers.

"You shouldn't have brought me here," Fikus said, fists over his ears.

"What's the big deal? You've been here before."

"This place is a sin against history."

"Whose history?"

"Yours. Mine. Everyone's."

"Oh, so you're an Indian now? Should I start calling you He Who Fluffs His Hair?"

"That's racist, Irv, and you know it."

Irv punched in his security code at the gate and brought the truck to a stop at the edge of the dump. The three seagulls circling overhead looked like bats against the gray. The dog sniffed the air and growled. Irv's heart hurt. He felt like it had been replaced with a rock, or spooned out roughly, the sides of his chest scraped raw and hollow. Why did it matter so much? Rita fucking other guys while she was fucking him? What was fidelity anyway? He pictured her face above his the way it was at the beginning, adoring and blushed up and so beautiful, and he felt his pizza coming back up.

"You should get out, make sure Daisy's not here," Irv said.

"Why would she be here?"

"Why the hell would she be in any of the spots we've checked today?"

Fikus had fished his list from the truck floor and smoothed it over his chest like a cloth napkin. "I don't know what's come over you."

"Save it, Fikus. I'm not in the mood."

Irv took a deep breath and looked out over the dump. It wasn't like a landfill. There was no system, although Irv had developed his own over the years. Big things first, small things last. Heads, tails, heads, tails, a coin flip before a football game. The animals he collected two days ago were still on top, and deer from the past month bloated around everything like saturated cereal flakes.

"You stay," Irv said to the dog. "You go," he said to Fikus, shoving him in the shoulder.

"Fine. But stop punching me. I'm feeling woozy." Fikus reluctantly stepped out of the truck and flipped on a flashlight he pulled from under his slicker.

While Irv dragged the coyote out of the bed and slid him on top of the pile, Fikus wandered around the hole, darting his flashlight beam at an otter, a mole, and finally a tabby cat with slivers of fur on its ribs. Irv followed him to the lip of the hole, imagining what it would be like to just chuck him in and drive off, but he knew he didn't have the stones, and besides, it wouldn't solve anything. He couldn't kill the ache.

"I'll find her, you know," Fikus said.

"Who?"

"Daisy. I'll find her."

"I'm sure you will."

"And when I do, it will be atonement. For the sins. For all the people killed here for the wrong reasons."

"Good for you. Now get in the truck. I want to go home."

"I didn't want to come here anyway."

"Just get in."

Fikus did so, but slowly and not without growling something under his breath about "that poor dead man, that worse-off dog."

After he dropped Fikus off, Irv drove. He drove as far as his anemic gas tank would let him, coming to a stop across the road from the now defunct Spencerville Fun Spot. He just needed to think a minute, so he killed the engine and leaned over the steering wheel, looking out on the frozen Ferris wheel and a patch of woods behind it, the tops of the maples like black thread on the horizon. The dog, who'd been sleeping with his head on Irv's thigh, started to bark and whine, paddling his way out of Rita's towel before Irv could do anything.

"What's wrong with you?"

The dog howled and the sound hurt Irv's ears. He hopped out of the cab into the wet, studying the white trail his headlights made through the darkening night, the two beams distinct at first and then blurring to a soft glow. At his feet was a dead rat, its long tail waffled with tire marks. Life was loss, Irv thought. That was it. The big secret. Loss upon loss upon loss until it was hard to know if waking up the next day made any sense at all. He'd left the door open and suddenly a yellow body shot past him and took off toward the Ferris wheel, kicking up leaves and scattering pebbles like there was nothing wrong with him. Rita's towel lay in a heap on the seat.

"Pooch!" he called. "Pooch! Stop!"

Irv shut the truck door and muttered under his breath. Fucking dog. He made his way across the road as the clouds opened up and the rain began to fall hard and steady, like a warning. Like, *Give up. Go home.* The bottoms of his pants were soaked and stiff.

"Pooch!" he yelled again, but all he heard was the rain and the growl of a semitruck jack braking on the interstate half a mile south. The braking sound faded, replaced by a high-pitched howl that cut through the night. The cry circled him, echoed and doubled on itself, like a musical note held too long. It became almost human. Irv thought of Hector Gonzalez and his untouched food, of Rita and her pretty legs. Always, always Rita. For a minute Irv couldn't move. What was Pooch up to? Irv didn't want to see. Didn't want to know.

Then he started running toward that howl. Fikus was a lying sack of shit. Sure he was. That story about Rita was a story. Fiction. Nothing more. And maybe Irv could win this one. Maybe, for once, he wouldn't be too late.

Paradise

You decide to sneak out of the house early in the morning before your mother gets up for work because if she knew where you
were going, she would laugh at you. She thinks all Christians are
cray-cray for all eternity amen and you used to agree with her,
but that was before the mermaid necklace she gave you started to
glow, to burn. You've got a pink, raw spot right above your heart
and when you touch it—the necklace, not the spot—your fingers feel like they might catch fire. Fucked up, right? Totes fucked
up, and, far as you can figure, your only option is to take the
things—the necklace and the spot—right to the source, to God,
the man upstairs with the beard and the flowing robes and the
booming voice you've only recently started talking to on account
of the silver mermaid with the ember eyes and Daisy Gone-zalez
and this weird sensation you have that the world, which once made
a modicum of sense, is now as out of whack as your busted front
door hanging from its hinges like a loose tooth.

You shove all your stuffed animals under the sheets, the tail of your best My Little Pony curling out on the pillow so that your mother will think you're sleeping in like usual and not sneaking out for Sunday service because a) you need to confess your sins, b) you want to pray for Daisy's safe return, and c) you overheard your cousin Dora tell your other cousin Bethie that if the devil is doing his work in your near vicinity your best bet is to ask for an exorcism of sorts. "A Devil Get Thee Behind Me" deal, overseen by an expert in such things.

"Aka," Dora said the last time you spent the night at her house, "a ministhter." Dora has buckteeth and spit on her bottom lip. Always. She's ugly and ashy all over but she's also older than you so who are you to question her facts? Especially now that the mermaid necklace, so pretty at first, has grown sinister, possessed. You're terrified of it. Plus, you wouldn't mind being saved.

"Better thsaved than thsorry," Dora said. "If you're not thsaved before you die, you'll thspend all eternity up to your thshins in molten lava. Hellths heat is like a billion thonths. It's like taking a bathth in the microwave."

You grab the mermaid necklace from the top of your dresser. You haven't worn it for five days now and the singed skin over your heart has begun to heal. The minute you touch the chain it grows orange and warm, so you drop it into a small box and put it in your pocket, pausing for a second in your doorway. The purple My Little Pony tail bears no resemblance to your nappy mop and the lumpy assemblage of animals looks less like you and more like shit on a shingle, but it doesn't matter. Your mom won't check, not really. She'll be in too much of a hurry to get to the hospital and anyway she knows you can take care of yourself. You've been taking care of yourself for as long as you can remember.

Which is the same amount of time you've lived across the street from Colliersville Baptist Church. Still, you've only seen inside it once and even then it was dark because you were there waiting out a power outage and a gas leak. You left before the lights came back on because the minister told your mom that God in his heaven was not on the side of single motherhood. "It marginalizes and emasculates the father who, according to scripture and divine right, deserves the head seat at the family table," the minister said. "If a man's home is his castle, you must vouchsafe him his throne."

Your mom, her face one big scowl, threw a plastic cup of raspberry lemonade in his face. "Vouchsafe that!"

God must be on your side this morning because you manage to get out the front door without waking anyone, not your mom, not her boyfriend, Tony, not even Tony's dog, Ruthless, who, once roused, is not satisfied until he's terrified the entire goddamned neighborhood, barking and whining and throwing his fat white body against the portable dishwasher. Ruthless is snoring outside the door to your mother's room, banished but standing guard. You watch him for a second. He's a sausage with ears, a pig with paws. You don't push your luck. You wait to put your shoes on until you're off the stoop and into the grass because the stairs bounce. Tony likes to say "I gotta fix that," but he says the same about the door and you know how that's turned out. Yeah, right, Tony. That'll be the fucking day.

The church lawn is different from yours and every other Maple Leaf Mobile Home Park yard you've ever seen or set foot on. There are no sun-bleached two-liter bottles, no soggy mail, no plastic wrappers or bent nails or broken water guns to contend with. Instead, all is dark green and smooth, like the carpet in the school nurse's office.

Dora told you it'd be like this. "I like churchth as much ath Dithney World. I like it more."

There are other kids your age climbing the stone steps to the front door, none from the trailer park, though, and they look so clean, their teeth so straight and white and even, that you start to think you might have made a mistake.

Then the minister, the man your mother still refers to as "Dick Divine Right," touches your shoulder. "It's wonderful to have you here," he says. He is tall and smells like pepper. "I'm Pastor Rush. And you are?"

"Tiara," you say.

"Welcome, Tiara."

You stick your hand down your pocket and check for the necklace. Still there. You figure now's your chance to tell Pastor Rush that Daisy's disappearance is all your fault because you were more concerned about a fish than a friend. Also that you have been hoarding a clue—Daisy's beloved mermaid necklace—that might lead to her being found because your mom gave it to you and it's pretty and your mom doesn't give you many pretty things. You open your mouth to confess, but before you can say anything more, Dick Divine Right tells you to go on inside.

"The service is about to start," he says.

You think of Dora, how she would say it, how she would spray it. "The thervith is about to thtart." You find a good seat behind a girl with long brown hair tied in a red ribbon. Her hair is thick and gives off an odor of strawberries. You'd bet your entire Barbie collection she's from Wyndham-on-the-River, and that's when you notice Asperger's Alex sitting right next to her. You wonder if they might be brother and sister, but she doesn't go to your school. You've never seen her before. You're mesmerized by the girl's ponytail, how it seems to sway in the breeze even though the stained-glass windows are shut tight. You follow the ponytail's path down her back and it seems to be pointing to a navy-blue hymnal, caged behind a wooden rail. Pastor Rush is at the front now. He coughs and the room goes silent. He asks you to pick up the hymnal and turn to page 22. The book is heavy and its pages are dipped in gold. The glitter comes off on your hands and you wonder if that is, in some way, a blessing.

"Lift up your voices," Pastor Rush says.

A bald man with a hole in his throat sits down in front of an organ and pounds out the first few notes of a song about angel wings and Emmanuel. You don't know the tune. You've never heard it. The only songs you know by heart are "Waltzing Matilda," your friend Fikus's favorite and, according to him, "the only worthwhile thing to have ever come out of Australia," and that sappy number your mom loves with the woman swearing over and over, "I've been to paradise, but I've never been to me." Even though you're a few beats behind the rest of the kids, you mouth the unfamiliar words anyway—who is the Holy Ghost? What is hosanna in the highest?—hoping Asperger's Alex, who spotted you a second ago and keeps looking at you over his shoulder, doesn't tell anyone your secret.

Your secret is you are a heathen. An unbaptized, unsaved bastard of a heathen. No Bible in the house. No father that you know of. No idea of what a burning bush is or an arc.

But it's okay, says Pastor Rush. Nothing matters but Jesus Christ, the body, the blood, the son of God who died on the cross so that we might be reborn. "Forget everything you've ever known about the truth," he says. His hands seem to catch fire from the candles on the altar. "Forget everything you've ever heard about the way and the light. This, my friends, is the way. The only way, the only light that guides your path to paradise. The rest is darkness, void, a vacuum of hate and ignorance and unlove."

He calls out to the congregation to be saved, to accept Jesus as their personal savior. The adults sit still. You suppose they've already been saved and accepted the light, the Jesus, the way. Most of the kids just look at each other, but Asperger's Alex jumps up, steps on a few feet, and hurls himself toward the altar. "Me me me me!" he says. A few other kids follow him at a slower pace—a redheaded girl with freckle-brown legs, a boy carrying a paper airplane. Pastor Rush palms each of their foreheads in turn, declaring them free of sin. They fall to their knees and kiss the carpeted stairs.

You almost go. You think very hard about going. You finger the necklace in its box, releasing a tiny smoke signal. Is the devil holding you back? And where the hell is Daisy? You concentrate for a minute, trying to pray, but you don't really know what it takes. Please God on your throne at the head of the table of the world, bring back my friend. I want to sit next to her on the bus and talk to her about my problems and her problems and take rides on the back of her wheelchair like we used to when Fikus wasn't looking. Also, God, please make my soul a light thing not a dark thing. And for Christ's sake, turn this necklace into something normal so I can wear it on dress-up days without dying.

Pastor Rush shouts, "Children! Children of God! Those who have not come to me today will come next week and the week after that and the week after that until all of you, like a sea of salvation, will pour down this aisle toward redemption. Waves and waves of belief and truth and love."

The ponytail of the Girl Who Might Be Alex's Sister shudders and goes still.

Then there's another song, this time about a woman named Mary and a dead guy named Lazarus, and when that's over you're told it's time for Sunday school. You follow a line of heads down an elbow-shaped staircase to a room painted pea green, the same color of your grandmother's attic, and that reminds you of the little girl you tortured there a few years ago because she had lice and no shoes.

"We're all loved by Jesus always remember never forget that," says a woman who introduces herself as "Miss Shellie for you new faces." You and the rest of the kids sit in four cross-legged rows in front of her. Miss Shellie is dumpy and white and old. A dark line of base runs along the bottom of her face and blends into her wrinkled neck. She looks a little like Mrs. Holt, who lives down the street from you and has a special house behind her trailer for her pet chinchillas.

"Today we're going to talk about the story of the loaves and the fishes," Miss Shellie says. "Can anyone tell me what this story is all about?"

Fishes and bread? Oh hell no. You love fish—Murphy's cool as shit—but this is not what you came here for. You came here to pray for Daisy and have your soul saved and your guilt exorcised. Last things first, you figure. You raise your hand.

Miss Shellie nods at you. "Yes, little girl?"

"Forgiveness for sins. How does that work exactly?"

"Excuse me?"

"So I did this thing. It wasn't a good thing. How do I stop being punished for it?"

Miss Shellie sits down in the teacher-sized chair. Even so, her hips spill over. "That depends. What is it you've done?"

You fess up as fast as you can to the "making Fikus drive away while Daisy was still basically alone and vulnerable" part, but you don't yet mention the necklace because as you speak, all the heads of all the kids swivel in unison and their blue and green and gray eyes stare at you like you're an alien and for a moment you feel like you are. There are only two pairs of eyes that look like yours and they belong to some other Wyndham-on-the-River pricks. You can tell by their cute dress/tights combinations and shiny hair. This makes you miss Daisy with a fierceness that surprises you. You miss your mom, too. And your bed and your My Little Pony and even Ruthless. You don't miss Tony. He sucks. His pizza sucks more. It tastes like dirty socks if it tastes like anything at all. But even if he's still there in your house sleeping off Sharkey's you want to go home and forget this day ever happened.

"Miss Shellie?" you say, but she doesn't answer you. While you told her about your sins, she stood up and got busy slapping felt fishes and felt loaves on an easel. You reach for the box in your pocket. The kids are still staring. Miss Shellie brings out the felt Jesus. He has white robes and a yellow halo over his honey-blond hair. Miss Shellie sticks him on the board next to what appears to be a trout and some French bread. Her fat back is to you. Her fat butt jiggles in her skirt while she works. Finally, she turns around. Her face is red with anger. She is saying something to you about soap and washing your mouth out with it, which means you must have cursed during your confession. The problem is, it's a habit now so you hardly notice it.

"That's it?" you ask. "Wash my mouth? That's all you got?

I tell you I probably killed my friend and you tell me not to say 'shit'?"

"Perhaps this is not the place for you," Miss Shellie says. "My Sunday school room is reserved for children who know how to behave themselves."

Excuse me? you want to say. But not excuse me. No. Fuck that. Fuck behaving yourself. Instead of sitting meekly in front of the stupid felt easel like the rest of the blond, reserved children, you take the necklace out of its box and throw it as hard as you can at Miss Shellie's pasty face. You pray it makes a permanent mark. Come on, God, brand her. Please, Jesus, a scar. Then you start running as fast as you can up the elbow stairs, through the church sanctuary, past Pastor Rush, and out the front doors into the cool world, where it's raining softly. You head for your dirty trailer with its broken door and bouncy stairs, its dusty carpet and duct-taped windows, its hard-water-stained bathtub, kitchen sink, dishwasher. The dishwasher that Ruthless likes to head butt from one end of the house to the other, often while shitting Tootsie Roll–sized turds in perfect ten-inch intervals. Paradise.

F5

(June)

The winds and rains were coming for Colliersville. Everything from Hate Henry Road in the south to Elm Street in the north to the dusty ends of Route 20 would get swept up in a funnel cloud and a flood and nothing would be left of the town but two telephone poles and maybe a lone pig left to squeal on a roof. It was inevitable and Trevor tried to tell the ugly policeman so, but the cop just sighed into his clipboard and said, "Fine, fine. That's fine, but what exactly did you *see*?"

Trevor balled his fists. His fingernails had gotten too long again. Facts. That was all anyone ever wanted from him. His boss was the worst. "How many carts in the parking lot, Trev?" He called him Trev. Trevor despised him for it. "And how many in the store? Do you think that's the right ratio for good business? Do you, Trev?" And his mother was forever asking about his paycheck so she could decide where to keep the thermostat. Numbers. More numbers. It didn't matter if she set it at sixty-three or sixty-seven. He was always cold.

"There won't be anyone left," Trevor whispered.

"What's that?" the policeman asked.

"Never mind."

Trevor knew records would be broken. There would be record winds, record rainfall, enough lightning strikes to power Colliersville for a year, if only it were still standing. The animals had told him—the first being the two dogs he saw on his way to work, a black bulldog and brindle mastiff mix, both big in the shoulders and short of snout. "Watch out," they said. "When the rains start, duck." The geese confirmed it. "We're gonzo," they squawked between wingbeats. "Gone. So. Gone. So. Gone."

Trevor worried for the chained, the caged, the otherwise domesticated. The wild ones could simply leave, but the two dogs had grown fat and happy behind a hurricane fence and now they whined at the wood every morning when Trevor walked by. "Help us," they said. "Do something."

The nightly news would try to tell the story, but the apathetic anchors would mispronounce all the names. They'd call him Taylor if they called him anything at all. They'd call the town Colorsville, which was funny because almost everyone who lived in Colliersville was white. Trevor thought that when the twister came, if he didn't die, he'd move to Mexico because in movies Mexico looked like a rainbow unfolding into the sea.

"Colorsville," the news anchors would say, "is history."

"Look, kid." The policeman shifted in his chair. "Think of the little girl."

The White Swan Grocery Store employee break room smelled like Lois's old lunch. Trevor sometimes wished the place where he ate his daily peanut-butter sandwich and apple weren't windowless and claustrophobic and lit with buzzing fluorescent bulbs, but the boss said natural light was a luxury he couldn't afford. "Who do you think I am?" he told anyone who complained, usually Lois. "Sam Walton?"

If the tornado didn't come Wal-Mart would and Trevor wasn't sure which was worse. He figured it was total destruction either way. Six one, half dozen the other, as his mother liked to say.

"I *am* thinking of the girl," Trevor said to the cop.

A centerpiece of fake African violets drooped onto the card table where Trevor bumped his balled fists together, demolition-derby style. Vroom. Crash. Burn. Trevor and the policeman were alone but they wouldn't be for long. Henrietta from deli took her break at twelve thirty every day so she could stay up-to-date on *General Hospital* and throw orange peels at any man who a) was sleeping with someone else's wife or b) wore a double-breasted suit.

The truth was Trevor couldn't stop thinking about the little girl. He saw her face on boxes in the cereal aisle, so cute, so dimpled, hovering above bowls of whole grain. He imagined he could hear her voice over the PA system, announcing a special on kale. He dreamed about her, too, and in his dreams she was older, no longer wheelchair bound, and beautiful. She had long hair and glitter on her face and seemed somehow to have grown wings. She invited him to take flight with her, to ride the currents out of town to someplace bigger, someplace better. *I'm thinking Disney World,* she often said. Trevor wanted to go with her but never did, sometimes because he had to work but mostly on account of his mother, who needed him to stay behind and fix something—the toilet, the cat's collar. He woke up convinced that if he'd only done something, anything, if he'd screamed when he saw the car and the spinning wheels out the window, Daisy would have had the chance to grow up into that lovely young woman, to fly, if not on her own at least in a plane, all the way to Disney World. The dreams made him even sadder than before.

When he wasn't thinking of Daisy he was thinking of Kurt in seafood, who had a black unibrow and hair like a bristle brush. Whenever Trevor stopped by the live lobster tank, Kurt talked his ear off about *Star Wars*—"the first three, correction, the *only* three"—and about how much he hated living with his mother, who, according to Kurt, gave all their money to TV preachers and paralyzed veterans.

"I'm dying," Kurt told him. "Dying a slow death of boredom and casseroles."

It was fate. He and Kurt had so much in common. It didn't matter that Kurt was ten years older and had a son to think of and student loan debt, too, on top of it all, which Kurt said was bullshit because education should be free. "Like air and sex." Trevor loved Kurt with a passion that made it hard to breathe. He worried that the crushing feeling on his chest might be due to the proximity of shellfish, which, if Trevor ever ate some by mistake, would send him into anaphylactic shock, but in his lucid moments he knew it was love combined with the terrifying thought that any day now Kurt might transfer to the Fort Wayne store.

The lobsters told him Kurt was short-timing it. "He can't wait to get out of here," they hissed. "Don't be such a fool."

Of course, when the storm came none of this would matter a bit. Love was nothing in the face of an F5. Neither was wood or glass or metal or concrete. Churches would end up as flattened as Miss Kitty's and the liquor store. God didn't cherry-pick. Kids would die, kids like Daisy Gonzalez, and grandmas who'd never done a thing wrong in their lives, and mothers like his own who might eat too much but who loved their children unconditionally and packed them plastic bags full of pills and a sack lunch every day because they never remembered to take their meds and were pretty much helpless in the sandwich-making department. The town would be destroyed, leaving only that one pig to tell the tale of what it was like to be inside the funnel cloud—*oink,* the pig would say to the handsome man from the Weather Channel, who understood nothing and cared only about his hair and pending contract. *Oink, oink.*

Trevor could translate those oinks but who would think to ask him to? "You wouldn't believe the whiteness," would be the pig's exact words. "Blinding white, is what I mean, and lightning flashes every few seconds and the smell of gas—which I'm used to but still—and little tornadoes spinning off the big one as geese and ducks and chickens whirl past on their way up and out. Poor devils. Too small. Too loved. I only lived because God didn't want me."

Trevor thought he might be spared for the same reason. Pastor Rush once sermonized that heaven spit out people like him, and then, during the intervention that his mother paid for with her Mary Kay money, the pastor prayed Trevor would abandon his sinful ways and maybe even marry one of the teenage cashiers at White Swan, preferably the out-of-wedlock pregnant one, killing, as Pastor Rush put it, "two doves with one stone." But Trevor just took greater care to hide his *Bronc* magazines from his mother, and when the two of them sat down with their popcorn to watch movies on the weekends he now threw things into the conversation he hoped put up a convincing straight smokescreen: "Look at that lady's butt!" he said. Or, "Those are some breasts on that lady."

His mother's cat, Mr. Greenjeans, called him out on it. "You're gayer than I am. Just admit it."

Ever since Mrs. Moody's third-grade class and the take-home gerbil incident of 1989, Trevor heard everything animals had to say. That was twenty years ago and his brain was an echo chamber, filled with the loves, disappointments, and complaints of the four-legged, the amphibious, the furry. The clamor was so loud it made it difficult for Trevor to do anything beyond watch movies with his mother and count shopping carts, some of them still holding little purse dogs abandoned for the moment by their owners, who said nothing when the pooches called Trevor "chubs" and "hopeless plebe."

The lobsters in Kurt's tank were even worse. They pleaded for their lives in high-pitched whines that made Trevor's eardrums ache. "Why let us swim now if all you're going to do is kill us? We know what happens after this. We're not stupid. We're not monsters. Do we not weep?"

According to the boss, the lobster tank had been installed to class up the joint. Trevor supposed it did. White Swan, half a century old and sans an organic food section, could use all the help it could get. It was just too bad that Kurt didn't work in deli, where everything was already dead.

"Hey? Are you listening to me?" The police officer waved a hand in front of Trevor's face.

"I'm listening," Trevor said.

"Your boss said you told him you know what's become of Daisy Gonzalez."

"Yes."

"Well," the police officer said. "I'm waiting."

Trevor supposed everyone was waiting, waiting for Daisy to be found, to be given back to her father, alive, smiling, in perfect health. Especially Trevor's mother. Viv followed the Daisy

Gonzalez case like a woman obsessed. She worried more about that little girl than she did her diet or her own son. Not that she ever joined the search party. She was too fat to do much of anything for too long, but she watched every newscast she could and saved the articles from the *Colliersville Record* in a gingham scrapbook, along with a few of the flyers volunteers stapled around town and photos of the girl she'd made Trevor find for her on the Internet. Viv's scrapbook had bulged to an alarming size. "It's going to be fat as my rear end soon," Viv said, squishing it shut under a mottled thigh. Trevor looked at his mother and then at the book and was silent.

"I'll repeat the question," the cop said. "What exactly did you see?"

"It will be like this place never existed," Trevor said. "The aftermath, I mean. People will walk out their front doors only they won't have front doors anymore. God's taking it all back."

The cop clearly wasn't interested in what Trevor had to say about the end of the world as they knew it. When Trevor tried again to suggest that the cop had better enjoy himself while he could because soon, maybe that very night but most certainly in less than a week, they'd all be fertilizer, the man shook his head. "The girl. I'm here about the girl. Daisy Gonzalez. Tell me what you know. I'm begging you at this point."

That morning, before the store opened, Trevor and Kurt were loitering in produce, the boss educating them on the top five ways to spot a shoplifter—"coats in summer!"; "shifty eyes!"; "backpacks!"; "coats in spring!"; "shifty hands!"—when Trevor, who'd been distracted by a Seeing Eye beagle bitching about his master, had a thought. He knew Kurt liked him okay, because Kurt made no secret about whom he despised and why. He hated Henrietta for her habit of sweating out the top of her nose, Lois for her tuna lunches, the pretty teenage cashiers for their habit of reading *People* magazine between customers, and the boss because he was a fat windbag with an exaggerated sense of his own importance. The only time Kurt criticized Trevor was when he thought he took too much of the boss's shit. Usually he just slapped him on the back and said he was all right, he didn't yak incessantly like every other half-wit on the White Swan payroll and so he "was good in his book." But Trevor wasn't content with lukewarm praise. He wanted fire, devotion, a reckless, stupid love that, it seemed to him from the movies he'd watched with his mother, belonged only to men of mystery. Men who knew things others didn't, men who harbored secrets that threatened to eat them up inside. So as the boss wrapped up his lecture and Kurt seemed poised to leave, Trevor shouted, "I know where Daisy Gonzalez is. I know what happened to her."

At first the boss didn't believe him. "Trev. Be serious," he'd said, but Trevor said he was serious, he'd never been more serious in his entire life. He'd clearly made an impression on the boss because the boss immediately called the cops—well, *the* cop— and now that man was here in the break room, his sad face turned for the moment toward Henrietta and her bulky figure, poised at the edge of the loveseat like a Slinky about to topple.

"Jerk-wad," Henrietta growled at the television. "Reprobate."

The cop focused again on Trevor. "Whatever happened to Daisy might not be an isolated incident. Her kidnappers might hurt others, do more harm. Your sitting on this information could endanger countless lives. Have you thought about that?"

"Yes," Trevor said. The soft skin of his palm gave way under his fingernails.

"Goddamn it." The policeman stood up and paced for a moment, kicking at a ripped gum wrapper. He sighed heavily and sat down again, his voice gentler this time. "All you have to do is tell me what you witnessed. That's it. Just tell me. Say the first word. I'll try to help you with the second. Okay? Deal?"

Trevor shook his head. The words would not come out. The picture was there, but the words weren't.

Henrietta threw a piece of orange peel at a doctor in navy-blue pinstripes. "Get a stylist!" she yelled.

The cop got a call on his cell phone. "Yeah?"

Henrietta tossed another peel at the screen. A tall blond woman with sharp collarbones and an even taller dark-haired man with a Fred Flintstone five-o'clock shadow were locked in an embrace behind a potted palm.

"He's married to Theresa the redhead with the job at the phone company," Henrietta said.

Trevor nodded. He remembered the redhead from the week before. She'd been crying into Fred Flintstone's shoulder, convinced he'd never love her the way she needed him to. "Tenderly," the woman said, "and with reverence."

Trevor supposed he'd never be loved that way, either. Especially now, because the cop was standing, the cop was on his way out, his skull pink under his crew cut. "I have to go," he said to Trevor, "but don't think for a moment that I'm done with you."

The people would scatter like flower petals. They would be scooped up by the wind and pushed on air currents to other states, other countries. New Yorkers would talk of a plague of obese people mid–microwave dinner falling from the sky, Canadians of televisions, big as boulders, cratering the Shield. Bostonians would complain to Katie Couric that their own houses were ruined by a hail of late-model American cars and corn silos and tulip trees.

Most of Colliersville's full-time residents would end up on dry land, draped over fences and half-buried in fields, but a chosen few, Mayor Rodgers and his family and the boss and the Yoders probably because they were rich or had been rich anyway, would be dropped in the ocean for the sharks and the mermaids to feast on. No news coverage for them, only swirling waters and a glimpse of Atlantis.

He had to warn Kurt. After the cop left, Trevor shuffled over to seafood, ignoring the nasally calls for extra help up front. "Trevor to checkout," Lois called. "Trevor to checkout." Lois and the pretty cashiers could bag their own groceries for once. The customers could walk a few extra feet to the corrals and get their own carts. He had more important things to do.

"So," Kurt said, spotting Trevor over the counter and wrapping up a pink wad of salmon, "how'd it go with Magnum, P.I.?"

Trevor shrugged. "We need to get out of here."

Kurt weighed the fish and told an old lady in navy polyester pants to pay at checkout. "You okay, man?"

"This place is going to blow."

"It already does."

"No. Listen. This is important. There's going to be a storm—"

Kurt came out from behind the counter and threw an arm over Trevor's shoulder. Kurt smelled strongly of fish, but Trevor didn't move away.

"You're overwrought, dude. You need to get your mind off that girl. How 'bout you come home with me after work? You can meet my kid, have a few beers."

Trevor wasn't supposed to drink. Alcohol reacted strangely with his medication, made him feel like a character in a video game instead of part of his own life. The last time he drank, after the intervention with Pastor Rush, he ended up dragging Viv into the yard in the middle of the night to save her from Donkey Kong. Booze meant more scenes, which meant more pill bottles, and more pill bottles meant Trevor floated a few inches above his shoes at all times. The carts got hard to grab.

"Sounds good," he said.

They stood for a few moments more, Trevor relishing the heavy feeling of Kurt's arm on his back. The store was full of summer shoppers stuffing their carts with hot dogs, hamburger patties, potato salad, chips, and pre-cut fruit. Trevor couldn't remember when the place had been so busy, packed as it was not only with customers, but with pre-holiday help in deli, floral, and cleanup. The poor kids, Trevor thought, watching as a skinny boy plagued with acne sliced roast beef into a plastic bag. They have no idea what's going to happen to them.

"Go ahead," said a girl lobster, banging an oversize claw against the glass. "Feel sorry for those assholes, but as for us crustaceans, you clearly couldn't care less. Very nice."

When the tornado came through, White Swan would be one of the first buildings to succumb to its fury, boxes of cereal and bulk bran and cartons upon cartons of eggs coating the town like batter. There'd be a blanket of laundry soap on the Ranasack, a river of mayonnaise where Main Street used to be. The store's supply of shopping carts would come crashing down in Akron, wheels up in a just-poured road, the child safety flaps banging in the breeze.

"You okay?" Kurt asked again.

Trevor cringed as Henrietta huffed past him. She'd told the policeman not to blame Trevor for stonewalling. It wasn't his fault she said. *He's a retard from way back.*

"Oink, oink," he whispered to no one in particular.

The day was almost over but not quite and Brianna Pogue was in aisle nine. She seemed to be staring into the grape juices. Trevor knew her for her stringy hair and way of squinting. He hoped he could walk by her this time without being seen but then he heard her holler his name and so he turned back, unable to disobey her even now.

"Trevor Hochstetler," she said, and her voice grew silky. "Killed any gerbils lately?"

Trevor looked at the floor, which was still sticky from a glass bottle of cranberry a kid knocked over that morning.

"I come in here every week thinking maybe, just maybe, Trevor Hochstetler will have moved on, found a real job, but it's always the same old story." Brianna dropped her purse at her feet. Glitter fell out. So did a pair of six-inch heels, a few joints, a roach clip, and a pack of cigarettes. She gathered everything up hurriedly and threw the purse back over her shoulder. "There you are now, looking just as hopeless as before, asking if we want paper or plastic. Paper or plastic. This is your life, Trevor Hochstetler. If you were ever on that old game show, it'd be the loneliest episode ever. Just a line of grocery carts coming out to greet you. Pathetic."

Trevor's shoe sole caught on the dried juice and he ground it around and around in the spot, enjoying the squeak and squish of cheap leather against the tile.

"How's it feel to be voted 'Most Likely to Be a Loser' and have it come true?"

The boss said something over the intercom. Trevor heard his name and the word *now*, but Brianna didn't seem ready to let him go. This was how it'd been years ago when he sat next to her in third, then fourth, then fifth grade, his desk slightly removed from the others because Brianna swore he smelled like poop and made her underperform on tests. She used to harangue him for eating paste and wiping his boogers on the bottom of his desk, and, because he'd drowned the gerbils, because he'd confessed to her that he'd flushed Adam and Eve, beloved pets of Room 226, down the toilet when they'd asked him to, Trevor felt compelled to listen to her until her words became barks, hisses, full-moon howls.

He started taking the pills that year, little green ones at night with a glass of milk. At first, they came in tinfoil-wrapped sheets. Later, bottles, so many bottles he used the empty ones as bowling pins. The colors of the capsules changed—from green to blue to orange and back again—but the feeling didn't. He'd stopped crying about the gerbils because crying would have required he do something with his face. When he wasn't dreaming of Daisy Gonzalez, Trevor dreamed he was a ship in a pill bottle, trying to rock himself out.

Brianna grabbed Trevor by his collar. She pulled him close. She whispered in his ear, "I know you think you saw something." Spit hit his hairline. "You didn't see anything. You understand?"

"I understand."

"If you tell anyone what you saw, it will not go well. For you. It will not go well at all. I just might have to tell the police about your experience with helpless animals. You know what they say about serial killers, don't you? It all begins with animals."

"There's going to be a tornado. . . ."

"What?" Brianna put a cigarette between her lips but didn't light it. "I can't hear you, Trevor."

He began to tremble and hoped he wouldn't pee himself. In his mind a vision appeared of Brianna being plucked from her pole at Miss Kitty's by the twister, fishnet thigh-highs ripped off and snaked around her neck until her face turned purple and she was dropped into the ocean, dry blond hair bobbing on the waves. "It's going to be an F5," he mumbled, looking up the aisle where Kurt was waiting for him near an endcap of half-off laundry detergent. "That's the big one—"

"Hey, buddy!" Kurt shouted. "Fuck the boss. Not literally. That would be disgusting. Ready to go?"

Brianna scowled, first at Trevor, then at Kurt. She started to walk away but turned back to Trevor and raised her pinky finger in warning. Trevor remembered that finger very well. *Gerbils,* she mouthed around her cigarette. *Adam . . . Eve . . .*

Kurt's mother's house looked like a chocolate cupcake. Round and low to the ground, it had brown walls and a pink roof and lime green–framed windows whose glass was foggy with canned snow.

"Don't say anything," Kurt said, parking his car next to a rusty pop-up camper. "This place makes me feel like Papa Smurf."

Trevor couldn't have said anything if he wanted to. He was still shaking from his meeting with Brianna, and being this close to Kurt for this long made him nervous. He quaked all the way up the walk to the front door and inside, where he could have sworn a tornado of country cuteness had already roared through, leaving in its wake a mess of ruffles and pastel teapots and little figurines of moon-eyed kids and bears in dresses and angels on their knees in dewy grass and wildflowers.

"This is Ma's sitting room. Hell, isn't it?" Kurt said. "Come on. I should introduce you to her or she'll be on my case all night long."

He led Trevor into a pie-shaped kitchen, where a woman in a turquoise smock stood at the stove, stirring a pot. She started when she saw them.

"Ma, this is Trevor."

It was clear she'd been crying. Her light green eyes, exactly the color of Kurt's, looked small and painful behind pink plastic glasses. With the exception of her eyes, she bore no resemblance to her son. Her light, fluffy hair stuck wetly to the base of her neck and a long cross necklace hung low over a flat chest. She had two bright spots on her cheeks like a doll. "Any friend of Kurt's," she said, holding out a bony hand.

Trevor took it and tried to smile at her but he had that crushing feeling on his heart again. Everything was a little too familiar— the warm, sweet-smelling kitchen, the pastel walls, the Bible under the phone, the phone under the crucifix, and the crucifix hung just so beneath a delicate border of pansies. He wondered if Viv and Kurt's mother were in some secret society together, a club that required its female members to adhere to a strict dress and decorating code. Maybe Kurt's mother had a scrapbook somewhere full to bursting with morbid memorabilia and a gay cat lurking in the corner.

She wiped at her eyes. "I'm sorry for the state I'm in. I've been listening to one of my programs."

It wasn't until Kurt flipped it off that Trevor realized the radio was on at all. "Fucking Amish love stories. How can you listen to that crap?"

"Hush," she said.

Kurt fluttered his hands near his cheeks. "Love among the zipperless."

"Kurt Allen. Please."

"Where's Charlie?"

"Dad!"

A boy about eight years old darted into the room, ramming a dark head into Kurt's thigh. Kurt grabbed him by the waist and flipped him upside down until he squealed.

"You'll drop him," Kurt's mother said. "One of these days. Mark my words. You'll drop him."

"Shut up, Ma. Jesus Christ."

She rolled her eyes skyward and turned back to her pot. "Forgive him, O Lord. Hate the sin, love the sinner."

The boy, a small version of Kurt sans unibrow, was right side up and on his feet again. "Who're you?" he asked.

"This is my friend Trevor. We work together."

"Lobsters taste good," Charlie said.

"I wouldn't know," said Trevor.

Charlie frowned. "Really?"

"I can't eat shellfish."

"No shit," Kurt said.

"Language," said Ma.

"Let's get out of here," Kurt said. He and Charlie grabbed a bag of chips from the top of the refrigerator and three cookies from a porcelain jar painted to look like a girl squirrel and a boy squirrel rubbing noses. Charlie dropped one of the cookies on the floor as he and Kurt jostled each other down a dark hallway.

"Five-second rule," Charlie said. Then he scooped the broken cookie up and popped it in his mouth.

"Do you have any pets?" Trevor asked, his chest tightening further as he followed them.

Charlie stopped and looked at Trevor. The gap in his two front teeth was the size of a pencil eraser. "Not a dog or nothing. Just two fish. Red Fish and Blue Fish."

"Charlie's allergic to dander." Kurt said. "It's like you and the lobsters."

They emerged into a small white room whose only ornament was a fake Tiffany lamp hanging from the ceiling and a poster of Princess Leia swinging a whip. While Kurt grabbed two beers from a minifridge in the corner, Trevor studied her, noted her perfect breasts behind the shell-like bikini and her long legs, her strong yet womanly waist. Pastor Rush had used a similar picture to try to woo Trevor away from the dark side, but the girl simply looked cold to him. Later, after Pastor Rush had left with his projector and dusty film strips, *Praying the Gay Away* and *AIDS: Gay Killer,* Trevor drew a shawl on her shoulders and Sharpied her a pair of sweatpants.

"This is our man cave," Kurt said, joining Charlie on a small plaid couch. "No doilies here, thank God."

Trevor sat down on a director's chair next to Kurt and watched while Charlie hooked up a video game system to a hulking television in the corner. The fish were on the floor in front of the TV, swimming in circles in their small tank and, as far as Trevor could tell, arguing about which direction they should take tomorrow. "Clockwise," said the red fish. "Counter," said the blue.

Princess Leia. Charlie's mom. Kurt liked girls. Plain and simple. Heaven, once it got its hands on Kurt, would keep him. In reality, Trevor had known this for quite a while, had understood in the back of his heart that Kurt just saw him as a friend, but still. He'd allowed himself to dream, to fantasize, and now, sitting in the middle of Kurt and Charlie's man cave, Trevor realized how ridiculous those fantasies had been. He popped a green pill onto his tongue and cringed at the battery-acid sting of it.

Kurt nudged his elbow with one of the beers. "Nintendo, my brother," he said, motioning with the beer toward the television, where a bright image of boxing rodents blinked and weaved. Trevor took the beer and gulped down what he could without gagging. The pill nudged its way down his throat, scraping a raw, wounded path as it went.

"Nintendo rocks!" Charlie said.

Kurt and Charlie played three games and then, just as Charlie was offering his controller to Trevor, Kurt's mother came in with a tray of cut-glass tumblers and cookies.

"Pudding's ready," she said.

Kurt threw himself back against the couch cushions and hid his beer between them. "For fuck's sake, Ma. I'm not twelve."

"Language."

"Thanks, Meemaw." Charlie dipped a finger into one of the tumblers and licked it clean. "I love pudding. I want to rub my balls in it."

"Your what?" Kurt's mother asked.

Charlie started to repeat his statement but Kurt interrupted him. "Storm's brewing," he said, parting the plain red curtains over the couch. "Gonna be a doozy."

Trevor edged up a bit in his chair and looked out. The sky seemed to tilt toward the grass under the weight of a black cloud. An open hand of fanned maple branches squeaked against the glass pane, leafless, and rain began to fall in fat drops onto a window box of weeds and wrought-iron wands bent to look like sunflowers.

"Do you guys have a basement?" Trevor asked.

But no one heard him. Kurt's mother leaned over Charlie to watch the storm and jumped when a bright bolt flashed over the neighbor's house. She fingered the cross on her necklace.

"I just heard on the radio they found poor little Daisy Gonzalez," she said.

"They found her?" Trevor didn't understand. He hadn't told the cop a thing. How had the case been solved so quickly? Who was the hero? Not him. He knew that for sure. Not him.

Kurt's mother nodded. Her eyes were still red and moist. "She's gone, I'm afraid. To meet her Maker."

Everyone was silent for a moment. Then Charlie said, "She went to my school."

Kurt tousled Charlie's hair. "I'm sorry, buddy." But he was looking at Trevor, searchingly. Trevor couldn't say it. He thought of Brianna, the threat she'd made back at the store. His throat kept closing on its own.

"They're not going to give a rat's ass about that girl in a second," said Blue Fish.

"What?" Trevor wished he hadn't drunk that beer or popped one of his pills.

"What what?" Charlie asked. "She went to my school?"

"No, that's not what I mean." Trevor leaned toward the fish tank.

"Let's leave asses out of this for once," hissed Red Fish.

"Give it a rest." Blue Fish blew a line of bubbles at her. "I'm trying to warn him."

"Warn me why? Of what?"

"You okay, buddy?" Kurt asked.

"Lightning," Blue Fish peeped. "Lightning strike. Imminent. Pick us up, half-wit. Pick us up or you'll be sorry."

"Hurry," said Red Fish.

"Hurry hurry," said Blue.

Trevor did as he was told. He lunged forward and grabbed the fish tank, raising it above his head like a barbell. Dirty water sloshed onto his White Swan polo in a heart-shaped stain.

"What the fuck are you doing?" Kurt asked.

"Language," Ma said, and then it hit, the bright light and the purple light, the fire and the traveling burn. The current jumped from the sugar maple next to the window to the TV antenna and traveled through the wall to the socket on the other side. Nails popped and drywall cracked. The window shattered into tiny pieces on the couch. The television fell to the carpet and an acrid smell of smoldering wire filled the room, which was silent now except for a hiss coming from the wall. Kurt and Ma were at Trevor's feet, both of them staring openmouthed at him from their puddle of spilled pudding. Charlie was on his knees over the Nintendo set.

"Shit, Trevor," Kurt said.

"I wasn't lying," Trevor said, his throat open now. His throat a whole road. You could drive a car down it. "I know who did it. Who kidnapped Daisy. It was Brianna Pogue and Josh Seaver. I saw them throw her body under the Spencerville Fun Spot Ferris wheel and bury it sort of."

"Bury it?" Ma asked.

"Sort of?" Kurt said.

"That's all I know, though. I don't know how it happened. I was hanging out at the Fun Spot. I do that sometimes, because, I don't know. It's quiet. Nobody's ever there. Except for that night, of course. And sometimes this teenage girl and her boyfriend. Anyway, it doesn't matter. She's dead. Daisy. She was a beautiful little girl and she's dead and everyone knows now." Trevor stopped and saw that Charlie was staring up at him with huge, admiring eyes.

"You saved them," Charlie said.

Only then did Trevor glance up at the fish, who, seemingly undisturbed, were swimming silently in a circle, working the water into an effervescent whirlpool. He watched them for several minutes, long enough for Kurt and Charlie to gather up the Nintendo set and declare it unscathed, long enough for Ma to stack the pudding dishes in a pyramid on the tray. The fish didn't say anything. They didn't tell him if the storm that had started outside was going to end in Armageddon. They didn't chastise him for waiting this long to tell someone about Daisy. They didn't say if Trevor should run, hide, stick his head in a ditch, or declare his love, because what, after all, did he have to lose?

They didn't even thank him.

Damage Waiting to Happen,
Collateral and Otherwise

(June)

1.

The roof flew off first. No. That's not right. The windows broke, came inside, turned to sparkling grains like sugar on the floor. The drywall died next, became flour. It was like God was saying, *Forget this storm. Make cookies.* Then she changed her mind because the paint cans and brushes and tarps I'd stacked so neatly on shelves in the corner started flying around the room, whirled into a separate and smaller but just as deadly tornado by my bed, which wasn't really a bed, just a futon mattress I borrowed from Rhae Anne. I hid, of course, did what my third-grade teacher, Mrs. Moody, and my mom taught me—I stopped, dropped, and rolled under the nearest couch. Only I didn't have a couch, either. No bed, no couch, just that mattress and a broken satellite chair that served the purpose at the moment.

It wasn't so much the wind as the roar. People like to say, "It was so loud I couldn't hear myself think." That can be a good thing. Things crashed against the concrete. Things smashed and spilled. I cowered. Not because I'm a pansy. Suck it, Benny Bradenton. But because I'm smart.

For a second I did wonder how Mom was. Not Dad. Dad is what Benny Bradentons turn into. But what about Mom in her new Wyndham-on-the-River landominium? Mom in her pearls. Those pearls would save her, I told myself. The pearls and the pills she still snuck although not as often. And maybe her bridge table.

While I worried, the roof left and the ceiling above me followed it, both pulled into the air by an invisible hand and now part of the roar. The hand was coming for me, too, so I clung to a cord I'd taped to the floor. My hair dryer. All that stood between me and certain death. Rhae Anne would love that.

It was all over in a minute and a half, maybe two. While it lasted, I held my chest, wished hard they were real. Someday. I felt my hips. So bony, hairy, too. Round out, I told them. Not that they listened. They couldn't hear me over the freight train barreling through. Round the fuck out.

The paint cans and brushes and tarps were still spinning. I could hear them whipping around my chair and ricocheting off the door and walls. I imagined for a second that I was standing there in the center of the storm in the center of the room, rolled over by the funnel cloud from feet to forehead, transformed like some superhero by the power of nature, stripped and polished and made perfect. No more back fur, no pimples, no penis, just pink, dewy beauty and legs that crossed at the ankles automatically. What once was Wally was now Willa. The end.

Not that this whole thing has ever just been about the looks part, the prettiness. It's a feeling, too, a knowledge, an entire body of it, and I made a promise to God that if she saw fit to let me live through this storm I would do it right, be the woman I was born to be, not the boy or girl everyone expected. I would embrace the sacred feminine, whatever the hell that was, and be a good sister friend to all the ladies, even ones like Una Prokus who hated to get too close to me in case my kind was catching.

But really, after this storm, it wouldn't be a big deal, right? My wig and face and fishnets. Nobody would care. How could they when the world was ending anyway?

Then it was done. Quiet. The roar left, gone as quick as it came. Rain fell in. Soft. Cold. I opened my door, now dented from the paint cans and a mess of white and beige and brown stains, and crept up the stairs. There weren't walls around them anymore. Or a second floor above. The stairs went nowhere. Juan was hiding in the hollow underneath, clutching his basketball. He sang to it like a baby, a Spanish lullaby or something. That Nina person in her trucker hat was next to him as usual. She wasn't singing. She said to me, "You don't pay no rent."

I said, "I live in the utility closet."

"Whatever," she said.

On the other side of the building, people were crying. The Bottoms had been turned upside down. The trees weren't trees anymore. More matchsticks, things you could play with. Cars were stacked on top of each other in twisted metal pillars, and the river had crawled right up on land and lay there like a lizard sunning itself, only there was no sun. Not yet. That would come later. Blue skies and birdsong and the digging out. The cleaning up.

For now, the water lapped at my feet. A huge fish swam out of the old Udall place and made its way across the street. There was something on its back, sort of stuck to it. I leaned in to get a closer look. It was a picture in a broken frame. A square-jawed baseball player with a pair of glittery panties on his face. I grabbed the panties, let the picture drift on by.

2.

Welcome to Miss Kitty's, where every girl's a princess and every man's a king, if not for a day then at least for an hour, or seven minutes. That's the lap-dance limit. Ask Stan McElroy. It's his rule. "Anything longer'll cost 'em more, and if they don't like it, they can lump it."

Is this your first time dancing? Oh well. You look young, is all. I hope you realize what you're getting into here. Miss K's is an institution. A few pervs have tried to have us shut down over the years, but no luck. We're untouchable basically, unless the Board of Health gets wind of what Beans does back there in the kitchen. Whatever you do, don't order the hot wings.

Do you have any questions so far? . . . Stan? Don't bother with Stan. He's in his office most of the day crunching numbers. That's what he calls it. Crunching numbers. Really he's doing coke and talking to his wife on the phone. They can't let an hour go by without talking about something, even if it's just what Stan should have for lunch instead of the hot wings. That's love, I guess. Or one way of doing it. Me and my boyfriend, we're less needy. We give each other our space. Oh, you wouldn't know him. He's a homebody type. Never comes here, thank God. Boyfriends should stay away. If you have one, tell him that. He probably thinks he'll like watching you but he'll hate it. He'll get all eaten up with jealousy. Trust me. It gets ugly around here no joke.

I'll show you the dressing room. That's where you'll spend most of your time between dances although Stan does like it if you mingle with the customers some and there's a little nook over there for giving private couch dances and even privater massages. It's up to you if you want to do that—there's money in it duh, but that's also how you get your stalkers. One stole a girl a few years back. Just took her to like Canada or Greenland or someplace and no one's seen her since.

Oh yeah, Daisy, well. I'm not living under a rock, am I? I'll tell you a secret. That Juan person did it, no doubt in my mind. All the signs point to him, but the pussy cops let him go. Just set him free to menace the rest of us to death and I sincerely hope they don't regret it.

Well, here we are, glitter ground zero. I like to call it the "shit-uation room," mostly because Maria Pinto leaves her shit all over the place for the rest of us to clean up. Maria thinks she runs and rules this place but she's just this side of delusional. Want to know who tips well or doesn't tip at all, ask me. Same goes for where to buy the best baby wipes, how to shave so you don't get bumps, and what to eat between sets so you don't pass out or puke or die. I can hook you up, is what I'm saying. It's no problem. I've done it for lots of girls. I'm by way of being a bit of an ambassador.

What's Colliersville like? It's small, but you probably already knew that. There are the tree streets downtown and the Bottoms at the bottom near the river and Maple Leaf Mobile Home Park in between. Oh, and Wyndham-on-the-River out a ways. Not on the river. Ironic, eh? Everybody knows everybody. Well, except the Ranasack Apartments people, who know each other and not us and us who know each other but not them. Whose fault is that, though, if they won't speak English?

Hey, hey, no offense. I didn't realize. You know what's funny? You actually kind of remind me of this woman who lived here for a while. She was from some island down south. No, not Cuba. I don't know. One of those islands the cruise ships go to. My boyfriend's uncle ordered her from a magazine, I shit you not. She was pretty in your way. Pretty and sad. Superstitious, too. She covered Rita Washburn's yard in plastic fork crosses one time to try to get rid of a pregnancy. Didn't work apparently because she and Josh's uncle have a kid who's probably your age. Or last I heard.

What? . . . That? That's just thunder. NBD. We get a lot of storms in the spring and summer and this season's been a doozy already, but we're fine where we are. Don't listen to Maria. She doesn't know shit about shit.

No, see, if there's a tornado there'll be a siren. And then we can hoof it to the basement. Trust me, you don't want to go down there if you don't have to. It's overrun with rats, and it's also where Stan keeps his mannequin collection. He started stealing them from stores years ago, mostly from the Fort Wayne Sears but JCPenney, too, and Hudson's and Ayres—those girls are the fancy kind, all pointy elbows and chins—and now he's got enough to start an army. Not sure how good they'd be against the terrorists. At the very least, they could scare them to death.

I love that sound, the thunder. Then the rain on the roof. Adds to the atmosphere, don't you think? I like to close my eyes for a minute and pretend I'm in *Flashdance*. . . . Oh. Before your time, probably. So this really beautiful girl welds by day and strips by night and eventually she tries out for the ballet or something but what I like is the love story, her handsome millionaire boss showing up with roses and sweeping her off her feet. I figure, if it can happen to her it can happen to me, right? When it rains like this, I close my eyes and pretend I'm Jennifer Beals dancing with like a waterfall in the background. The problem is, when I open my eyes there aren't any millionaires or waterfalls, just the same loser old men and college boys I see every day, and since I can't really weld I know that I'm pretty much doomed to rot here on this mirrored floor in six-inch heels, getting calluses in my armpits from the pole for the rest of my life.

It'll be different for you, though. You're smart. You give off that vibe. Also, you have the heart-shaped face and teardrop tits guys like. My tits are a mess but no one seems to care that much. It's all about confidence. The strut. Faking it. Hot chicks are a baker's dozen. Guys can't tell hot from fugly, and I'm not really sure they care. . . .

Honestly, I don't really remember. High school happened and some random retail gigs, then this. I was going to go west with my best friend, Frannie, but the night she showed up wasn't a good one and here I am. Just do what I do: tell people you're working your way through medical school. They love that.

Fine, fine, but don't say I didn't warn you about the mannequins. One of them's dressed like the queen of England. Stan has a thing for her. Grab that flashlight, will you? If we make it down there quick we can grab the corner with the least amount of mouse shit.

You shut up, Maria Pinto. Bitch. I wasn't talking to you anyway.

3.

The house was dark and quiet and Daisy was nowhere and Hector was walking from room to room, yelling her name. He was looking in empty closets and throwing blankets on the floor and telling her this wasn't funny, this wasn't a game, she better come out or else. He was throwing open windows and calling for her over and over and then he was outside—how had he gotten there?—and he was jogging around the house, tripping on his lawn furniture and a doll Daisy had left out in the rain. The rain was falling sideways. It pushed against him. Trees were falling, too. He dodged them. Slipping in his socks, Hector promised himself and his dead wife that he would get their girl out, out of the Bottoms and Colliersville and Indiana, out of the entire Midwest bread basket/Bible Belt if he had to, give their Daisy a chance to blossom. Ugh, sorry, Tina baby, he thought. Sorry for the mixed metaphor slash cliché. Bread baskets and blooming flowers. He was not at his best. He was running right into someone's overturned trashcan. *People* magazines and empty cigarette packs and Diet Mountain Dew cans spilled onto the street from its rusty mouth. How had he ended up here? Not just Colliersville but the Bottoms where the Seavers from down the street and the Tucker boys from Maple Leaf often used national holidays as an excuse to turn the entire neighborhood into one big midnight brawl, an adult game of cowboys and Indians, the cowboys (Seavers) armed with BB guns and the Indians (Tuckers) with air cannons that shot potatoes? I hate all of you so much my heart burns, he thought. I hate you with my whole heart. I hate you with the hole in my heart. He wasn't making sense. He didn't have a heart murmur. Not that he knew of anyway. He wanted to throw up.

Hector hadn't eaten much of anything since the sort of tacos at Renee Seaver's. He was starting to see things when he stood up too quickly and his limbs felt full of air. He wasn't teaching anymore. Or was he? Sometimes, when he woke from a fevered nap and floated down the hall, he would find his sophomore history class there waiting for him. The room anyway, the desks in neat rows, and the computers, too, their screens dusty, dark. But no students. The emptiness felt like his fault. In his guilt, he dropped erasers. He was always dropping erasers and when they fell the white dust rose upwards, choked him for a moment, made a pattern on his glasses in the shape of the man on the moon.

He wasn't dropping an eraser now. Too busy. Too needed. He was darting around his yard while the sky came apart around his head. He was looking for her, calling for her still. Daisy. Daisy Face. Flower Power. Powder Puff. Pretty Pants. Honeybreath, Tigger Tail, Bug Bug, Pookie Pie. He remembered the nickname "Pookie Pie," made up when she smashed a piece of pumpkin pie in his face as a joke, but had forgotten *her,* his own daughter. Thanks to a ridiculous phone call from Renee Seaver's uncle during his planning period, Hector had forgotten to pick Daisy up at the bus stop that fateful day, and then Marissa Marino, whom he hated now more than any Seaver, had forgotten her, too, no doubt caught up in her own little world of transcripts, grade inflation, and prom dresses. Daisy was only supposed to be left alone for an hour. After school, Marissa would take over and together they'd watch Little Mermaid, or, at the very least, "Under the Sea" and "Poor Unfortunate Souls" and "Kiss the Girl." That was the plan. What had happened to the plan? What had happened to Hector's entire world? It didn't look like a world anymore. It looked like a soupy fog he was pushing through. He bumped into a wheelbarrow, a clothesline, a car door. Behind his shed, he nearly collided with a group of four figures marching in a line, all of them dressed in Revolution-era garb. There was General Henry Colliers holding a musket and his ditz of a daughter holding her heart and Chief Talking Stick holding a bow and arrow. Horace Beancoop, the eccentric credited with planting all of the trees on the tree streets, was there, too, spreading his seeds and glancing up at the sky every once in a while as if to ascertain whether the falling rain would set them in their spots and give them a chance to grow or wash them out completely. Here they were, in the fog—the entire Colliersville, Indiana history unit in the flesh, prepackaged for easy digestion by his sophomores. The reason he was placed on "administrative leave, indefinite." Hector blinked. They disappeared. He was in his nice neighbor's backyard but didn't know why. The nice neighbor, whose name he suddenly couldn't remember, was yelling at him from her doorway to go inside because "there's a tornado on."

There's a tornado on. Hector swore that's what the woman said. Hector yelled back, I know, I know, that's why I'm here, I'm trying to find my daughter, she can't be out in this. Hector ran down the hill toward the river. It was swollen and foamy and filled with trash and trees. He was scanning the water for a glimpse of black pigtail, metal chair, small hand. He was watching a great blue heron, spooked from the shallows, lift its way into the air and disappear around the bend, body like a compass needle pointing north. He was pulling off his shirt and pants and preparing to jump in when his neighbor grabbed him and held him back.

"She's not there," the nice neighbor said. She had cut her hair. She looked younger and smaller somehow. "She's not here. Come on, Hector. Now. I mean it. You need to come with me."

4.

Once I had two sons. Now I have none. One son died. The war. He didn't know I existed. The other thinks he's a girl so I guess in a way you could say I have a daughter but she won't talk to me—considers me the devil incarnate—so there you go.

Once I had a whole farm, a booming business. That can be taken away, too. Even here in America, land of the dream and the free and the brave, what you work so hard to build from the ground up can be snatched away and given to someone else. Just like that. All my cows. The machines. Years and years of labor. My father's land, in my family since William Henry Harrison was governor of the Indiana Territory, gone. Frannie said she heard the farm was going to be cleared for a shopping center, a tacky strip mall with a Wal-Mart and a Shoe Carnival and a Subway. A once noble plot turned into a playground for the poor. I don't know where Frannie gets her information, but I guess that's what's called "spreading the wealth." Robbing from the rich and giving to the undeserving. Hey, Robbing Hood. Hey, Barack Hussein Obama, why don't you go back where you came from?

I have nothing left to lose. The tornado, wide as my old barn, is over my left shoulder. I'm racing it. It looks like a wall of insects, a spinning spiral of ticks, and out of habit I start talking to Birdy in the passenger seat about the year all the cows got heartwater and died before we could vaccinate them. Convulsing in the fields, the poor fuckers, legs up and moaning. Terrible. The worst night of our lives. Right, babe? Only Birdy's not there. A handful of turkey jerky is. And a gallon of Mountain Dew and some PowerBars. It's what I wanted and I have to remember that.

Frannie said no one will find me where I'm going. There's a wall around the place two stories high and three feet thick. Turrets here and there. They make their own guns and everyone has one, Frannie, her eighty-five-year-old neighbor lady, even the kids. Three-D printers, Frannie whispers to me at night over the phone, her voice deeper than I remember. There's nothing they can't do. She says Hank Seaver and his militia are nothing, are basically Greenpeace compared to her people. Let my people be your people, she says.

State lines, here I come. I'll cross five before I'm done.

The thing I don't understand are the birds I hear on my way out of town. Shrieking like there's no tomorrow. Three hit my windshield, crack it so it's hard to see. What the hell. The birds fall dead and broken necked to the concrete. Red first, then yellow, then green like a traffic light. The only one for miles.

5.

Dear Frannie,

There's a tree in my bathroom and a fishing boat in my bedroom and I'm in this shelter, which is really the elementary school, wondering where you are.

Randy's not here, either. Got a call, I guess. Emergency at the Fun Spot. Emergency at the Fun Spot. Sounds like a porn video. Or a really bad horror movie. Remember when we used to waste whole weekends watching *Friday the 13th* and *A Nightmare on Elm Street* with Brianna Pogue? All those dead pretty girls. You said you wanted to be one, and while Brianna didn't get it, I did. You wanted to disappear when you were still young and beautiful and leave behind a whole town to mourn. Well, mission accomplished.

I don't know why I write to you. You never answer me. I'm not even sure you see my messages. It's like e-mailing a ghost. Your mom told me the people/cult members you're living with screen all your calls and read your mail and don't let you have Internet because it's the devil's playground.

Randy would probably agree with them about the Internet. He thinks all I do is play *Candy Crush* and get on Facebook and that's sort of true. What else is there to do?

Anyway, I just wanted to tell you about the tornado that came through tonight. Hence the tree and the boat. My woods are gone and I watched them leave. There was no siren, no warning. I thought I might die, see Kenny soon, but some nice firemen came to rescue me and bring me here and so I lived to write to you another day. Which is ridiculous I know because even if you hear about this storm somehow, you won't worry about me. You'll be thinking of Helman and his cows. Here's some news for you—the cows don't live here anymore and Helman's still an asshole. He's always been one and always will be one and the fact that you can't seem to accept that proves love is nothing but damage waiting to happen, collateral and otherwise.

Speaking of damage, everyone here is saying insurance won't pay to fix our houses. An act of God, they say, eyes rolled upward. A couple people from the Ranasack Apartments are in the corner crying because someone died when the second floor collapsed. Two someones, I think. A few bit it at the Maple Leaf Mobile Home Park, too. Tossed, crushed, smothered, like a salad. Or a Waffle House scramble. Order up.

Everyone on the tree streets and in Wyndham-on-the-River survived unscathed, I guess because Jesus loves rich people? What would your fellow cult members say to that? And why did your lovely God see fit to spare me?

My home for the night is a canvas cot and a musty blanket in the middle of the gym. No privacy, but Pastor Rush, who made us all join him in prayer a few minutes ago, thinks we should be grateful for our lives. To my right is a girl who keeps saying, "Fuck this." She's got a book bag and a fish in a bowl. To my left is a middle-aged dude stinking of whiskey. Yuhl Butz seems to be running the operation, which isn't really an operation at all. No triage, just chaos. And the girls' bathroom toilets are clogged because, according to Yuhl's wife, Pearl, a "Maple Leaf skank" flushed a bunch of pads down them.

"Can't they read the signs?" Pearl says to me. She's holding her sticky-eyed poodle.

"There aren't any," I tell her. "This is the elementary school."

"I got my period when I was ten," Pearl says.

"So did I," I say.

And so did you.

A man from Fort Wayne came to drop off a metric ton of bottled water and some Meals Ready to Eat. How nice. And oh dear Frannie darling, I hate to be the one to break it to you, but that same man just announced to the room that Helman Yoder's missing. MIA. It was all I could do not to clap. A few Ranasack Apartments people did clap. And they woohooed, too. Screw Helman. You know what he did to you. Don't talk to me about gray areas and romantic fogs and things open to interpretation. Don't you dare say anything about forgiveness or bygones being bygones. I've heard all that before and I'm tired of it. I'm so tired.

What I'm really trying to say is come home. Care or something. And call your mother.

6.

In the blackness and the wind, Randy's flashlight seems a strobe. But it's really his nerves that make it shake. We can't believe our eyes. This whole time, she's been right here. This whole time. Jack leaves, can't handle it, but Irv Peoples's little dog doesn't move a muscle. He sits ramrod straight, nose in the air, guarding her. Anyone tries to get close, he snaps. It's the little dogs you have to watch out for.

"Call him off," Randy says to Irv. Randy's yelling but still it's hard to hear. The wind and the rain are drowning out almost everything. The Ferris wheel and its parasite tree groan above us. "We have to get her and get out of here." There's radio talk of a tornado touching down in Spencerville but I couldn't care less. Not now. Bring it on.

"But isn't she evidence? We can't move her."

Randy looks at me like I did this. "We can and we will."

We're all soaking wet and I'm so sad I want to join Jack, who's leaning his fat head against the ticket booth, but I stay where I am and look. I don't know why I look. The wind's trying to cover my eyes with my own hair, but I go ahead and follow the flashlight beam because. I don't know. I can't explain.

Randy's the one with the bag. He brought it from the station. Em found it under a pile of old phone books in the back room. The only one in stock. It's clear plastic, which why the fuck? But never mind. Not important. Irv and Randy and I go in and grab what's there. Randy zips the bag around the body and Irv and I lift her. It's so dark we can't tell where our own feet are and there's some tripping, some stumbling. We do not drop her, though. We do not do that. Randy goes back for the wheelchair and throws it in his trunk. Then we're all in our own cars where we wanted to be all along because we can cry in quiet and privacy and that's when I called you, baby, because it's when I feel like this that I need you the most.

The thing is I can't unsee what I saw. A bony shadow of a girl and the wheelchair in the background holding her together. Like a frame or something. A picture frame. I want to see her the way she was, the way she looks in all the flyers all over town, but now there's this image in my mind and I don't know what to do with it. Please tell me what to do with it.

Book of Shame

(July)

Viv stoked the fire blue hot and high in the neighbor's burn barrel late at night when she knew Trevor was dead asleep and the Smiths all far away on a camping trip to Michigan. She'd gotten a postcard from them that very morning—*Tahquamenon Falls State Park!* it said on the front in fat yellow letters. *Wish You Were Here.* She would burn it, too, along with the scrapbook and her favorite housedress and *Olé! Mexico from Agua to Zapata*, the DVD about Mexican cultural traditions Trevor'd ordered for her off the Internet.

All of it in some way reminded her of Daisy, poor little Daisy Gonzalez, whom Viv Hochstetler had never met but felt she knew, inside and out, like she knew Trevor and Lina Lordell, the no-nonsense detective from the Women's Channel *Primetime Mystery Movie Nights*. Unlike Trevor and Lina, though, Daisy was dead and so there was no more knowing her, and the scrapbook Viv had kept since the day she disappeared now seemed not only tacky and voyeuristic, but also unkind, ridiculous, sinful.

Viv's father had taught her how to build a fire. Newspapers then sticks then more papers. Like a lasagna. *Always use dry wood,* he said. *Never turn your back on the flames.* She burned the housedress first. The faded pansy smock had served as Viv's veritable uniform for the last several weeks and now the sight of it and its white buttons and yellow scalloped sleeves was hateful. Viv was amazed how long it took to flake to ash, the size 22 tag staring her in the face the entire time like an insult or a dare. How had Viv let herself get so fat? Henry, had he lived past forty, would be stunned, she thought, to see her now. She'd always been plump and he liked her that way—said she was like a sturdy glass of good beer: *My little mug of imperial stout!* he'd said—but this was too much. She never got near her scale anymore, afraid the needle would fly past the 250 mark and right out into space. Even standing at the burn barrel hurt. Her knees wanted to buckle but she wouldn't let them. Not today. Starting now, things would be different. No more food comas. No more falling asleep with a mostly eaten pie in her lap. No more living vicariously through motherless wheelchair-bound girls. She was a mother herself, wasn't she, and it was time she started doing her job. Clearly Trevor needed her to do more than pack his lunch and remind him to take his meds. Somewhere along the line, she'd failed him. How else to explain the fact that Trevor, her Trevor Lever, had known all along what had happened to Daisy and somehow found it fine to say nothing? How else to account for the fact that her sweet son had gone to work every day and fallen asleep in his recliner every night like he wasn't harboring a dark and horrible secret? Instead of going to the police immediately with what he knew, Trevor had watched as Viv padded her Book of Shame. He'd even helped her add to her stash of morbid memorabilia. It was her fault. It was all her fault.

The crescent moon hanging above her house sent out a bright, crooked smile of agreement. Seriously, Viv Hochstetler. What have you been doing with your life? Even before you let yourself become obsessed with a missing crippled girl, you were up to no good. Cooking and cleaning some, sure, but less and less with each passing year and gained pound, and no job or direction to speak of. Living off Henry's insurance money and Social Security, volunteering at the church when asked but usually preferring to stay home with Lina Lordell and Trevor and Mr. Greenjeans because . . . well, why? Because, when one ventures into the outside world, one is almost sure to meet a twelve-year-old boy or even three of them and everyone knows twelve-year-old boys are cruel to fat people, fat women especially. Viv didn't think she could bear one more whale joke, one more "Your mama's so fat . . ." At home, no one noticed her weight. The TV didn't talk back and Trevor rarely spoke unless spoken to. Likewise as silent were the pictures of Daisy she glued in her scrapbook, but Viv knew, just from looking at the girl's round black eyes, that she understood. What had twelve-year-old boys said to her as she wheeled herself around town? Did they tape terrible signs to her back? Throw things at her useless legs? Firecrackers. Spitballs. Sticks.

Viv imagined these things and rotted inside the walls of her home, pinning all her hopes on someone, anyone, finding Daisy Gonzalez alive. The scrapbook was her way of gathering evidence, of being a part of it all. Making a difference, at least that's what she thought as she painstakingly glued every article, every photo, every fragile piece of newsprint and MISSING, REWARD flyer and clue she could find to the scrapbook's bright white pages, securing each souvenir with yellow, daisy-shaped stickers that, when scratched, gave off the smallest hint of sweet scent.

What folly. What vanity. What madness.

And who was to say that Viv's sinfulness hadn't helped bring the Lord's attention to, and fury down on, the town in the form of the F5 that had turned Colliersville, or parts of it anyway, into a veritable wasteland? Viv could not say this for sure, because God had seen fit to spare her house at the last minute. All she and Trevor had to deal with were some branches littering their front walk and several hours without power, whereas people like the Smiths were looking at months of homelessness and expensive roof repairs and mold removal. As she stood there, Viv could hear bucket trucks roaring down Beacon Street. Probably to work on the power lines downed during the storm. She thought of the suffering of the poor people living in Maple Leaf Mobile Home Park and prayed for the souls of those who lost their lives not just in that neighborhood, but in the Bottoms and downtown as well. There was Greg Steele and Pam Seaver and Jason Nelson and Stan McElroy and some poor wayward girl named Cherry. Also a man named Ulises and a woman named Elena, living at the Ranasack Apartments, and Gina Holt and every single one of her pet chinchillas. Helman Yoder, too. Found in his car, which had been tossed into the river and then got hung up on a log, water streaming through the windows, stripping Helman naked as a baby. Randy Richardville was quoted in that morning's *Record* as saying there would probably be more dead to add to that number as search-and-rescue teams combed through the wreckage. A travesty. And one for which Viv might be at least partly to blame. . . .

She glanced back down at the burn barrel. When the housedress was nothing more than embers and a few sheets of gray pansy-patterned cotton, she tossed in the postcard, on which her neighbors had written, as a postscript, *How are the cleanup efforts going? Any new Daisy developments?* Everyone, even the atheistic Smiths with their Buddha statue out front and their maypole out back—both, incidentally, destroyed in the storm, carried off, in fact, to parts unknown—knew about Viv's obsession. It was embarrassing.

Thou shalt have no other god before me. Viv had had many gods before him. Trevor. He was her first. Her little angel on earth. How she'd worshipped him, even with his faults, his little slips into strange silences and unexplained bursts of anger and despair. The drugs and Dr. Nelson had helped and later the job at the grocery store. Still, even a doting mother had to admit Trevor hadn't quite turned out exactly as she'd hoped. There would be no grandchildren. She was sure of that. And no wedding to plan and lose weight for.

Food. That was another false idol of hers. Cakes, mostly, and ice cream and sometimes, in a pinch, candy. Puddings, too. Anything sweet. Not that she didn't enjoy every now and then a fried chicken or a good roast, but she could say no to those things. She had no power over sugar. Just the smell of it made her heart beat faster. Especially after Henry died and all those nice people from the church piled her countertops high with condolence. So many cakes, so little time. There'd been cold cuts and veggie trays and chips and dips, of course, but the cakes. Yellow, red velvet, carrot, white, confetti, spice, pineapple upside down. Chocolate, obviously. The cakes had crowned the whole offering like iced jewels and Viv approached them each morning with what she hoped was the proper amount of reverence. *Thank you, Lord, for the bounty I am about to receive. Here's to you, Henry.*

She planned to put several in the freezer for safekeeping, but instead she and Trevor devoured them all in a matter of days, and when the last piece of carrot cake disappeared, they both stood up from the table at the same time and wandered outside to lie in the backyard in a daze of sugar sweat and shame.

Daisy. Her final god. For the past month Daisy Gonzalez had controlled almost every aspect of Viv's existence. She used the girl as an excuse not to shower at regular intervals—who knew when the news might interrupt one of Viv's soap operas with an update, a break in the case?—or cook nutritious meals or keep her home in tolerable order. Viv and Trevor had lived exclusively on store-bought confections and microwave dinners. The trash can overflowed with plastic containers flecked with food and mold. Cat hair and dust bunnies had taken over. They rolled on the floor like tumbleweed. Mr. Greenjeans complained constantly. He liked things neat. So had Viv, but that was before. Before Daisy disappeared and Viv had succumbed to a kind of sick excitement not unlike what she'd felt on her wedding day—terror and anxiety mixed with a delicious anticipation and a sense that the boredom, the suffocating sameness of the day-after-day existence in Colliersville, Indiana, had finally come to an end. Viv Hochstetler now lived in a place where things happened. Not to her, but all the same, she was a witness, like the funny and sad and funny/sad characters who, each week, orbited around Lina Lordell in a dizzying circle of half-truths and fake testimony and, sometimes, real and estimable grace. Viv, too, was a witness to history. Hence the scrapbook. Admittedly, Viv had splurged on the pretty gingham cover and acid-free paper, but didn't a little girl being kidnapped warrant a little extravagance, not to mention a few more applications to her God than might be considered strictly necessary or in keeping with his teachings? She had hoped and prayed for Daisy's safe return so often, cast her eyes up to the crucifix in the kitchen with such concentration and vehemence, she wondered if even Jesus himself might tire of her constant requests.

"Please, Jesus, save little Daisy and deliver her back to the loving arms of her poor daddy. Please, Jesus, lord in heaven, hallowed be thy name. Thy kingdom come, thy will be done . . ."

She prayed to Jesus but thought only of herself, and that was blasphemy. That was vile wickedness, as was her fantasy of Daisy's eventual discovery by a nice teenage volunteer who would find the girl perhaps in a park or a shed somewhere, shaken but largely unharmed and fully ready for her cameo on the evening news, after which Viv would stride out her own front door, upright and healthy as you please, and walk—yes, walk—the full four miles to the Gonzalez place in the Bottoms and hand Mr. Gonzalez her scrapbook, wrapped up tight and pretty in a pink ribbon, a token of her joy and sisterly love. The sheer arrogance of such fantasies! Like she was some sort of latter-day Moses humping his tablets down the mountain, only this book wouldn't be instructional per se, it would be atonement—a fat, sticky-in-places apology for all the unkind words hurled at Daisy and her people ever since Helman Yoder had recruited a hundred illegal immigrants to milk his cows and then left them to their own devices when the dairy was shuttered. Viv was well acquainted with the prevailing opinion of Colliersville's native population toward Mexicans of all kinds, even Daisy and Hector Gonzalez's kind, which was legal and documented and pretty much as American as apple pie, and it was a hateful thing to behold. Had a gaggle of twelve-year-old boys called Daisy a dirty spic? Told her to go back where she came from, even though where she came from was here? This very town. This very state. This very soil with its clay and silt and sand. Oh Daisy. Poor Daisy. No wonder she had wilted and died.

Viv had bought the DVD *Olé! Mexico from Agua to Zapata* as a way to educate herself against the ignorance of people like Shellie Pogue and the entire Seaver clan, who thought the solution to illegal immigration was to build an eight-hundred-mile humming fence along the Rio Grande that would electrocute men, women, and children upon contact. That or just shoot to kill anything moving in the desert. "Lizard or otherwise," Shellie had said once, and Viv had cried that night alone in her bedroom because she'd said nothing. Like mother like son, she thought now. It was all her fault.

Viv watched *Olé!* three times all the way through and many times in fits and starts, pausing to ask Trevor questions and turning on the subtitles when the accents of the nice lady narrator and her sombrero'ed puppet friend got a little too thick for her to understand. The DVD, which didn't so much burn as melt over the sad remains of her housedress, gave an overview of everything from Mexico's most beloved artists and holidays to its main exports and key historical figures. Viv kept returning and returning to the part about the Day of the Dead, all those beautiful, sugared skulls. "That's how we should do it," she'd told Trevor one day while they wolfed down Hot Pockets in front of the television, and what she meant was *not forget them.* Not forget men like Henry who died young simply because remembering them was too painful. We should dance on their graves, she thought. Sing their favorite songs. Talk about them to anyone who will listen. Tell stupid stories and cry on shoulders and wail through the night. Laugh out loud because, in the end, we're all in this together. This perverse idea of dealing with death like we're proper people, like we're decorous and genteel and well mannered, and death is something to be buried cleanly and without feeling, is killing us, she wanted to shout. Killing us.

Daisy's funeral would take place in two days. Viv read about the arrangements in the paper that morning right after she finished the article on Brianna Pogue and Josh Seaver being indicted for manslaughter. Both had attempted courtroom confessions of a sort and Viv read their stories clean through, trying to think of the two with something like Christian kindness but couldn't. Brianna Pogue and Josh Seaver abducted Daisy Gonzalez on a lark. They took pictures of the girl playing basketball and spending time with Juan Cardoza and, having coaxed Daisy into the old Udall place for the night, sent the photos to the police station. They thought if they built up enough suspicion against Juan and were successful in talking Daisy into blaming Juan for the incident, they would at the very least get Juan fired from the janitorial post he "stole" from Josh. They knew Juan wouldn't be a good advocate for himself and hoped the police would hand him an attempted kidnapping charge, maybe even slap him with an intent to harm. They planned to send Daisy home to Hector the next day. "So we get our revenge," Brianna said, "and nobody gets hurt." But then they woke to find Daisy killed by a support beam that had fallen in the night. It was an accident, Brianna swore. A stupid, horrible, tragic accident, and Brianna said she and Josh would never be the same. "So really we've had our punishment already," Brianna said. "You don't even have to put us in jail. We're, like, in jail already. The jail of our own minds."

Viv tossed that morning's paper onto the blaze and watched Brianna's face and Josh's five o'clock shadow curl to black, then bone white. Viv supposed the devil was getting a room ready for them in hell.

She'd saved the scrapbook for last because the fire was at its hottest and it hurt her the most to give it up. The book was almost as fat as Mr. Greenjeans and its contents spilled onto the ground. Viv had to crouch next to the barrel and gather up a handful of articles and photographs bleeding ink onto her hands. Bending over was a catastrophe. Her hair stuck and melted to the side of the barrel. Her back ached with the effort of hoisting herself upright. I am a joke, she thought. I have grown ridiculous.

She held the book, pages down and fanned out over the flames, watching as they ate up Daisy's pretty face and a story about Hector Gonzalez's private pain. Next to burn was an article about a rash of anti-Mexican vandalism that had broken out in the Bottoms. Then some recipes for Mexican hot chocolate and flan and another article about Hector, who had been put on temporary leave from the school. Viv held on to the book as long as she could, until the heat singed her skin and her fingernails seemed to expand. Then she let it drop down into the ash, a gray cloud bursting upward into her open eyes. The sting. The choking and falling back. It was what she deserved.

When it was all gone, when everything was smoke and trash, Viv flopped down onto the cold grass and stared up at the sky, thinking about Mexico, all their dead, of suns and sons, marigolds and mothers. Daisy had had a mother but she died in the same accident that left the little girl a paraplegic. Trevor Hochstetler had a mother and it was time she started showing up.

The moon looked like a scooped hand reaching out to cup a neck. To support or to strangle? Viv didn't know which. She'd have to stand up eventually. She'd have to go in. She closed her eyes. Her stomach growled. Down, boy, she thought, rubbing it in a circular motion. Down.

Enemies

(July)

He hadn't put flowers on Joy's grave for weeks, not since the tornado and the Mexican mess and the drawn-out settlement sessions with Maria Pinto and her lawyer. Today he brought tea roses because they'd been on sale at White Swan. Also, with their small buds and delicate coloring, they struck him as something a little girl might like. Not that Joy ever had the chance to be a little girl. Dolly delivered her stillborn at eight months, so Joy never got to open her eyes or kick her legs or cry out against the injustice of it all. He would never forget as long as he lived her tiny perfect face when they wiped it clear of blood. The bloom there.

He put the roses, slightly wilted now from the heat, on Joy's headstone and said a short prayer. The prayer was always the same—Dear Lord, bless her and keep her. We loved her so. She brought us joy. Amen.

Which was true. She had brought them joy. Those were probably the happiest months of his and Dolly's life together. All that planning, all that hope. Decorating the nursery, which was now

Dolly's sewing room. They'd tried to have another but it had come to nothing and so they didn't have a family; they simply had a life. They watched TV most nights, fell asleep in front of Jay Leno. They cooked on weekends, big meals that took a lot of time to make because they had so much of it to use and get through. And they went for drives in the country while listening to talk radio. They dreamed about getting a farmhouse and a few acres. Dolly said, "How about horses? Two to start. And maybe a few goats." Chuck nodded his head sure, knowing that they'd never get around to any of it. It was nice to think about it, though. To imagine a different sort of day.

"Mr. Breeder?"

Chuck turned and there was Maria Pinto, clutching a bouquet of carnations. Also crying, by the shadowed look of her eyes.

"Hello," he said.

He hadn't seen Maria since the final settlement conference, when, on the advice of his lawyer, Chuck agreed to give her the full amount she asked for. Eighty thousand dollars, to be paid in installments over the course of eight years. He wasn't, as he'd burst out, made of money. Did they think he was some kind of gangster? "I run a Laundromat, for God's sake!" He was ashamed to find he was shaking. "You wanted to break me? Congratulations. I'm broken." He was even more ashamed of that admission. Why had he shown such weakness in the presence of his enemies?

Maria was paying her tardy respects to Nina Morales, the woman behind the blood curse, who had died of a heart attack at the height of a heat wave. Mr. Aguilar and Mrs. Gutierrez discovered Nina's body on the Fourth of July. They found her, slumped over a chair near a leaking window, fireworks exploding just outside and painting her already blue face bright blue. And red. And white. It was a smell situation. Sad. The whole thing. Sad. But Mr. Aguilar and some of the other men thought it funny—a nurse dying alone in the condemned apartments with no one to help her. Ironic, they said, also because Nina hadn't died in the tornado like Ulises and Elena. Maria slapped them upside the head every chance she got. "You don't even know what that word means."

Maria hadn't been able to attend Nina's funeral because of the settlement conference and so every Saturday since she placed a bouquet of carnations on the small pink stone they'd all pitched in for. It was the least she could do. That, and give $100 toward the headstone fund Mrs. Gutierrez got going because Nina had no family. Even Basketball Juan had forked over $50. He and Nina had been friends of a sort.

"How are you?" Maria asked Mr. Breeder. The question was a matter of politeness, a habit. She wasn't really interested in his answer.

"Fine," he said. "Just fine. And you?"

"Fine, too," she said.

Seeing Mr. Breeder here was strange and Maria didn't like it because he looked sad and like he might have a secret. She preferred keeping things simple between them—he was a bigot, she was a warrior on the side of right, but she worried she hadn't really done much to advance any cause. The blood curse had been Nina's idea anyway—Maria didn't really understand it—and walking by the Beacon Street sidewalk blotch was a little like waking up with a hangover and shameful flashbacks of sluttish behavior the night before. The stain reminded her of things she would just as soon forget.

An unintended consequence of the blood curse was that Hector Gonzalez now had a daily reminder of the very place where his wife had died and his daughter was made a cripple. Had Nina known, she would perhaps have had second thoughts about spilling blood just there. It was Brianna Pogue who brought that piece of town history back to the forefront of people's minds. Maria heard all about it a week ago while flipping channels. What she'd wanted was the weather but what she found was a morning cable access talk show with Brianna, pasty in prison-issued orange, as the guest. Seated on a beige couch next to a large fake fern and an empty bookcase, Brianna looked thinner but otherwise unchanged by her month behind bars. Just as Maria was going to turn the TV off in disgust, Brianna blurted out that three years before, she saw Tina, Daisy's mother, and little Daisy herself get run over by Diana Seaver and her Irish limb-salesman lover. They were in the man's truck, Brianna said, and she knew that because limbs kept falling out of it. Arms, hands, legs. "You name it," Brianna said.

"Are you positive?" asked the soft-voiced host. "You want to be careful not to falsely accuse people on live TV."

"Why?"

"You could be sued."

"Do you think I care about that now?"

Brianna admitted that at the time of the hit-and-run, she was tripping balls and did not trust her own eyes, but that over the years she'd grown more and more convinced that what she saw was what really happened. "I'm as sure about that as I'll ever be about anything." Then she shared with the host, a demure woman in a black skirt suit, a stage-whispered theory that if she and Josh had left town after Daisy died they would not simply be committing the same sin as Diana Seaver and the Irishman but would, in effect, become them.

The host was confused. "Can you elaborate?"

"It's like we wouldn't be just ourselves anymore," Brianna explained. "We would be Diana and that salesman, too. We would inherit their sins. Our souls would merge. Maybe our bodies, too. You know, the Doppler effect?"

"I think you mean 'doppelgänger,'" the host said.

"Whatever," Brianna said. "Magic is what I'm talking about. The black kind."

Maria shook her head to rid it of the memory—of course Brianna Pogue had found magical thinking in prison—and peeked past Mr. Breeder's shoulder at a small stone angel.

"So," he said. He shuffled left to hide the grave, but Maria had already seen it: JOY BREEDER, BELOVED DAUGHTER, 1976. No second date. The stone, next to Nina's and just as modest, was somewhat sunken. Gray granite. A reluctant grave, whereas the monument right to the west, Daisy Gonzalez's grave, was large, looming, stacked high with fresh flowers and ferns.

Thirty-four years ago, Mr. Breeder had had a daughter. So long ago. Maria wondered if Mr. Breeder's memories of Joy were like those Maria had of her childhood home in Mexico City and the ones her Ranasack friends cherished of their lives before Colliersville—wavering images at the back of the mind, brief and shifting flashes of beautiful and sad and funny moments mostly divorced from pain because it was hard to imagine they'd ever happened in the first place.

She had assumed many of her neighbors would finally go home to Mexico after the tornado, but instead all decided to stay, in large part because the Ranasack Apartments were being renovated to be both "livable" and "green." Willa Yoder of all people had launched a Go-Fund-Me campaign to raise money for a new roof and then, thanks to some Facebook shares and a spot on MSNBC about the tornado damage and the former dairy workers left homeless, a few anonymous donors kept on giving until there was enough to gut the place and redo the wiring, the plumbing, and the interiors. There was talk of putting in a laundry room, a play area for kids, maybe even a gym, and Pastor Rush and Ruby Rodgers had seen to it that the building was handed over to the county for Section 8 status. Everyone was going to be allowed to keep their original apartments, only those apartments would look nothing like the ones they'd moved into. There would be up-to-date appliances and large windows that let in a healthy amount of natural light and bathtubs instead of camp showers. The work, much of it done by the residents themselves, was scheduled to be completed the following spring. In the meantime, Helman Yoder's former workers/tenants were being housed by volunteers around town. Maria was staying in Helen Garrety's spare room, Juan and Mr. Aguilar were with Irv Peoples, Rosa Torres and her two kids, the now infamous family booted out of the Laundromat by Mr. Breeder, were with Shannon Washburn. The housing program, also engineered by Willa, had likewise garnered some national attention. Colliersville was being hailed as a triumph of "tolerance and caring" in a country ripped apart by racial tensions. A Stetson-wearing musician in Nashville was writing a song about it.

The whole thing had turned Nina's stomach. She told Maria that, far from being a show of empathy and man's humanity to man, the housing program was "bullshit white-guilt charity bullshit" and the news coverage of it and the apartment building remodel was "bullshit just plain shitty bullshit." She refused to leave the apartments and settle temporarily with Shellie Pogue, who'd invited her to stay in Brianna's old room, saying she might hate white people, but she hated being a houseguest even more. And then she died before the cranes came out.

What would Gordy/Ramon have thought of this unlikely turn of events? This transformation in town sentiment, brought about, Maria supposed, by the tornado, Daisy's death, and the national spotlight focused right on Colliersville's worst warts? Gordy's article, in which he referred to her as "Yolanda" (Yolanda?!) and "both the siren and the song," certainly could take no credit. Maria hated it, the entire piece, found it insulting and condescending, short-sighted and long-winded. Talk about your bullshit shitty bullshit. It didn't even mention Daisy or Hector Gonzalez or the so-called blood curse, even though it was published just as the search parties were gearing up and the blood was still drying. Probably, Maria assumed, because the minute Ramon/Gordy left Colliers-ville, the town ceased to be real to him. Pretentious prick.

Still, she missed him, truth be told longed for him. Not for the days at the dairy. Those were awful. Those were hell. But for their nights in their apartment, the movie watching they did and the cuddling and the sex. More than that, though, she just wanted to sit at the kitchen table and eat with him. To see him across from her looking at her the way he did. No man had ever made her feel so cherished. Or so cast off. Not even Larry Peters, who the min-ute Maria dumped him took up with another former Miss Kitty's stripper, a young clueless girl from Tennessee with skin like a peach and a habit of saying "all y'all." All the time. With Larry, out of sight was out of mind. Gordy, on the other hand, had tried to reconnect, to reconcile. Maria had a mountain of letters from him at home. Real letters. All of them saying basically the same thing—I love you. Forgive me. Come to New York. They were good letters and that was the only reason she hadn't burned them or thrown them in the trash along with the baseball cap and deodorant and mix CDs he'd left behind.

"When do you suppose they'll get around to fixing that?" Maria asked Mr. Breeder, who was hitching up his pants and staring at a twenty-foot section of wrought-iron fence on the west side of the cemetery, bent and twisted toward the sky by the tornado. The cemetery's only storm-related casualty, it looked like an enormous tree trunk. A few cardinals perched on the uppermost tendrils.

"I heard they're taking bids right now," Chuck said. "They want it to be up before the cold weather hits."

"That's nice," Maria said.

"Yeah," Chuck said.

"Well." Maria pulled her hair off her neck and fanned the sweat away. "I was just leaving."

"Me too," Chuck said. "Me too."

The sun was hot and bright behind Maria's head and Chuck found it difficult to look directly at her. It had always been hard to look at her, both because he hated her and because she was so beautiful. He knew that if he spent too much time on her face he wouldn't hate her anymore. He would want her and then what? He would dream of her? He already did and in his dreams she hovered over him like an angel, naked and soft skinned and glittery, black hair blowing upward, breasts hanging down, and what was wrong with him anyway he needed to have his head examined he was at his own child's grave for God's sake and what if Dolly knew what he was thinking she would kill him and she had every right. Sometimes it was terrible being a man. It was the worst thing.

For a long time after the "No Mexicens" mess, Dolly wouldn't speak to him. She said that the man she married would never have done such an ignorant, racist, unfeeling thing. Then she moved out of their bedroom into her sewing room and stopped having her meals with him. Chuck had thought he would never experience the kind of misery he felt after Joy's untimely death, but being shut out by Dolly was worse. She was his best friend, his only friend really. He couldn't eat or sleep or finish a crossword without her. So, gradually, he became disconnected from his life, and the Laundromat, which, like Dolly, seemed almost an extension of himself, was no longer a safe space. To begin with, there was that bloodstain to step over every day. And sometimes people protested in front of the shop, only a handful and they were generally peaceful but still. Chuck started staying home more, paying Shannon Washburn overtime to open and close and make the bank deposits, and he hired one of the Tucker boys, the nice one, to help her.

And then the e-mails started coming in. E-mails and letters and phone calls from Bob in Tennessee and Cheryl in Alabama and Roy in Utah and Lori in West Virginia and Lee in Idaho and George in Ohio and Travis in Arkansas and the overwhelming Texas contingent—Becky from San Antonio and Wes from Lubbock and Vic from Fort Worth and John from Waco and on and on and on. Hundreds and then thousands of e-mails and letters and calls from people who swore allegiance to Chuck's "cause" and vowed to defend him, with force if necessary. And to donate money should he need it to pay his legal fees and get "that Pinto bitch to shut her wetback cakehole."

"You know who these people are, right?" Dolly asked in a rare moment of loquaciousness. She had a pile of letters in her hand and was headed for the recycling bin. "The 'organization' they belong to? The cause they're so eager to trumpet? The KKK. Congratulations, Chuck. Your biggest fans wear white sheets and burn crosses and lynch people. Good work."

He got a new phone number and e-mail address and threw most of his mail right into the trash. He dreamed of being part of the witness protection program.

"I don't like it here," Maria said to him now. It was as if she could read his mind. "I never did. I think I might be moving." Then she clamped her hand over her mouth, surprised to have confided that much to him.

"Oh good," Chuck said. "I mean, I'm not glad that you're leaving. Only that you have the opportunity."

"Thanks to you," Maria said, laughing awkwardly.

Chuck bowed and some coins fell out of his pocket. A few were pesos, the edges scarred by Scottie Horne's screwdriver. "You're very welcome." He picked up the coins.

"Well," Maria said.

"Well," Chuck said. "So, where?"

"Where what?"

"Where might you be moving to?"

"Oh." Maria twisted a lock of her hair. "New York, I think." Now that it was out, she realized it was exactly what she wanted to do. To go to Gordy, to give their love a chance. "Might as well take my bite out."

"While you're still young."

"Right."

Chuck and Dolly were talking of taking a trip to New York themselves, at Christmastime maybe, to shop and see a Broadway show. Dolly had thawed to him after the settlement conference and because he refused any and all help from the e-mail and letter writers. Things between them were almost back to normal, not quite, but getting there. To the east of Joy's grave were Chuck's and Dolly's plots, just waiting for them. Chuck sighed. How long would it be? He hoped he went first.

Maria felt the sweat starting on her back now. She'd be a sticky mess by the time she showed up for her shift at Sharkey's. On second thought, maybe she wouldn't show. No one would care anyway. Since the tornado had turned Miss Kitty's into a condemned rattrap, Sharkey's had added a pole in the corner where the jukebox used to be. The idea was to cater to the now defunct strip club's most loyal clientele, but no one came to Sharkey's to watch half-naked girls. They came to drink cheap beer and eat peanuts and argue about the Bears and the Colts and the White Sox versus the Cubs. They wanted nothing to do with Maria or the girl from Tennessee with the perfect tits. The tip situation was abysmal.

Chuck visited Sharkey's some and, like the rest of the mostly balding beer drinkers at the bar, scowled and turned his back when a dancer's name was announced. "Real tragedy what happened to that girl," he said to Maria. "Daisy was her name, if I'm remembering correctly."

"Yes," Maria said. "A tragedy."

"And then that tornado coming right on the heels . . ."

"Crazy," Maria said.

"You lost some of your friends in the storm, I think."

"My friends?"

"Well, some neighbors, at least."

Maria had never liked Ulises. Too much swagger there, a tendency to lie and get away with it, and Elena was a passive-aggressive nightmare and a horrible mother. Her daughters, now in the custody of Mrs. Gutierrez, were better off without her. Harsh, but true. "May they rest in peace," Maria said.

She and Chuck stood there a little longer, both looking at the grass, both thinking of what was under there. A heron flew over, made a sharp shadow on the ground, and a man came to mow. Across the road at the trailer park Fikus Ward and a little girl in a pink bathing suit seemed to be holding a kind of ceremony under a bird feeder. A shoebox was involved. And some praying.

"Well, good-bye, Mr. Breeder," Maria said. She held out her hand.

He took it. It was so small and dry. They hadn't shaken hands at the settlement conference. Chuck had left too soon and too angry. "Good-bye, Miss Pinto."

They walked back to the parking lot, Maria leading the way, stepping gingerly in her high heels. Chuck followed with his head bowed and hands clasped behind his back. Neither of them spoke. They read the stones. Names. Dates. Bible verses. They watched as engravings of cherubs and ivy and trumpets flashed by. They got in their separate cars and drove away, Chuck home to Dolly and Wyndham-on-the-River and Maria eastward, maybe toward a new life, both thinking they knew too much now, of men and women and the world, to hate each other any longer.

Murphy

"Hey, Fikus?"

"Yes, Tiara?"

"You don't have to be so sad. It's not your fault."

"It's not?"

"No. I don't blame you. And you shouldn't blame yourself, either."

"But I do blame myself. Every day I wake up and I blame myself."

"Then I'll pray for you. We should pray anyway, cuz this is a funeral."

"Of course."

Tiara took the shoebox that held the limp remains of Murphy the goldfish and placed it in the hole they'd dug below Fikus's bird feeders. She covered up the lid with dirt and placed a single daisy on top. Then she closed her eyes, clasped her hands, and knelt in the grass beside Fikus, who was already crying.

"Slow down," Tiara said. "This is going to be a full Christian burial. You got to pace yourself, for shit's sake."

Fikus nodded, snot billowing out his nose.

"Okay, here we go," Tiara began. "Dear Lord, who art in heaven, hollowed be thy name, thy will be done if kingdom comes, on earth as it is times seven. Give us this day our daily bread and forgive us our messes as we forgive those who mess up against us and lead us not onto plantations, but deliver us from evil, for thine is the kingdom and the flower and the gory, forever and ever. Amen."

"Amen," Fikus said.

Reincarnation

(One year later)

They talked about what was ruining this country. The woman with the stringy blond hair who'd once stolen money from the high school cafeteria cash register and the man with the scruffy face and green fingers. They talked all night of ruin and rot and people taking their j-o-b-s. The woman kept saying the man had a choice to make. It seemed like a very important choice. "You need to decide," the woman said. "You can't have us both. Do you want me or do you want her?"

"I want you," the man said.

"Then do something. Christ. Do something. For once in your life or I'll kill you myself."

"Okay okay okay."

The little yellow dog that had followed Daisy away from the bus stop barked and yipped circles around them. Their conversation made circles, too. Bubbles that expanded and contracted. Burst sometimes. They talked about what would happen after they died. The woman seemed to think she'd meet God at a gate.

The man said that was all a bunch of superstitious bunk and that what awaited them all was nothingness. A big black screen over their eyes for all eternity.

"You suck," the woman said, sticking her tongue out at him.

"That's not all I do," the man said.

The blond woman and the scruffy-faced man talked all night but rarely *to* Daisy. More they talked at and around her. They said a lot about Basketball Juan, about how he was responsible for what was going to happen to her, but Daisy didn't understand. How could he be responsible? He was home, probably watching a tele-novela with Nina. And what was going to happen to her?

When they weren't talking death and Juan and j-o-b-s, they smoked sweet- and sour-smelling stuff and ate white powder and snorted it, too, and decided between themselves that when Daisy died she'd return to the world as a mermaid. "Because you can't walk," the woman said at Daisy.

"Stands to reason," the man agreed.

But the man and woman were wrong. Daisy hadn't come back as a mermaid. She came back as a great blue heron, and now, in-stead of a wheelchair or fins, she had slick yellow legs, broad wings, and a trout inside her belly, half-digested.

Swim? she thought. Thanks but no thanks. I'd rather fly.

It had all happened so fast, that beam falling from what seemed like the sky but was really the ceiling. The blackness and the light. The dog lying next to her, silent. Protective. The man and woman waking up and panicking over Daisy's motionless face, arguing and crying and throwing her limp body and busted wheelchair in the back of a car. The long drive to nowhere, during which the man dumped the dog on the side of the road because he said they needed to lighten the load, to cut all ties. The woman crying some

more, saying, "He's going to get hit and then we did that, too."
The man throwing up his hands. "We did not do that. Do you hear
me? None of this is our fault."

The car ride ended in a jerky journey through a stinking
meadow to a grass-choked ditch with a view of soaring metal
above and a tree whose bark was all but gone. Days of flies followed. Sun. Blue with white in between. Then came rain and wet
grass bent over, tickling. There were nights of stars and mosquitoes and low, fat moons. And quiet. So much quiet. Finally, the
little yellow dog came back from the dead, its black nose digging
around. It barked and howled, and the man with the big belly said,
"Oh my God," over and over and over. The rain came again, this
time for real, and the wind howled, and a few other men joined
the big-bellied man in the darkness. They picked her up and took
her away and later cried alone in their cars.

Daisy hadn't really wanted to see any of it, but after the beam
fell she was everywhere and nowhere all at once. She wasn't yet a
body or a bird, more an idea buoyed around like a seed that might
never take root. She was witness to her own funeral at the Baptist church. She watched as Hector lost use of his legs in grief. A
nice fat woman in a red necklace caught him as he fell, and Hector said to her that it was strange, wasn't it? He'd always wondered
what it was like for his sweet little girl confined forever to that
stupid wheelchair and now he knew. The graveyard attendant
fetched him a chair they kept around for emergencies. "Now,"
Hector told the fat lady, "I know everything."

But he didn't know that right after they buried Daisy, someone or something whispered to her that nothing would be what
she expected but that was the way of the world and soon, very
soon, the ground would fall out from under her and she'd make

296 Deborah E. Kennedy

friends with the clouds and the orioles, the rainbows and the black-
birds, the mallards and titmice and woodpeckers. *Not the geese,
though,* the voice said. *Geese are awful.*

"Fuck you, fuck you, fuck you," said the geese anytime
anyone got near them or their precious air pockets. "Mine,
mine, mine."

In the spring, Daisy became an ovum, a mass of blood vessels
in a blue shell, then a downy hatchling eating right from her new
mother's gullet. She ate and chirped and grew. She left the nest
and the geese taunted her as she learned to fly because, unlike the
other sleek-feathered juveniles born that April in the rookery off
Route 20, she ran into telephone poles, trees, the sides of buildings. She defecated upon liftoff, almost every time, and ruined two
nests too, practicing a glide.

"Yoiks and away!" the geese honked at her from the banks of
the Ranasack, the shallows choked with their feathers. "Yoiks! And
away!"

The instinct she'd been born with took over and flying felt like
the one time Hector said it was okay to coast down a small hill
on her wheelchair—the whir in her ears, the dip in her tummy,
bugs whirling past, and sparks shooting upward—only now there
was no dip and she could see the whole world in focus and as it was
with her bulging yellow eyes. Fish, mostly, gleaming in the water
and smooth bellied, but also coins in fountains and bugs in fur and
shirt pins in haystacks.

Daisy's bird mother taught her how to find fish. She wasn't at
all like Daisy's human mother, who had cradled Daisy and kissed
her and sacrificed her own life so her daughter might live a little
longer as a girl. The bird mother was never affectionate, but she
was fierce and protective and made sure Daisy left the nest all in

one piece. Daisy had had a bird father, too, a tall and much-sought-after male with a bright, impressive head plume and the orangest legs in the rookery, but both he and Daisy's bird mother were eaten by a fox in Florida shortly after they'd migrated there, and now rumor had it that they were wolf cubs dodging bullets in Alaska.

Daisy supposed she should have felt sadness when she and her brother found their parents' remains, dropped bloody and fly-ridden at the base of a mangrove tree, but she'd never really cared deeply about them, was drawn to them only out of instinct.

It was Hector she loved.

Daddy, Daddy, stand up, she'd wanted so badly to tell him at the funeral and afterward when he didn't get out of bed for weeks. *It's okay. I'm okay.*

But he couldn't hear a spirit or a seed. He couldn't hear a heron either. And anyway, by the time she thought to try to talk to him, it was time to leave. One night she was perching on her old wheelchair outside Hector's house, kuk-kukking at his grief-dazed figure, and the next her bird mother was bullying her back to the nest to rest for the long flight south.

Daisy had wished hard that she'd had her girl mouth so she could tell Hector all about her new life, thrill him with stories of near midair collisions and storms pounding through the trees and fish stabbed through the heart, about the rookery, how it looked like something out of a cartoon during the day but at night be-came a ghostly place filled with rustlings and howls and echoes. Weasels came out and slithered around the tree roots, licking their lips. Coyotes cried from the undergrowth, but herons didn't worry about them. Too slow, too stupid. They worried about the wea-sels, and about hawks, too, and fishers, though they were rare. Still, Daisy hardly ever felt scared. She had a brother and a sister now. They hunted together and preened at the same time. Her brother had once been a Jersey cow, her sister a manatee. They loved to fly and looked beautiful doing it, their shadows on the ground straight and clean as arrows. They told Daisy her flying was coming along nicely. "You haven't run into anything in ever so long," they said.

Daisy was no longer the rookery's worst flier. On both of her migrations—first south and now north—she proved herself more like its fourth worst, behind a few young birds and one old-timer with a fishhook stuck permanently in his right wing. Fourth worst was good enough to get around, especially home in Colliersville where the currents were kinder than the Florida winds and there weren't as many small-engine planes and kites to contend with.

Daisy had worried about Hector all the Marco Island winter, and between flights to the shore and whole days spent up to her knees in sea oats, she pined for their old life of silly games and fattening food and bedtime stories. The rest of the rookery fwanked on and on about how winter in Florida was really the life. "Shangri-la," they croaked, if you blocked out the noisy tourists and avoided the Burmese pythons, but Daisy couldn't wait to get home, to Colliersville and the nests that waited for them there, stacked three to a tree and wide as her twin bed, only wild with twigs and tasty beetles and sometimes even fast-food wrappers and human hair, sluffed off in small piles from brushes and drains.

On the flight from the island to Indiana, Daisy had finally told her brother and sister all about her human daddy. She hadn't told them before because it was too painful, it was too soon, and she didn't know them well enough, but now they understood and, in turn, they told her their stories.

"I left a whole herd behind me when I was struck by a semi on a highway outside of Philly," her brother said.

"I'd just birthed a calf when part of my right side got chopped off by an Evinrude," said her sister.

"Life is so awful. It hurts so much," Daisy told them, somewhere over Georgia. Georgia went on forever.

"This is your first reincarnation," said her brother, who in addition to a cow and a heron had been a tea rose and a butterfly and a beaver. "You get used to it."

Daisy thought she could get used to anything, just as long as she knew Hector was okay. Nothing else mattered. Not mating, not knowing where her next fish was coming from. All her instincts were trained on her daddy, so on her first night back in Indiana she took off for the Bottoms, eager to check up on him, to see how the seasons had treated him. Her brother and sister were surprised. Wasn't she tired? Didn't she want to sleep and sleep and sleep and maybe, when the sleeping was over, mate? But Daisy was adamant. She had someone to see. And so she set off, taking the same path the tornado had a year before, keeping her eye out for tension wires and geese, wind turbines and too-close-together trees. Route 20 was tricky but she didn't mind and she didn't look away when she spotted the Ferris wheel with the tree growing through. The rest of the Fun Spot was leveled, was nothing but planks of rotting wood and twisted nails, but the storm had spared the Ferris wheel for some reason and so she flew in and out of the uprights, gazing down on the spot where her girl body had lain for days and weeks, becoming air, becoming earth. She studied the damp, dead grass, saw a cornflower peeking through and an army of marching ants on their way home, fragments of a dead worm on their backs.

Her bird brother and sister told her that every living thing, even slugs, worms, bacteria, were building on themselves all the time, layers like onion skin, and taking those layers into their next life, so she lingered. That Ferris wheel was part of her. She had the peeled paint in her blood.

After the Ferris wheel came a brand-new shopping center wreathed in red, white, and blue bunting. Cows had lived there once and her friends Juan and Maria and Nina milked them in a big blue barn, but it was all concrete now and GRAND OPENING signs and lights on poles where seagulls perched. There were no cars yet, no consumers, just a lone man in a yellow hard hat strolling up and down the sidewalk making notes. Daisy pooped on him. By accident.

And soon she was downtown. There was the high school sitting like a sprawling brick amoeba, its brand-new roof bejeweled with shining silver fans the shape of chef hats. Someone had set up a lemonade stand on the sidewalk. A sign declared, DAISY GONZALEZ MEMORIAL SCOLLARSHIP FUND. Tiara and Fikus Ward, Daisy's bus driver, handed brimming Dixie cups to Tina Gonzalez's former boss, the ugly beautician, and a girl with hairy legs and large, perfect breasts. Also to Basketball Juan, who had to put his basketball down so he could hold his lemonade. Daisy sighed over him. Juan, her buddy. Daisy wondered if he was lonely without her, without Nina, without Maria. All his friends gone so quickly.

But then Juan and the girl with the hairy legs finished their lemonade and started tossing the basketball back and forth, back and forth. Bounce passes at first, then chest passes. Tiara yelled at them, said they sucked donkey balls, and ran in on the game, arms waving wildly. "You can't play keep away from me!" she said. "I invented keep away."

Daisy kept on. Up Main Street and Beacon, over what was once Tony's Pizza (the tornado took out that entire building) and was still the Hair Barn and Breeder's Laundromat. Miss Kitty's was boarded up. The tornado did that, too. There was a sign on the sidewalk that said FOR SALE. She swooped in over the spot where her human mother was killed and Daisy was left without legs that worked. A rusty brown stain bloomed there still. A spider scuttled over it, and an old lady dodged it, careful to keep to the edge of the sidewalk. That part of town used to make Daisy and Hector sad. They drove around it if they could, gave it a wide berth, but Daisy looked hard at it just as she'd studied the spot below the Ferris wheel. In the end, it was just another layer. It had to do with history.

That's why it doesn't matter if you get rid of the wheelchair or not, she'd wanted to tell Hector back when her transformation was just beginning. *Stop torturing yourself. Let it rust or don't. Take it to the Goodwill or bury it in the backyard. It's all the same. Everything will be all right. You'll come back as a giraffe or a big black dog and children will love you all over again like I did. Do you hear me?*

He hadn't, of course. The problem was that even when given a body and a voice, the sounds that came out of her beak made sense only to the winged.

Kuk-kuk, she'd told the stringy-haired woman on her way out of the courtroom. She said the same to the scruffy-faced man as two deputies shoved him into a police van. *I forgive you. Forgive yourselves.*

Raa-raa, she said to the dog and the man with the belly. They no longer took long walks alone. They were always with Shannon Washburn now, Hector and Daisy's Bottoms neighbor. Since the storm there was a lot of work to do around the house,

Shannon's house mainly, and they did it together, Shannon in her short hair and the man with the belly, repairing gutters and reat-taching shutters and replanting plants, and the dog on the ground looking up. *Be friends.* That's what Daisy meant. *Be best friends. You know you want to.*

Aroo, aroo, she said to the mean girl who wasn't really mean and who'd spent much of her summer dismantling backyard tar-gets of the president's face and stowing them in her garage behind some lawn furniture. The girl turned one of the targets into a painting. She slapped oils on, used watercolors to draw a version of history only she understood. She did not know she had it in her. When she was finished, the president looked surreal, beautiful, the leader of a free world. She showed the painting to her dad and he cried and put away his gun for the night. *Aroo, arroo,* Daisy said to the girl. Translation: *You'll get out of here someday. Don't ask me how I know but I know. You'll get out and you'll do it on your own and no one will be able to take that away from you.*

Fwank, fwank, fwank, Daisy said to Shellie Pogue, her old sort-of babysitter, and the rest of the middle-aged white ladies drink-ing tea and knitting scarves in a bright farmhouse kitchen. Later, when the ladies gathered around a plot of earth under a broken treehouse, Daisy tried to tell them, *The boy you love is fine. He's okay. He's not scared anymore.* The women clasped hands and prayed. They didn't understand her. No one did. She could no more reach them than she could have convinced the search team to call it off and go home back when there was still hope they'd find girl-her alive. All those fathers of other kids with their flashlights and hip waders and safety orange hats, all those mothers stapling flyers to telephone poles, then praying at night for poor Daisy Gonzalez and her dad, who, they thought sweetly, could really use a woman in his life. Now more than ever.

Daisy took a left out of downtown and headed toward the Bottoms, flying first over Maple Leaf Mobile Home Park, whose sign, a year after the storm, still read MAP AF M ILE ME K. The absent letters were nowhere. It was as if they'd never existed. Even now, with the cleanup far behind them and much of the rebuilding effort finished, many of the Maple Leaf lots stood empty because the tornado had tossed the trailers into a nearby field and people who might have moved there thought there was something distasteful or unlucky about squatting in the same space as your friend who'd died when his closet fell in on him.

The empty lots were like missing keys in an old typewriter. Daisy blinked at them and glided by the concrete plant spitting dust and a small patch of woods just starting to grow back. There was a line of new scrub and brush through the center, a Mohawk in reverse. Daisy wasn't concerned about the woods. Nature would repair itself. It always did.

She passed over the Ranasack Apartments, which even from the air were almost unrecognizable on account of the roof garden and clean lawn and new basketball hoops hanging over a recently blacktopped parking lot. A woman and her children were outside, covering the sidewalk in chalk pictures of flowers and hearts and trees. The mother carefully drew a hopscotch grid, and while the little boy went to find a rock, the girl ran her foot through one of the hopscotch squares and laughed at her mother's frustrated face.

When Daisy got to Hector's little yellow house, the wheelchair wasn't in its usual spot outside. In its place was a clean spot of green lawn. She perched instead on someone's antique tractor, which gave her a good view of a long hall and a straight shot through to the living room.

Daddy, she tried to say. It came out as *Aroo. Aroo.*

What she saw shocked her, almost sent her toppling off the tractor seat. With her new eyes she spied Hector sharing his couch with the nice fat lady from the funeral, only she wasn't as fat as she used to be, and a chubby man in a black T-shirt. They were watching a movie and laughing. Hector had a bowl of popcorn in his lap. Fizzy sodas crackled on the floor at their feet.

Everything was as it used to be—the kitchen table covered in papers, the stove in used pots, the living room floor in books and magazines—but everything was different, too. The kitchen walls, which used to be white, were painted a brilliant yellow. The wood paneling in the living room was a light green, and the wheelchair, polished to an almost blinding sheen and pushed up against the north wall of the living room, held an earthenware pot of daisies—orange, pink, red, and blue. Hanging above the chair was Daisy's kindergarten picture, framed with blinking Christmas lights.

Daisy watched her human daddy and the two strangers for a long time. They were happy together, acting almost like a family would, touching one another politely and making sure everyone had enough to eat. Once in a while, Hector's eyes would stray to the chair or the photograph and then he would put his big fist over his heart, sigh, and look down. When he did this, the fat lady would say something funny or point to the television, where a pretty woman in a fedora chased criminals in her electric car.

Aroo, aroo, Daisy said, and for a moment nothing happened. *Aroo, aroo,* she said again, and all three of them looked up at once.

They must have seen her in the gleam of the neighbor's dusk-to-dawn light because their mouths went slack and fascinated. Humans often looked at herons this way. Daisy was used to it. The fat lady pointed at Daisy and whispered something to Hector and the man beside him. They stared for a while, their lips turning up in faint smiles. Then the lady tugged on the men's sleeves and they rose very slowly from the couch, creeping down the hall in a huddle.

The hall window was open and through it Daisy heard the lady shush the chubby man when his elbow dislodged Tina Gonzalez's picture from the wall.

"We don't want to scare him," the lady said.

Daisy stayed where she was, by this time an expert at freezing in place. *Him?* She wanted to laugh out loud but that was the only downside to being a heron. Herons couldn't laugh. It had something to do with dignity.

Hector and his guests pressed their faces to the window screen to get a better look, and Daisy, knowing it was probably futile but unable to stop herself, tried just one more time to say what it was she wanted to say, to unburden her heart. *Fwank, fwank, fwank!* she said. *I'm okay, Daddy. I'm fine. I miss you so much, but the skies are blue in my new life and when they aren't blue I just fly higher. When you die, try and find me. Or I'll find you and together we'll hunt for Mom. By then I might be a cat, you might be a mouse, and Mom might be a bear. We might all be Christmas trees. Or sycamores. Or cornstalks.*

Be happy. Teach kids what you know. Give the mean girl a recommendation and a chance. Flunk Benny Bradenton because he has it coming. Forget about Marissa Marino. She can wait her turn. Forget about all the times you yelled at me, or grew impatient. They don't matter either. Forget about leaving me at the bus stop to fend for myself. You did the best you could. You were the best daddy a girl could ever ask for. And just remember that I love you. I love you. I love you.

Hector gazed out at her, unblinking, his face a melancholy mask. The fat lady covered her ears and screwed up her face. "Such ugly sounds from such a pretty bird," she said, but the chubby man in the black T-shirt was weeping. Tears ran down his neck onto his shirt collar. He made small choking sounds like Daisy did now when her powder down caught in her throat.

"I'll tell him, Daisy," the man said. "Don't worry. Don't worry anymore. I'll tell him everything."

Acknowledgments

Thanks are due first and foremost to Yishai Seidman, tireless advocate, rock star agent, and friend, and Christine Kopprasch, editor extraordinaire and chance taker. Also to Amy Einhorn and Caroline Bleek and everyone at Flatiron books. I can't adequately express how grateful I am for your hard work, expertise, and passion.

I would also like to thank my kindred spirits at the Iowa Writers' Workshop, too numerous to name here, so I'll only say particular attention must be paid to Jill Logan, Susannah Shive, Sinead Lykins, and E. J. Fischer. I am deeply indebted to my Iowa workshop instructors as well. Benjamin Percy, Lan Samantha Chang, Kevin Brockmeier, Julie Orringer, Ayana Mathis, and Charles Baxter—thank you for pushing my writing into more challenging and, I hope, more truthful territory.

Writing teachers and mentors come in many forms, and I have been lucky enough to study under, and learn from, the very best. All my gratitude to Jonathan Smith, Marsha Dutton, Kathy Barbour, Dee Goertz, Kay Stokes, Melissa Pope Eden, Peter Orner, Nancy Zafris, Kay Sloan, Keith Banner, Eric Goodman, Tim Melley, Jim Palmarini, Don Corathers, and Doug Driscoll.

Thank you, too, to the Loechle family: Sue, Paul, Eric, and Annie. Were the rest of the world more like you. And to Jason Skipper, Evan Kuhlman, Ramon Jones, Liana Manukyan-Crosby, Randy Steckevicz, Angelo Veneziano, Mark and Olivia Hunter, Susan Doremus, Jhon Marshall, January Simpson, and the Rooksberrys. With friends like you, who needs armor?

I've dedicated this book to my parents, but other members of my family deserve recognition as well, including my brothers, Dean and Brian, who, over many years of backyard baseball games and going long, helped me grow a thick skin—essential in this business—and their wives, Anne and Phirin, and children, Samantha, Alex, Luke, and Lillian, who every day have a new lesson to teach me about what it means to love. The same can be said of my Zurbrugg and Ramsey and Uhrick aunts, uncles, and cousins living in and around Fort Wayne, Indiana, which was and is and always will be home.

Most of all, my love to Eric Meeuwsen, my soul mate and best friend, whom I'm pretty sure I've loved since hunter-gatherer times.

About the Author

Deborah E. Kennedy is a native of Fort Wayne, Indiana, and a recent graduate of the Iowa Writers' Workshop. Kennedy has worked as a reporter, editor, and teacher, and also holds a master's in Fiction Writing and English Literature from Miami University in Oxford, Ohio. She currently lives in Forest Grove, Oregon. *Tornado Weather* is her debut.